THE DESTROYERS

DOUGLAS REEMAN joined the Navy in 1941. He did convoy duty in the Atlantic, the Arctic, and the North Sea, and later served in motor torpedo boats. As he says, 'I am always asked to account for the perennial appeal of the sea story, and its enduring interest for people of so many nationalities and cultures. It would seem that the eternal and sometimes elusive triangle of man, ship and ocean, particularly under the stress of war, produces the best qualities of courage and compassion, irrespective of the rights and wrongs of the conflict . . . The sea has no understanding of the righteous or unjust causes. It is the common enemy, respected by all who serve on it, ignored at their peril.'

Douglas Reeman has written over thirty novels under his own name; he has also written twenty-four bestselling historical novels featuring Richard and Adam Bolitho, under the pseudonym Alexander Kent.

Also by Douglas Reeman

The Greatest Enemy
The Last Raider
With Blood and Iron
H.M.S. 'Saracen'
A Prayer for the Ship
Dive in the Sun
High Water
The Hostile Shore
Rendezvous – South Atlantic
Send a Gunboat
The Deep Silence
Go in and Sink!
Path of the Storm
The Pride and the Anguish
To Risks Unknown
Winged Escort
Surface with Daring
Strike from the Sea
A Ship Must Die
Torpedo Run
Badge of Glory
The First to Land
The Volunteers
The Iron Pirate
Against the Sea (non-fiction)
In Danger's Hour
The White Guns
Killing Ground
The Horizon
Sunset
A Dawn Like Thunder
Battlecruiser
Dust on the Sea

Douglas Reeman
THE DESTROYERS

arrow books

First published by Arrow Books in 1976

19 20

First published in the United Kingdom in 1974 by Hutchinson

Arrow Books
Random House, 20 Vauxhall Bridge Road, London SW1V 2SA

Random House Australia (Pty) Limited
20 Alfred Street, Milsons Point, Sydney, New South Wales 2061, Australia

Random House New Zealand Limited
18 Poland Road, Glenfield, Auckland 10, New Zealand

Random House South Africa (Pty) Limited
Endulini, 5a Jubilee Road, Parktown 2193, South Africa

The Random House Group Limited Reg. No. 954009
www.randomhouse.co.uk

A CIP catalogue record for this book is available from the British Library

The Random House Group Limited support The Forest Stewardship
Council (FSC), the leading international forest certification organisation.
All our titles that are printed on Greenpeace approved FSC certified paper
carry the FSC logo. Our paper procurement policy can be found at
www.rbooks.co.uk/environment

ISBN 9780099547679

Printed and bound in Great Britain by
Cox & Wyman Ltd, Reading, Berkshire

For Audrey and Elizabeth,
Barry and Richard,
with love.

Contents

Author's Note

As I gather material and do research for each new book I am quite frequently asked how I continue to unearth themes for the next manuscript, and the one after that.

In fact, the breadth of sea history, both ancient and contemporary, the many experiences of ships and sailors, never fail to awe me. Far from being denied plots for future stories, I sometimes seem unable to keep pace with those which I discover in my endless search.

Small but incredible acts of courage and endurance seem to rise up from the grander records of campaigns and barely remembered wars. When I was writing this book it was hard to accept that such deeds were in fact carried out by British warships in the Second World War, not least by the old destroyer *Cambeltown* at St. Nazaire.

My story, like the title, is double-edged. It is about a flotilla of out-of-date warships, destroyers, which because of war's incessant demands and greed were pushed against terrible odds, almost without regard to losses. But it also concerns the men who controlled their destinies. Men driven to the edge of endurance who in turn became *the destroyers*. Forced by various reasons to face each hazard, they still retained their more personal standards. Duty, fear, the need to destroy the enemy, each other if so ordered, these men were a part of history. Of war itself.

D.R.

I

The Destroyer

LIEUTENANT-COMMANDER KEITH DRUMMOND kept his head lowered as he walked around the deep puddles left by overnight rain. It was nearly dawn and the air had a bite like mid-winter. He hesitated and looked up at the departing clouds, the dull greyness of which matched the worn dockyard buildings and the looming shapes of vessels which still lay quietly at crowded jetties or protruded above nearby wharves and basins.

But it was early June, and the year 1943.

He stretched his arms and yawned, tasting the dampness, the smells of salt and oil, of wet metal and discarded waste. The untidy sprawl of the Royal Naval Dockyard at Chatham seemed almost peaceful in the gloom, he thought. In a short while all would be different again. The resting ships would come alive to the din of rivet guns and screeching saws, while above the open basins the tall gantries would sway and then plunge down like gaunt herons searching for food as the work of building and repairing, boiler cleaning and restoring got under way.

Two shadowy figures detached themselves from a wall, and a voice asked irritably, 'Who's this, then?' They were dockyard policemen.

Drummond stepped over some railway lines and approached them.

The first policeman said, 'Oh, it's you, sir.' He touched his cap. 'Surprised to see someone about so early.'

Drummond nodded. It was unusual to see dockyard policemen so far from their cubby-holes and fires, for that matter.

The other one said importantly, 'The tugs brought a destroyer in last night, sir.' He gestured to the dry dock at his back. 'Too dark to do much. We're just here to make sure that . . .' He looked at his companion and added awkwardly, 'Well, you know how it is, sir. She hit a mine in the estuary. Most of her engine-room blokes were killed. They're still inside. Can't get 'em out till daylight.'

Drummond walked to the side of the dock and peered down at the long, narrow hull. Even in the poor light he could see the damage. Could even see it happening, as if she had been his own ship. The bridge superstructure smashed half over the side, as if pounded by some giant hammer. Buckled guardrails, and one funnel laid out on deck like a huge coffin.

He said coldly, 'Yes, I know *exactly* how it is.'

A destroyer had been mined and towed into another dockyard nearby. She, too, had had dead sailors trapped below deck, left to wait for the water to be pumped clear, for the men with cutters to hack their way through. But when daylight had found them the dead had been robbed. Money and watches gone. No wonder these policemen sounded embarrassed.

Everyone had been most insistent that somebody else had been responsible. *Just one of those things.*

He added, 'Might be a fine day.'

He nodded and strode on towards the next line of basins, knowing they were staring after him, thinking he was bitter towards them or just one more hard case.

Drummond glanced towards the east where a moored barrage balloon showed itself through a gap in the low cloud. Beyond it and Sheppey Island lay the Thames Estuary and the North Sea. Despite everything which had happened, or because of it, he was glad to be going back.

His own ship had been in the dockyard for a month, and not a moment too soon. She had needed every hour of every one of those days, and he found he was walking faster, as if some doubt which had been in his mind was departing with the night.

He reached the basin and stood quite still on the edge, the chill air exploring his legs and whipping the oily dock water into nervous movement below him.

She was moored in the centre of the basin, and unlike his last visit three days ago, she was afloat again, a living ship. A destroyer.

He walked very slowly along the wet stonework, his eyes never leaving her lithe, familiar shape. Against the filthy water and dark dock sides her new coat of dazzle paint made her shine eerily, and her pendant number, I.97, stand out as if she were brand new. But daylight would show the lie, he thought. The paint would not hide the many dents along her three hundred and twelve feet of narrow hull. Nor could it disguise her outdated and quaint silhouette which had made her and the rest of her class so familiar throughout their long service. Unlike her more modern consorts, and especially the hastily constructed vessels which had been designed and built since the outbreak of war, she had an appearance which betrayed all of her twenty-five years. Behind her sturdy, open bridge her two funnels were unmatched in height or breadth. The foremost was tall and thin, the after one short and squat. Her main armament of four four-inch guns had open shields which left their crews unprotected from behind. Once, at the peak of her fame, she had carried two triple mounts of torpedo tubes, now she had only one set, the other removed to make room for more short-range weapons to fight off attacking aircraft.

Drummond smiled, despite his uneasiness. As Frank Cowley, his first lieutenant, had once remarked, she was like an old Chatham prostitute. Past her best, but, with a new paint-job and a wealth of experience behind her, carried a sort of jaunty arrogance which appealed far more than younger competitors.

He looked at the water below the steep wall. Except that Frank was no longer first lieutenant. He was over in Canterbury being watched by some grave-faced nurse in the naval hospital.

Drummond had spent the night, or part of it, in a Canterbury hotel. Helen, Frank's wife, had asked him to stay at her house near the hospital. But her eyes had told him the opposite. Just as they had asked, 'Why Frank, and not you?'

Drummond had tried to break the stillness between them. But it always seemed to return to the ship. But then, it was all he knew. They would be off to sea again soon. That had been wrong. He had seen the pain in her eyes. He had tried to tell her about the difficulties of getting a ship back to normal after a month's refit and repairs. There would be new faces to replace those who had gone elsewhere. For courses or promotion. For special leave or, like Frank, to a living death.

He could remember when Frank had got married. The party in the wardroom while the ship had been at Harwich between convoys. She had asked him why he had not got married. He had replied, 'Not in wartime.' Now she was probably remembering that, too. Hating him for being whole when there was no one to care. While Frank had no legs.

He walked down the steep brow and stepped on to the destroyer's deck, feeling its stillness, its watchfulness. He saw the bell hanging from its newly painted bracket, the night's rain misting it like steam. He touched it with his finger. The inscription was almost worn away. Years of polishing. All those men. All those years. *H.M.S. Warlock 1918.*

A figure clumped from the lobby below X-gun. It was Leading Seaman Rumsey, the chief quartermaster, a great bear of a man, always cheerful, with a sleepy grin which could overcome even the roughest reprimand. Drummond was glad he at least was still aboard.

Rumsey said thickly, ' 'Mornin', sir. Wasn't expectin' you just yet.' He banged his gloved fists together. 'I was just goin' to call the 'ands.' He grinned. 'Start another day like.'

Strangely sad on the damp air, a bugle echoed amongst the sheds and sleeping ships, to be joined instantly by others from the barracks nearby and the heavier ships of war which carried such luxuries.

Wakey, wakey, lash up an' stow! Rise an' shine, the sun's scorching your bleeding eyeballs out! The age-old joke at half past five of a spring morning.

Drummond stepped into the lobby and glanced at the board by the quartermaster's little desk. All the officers were ashore except the engineer and the torpedo gunner.

He swung round, suddenly and without warning on edge.

'Where is the new first lieutenant?'

Rumsey paused with one finger at the tannoy switch, his silver call resting on his lower lip.

He said carefully, 'Ain't 'ere yet, sir. We got a call to say 'e was detained. Train 'eld up by a derailment outside London.' He hesitated. 'Or somethin'.'

Drummond clattered down the ladder and heard Rumsey bellow into the microphone, 'Wakey, wakey! Rise an' shine!' In a moment he would rouse the duty petty officer and go to the messdecks and haul any malingerer out of his hammock, bedding and all. There was little pity from those who had the night watches.

Drummond groped his way into the deserted wardroom. He

knew every step blindfolded. Even the patch on the worn carpet was familiar as he stepped into the wardroom and switched on some lights. New paint everywhere, but the furniture was the same. Dark red leather which would be carefully covered when the ship was at sea again. When officers, chilled from an open bridge and dog-weary from watchkeeping, would slump down and probably fall asleep until they were needed. Like that last time. The clamour of alarm bells, the sudden crash and shriek of cannon shells. Frank falling against the side of the bridge, unable to cry out or even draw breath in his terrible agony.

One side of the wardroom contained the dining space. The well-polished table, the sideboard, and a pantry hatch through which the stewards listened to all the gossip before trading it forward to the messdecks.

Drummond let his eyes move to the other side. The battered armchairs, a picture of the King, the letter-rack and the cabinet which held a set of revolvers. The ship's crest above the old-fashioned fire, the staring warlock, and the motto which when translated read, *Who touches me dies.*

He walked out of the wardroom and past the pantry door. It opened slightly, and he saw Petty Officer Owles, the senior steward, watching him with surprise.

' 'Morning, Owles. Any coffee going?'

He bobbed his head.

'I'll open your cabin, sir.' He tugged a great bunch of keys from his pocket. 'Got to lock everything or screw it down in this place, sir.' He continued brightly, 'Have a nice leaf, sir?'

Owles always asked the same question. Just as he always called it 'leaf' and never expected or listened to an answer.

Drummond did not reply, and Owles said cheerfully, 'That's the ticket, sir. Glad to know that.'

He unlocked the last door in the passageway, the one marked *Captain*, and switched on the lights.

'Coffee in a jiff, sir.'

Drummond closed the door behind him and leaned against it. He was back.

Lieutenant David Sheridan, R.N.V.R., returned the salute from a party of seamen who were marching through the dockyard on some mission or other and then continued on his way. He was tall and broad-shouldered like an athlete, and below the rim of his cap his hair was dark, almost black, as it curled rebelliously above his ears. As he turned to watch some dockyard workers meandering along the littered deck of a refitting cruiser he felt his chin rasp against his greatcoat collar. That bloody train, he thought savagely. Sitting in a cramped, unheated compartment with some moaning civilians and an army subaltern who had looked as if he were just recovering from a terrible binge. He grinned, despite his irritation, the change pushing the lines from his mouth. Making him look his age, which was twenty-six. He had done a fair bit of moaning himself during the long, unexplained wait in that cheerless train. A bad air-raid, a derailment, nobody really knew. Or cared, it seemed.

His uncomfortable night made the air seem colder, and the sky was clouding over already. More rain. Funny how it always seemed to be raining whenever he was in Chatham.

He strode past another basin. This time there was a destroyer, and he hesitated to look down at her. She was old, a veteran from World War One, one of a design of nearly seventy ships known as V and W class destroyers. Like the one he was about to join as first lieutenant. The difference was that this one, already partly gutted by flaming torches and screaming saws, was part of his life, or had been. Now she was being cut down to receive larger fuel tanks, to become something else. A long-range escort. Not a real destroyer any more. He watched the growing pile of jagged metal on the docksides. Pipes and strips of newly cut steel. Wire and gun-mountings, a whole tangle which had once been part of a living ship. Part of him, too. But in time the wires and cables which now snaked ashore in every direction would grow fewer, the poor, hard-worked hull would get a coat of paint. A fresh company would arrive. A captain to command and carry ship and men from one call to the next. Convoy escort. Dreary and vital. Wearing and deadly. He felt the same old bitterness welling up inside him. He had been her first lieutenant for nearly a year. Learning the job and then teaching others. Drawing their confined, dangerous world together, handing it to his captain as a going concern.

The captain had called him to his day cabin to explain. It had sounded more like an apology.

'I had hoped to get a command of my own, sir.' Sheridan

could almost hear himself saying it. *Pleading.* It was so damned unfair. A slap in the face. Several of his opposite numbers in other ships had already got commands, temporary officers or not. He, it seemed, was to be given another run at the same old job, under some other captain. Lieutenant-Commander Keith Drummond, Distinguished Service Cross, Royal Navy. Sheridan had seen him once at a convoy conference and had remembered him despite all that had happened since. He recalled his grave, calm manner of speaking, the way he could hold a mixed gathering of merchant service captains, most of whom had been old enough to be his father.

Drummond was about twenty-eight or nine, but had the experience of a veteran, which indeed he was. When Sheridan had mentioned his name to some of the others, one of them had remarked, 'Drummond, you say? He's a bit of a goer, I believe. Runs a good ship, but he's a regular, David, so watch yourself.' They still spoke like that, after nearly four years of war, when the hostilities-only and ex-merchant navy men outnumbered the regulars by an overwhelming degree.

Sheridan had seen it in his own ship. The regulars had been sent to other vessels, promoted ahead of their proper time in a desperate effort to train the inflow of newcomers. To make a navy out of amateurs while day by day the losses to bomb and torpedo mounted and the convoys faced the ravages of sea and enemy alike.

The worst of it was, H.M.S. *Warlock* had just completed a refit. That meant many more new hands. No captain would be eager to recommend his first lieutenant for promotion at this stage.

Sheridan quickened his pace again. Before the war he had been hopeless at holding down any sort of work for long. He had wanted to go to university, perhaps to study law eventually, but he had been the family breadwinner. His father had been crippled in that other war, it had been the least he could do for him. Now all that seemed like history. He had taken to the Navy like a duck to water. Nothing else seemed ahead of him. It could go on forever. Except that 1943 had offered some small sparks of success. The North African campaign was at last ended, and the remains of the battered Afrika Korps had quit the desert just a month ago. After years of reverses and retreats, 'strategic withdrawals', as the journalists called them, the Army was getting a chance to hit back. There was talk of an invasion of occupied Europe. There was even a *demand* for it, especially from those who did not have to wear a uniform.

Through it all Sheridan had seen the Navy carrying on, from one disaster to the next. Norway and Dunkirk. Crete and Singapore. Great ships gone in the twinkling of an eye. Names which had been household words in those far-off days of peace. *Hood* and *Royal Oak*, *Repulse* and *Courageous*. Even the newer ones, like *Prince of Wales* and *Ark Royal*, had not been spared in the savage fight to keep the sea lanes open, to keep supplies and men moving.

It would have been something to get a ship of his own. To finish the war with a command to show for it, he thought. Anything would have done for a start. A stubby corvette, a trawler even. Or one of those weird paddle-steamers which had once taken passengers on day trips to Southend and were now classed as minesweepers. *Anything*.

'I say, sir?' A youthful voice made him turn. 'I was wondering if you could help?'

It was a midshipman. Very young, out of breath, and, from the cut of his uniform, brand-new.

'Well?'

The midshipman gestured to an untidy cluster of sailors who were grouped round a large rain puddle, their hammocks and bags piled up on two ungainly trolleys. Most of them were smoking.

Sheridan said, 'Tell those men to douse their cigarettes. It's close eight o'clock.' He waited, seeing the growing uncertainty on the boy's face. 'Colours are about to be sounded.'

Cigarettes vanished as if by magic, and Sheridan asked, 'What is the problem?'

'I—I was asked, er, *told* to accompany these hands to the *Warlock*.' He straightened his back and added firmly, 'A destroyer, you know, sir. I'm joining her.'

'Me, too.' Sheridan said dryly, 'She's in the next basin. Better get a move on.'

A bugle blared out again and from staffs and masts in ships and encircling depots and barracks the White Ensigns rose sedately to mark the day's official beginning.

Sheridan ground his teeth. Bad enough being late on the first day. To arrive after colours was even worse.

The midshipman fell in step beside him and added, 'I'm Keyes, sir. Midshipman.'

'I'm Sheridan.' He grinned. 'First lieutenant.'

'Oh!'

Behind them the new men shuffled along with their piles of baggage, watching the ships, preparing themselves like new boys for a school.

'Just starting?'

'Yes, sir. From *King Alfred*.'

Sheridan looked away. Another one. Nice enough youth, but knowing nothing, would have to be led by the hand.

He said, 'First ship then?'

'Oh no, sir. Actually, I did nearly three months in a cruiser before going to the training depot.' He added lamely, 'Mostly at anchor though.'

They reached the side of the basin and the midshipman exclaimed, 'Is *that* the *Warlock*?'

Sheridan studied him calmly. 'Disappointed?'

'Well, sir.' Keyes shifted under his stare. 'A destroyer, I mean, it's what everyone wants, isn't it?'

Sheridan smiled. Any minute now. He'll be talking about the greyhounds of the ocean. They always did.

But another voice spoke instead. A short, square chief petty officer with a coxswain's badges on his lapels was standing on the brow, his arms folded and his face like a thundercloud.

'And what are you lot then?' He had a Newcastle accent you could cut with a knife. 'Bloody comedians?'

The little party of men flowed towards him, already lost.

The coxswain saw Sheridan and threw up a stiff salute.

'Mangin, sir.' He ignored Keyes. 'Glad to 'ave you aboard.' He glanced at the men who were stumbling down the steep brow. 'An' don't forget yer bloody bags an' 'ammicks then!' The roar brought them running back again. He added calmly, 'Soon 'ave 'em into shape. Poor little sods.'

The coxswain watched until a leading seaman had sorted the newcomers into some sort of order and then said, 'Captain's aft, sir. Expectin' you.'

Sheridan nodded. I can imagine.

He answered, 'Thanks, 'Swain. The ship looks pretty good. Considering.'

'Aye.' Mangin watched him curiously. 'Saw your last ship over yonder. Poor old girl. They're takin' the 'eart outa 'er.'

Sheridan studied the coxswain. The mainstay of any destroyer. This one certainly had his wits about him. He already knew more about him than he did about them.

'She was a happy one.'

'This, too.' Mangin glanced aft where a crisp new ensign floated in a sluggish breeze. 'An' I've seen a few on 'em. Old but dependable.' He looked at Keyes for the first time. 'Unlike some.'

Together and in single file they walked down the brow where the quartermaster and gangway sentry watched them with neither interest nor surprise. A few dockyard men were still in evidence, but the ship was feeling alive, and there was some sort of machinery throbbing quietly below, a touch of warmth from one of the vents near the after funnel.

Keyes ventured, 'Where will my cabin be, er, 'Swain?'

Mangin smiled gently.

'*Cabin*, sir? I believe they're fittin' you into a cupboard down aft.'

Mangin added to Sheridan, 'Not much for you to bother about yet, sir. The bulk of the 'ands'll be comin' aboard this afternoon. There's only the duty part o' the watch 'ere at present.' He glared at the waiting men with their hammocks. 'An' this shower o' course.'

'Wardroom?'

'Some replacements, sir.' Mangin tugged his hat over his eyes. His head barely came up to Sheridan's shoulder. 'Gunnery officer an' navigatin' officer 'ave been with us for some while, as 'ave the engineer an' gunner (T). But the subbies, the doc, *this* young gentleman, an' o' course yourself, are new arrivals, so to speak.'

They walked aft in silence. Sheridan thought how spacious she now appeared. But once filled with her new complement there would be barely enough room to think.

Excellent sea boats, easy to handle, the old V and W's had once been the pride of the Service. Now, overloaded with modern equipment and weapons to fight a different sort of war from the one against the Kaiser's navy, their companies had swollen

20

accordingly. From about one hundred to nearly one hundred and forty, and with less space than ever.

Mangin said, 'I'll be off then, sir. I'll see your gear is stowed when it comes aboard, an' will take you round the ship after "Up Spirits".'

'I think I'd better snatch a quick shave.'

Mangin grimaced. 'I'd go to the captain now, sir, if I was you.'

Keyes asked, 'What will I do?'

Mangin beamed. 'Follow me.' The merest pause. 'Sir.'

Sheridan ducked through a screen door and sighed. *Here we go again.*

Drummond sat at the desk in his day cabin and put his name to yet one more document. He was conscious of the ship murmuring around and above him, the busy clatter of feet along the iron deck, the squeak of tackles as more stores were cradled aboard to be sorted and checked.

He was also aware of Leading Writer Pickerell's heavy breathing by his elbow as he folded reports or prepared another paper for his captain's attention. Pickerell was a good writer, usually overworked, and very conscious of his small confidences. He was more like a confidential clerk than a schoolmaster, which was what he had been just two years ago.

More feet on deck, and the coxswain's harsh voice, muffled but easily recognisable. Good old Tommy Mangin. Hard as nails, quick with tongue and fists, but strangely popular with nearly everyone.

'That's about it, sir.' Pickerell gathered up the signal log and some of the other files. 'The dockyard manager will be coming to clear things with you about lunchtime.'

'Thank you.'

Drummond stood up and walked into his sleeping cabin. His quarters were almost as large as the whole wardroom. A sign of less democratic days. When a captain was expected to entertain, to be *seen* for what he was. He crossed to the mirror above his handbasin and studied himself critically. He would make the most of his quarters while he could. He always did in harbour. Once clear of the last marker buoy he would be on the bridge. Either in his chair by the screen, or snatching cat-naps in his tiny sea cabin abaft the wheelhouse. These old ships had all their officers' accommodation right aft. Separated from the overcrowded forecastle not merely by rank but by the boiler- and engine-room bulkheads. On more than one occasion he had been marooned on the bridge by savage storms in the Atlantic, standing watch by watch with the luckless O.O.W. while the rest of the officers were battened down in their wardroom, un- able to make the dash along the narrow iron deck for fear of being swept overboard.

He touched his face, feeling the lines around his eyes. Some of the strain had gone, he decided doubtfully. He had brown hair, which was unruly within minutes of combing it. Level eyes, dark brown, giving him an almost wistful appearance. He grimaced. He would be twenty-nine next month. He felt about eighty.

He thought of his new company. It would not take long for the personalities to emerge. The willing ones, the jolly-jacks, those who would stay cool in action. Those who would break. He wondered about his first lieutenant. Frank had been a regu- lar, not that that meant much any more. The efficient survived. The careless soon bought it.

Most of the officers would be temporary ones when *Warlock* dipped her stem into open sea again. The gunnery officer, Lieu- tenant Giles Rankin, had been a car salesman, the sub-lieutenants were too young to have been anything before the war. The doc- tor was apparently a newcomer to any sort of ship, and had hardly qualified before entering the Navy. The navigating officer, Lieutenant Richard Wingate, was an unusual bird. He had joined the Navy as a boy, and had obtained his commission just prior to the outbreak of war. A scholarship boy, a very unusual achievement in times of peace. Young, cheerful and outwardly unruffled by almost everything, he was a godsend.

Like Bruce Galbraith, the commissioned engineer. Although he wore only a single stripe on his usually grubby reefer, he was almost the oldest man aboard. They got on well together.

Another old-timer was Mr. Noakes, the gunner (T). He *was* the oldest man aboard. He had been retired and had been re- called when it was at last realised that Hitler had meant all that he had said. Noakes had joined the Navy as a boy in 1911, before even the Kaiser had been seen as a real enemy. But unlike the navigating officer he had worked his way up to warrant rank step by painful step. A bitter man. Usually so full of resentment against 'young bloody amateurs' who had been promoted over his head that he could barely conceal it. It never seemed to occur to him that they might be more intelligent. But he ran his part of the ship like a piece of oiled machinery. And that was something.

Drummond tugged the comb through his hair and touched the blue and white ribbon on his left breast. An average wartime ship's company. He grinned, the effort pushing the strain from his face, revealing him as the man underneath. Youthful, reckless, and with little to hope beyond tomorrow.

He heard the other door open and Pickerell leaving, speaking to someone.

Drummond walked through to the cabin and said abruptly, 'You must be Sheridan?'

'Yes, sir. I'm sorry about being adrift. I'll see it doesn't happen again.'

Drummond gestured to a chair. 'Good.'

He watched him as he sat down. He had the look of experience. Well balanced, but a man who gave little away. A lean, hawkish face. One which would interest women.

He said, 'You were Number One in the *Venture*, I see.'

Sheridan had an easy voice. No accent. Difficult to place. 'Yes, sir.'

He added briskly, 'You were aboard during the Russian convoy affair.'

The reply was equally sharp. 'And a lot of others, sir!'

Drummond relaxed slightly. That was Sheridan's problem. *Venture* had been part of the escort on one of those convoys to Russia. He had done two himself and needed little reminding. A living, tormenting hell of ice and blinding snow, screaming gales and cold which got right inside the marrow of every bone. And whenever there was a lull the long-range bombers came. Or the U-boats, or, like *Venture*'s convoy, there was the threat of the big German battleships sneaking out from Norwegian lairs to decimate overloaded merchant ships with their mighty armament.

That particular convoy had been beset with troubles after mustering near Iceland. The weather had been worse than usual, and the only escort carrier had had to return to harbour with half her flight deck stove in by tremendous seas.

One battleship had been sent as covering force, just in case. She had been the *Conqueror*, a familiar sight in peacetime at reviews and on world cruises. Built just after the Great War, she had been something of an oddity, and had never fired her eight fifteen-inch guns in anger.

In wartime, signals sometimes got confused, like the men who made or received them. It was reported that a German battleship, escorted by the Navy's old enemy, the battlecruiser *Scharnhorst*, and powerful destroyers were out of their fjords in Norway and already dashing to attack the slow-moving convoy. The order to scatter had been given, although it was now being said that the man on the spot should have waited a bit longer. It was easy to say that from a safe fireside or a barracks wardroom.

The convoy scattered to the winds, the escort spread its thin resources and then followed suit. Only the *Conqueror* remained. Without air cover, and too slow to escape as the German warship loomed through a snow squall, its great guns already homed on to the elderly British ship by radar, which *Conqueror*'s builders had not even dreamed about. It was not even a battle. It was a massacre. Of the *Conqueror*'s thirteen hundred officers and men, three were recovered by a terrified neutral Swedish freighter, the only witness.

The convoy survived, or most of it, but the escorting destroyers bore the brunt of *Conqueror*'s fate like a personal disgrace.

Sheridan said harshly, 'I still think about it.'

Drummond walked to a scuttle and watched a Wren riding a bicycle along the side of the dock. Most of the seamen nearby stopped work to admire her.

He said, '*Conqueror*'s fate was decided long before she crossed swords with that German battleship.' He was thinking aloud. 'Built in peacetime, with little thought for real protection. One shell through those thinly armoured decks and . . .' He turned and added quietly, 'Well, that's what happened.'

Sheridan was watching him, as if gauging the right moment.

'I suppose it's why I've not been offered a command, sir?' He could not hide the bitterness any longer. 'My ship was there, as were a good many others. Does it mean we're all branded?'

'Is that what you think?'

'As a matter of fact, I do. My captain at the time was the

24

senior officer of the escort. He was obeying orders. You know he killed himself after the enquiry, don't you?'

'Yes. He was stupid to do so, in my opinion.'

Sheridan stared at him as if he had struck him in the face.

'He was a damned good captain, sir!'

Drummond strode to the desk and leaned on it, both hands gripping the edge until the pain steadied him.

'We are not here to discuss either *Conqueror* or your last ship! *Warlock* is my command, and what she does, how well she does it, is my concern! And I hope it will now be yours, too!' He was talking loudly but could not help it. 'You have been appointed as Number One because I *need* a first lieutenant, not because this ship is only good enough for you. She's a fine destroyer and her record will stand beside those more modern creations which swing round their buoys in Scapa waiting for the enemy to come out of hiding!'

Sheridan's eyes followed him as he strode restlessly to the opposite side.

'Don't show any contempt for this or any other old destroyer in front of me. In February last year, when *Scharnhorst* and *Gneisenau* and the cruiser *Prinz Eugen* broke through the English Channel and made a laughing stock of our intelligence system, it was a bloody handful of these old V and W's which were sent to stop them! The new ones were up at Scapa, like they were when *Conqueror* went down. So don't lecture me about anything so petty as your chances of a command!'

'I'm sorry, sir.' Sheridan stood up. 'I really am.'

'*Sit down*, Number One.' Drummond looked away. 'My fault entirely. Rank has its privileges, but insulting your opinions is not one of them. Not in my book.'

They studied each other for several seconds.

Then Drummond said, 'I came aboard early. If I'd been sensible I'd have stayed in that draughty hotel until now. Then you'd have been aboard first.' He smiled gravely. 'And you would not think, as you do now, that your new captain is halfway round the bend.'

Sheridan grinned.

'Like the rest of us, sir.'

Drummond pressed a button and waited for Owles to peer through the door.

'Drinks, sir? Right away, sir.' He saw Sheridan. 'New first lieutenant, sir? Hope you had a nice trip down, sir?'

He was gone before Sheridan could reply.

Drummond smiled. 'Don't bother. His is a different world.' He looked at the bulkhead clock. It was nine o'clock. He said, 'Early for drinks, but after yesterday I think I need one.' He studied Sheridan's stubbled chin. 'And I'm certain you do.'

Later, after Owles had brought glasses and a decanter, Drummond added, 'Our orders have arrived. We will proceed to Harwich, day after tomorrow. There's to be some sort of conference on the flotilla's future.'

Sheridan watched as he poured the drinks.

'Harwich. I've been there several times. I expect your flotilla has got a new Captain (D) since I was last visiting the place?'

Drummond held out the glass very carefully.

'Actually, Number One, there has been a new Captain (D) appointed more recently than that. Last week, to be exact.'

Sheridan hesitated, knowing there was more.

'Thought you should know. He is Captain Dudley Beaumont.' He saw uncertainty giving way to dismay as he added, 'The only officer to survive from the *Conqueror*.' He raised his glass. '*Cheers*.'

2

Scrapyard Flotilla

DRUMMOND leaned back in the desk chair and carefully filled his favourite pipe before slipping it into his reefer pocket. Only one scuttle was still uncovered by its deadlight, for, like the rest of the ship, all unnecessary openings were sealed, watertight doors clipped home in readiness for leaving harbour. It was doubly necessary to be careful with a company partly made up of men who had never been to sea before.

The deck trembled to the engines' steady beat as Galbraith carried out his usual tests. No need to worry there. A scraping thud announced that the brow had been swayed ashore, that the very last man, the postman, was safely gathered into the hull. He glanced again at Sheridan's neat message pad. Only two men adrift, both of whom he knew. One had been granted immediate compassionate leave, his home having been bombed three nights ago. The other had merely failed to arrive. Probably drunk somewhere, or fast asleep on the wrong train. It would all be sorted out later.

He thought of Sheridan's efforts in the last two days. He had more than shown his ability and energy, and he could understand his bitterness at not being given a chance of command.

From the moment the bulk of hands had returned from leave the work had never stopped. Ammunition to be loaded and sorted into its correct stowage, from heavy four-inch shells to the masses of cannon and automatic weapon magazines. Stores and crates of tinned milk, jam, tobacco and paint. Rum and wire hawsers, canvas for just about everything from repairing bridge dodgers to sewing up bloated remains found drifting in abandoned lifeboats. It never failed to impress Drummond that a hull could take so much. Then the oil fuel pumped across from a nearby tanker, while Galbraith and his chief stoker watched the pulsating hoses as if able to judge the capacity to the exact pint after so much practice.

The work had ceased after dusk the previous evening, and Sheridan had asked him along to the wardroom to meet the rest of the new officers informally over a glass. He had refused, not because he had not wanted to go, but because he had known that as Sheridan had not yet had time to get to know his own wardroom companions, he, and not the captain, would feel an outsider.

In the muffled distance the tannoy squeaked to a bosun's call and a voice said, 'Special sea-dutymen close up! Hands to stations for leaving harbour in ten minutes.'

Drummond found he was waiting, almost poised in his chair. The next announcement would tell him a bit more about his first lieutenant.

The quartermaster's voice continued, 'Both watches will be required. Fo'c'slemen on the fo'c'sle, quarterdeckmen on the quarterdeck. Dress of the day, Number Threes.' The tannoy went dead.

Drummond stood up and crossed to the uncovered scuttle. Sheridan was on the ball. Normally, one watch would be sufficient to stand at harbour stations, while the other prepared to man the defences. But with so many untried men, and officers, he was taking no chances. It would help them to move as a team, and, anyway, it would be a while before they had worked down the Medway, past Sheerness into open water where trouble might be expected at any time.

The important thing was, Sheridan had used his intelligence. He had not asked. He had acted as he saw fit.

Owles entered the door and watched him gloomily.

'Off again then, sir.'

Drummond patted his pockets and glanced quickly round the cabin. Freshly washed grey sweater. Leather sea boots and binoculars. Duffel coat, the latter still bearing the paint stains from the last refit. A year back. It seemed like a lifetime.

He reached for his cap and then sat down again. It would not do to appear impatient.

He said, 'Harwich in time for supper, Owles.'

If they were lucky, he thought. The calendar on his desk said it was June 13th. A Sunday. It might take a bit longer today. The Navy was strange like that. Peace or war, Sunday was always a special, confusing occasion.

There was a tap at the door and Fitzroy, the petty officer tele-graphist, stepped over the coaming, a pad in his fist.

'From tower, sir. Proceed when ready.' He grinned. 'I think they mean right away, sir. There's another destroyer hovering about. Needs our berth.' It seemed to amuse him.

Overhead the tannoy again. 'Hands to stations for leaving harbour! Stand by wires and fenders!'

The deck gave another, more insistent quiver, and Drummond pictured the engineer with his men sealed in their world of gleaming steel, dials and gauges, steam and sweat.

He looked at the clock. Four minutes to go. Sheridan was cutting it fine. He appeared at that moment, cap under his arm, his hawkish features set in an expressionless mask.

'Ready to proceed, sir.'

Drummond jammed his cap on his head and nodded.

'Fair enough.'

It was a fine day at last, the air clean and crisp. No clouds, but the sun was watery and gave little warmth as Drummond strode along the port side towards the break in the forecastle and the straight, uncovered ladders which led to the signal bridge, where the slender-barrelled Oerlikons had been mounted on either wing, cutting down the space even more. Then up further to the place where he would probably remain until they moored again.

The bridge was crowded. Lookouts and bosun's mates, Lieutenant Wingate, the navigating officer, standing dead-centre on the compass platform speaking quietly to his yeoman. Giles Rankin, the gunnery officer, was compressed into the centre of a small group consisting of the two sub-lieutenants, Midshipman Keyes and, surprisingly, Surgeon Lieutenant Adrian Vaughan, the new doctor. He was a strange, unsmiling young man, with hair and features so pale he could almost be an albino.

They all turned as Rankin drawled, 'Thought it might be a good idea for them to stand up here on the forebridge as we get under way, sir. Just this once.'

Drummond nodded to them. 'Good morning, gentlemen. Watch everything and ask if you want to.'

He turned as a voice said, 'All closed up, sir. Coxswain on the wheel.'

Wingate called, 'Number One's singled up, sir.'

Drummond walked to the forepart of the bridge and laid his

29

binoculars behind the glass screen. The newly painted forecastle, the long barrels of the two forward guns, reached towards the stem where Sheridan was standing in the eyes of the ship. Beside him was a signalman waiting to haul down the Jack once contact with the land had been cut.

'Stand by.'

He ignored the watching officers and concentrated on the dipping and tautening mooring lines. The forecastle was a litter of wires, amongst which the seamen moved like creatures being stalked by an endless serpent. It was an illusion. He saw Leading Seaman Eaden, captain of the forecastle, striding through the apparent confusion, his gloved hands pushing a wire into a man's fist here, or whipping off a lashing prior to letting go. Even from the high bridge it was easy to spot the new men, Drummond thought. They held wires without recognition, waiting to see what the others would do.

'Standing by, sir.'

Petty Officer Tucker, the yeoman of signals, said gruffly, 'From *Observer*, sir. *How long will you be?*'

Tucker was an old hand. Short and stout, with a beard so thick it was hard to see what he was thinking.

Drummond glanced at the waiting destroyer. Brand-new, single funnel, twin mountings for her powerful armament, she was idling impatiently towards the jetty. She even had her fenders down. Drummond could see her captain, the scrambled egg on his cap as he peered at the moored *Warlock*.

'Tell him, about three hundred and twelve feet.'

He forgot the other ship and snapped, 'Let go aft!'

He saw Sheridan acknowledge as the order was passed, the men with heavy fenders moving them nearer to the flared bows.

A bosun's mate called, 'All clear aft, sir.'

He could almost feel the other destroyer breathing on him.

He turned on the grating and looked down at the new officers. One of them had 'New Zealand' on his shoulder.

'Space here, or lack of it, means we will have to go ahead on the back spring and get the stern to swing out into the stream.' He saw them nod in unison. 'Remember it. Take your time. You've plenty of chances, but only one ship.' They laughed, as he knew they would.

'Slow ahead starboard.'

The bridge vibrated evenly, and a pencil rolled across the uncovered chart table and fell to the deck.

Drummond stood up on the side of the bridge watching the spring tightening and slackening as Sheridan's forecastle party eased it carefully around the bollards. Too much strain and you could snap a wire like a thread. Then it would flail inboard like a lethal whip.

He turned aft, watching as the outboard screw churned the sluggish water into froth. Noakes, the gunner (T), had his wires already neatly made up into coils, his men fallen into two lines for leaving harbour. He breathed out slowly as the sunlight lanced down on to a narrow sliver of water between quarterdeck and jetty which had not been there before. The stern was starting to swing out, angling away, while the solitary spring took the ship's slow thrust ahead like a halter.

Across the water a loud-hailer squeaked and then the other destroyer's captain exclaimed loudly, 'Thank God! You were there so long, I thought your ship was holding up the jetty!'

Drummond waved without turning his head.

The *Warlock* was now standing out from the jetty at about forty-five degrees, the nearest stonework hidden below the great flared forecastle.

'Stop starboard.' He waved to Sheridan. 'Let go forrard!'

The Jack had vanished, and Drummond saw that same Wren sitting on her bicycle watching them leave. A few dockyard workers were waiting to receive the other destroyer. Otherwise it was pretty quiet. Here, it was all too commonplace to comment upon, let alone show emotion for one more elderly destroyer going back to war.

'Slow astern together.'

He heard the coxswain's reply up the brass pipe where Wingate was watchfully contemplating other shipping nearby.

Sternfirst, the *Warlock* thrashed past the new destroyer, between two moored storeships and a dredger, her small wash stirring up waste and shavings, leaking oil and flotsam which were part of any dockyard.

'Stop together.'

Below his feet he heard the jangle of telegraphs, then, 'Both engines stopped, sir.'

Drummond took a quick look around. Two small harbour

launches. A cruiser moored further downstream. The latter would need a salute, but he had already seen Vickery, the chief bosun's mate, and his acolytes standing in line ready to pipe their respects.

It was all like a pattern. His mind recorded everything, discarding normality, noting only possible flaws.

He saw Keyes staring up at him, eyes filling his face. It must be a big moment for him. The greatest thing in his life. Eighteen years old. Not in a barracks or a classroom with some grey-haired instructor. At sea. On the bridge of a destroyer.

Impulsively he said, 'Up here, Mr. Keyes.' He saw the indecision and added, 'Chop, chop! We'll be astride the sandbars in a moment!'

The boy stood beside him, his hands in tight fists, as if expecting a blow or a reprimand.

'Right, Mr. Keyes.' Drummond pointed over the screen, seeing Wingate grinning from beside the voice-pipes. 'Take her out. Slow ahead. Starboard ten. Steady her, and then leave it to the coxswain. He can follow the buoys without constant wheel orders.'

There was a stunned silence. Then Keyes whispered, 'Slow ahead together.'

Nothing happened.

Wingate tapped the voice-pipe with some brass dividers. 'In *here*, Mid!'

Keyes tried again. He was shaking, his face was like chalk.

He said, 'Slow ahead together.'

Drummond felt the immediate response, remembering his first time. The ship charging away under him. Running wild.

He said quietly, 'That can-shaped buoy, Mr. Keyes, do you see it?' He saw him nod jerkily. 'Keep it to *starboard* as we leave the dockyard boundary.'

Keyes seemed to recover. 'Starboard ten!' He groped across to the gyro repeater. 'Midships! Er—*steady!*'

Mangin's voice came up the pipe. 'Steady, sir. Course zero-four-five.'

Drummond looked away, hiding a smile. Mangin had ignored the orders and had taken over control as soon as he had recognised the midshipman's voice.

The cruiser's craggy bulk moved ponderously towards them,

a marine bugler at the guardrails beside the officer of the day.

Drummond nodded, and a bosun's mate pressed down the tannoy switch.

'Attention on the upper deck! Face to starboard and salute!'

Warlock pushed her way slowly towards the watery sunlight, her men fallen in on forecastle and quarterdeck in swaying blue lines, the officers with hands lifted in salute. High above the forebridge, on the little catwalk which ran around the glass radar lantern, known as the 'jampot', the saluting party raised their silver calls, and across the narrow strip between cruiser and destroyer echoed the shrill mark of respect. It in turn was returned by the blare of a lordly bugle.

Drummond said, 'Very well, Mr. Keyes. Now that you have got us safely out of harbour, you may rejoin the others. You'll get more practice later on.'

Wingate said softly, 'You made his day, sir.'

The navigator was a dark-faced, gipsy-looking man. There was something theatrical about him. About his black leather coat he always wore at sea, his sheepskin-lined boots. Even his cap seemed different from everyone else's. Perhaps he was enjoying his commission to its full. Either way, he was a very good navigator.

Strangely enough, Rankin, the ex-car salesman, was far more of the regular officer in appearance than any of them. He had a sleek, glossy head with an exact centre parting. Narrow, haughty features, and a drawl which could have come straight from Bertie Wooster. He must have sold very expensive cars to have learned so much, Drummond thought.

Rankin was saying airily, 'Tour of the ship, inspection of forecastle and main galley, then you can carry on about your allotted duties.' His sharp nose came round with a jerk. '*Got it?*'

They shuffled to the rear of the bridge, suitably impressed.

Drummond sat down on his tall wooden chair which was bolted to the port side of the bridge.

'Fall out harbour stations, if you please. Port Watch to defence stations.'

Sheridan clambered into the bridge and saluted formally.

'All secured forrard, sir.'

'Very good.' He leaned back in his chair and groped for his pipe. 'They did quite well, I thought.'

'I thought so too, sir.' Sheridan sounded pleased. Then he added, 'That new destroyer, the *Observer*. Quite a ship. It would be something to command her.'

Drummond threw his match into the little tin which was tacked to his chair. Across the screen he could see small houses dotted about on the shoreline, the clouds of gulls diving and circling above some invisible fishing boat in the narrows. He watched the pipe smoke plucked away over the bridge and motionless lookouts.

He rarely thought about the thing which was obviously uppermost in Sheridan's mind. Perhaps because he had been so long in different ships under such varying conditions. Twenty-nine next month, and yet how full his life had been. To the Naval College at the age of twelve and on into his own specialised world. A battleship, a cruiser, two destroyers, a sloop, and others he had almost forgotten. He would well appreciate how Keyes must feel, even though his new life was so spartan because of the war. To Drummond, those early days had been quite different. Ships at anchor, awnings spread, bands playing. The harbours and bays made bright by glittering scuttles and fairy lights. The show of Britain's naval might only thinly hidden behind cocktail parties and regattas, visitors in beautiful gowns, bare shoulders and bold glances.

He said slowly, 'I suppose so.'

Drummond touched the worn teak rail below the screen. Why this ship? What was so special about her? Sheridan's remark made him vaguely uneasy. It was stupid, and he knew it. He was a regular officer. A professional. Provided he lived to see it, promotion must inevitably come. Other ships, greater responsibility.

Feet clattered over the gratings and Owles said, 'Brought the remains of the coffee, sir.'

From port to starboard, very low down, three Spitfires streaked through the sunlight with their familiar whistling drone.

Perhaps because *Warlock* was born in his own time, he thought vaguely. When he had entered the Naval College she had already been nine years old. Her record of service was quite amazing. All those miles, pounding away, year in, year out. She had been born too late to fight the Kaiser's fleet, and had steamed on the sidelines merely to watch as it entered harbour to sur-

render. 1919 found her at Odessa, helping to evacuate the terrified aristocrats fleeing in the face of the Russian Revolution.
The China Station, to guard British possessions, watching helplessly as the Japs bombed the Chinese settlements. To Spain for
the Civil War, where she had worked in perfect unison with
another destroyer to carry off trapped neutrals from that savage
encounter. The other destroyer had been German. She had been
sunk by the R.A.F. a few months back.

When this war had exploded across Europe, *Warlock* had been
well past her prime, but with her sixty-odd consorts she did her
best whenever the occasion offered itself. Lifting off exhausted
soldiers from abandoned beaches. East coast convoys and E-boat
Alley, the Atlantic, North Russia.

He ran his fingers along the smooth wood. And she could still
give thirty-four knots. *With a following wind*, as Frank used
to say.

Sheridan asked suddenly, 'The Captain (D). Beaumont. Have
you ever met him?'

'I served with him once, as a matter of fact.' He turned and
saw the astonishment on his dark features. 'The Andrew's a small
world. Years ago, it was. I was a snotty in the battleship *Agincourt*. He was the gunnery officer, if I remember rightly.' He
leaned sideways to the voice-pipe. 'Who's on the wheel now?'

'Chief quartermaster, sir.'

He could picture Rumsey's lazy grin.

'Good. Watch the next leg. There are some practice targets
moored to starboard.'

He looked at Sheridan. 'What was I saying?'

'Beaumont.' He seemed unsure of how to continue. 'I've heard
plenty about him, of course. All those write-ups in the paper.
A lot of people said he should have got the V.C. for what he
did.'

Drummond examined his pipe. *For what he did*. He would
not tell Sheridan it had been bothering him, too, although for
other reasons.

He could only remember Beaumont as a sarcastic bully. The
new hero image just did not seem to fit. Maybe he had changed?
And what exactly had he done on that dreadful day? It was
about eight months ago now. He could recall the horror at hearing of *Conqueror's* destruction, the pity at the pictures of the

three blanketed survivors being landed in a Scottish port. It must have been terrifying to have that great ship blasted away beneath you. To be left in angry seas, bitterly cold, without hope. Three out of thirteen hundred. But what, apart from survive, had Beaumont done?

The yeoman stepped forward. 'Signal, sir. We are to berth alongside *Lomond* upon entering harbour. Captain (D) requires our E.T.A.'

'Very well.' He looked at Wingate. 'Give the yeoman the time of arrival and make out a reply.'

Sheridan said ruefully, '*Lomond*'s the flotilla leader, I take it. It'd be a good beginning to ram her as we go alongside.'

'An end, more like.'

Sheridan moved away. 'I'll get on with my work, sir.' He climbed over the side of the bridge.

Wingate said, 'I wonder if we're going back to the old job, sir?' He frowned. 'Bloody east coast convoys get on my wick.'

Drummond shrugged. 'We'll see.'

He settled down in the chair, his eyes distant as he watched the channel swimming slightly across the screen under the helmsman's hands. Reflected in the glass he could see the steel gate through which Sheridan had just departed. It was clipped open to avoid the constant rattling. It was a new gate. But, like the other one, was a quarter of an inch thick.

The German E-boat had been moored to a navigation buoy, some miles east of Flamborough Head. It had been raining at the time, and the night had been as black as a boot. *Warlock* had been senior escort to a slow north-bound convoy. Fifteen assorted ships, some of which had been many years older than this one. The escort, apart from *Warlock*, had been a sloop, two trawlers and an armed yacht. You had to make do with what you could get.

That was the trouble with convoy work. *Strain.* Fear of running down the next ship ahead. Even more fearful of losing her as you steamed without lights between the protective minefields. The east coast was lined with protruding mastheads. Forlorn memorials to vessels lost to enemy and minefield alike.

The radar operator had picked up the blip, but perhaps they had been too long on the same job and saw only what they expected to see. The plot had reported the blip as the buoy. It was where it should be.

The convoy had sailed on through the sheeting rain.

The E-boat's powerful diesels had roared into life spontaneously with her cannon fire, and as she tore through the ponderous merchantmen she fired her torpedoes for good measure.

It was all in the report. Almost commonplace. A cultured newsreader on the B.B.C. had eventually announced, *'During the night, enemy E-boats attacked one of our convoys. There were some casualties, but one enemy E-boat was sunk.'* That had been the sloop's work. She had almost been rammed by the thirty-knot E-boat as she had loped along at the rear of the convoy. *Tail-end Charlie.* And she had slammed two shells into the other vessel within minutes of the original attack.

But that one burst of cannon fire had swept over *Warlock's* bridge like hammers of hell. One signalman and a messenger who had been carrying a fanny of cocoa to the bridge had died. Without effort Drummond could see the blood and cocoa thinning in the torrential rain, see Frank's eyes glinting in the reflected glow from the blazing E-boat.

Both legs. He shuddered. It would be better to die.

From the opposite corner of the bridge Wingate watched him thoughtfully. He guessed what he might be thinking. How close the skipper and Frank had been.

He smiled wearily. Like that bloody girl in Maidstone where he had spent his leave. Kept going on about the war. What was it like? Have you ever had to kill anyone? When all he had wanted to do was . . .

He leaned over the voice-pipes. 'Port ten.' Pause. 'Midships. Steady.'

Quite a girl. He had managed it in the end, but she had burst into tears. His smile spread to a grin. Silly cow.

'Aircraft, sir! Green one-one-oh!'

An instant's chill. The creak of metal as the slender muzzles swing towards the washed-out sky.

Then, 'Disregard. A Beaufighter. Carry on with the sweep.'

Drummond relaxed again, seeing two grubby Asdic trawlers heading up channel. He felt the pressure of the chair against his ribs as *Warlock* lifted slightly in a sudden swell. Open water ahead. She seemed eager to get back, too.

During the last dog watch, as *Warlock* moved slowly between the lines of moored escort vessels, trawlers and all the motley collection of ships which went to make the Harwich Force, Drummond was certain he had never known a finer evening. The sky was salmon pink, and it had all the makings of a fine sunset. No breeze, and even the turbulent current caused by the entwining of the rivers Stour and Orwell, so often the nightmare of less experienced captains, was barely noticeable.

As before, the newly joined officers were grouped in one corner of the bridge, trying to see everything, and at the same time endeavouring to keep out of everyone else's way, as with careful deliberation Drummond conned his ship towards Parkstone Quay and the moored flotilla leader, *Lomond*. Despite her familiar dazzle paint, the other destroyer looked almost orange in the warm glow, and Drummond saw the duty watch gathering along her decks to receive heaving lines when they nudged alongside.

The passage up from Chatham had been uneventful. Just as if the enemy was giving them time to get settled.

Drummond glanced quickly at the small group below the compass platform. One more exciting moment, he thought. All these ships, old and new, scarred and worn from constant service around one of the war's most dangerous pieces of coastline. Within reach of air attack and the more hated sneak raider which swept inshore, dropped bombs and was away before a warning could be sounded. Mines, E-boats, even German submarines, had been tempted to hunt in this busy and vital area.

'Port ten.'

He heard Mangin's calm acknowledgement, imagined him watching the nearby ships and jetty through his wheelhouse scuttles.

'Midships. Steady as you go.'

Fore and aft the hands were fallen in again, the wires laid ready to be released and then made fast. For how long this time? he wondered. Sheridan was in the bows, his head slightly turned to watch a trio of motor torpedo boats growling throatily towards the sea. Low-lying, their tattered ensigns flapping impatiently, as if they were irritated at being throttled down by harbour regulations. Once clear of the base they would be off, perhaps to the Hook of Holland. Tomorrow, if they survived, they would return, their tubes empty, their young crews only then beginning to realise it was all over for another short while.

Drummond studied the *Lomond*, thinking about Captain Beaumont, and what the change of control might bring. The previous Captain (D) had been a veteran of destroyers, but had begun to show the signs of exhaustion. He had been appointed to a training depot in the north. To make sailors out of milkmen and solicitors, to help feed the ever-hungry fleet with its greatest need.

Leading Seaman Eaden was poised at the forecastle guard-rails, a heaving line in his gloved fists. Sheridan was taking no chances. Aft, and on the iron deck by the unmatched funnels, others waited to move when ordered. He leaned over the screen and saw the gunner (T) on his quarterdeck, one foot on a depth-charge rack, hands on his hips, making him look almost deformed. Noakes was square in shape and had no visible neck at all. His cap, as always, was worn flat on the top of his bald head, like a lid, screwed down to contain the working furies within the man until some safety-valve in the shape of a clumsy rating presented itself.

He turned towards the ships moored ahead of the flotilla leader. Old, familiar, their similarity in outline and design did not deceive him one bit. In pitch blackness he could find his way about any of them, and yet each had become an individual over the years. Or perhaps ships were born with varying characters, he thought vaguely. It was odd that one destroyer might bring fame to a man. The same ship could ruin another. Everyone scoffed about it, of course. Coincidence, luck, bad management, or an ever-changing scale of odds, but inwardly many thought otherwise and took no chance.

'Stop starboard.'

He watched the *Warlock*'s shadow creep across the *Lomond*'s quarterdeck. She was typical of her class, and somewhat larger than *Warlock*. Better armed, too. Two men crouched on her searchlight mounting, paint brushes poised while they watched *Warlock*'s careful approach. Working on a Sunday. They must be under punishment. A cook in shirt-sleeves and apron scurried along her iron deck with a heavy enamel bucket. Some delicacy for the wardroom, or his dirty underwear, it was hard to tell.

'Starboard ten.' He craned over the screen. 'Midships. Slow astern starboard.'

The water between them had lost the sunlight, and he saw Eaden's arm going back, and then watched the first heaving line soar across to the waiting hands. He could sense Keyes and one of the sub-lieutenants watching him in those last moments. They would learn more by keeping their eyes on the deck below.

'Stop port. Half astern starboard.'

He controlled the edge in his tone as the flared forecastle swung too sharply towards *Lomond*'s hull, and then, caught by the sudden thrust astern, hesitated and came under control again.

The headrope was already being hauled across on the heaving line, and when he peered aft he saw the men scrambling to follow suit with sternrope and spring.

He heard the harsh tone of some invisible leading seaman. 'Grab that fender! Move yer bloody selves, or Number One'll 'ave yer guts for garters! An' I'll *weep* meself if you scratches our lovely new paint!'

'Stop starboard.'

The deck shuddered as the backwash from the starboard screw surged noisily along the ship's side.

Fenders screeched, and as more lines were passed across and turned quickly on to bollards, *Warlock* came to rest.

He heard the New Zealand sub-lieutenant, Hillier, say quietly, 'Hardly felt it. We could have cracked an egg that time.'

Drummond returned the wave from an officer on *Lomond*'s bridge and said, 'It isn't always that easy.'

There was bustle everywhere while wires were slacked off or tautened until the trim was to Sheridan's satisfaction. A small brow was being hauled across from the other ship's deck, and he saw a postman from the base standing by the guardrail waiting to come aboard. Back mail perhaps which had at last caught up with them. Parcels from home. A birthday cake for someone, lovingly made from carefully hoarded rations by a wife or mother.

He smiled gravely as he watched the foreshortened shapes of seamen hurrying back and forth below the bridge. Mostly mothers. The average age of *Warlock*'s company was about twenty-three, at a guess.

'All secure fore and aft, sir!'

'Very well. Ring off main engines.'

He watched the hurrying figure of Lieutenant-Commander Dorian de Pass, *Lomond*'s Number One, and therefore Captain (D)'s right-hand man, striding towards the brow which had only just been made fast. Thin as a stick, he had a huge nose which he moved from side to side as he walked. As if searching for some unidentified smell or gas leak. Fastidious and fussy, he was known as the Informer by most of the flotilla.

Within minutes he had reached the bridge, the nose seeking out the group of new officers, examining and then discarding them as he saw and saluted Drummond.

'Welcome back, sir.' He was always formal. Even when drunk. 'Everything in order, I trust?'

Drummond smiled. 'But of course. How are things here?'

De Pass threw up his hands. 'A madhouse. But I—that is, we, Captain (D) and myself, have got some semblance of order.' He shook his head worriedly. 'Big changes afoot.' His eyes moved over Drummond's faded reefer and scuffed sea boots. 'He'd like to see you as soon as convenient.'

Drummond handed his binoculars to a bosun's mate.

'You mean now, I take it.'

'Well, yes.'

Sheridan appeared on the bridge and saluted.

'Any instructions, sir?'

Drummond looked at de Pass.

'Well?'

The other man glanced at Sheridan, the nose hovering for a few extra seconds.

'No shore leave. Not tonight anyway. Otherwise . . .' He shrugged.

'Carry on, Number One. I'm going across to the leader right away.'

De Pass followed him down to the iron deck where, mercifully, Vickery, the chief boatswain's mate, had mustered a side party.

De Pass said irritably, 'Your new Number One. Another temporary. Dear me.'

Drummond grinned. 'Better watch out. One of them might get your job.'

The calls shrilled and salutes were exchanged as Drummond

walked briskly across the small brow to the other ship. He nodded to the *Lomond*'s O.O.D.

'How's the wife?'

The lieutenant grinned. 'Another kid, I'm afraid, sir.'

He could feel de Pass's disapproval but did not care. It was like a homecoming.

Before entering a screen door he paused and glanced back at his own ship. They were still busily stowing wires, clearing up the tangle. Thin tendrils of smoke drifted from both funnels, and he saw Lieutenant Rankin climbing up to X gun, followed at a discreet distance by an ordnance artificer. How he loved his guns. Even expensive cars might seem dull after the war, he thought.

Between decks it was noticeably more roomy than *Warlock*, for the leader carried extra accommodation for a variety of officers who managed the flotilla's affairs. He heard the buzz of voices and laughter from the wardroom and the clatter of glasses. Sunday in harbour always carried some heavy mess bills. Visitors from other ships, old friends. Anyway, the Sunday supper was usually the same, and needed something to ease it along. Cold Spam, pickles and dehydrated potatoes.

De Pass said, 'Go right in.' He hung his cap carefully on a hook outside the wardroom. 'I expect he'll have a lot to tell you.'

Drummond tapped on the door, pushed it open and stepped into the broad day cabin. All the lights were on, for with the jetty on one side and *Warlock*'s hull nestling against the other, the space would be like a crypt without them.

Captain Dudley Beaumont was standing at the after end of the cabin, one hand behind his back, the other hooked around the buttons of his reefer. Medium height, thick build which might show overweight but for the superb cut of his uniform, Beaumont made an imposing figure. Early forties, but had a face which would now remain much the same for a long while, Drummond thought. A pink face, very smooth and clean. Fair hair, cut short and brushed straight back. He looked as if he had just emerged from a shower or hot bath.

Beaumont said warmly, 'Good to see you, Drummond.' He thrust out his hand. 'The last of my brood, eh?' He chuckled.

Drummond watched as the other man pushed a chair across the carpet. Everything about Beaumont was perfect. The shirt cuffs which shone below his sleeves with the four gleaming stripes were exactly equal, and each had a heavy link which looked like a gold nugget. He had a way of moving, holding himself, as if he was very conscious of each action, like a dancer, or actor. It was difficult to picture him relaxed.

He sat down opposite Drummond and laced his fingers across his stomach. Powerful, large hands, but with pale, almost delicate skin. Manicured.

He said, 'De Pass will have told you we've had a few changes since you were last here.' It was a statement. 'The commodore will be holding a commanding officers' conference tomorrow, but I like to tell my chaps myself. First.' He unlaced his fingers and examined one of them carefully. 'I've been given this appointment to *make* something of the flotilla.' The hand shot up like a traffic policeman's, as if Drummond had just started to interrupt. 'I know what you're going to say, Drummond, and I don't blame you. You'll tell me that the record of our ships is first-rate, that they've done all, no *more* than could have been expected of such, er, *senior* vessels. It is true, of course. But the flotilla has in the past acted as a lot of cantankerous old veterans, as individuals, or part of a larger pattern.' He leaned back in the chair and regarded Drummond calmly. He had very clear blue eyes. Like a child's. 'I am to alter all that. These destroyers are being given a new role. More like that for which they were conceived.'

Drummond cleared his throat. Before the other man he felt like a tramp. Perhaps that was Beaumont's policy.

He asked, 'No more east coast convoys, sir?'

Beaumont patted his pockets absently. 'Correct. I've made a study of these ships. Ever since I was told what their lordships had in mind. They call them the Scrapyard Flotilla round here, don't they?' He frowned. 'I intend to change all that, too.'

Drummond had never thought of their nickname as a slur. It had a sort of affection, an admiration which anyone has for a ship which keeps on going. No matter what.

Beaumont shot out one starched cuff and looked at his watch.

'Can't stop now. Dinner with Nick Brooks tonight. Always has a good table.'

Drummond stood up. 'Then I'll see you at the conference, sir.'

Nick Brooks. So casually mentioned, or was it? To everyone else, that particular being was known as *Admiral* Brooks. A very important person indeed.

'Good. Just wanted to meet you. Straight off the dock, so to speak.' Beaumont rose and flicked his jacket into place. 'You've changed a bit since the old *Agincourt.*' He smiled, showing a set of small white teeth. 'Still, command sits well on your shoulders.'

'Seems a long while ago, sir.'

'I've an excellent memory.' Beaumont regarded him bleakly. 'I hear that your new Number One was in *Venture?*'

Drummond tensed. Nothing *casual* about this one.

He replied, 'Yes, sir. He's settling in with me very well.'

'Hmm. Early days.'

Beaumont walked to a scuttle and bent as if to seek out the sky between the two hulls. He did not speak again, and the sudden tension was almost physical. Beaumont seemed to have switched off, like a machine. He was still by the scuttle, the fading sunlight playing across his hair and shoulder, one pale hand resting against the cabin side. Motionless.

When he did speak, his voice came from a long way off.

'I'll not forget that day. It leaves a scar, you know.' He straightened and turned to face Drummond again. 'But at least they died knowing they were meeting impossible odds.' His eyes seemed to shine more brightly. 'God, I was so proud, so damned *proud!*'

A chief steward peeped around the door.

'Admiral's car on the jetty, sir.' He glanced at Drummond and added, 'I've had the wine sent over to it, sir.'

Beaumont nodded, his mind partly elsewhere.

'Tell the O.O.D. I will be up right away.' He thrust out his hand again. The skin was dry and very smooth. 'Tomorrow then. All commanding officers. Immediately after breakfast.'

Drummond forced a smile, out of depth with this impenetrable man.

'I'd like to tell my officers if we're going to—'

Beaumont snapped, 'Tell them we're going to fight a war!' He tapped Drummond's breast. 'Our way! *My* way!'

Drummond returned to the upper deck, his mind dragging

on Beaumont's strange mood. What in hell's name did he imagine they had been doing all these years?

He saw Sheridan and Wingate waiting to greet him at the brow and was glad of one thing. That, temporarily at least, *Warlock* would get the chance to avoid the drudgery of east coast convoys. Whatever Beaumont had to tell them, convoy work was not going to be included, that was obvious.

The call shrilled again and Sheridan saluted, his eyes anxious.

Drummond turned, and through the canopied guns on *Lomond*'s deck he saw Beaumont climbing into a resplendent staff car, a marine driver snapping to attention by its open door.

Whatever Beaumont's sort of war was going to be, it would certainly be different, he thought.

3

Wondering

SHERIDAN stood with his back to the unlit wardroom fire and allowed the din of conversation and laughter to wash around him like spray. Beyond the half-drawn curtain he could hear the stewards preparing for lunch, so that the rest of the wardroom seemed extra crowded and confined. Including the captain, *Warlock* carried ten officers, nine of whom shared the wardroom, and nine of whom were now either standing or lounging below an unmoving ceiling of tobacco smoke.

'How are you settling in, Number One?'

Sheridan looked down to one of the battered leather chairs. Galbraith, the engineer, was watching him, his long legs thrust out and resting on the fender which protected the fire. He was a gaunt, untidy man, with an exact, circular bald patch, so that from behind he looked much like a monk.

Sheridan smiled. 'Pretty well, thanks. How's your glass, Chief?'

He did not really want to talk, not just yet, although he liked what he had seen of Galbraith. The chief was not much of a talker, and used words economically, like fuel or engine-room grease. Sheridan had been thinking about the captain. He was still aboard the leader alongside, where with the other destroyer captains he had been since breakfast. What the hell could they be discussing? Policy, changes of strategy, the cost of gin?

Galbraith held out his glass to a passing messman.

'Usual, Napier.'

His usual was apparently rum and sherry. It sounded terrible, and nobody seemed eager to test his strange fancy.

Sheridan said, 'You've been aboard quite some time. The longest of anyone.'

'Aye.' Galbraith took his refilled glass. 'Down the hatch.' He licked his lips. 'Since she first commissioned in this war.' His eyes were distant. 'Seen some hard days. And some good 'uns.'

'The Old Man's been in command for eighteen months.'

Sheridan thought how ridiculous it sounded. *Old Man*. Drummond was only a couple of years older than himself.

'That's true.' Galbraith gave a slow smile. 'If you're asking me what he's like, *really* like, I canna tell you. To me he's one thing. To you, maybe something else again. I like him fine. Not just because we're both Scots, but because he's fair. I've served with a few right bastards in my time. Nice as pie one minute. Wild men, screaming for blood, the next.' He sighed. 'This skipper's all right. But . . .' He hesitated, studying Sheridan as if to make up his mind. Then he added bluntly, 'But he's stretched like a bloody wire. I hope you can help share his load. He deserves it, believe me.'

'I expect he's used to better things.' Sheridan saw the gunner (T) downing what must be his tenth gin. 'My predecessor, Cowley, must have been on top line.'

Galbraith stood up.

'I'm just going to share a tot with my chief stoker. It's his birthday. Not supposed to go boozing in their mess, but I was a petty officer myself not too long back. I'd not want to forget that.' He touched Sheridan's sleeve, his face suddenly grim. 'You and me will get on well. So listen, I'll not repeat myself. I'll deny I said it, if you bring it up again.'

Sheridan waited, watching the bitterness in his eyes.

Galbraith said quietly, 'Lieutenant Frank Cowley was the skipper's best friend. But he was a bloody fool, and but for the skipper's action that night we'd have lost more than two killed and the first lieutenant wounded. We'd have lost the whole ruddy ship!' He tapped the side of his nose. 'So think on, and act accordingly.'

He left the wardroom.

Sheridan moved to where Lieutenant Wingate and the new doctor were in conversation by an open scuttle. If Galbraith was right in his assessment, it could not have been easy for Drummond. Carrying the ship and his first lieutenant. Because of friendship. Or something from the past perhaps.

He nodded to Wingate. 'Like me, Pilot, are you waiting to hear what's been going on at the C.O.'s conference?'

Wingate grinned. 'It helps. I might need a new chart.'

The navigating officer was always friendly enough on the surface. But Sheridan could not help wondering if he resented being placed junior to him, a regular beneath a reserve officer. He might even harbour a greater grudge because of his humble beginnings. An orphan, pushed into the Navy as a boy seaman, he had done it all on his own. It was not hard to picture him in an old oil painting. A reckless privateer, one of Drake's men at Cadiz.

The doctor said carefully, 'I must say I feel very raw amongst all you *professionals*.'

Wingate said cheerfully, 'Not to worry, Doc. You're being detailed to censor the lads' letters. You'll soon discover they're even more professional at things other than bloody fighting!'

Sheridan felt Rankin at his elbow. The gunnery officer's mouth was set in a thin line of disapproval.

'Paint all over X gun, Number One.' He almost snatched a pink gin from a messman. 'I *told* my artificer about it. The bloody man. Doesn't know a breech-block from a bull's arse!'

Wingate chuckled. 'Take it off your back, Guns. Next time I'll get the old *Warlock* so close to the bastards you can drop the shells straight down on their little Kraut heads!'

Rankin sniffed. 'It's no joke. Some people have no sense of—'

They all turned as Noakes' harsh voice filled the wardroom. He was on his feet, his face brick-red as he swayed in front of the midshipman.

'What the 'ell do you know about it, *Mister* Keyes?' Noakes thrust his head forward, some gin slopping over the faded carpet. 'Young know-it-alls with their nappies still wet tryin' to tell me what's what!'

Keyes looked terrified.

'I'm sorry. I was only saying that I thought—'

Noakes bellowed, 'I don't *care* what you think!' He peered around at the others. 'Tellin' me that the battle of Jutland was a failure! 'Ow does 'e bloody well know? 'E wasn't there, was 'e!'

Hillier, the New Zealander, said quietly, 'But *you* were.'

''Course I was!' Noakes seemed doubly irritated by the interruption.

'Then, according to a rough calculation,' Hillier's voice was very calm, 'you must have been about the same age as young Keyes here, right?'

48

Noakes blinked. 'Er, yes. I suppose I was.'

'Well then.' Hillier winked at Keyes. 'I'll bet you were moaning about all the silly old sods in high places who had got you into the battle in the first place.'

Wingate remarked, 'Good bloke, that Hillier. Never seen Bill Noakes caught out like that.'

The bulkhead telephone buzzed and a messman called, 'First Lieutenant, sir! Captain's coming aboard!'

Sheridan nodded and hurried from the wardroom, snatching his cap as he bounded up the ladder and through the quartermaster's lobby.

In a very short while he had learned a lot about his companions. Outwardly they could have fitted into any ship, anywhere. But in time their other, private selves would emerge, to be shared by no one beyond this long, outdated hull. Something special, upon which they would all have to depend.

He saluted as Drummond strode over the brow. 'You've had a long day, sir.'

Drummond halted in his stride. From the look on his face Sheridan guessed he had not heard a word. Nor had he even noticed the salutes of the side party. His reactions had been automatic. A protective front.

Drummond asked, 'What time is it, for God's sake?' He did not wait for an answer but said, 'The flotilla is being reorganised, given a different role. Before that we are to work together, but be independent of other groups.'

Sheridan asked, 'Will it be a bit like the new anti-submarine groups we've been hearing about, sir?'

He watched Drummond's grave features, remembering the engineer's remarks. *Stretched like a bloody wire.* It was all there in those brief seconds. Strain, apprehension, doubt.

Drummond said, 'Something like it. I'm still not quite clear myself.'

Owles appeared in the lobby door.

'I've got your lunch ready, sir.'

'Later.' Drummond looked suddenly desperate. Trapped. 'Later.'

Sheridan said, 'We hoped you might drop in for a gin, sir.' He waited, feeling the other man's tension. 'You know how it is. First time all together.'

49

'Yes.' Drummond looked along the iron deck towards the bridge. 'I don't get too many chances.'

As he stepped over the coaming, Sheridan whispered to the quartermaster, 'Fetch the chief from the P.O.s' mess.'

In the wardroom everyone fell silent as Drummond walked through the door and said, 'Relax, gentlemen. I've been asked in for a drink.'

Owles appeared as if by magic. 'Here you are, sir. Horse's neck. Just how you like it.'

He raised the glass. 'Cheers.'

Then he looked at their varied expressions, seeing the unspoken questions, and the carefree excitement of those who still did not know.

Sheridan said quietly, 'All present, sir.' He had seen Galbraith ease his lanky figure around the door.

'I've not been able to speak with the new arrivals. Except for Number One, that is. So I bid you welcome now. And hope you'll settle down without too much hardship.'

He saw Keyes watching him with fascinated attention. And the dull-eyed sub-lieutenant, Tyson, whose brother had just been reported missing in Burma. Rankin, straight-backed, as if on parade, his narrow face completely blank. He was probably on another plane entirely. When he got his orders he obeyed them. He had made life very simple for himself. And Wingate, outwardly relaxed, eyes slitted against the reflected glare from an open scuttle. But his mind would be preparing, calculating. How many miles, which charts, when did they have to get there?

He thought suddenly of the conference. It had been more like a speech. Even the commodore had remained silent after his introduction and summary of the present strategy, *the war at sea*.

Beaumont had begun quietly, in an almost matter-of-fact way. Touching on some of the commodore's comments, sharpening them and leaving little to doubt. The war in the desert was over. The battle for Europe would soon begin. This year, early next year at the very latest. It would have to succeed. The enemy had had too long to dig in, to learn what to expect.

Help to Russia would be stepped up. Supplies, arms and vehicles. That meant more Arctic convoys. Drummond had felt the mention of them move round the gathering like a threat, a dread. He had watched the faces of the other commanding officers. Gauging, trying to see one step ahead of Beaumont's words. Like his own officers were doing to him now.

The flotilla was to work as a team again, not in a hotchpotch of escorts and patrols. That had got their interest all right. Beaumont's voice had become sharper, incisive as he had outlined his plans. It had sounded as if each ship was to be put on trial, to prove if her ability was up to this new scheme. It still sounded like that. And yet Beaumont had held them in the palm of his hand. Serious one moment, excited and passionate the next, he had overcome almost every doubt.

One man had voiced the only open opposition.

Ventnor's captain, Lieutenant-Commander Selkirk, a tough reservist, who in peacetime had been first officer in a freighter running back and forth to Argentina, had asked, 'What if we find this new role too demanding, sir? I mean, these old ships are better than most for routine work, but to compete with brand-new fleet destroyers seems, if I may say so, a bit optimistic.'

Beaumont had regarded him coldly. 'A ship is only as good as her captain. I am empowered to make changes if anyone fails to measure up!' The chill had gone, to be replaced instantly by that other Beaumont. Eager, persuasive. 'But let's talk of *success*, eh?'

If charm was a weapon, the battle at the conference was over before it had got off the ground. He had finished by wishing them luck, after talking almost without a break for four hours.

Drummond continued, 'We will be leaving Harwich in two days. In the remaining time I want all of you to get as much work done as you can. Get to know the new hands, change them around if you think they are badly placed. Ask Number One first, of course. I don't want him nagging me.'

Several of them laughed.

He saw the curtain across the dining space quiver, and guessed the stewards would already have a new 'buzz' on way to the messdecks. Going to Russia. To the Med. To blazes.

Wingate asked, 'Can I ask where, sir?'

'First to Falmouth.' He saw the surprised glances. 'After that, well, you'll know soon enough.' He smiled gravely. 'When I do.'

Wingate whistled softly. 'It'll make a gap in the old Harwich Force.'

Drummond looked away. 'Replacements are already coming. Four new destroyers from Rosyth. Two American escorts, and some Free-French corvettes. I think they'll manage.'

But he knew what Wingate meant. The old crowd. Familiar ships and faces. Pain at seeing one of them trying to get back, listing and pitted with splinter holes. The companies lining the rails to cheer like madmen when one returned after sinking a submarine. Remembering those who never came back at all.

But perhaps it was all to the good. Too long on the same job meant weakness when it was least expected. Familiarity brought disaster. He thought of Frank falling. Of Helen's accusing eyes. *Why him?*

He suddenly felt tired without knowing why. He wanted to go to his cabin. To think. To try and see behind Beaumont's words. It was obvious he had a lot of pull in high places. *Nick Brooks*, for instance. But what could a flotilla of veteran destroyers do that it was not already doing?

The flotilla would slip through the Channel in two separate units. *Lomond* was remaining here to complete certain repairs, but Beaumont intended to sail with the rest of his brood in *Warden*, the half-leader. Her captain, Hector Duvall, a bearded and fruity-voiced commander, would love that. To have his new Captain (D) as passenger, tutor and possible executioner all in one package.

Hillier said cheerfully, 'Well, my folks will certainly hear about me now! With a man like Beaumont in command we should soon make a name for ourselves!'

Galbraith said dryly, 'I hope it's a name I like.'

Drummond glanced at Sheridan. 'I'll leave you to it.' He nodded to the others. 'We'll all know each other better before long.'

He paused by the door. 'Thanks for the drink, Number One.'

As the door closed behind him the conversation swelled out louder than before.

Wingate asked, 'What d'you reckon, Number One? The Med or Western Approaches?'

Sheridan shook his head. 'Neither. That's what I think. Beaumont's got other ideas.'

'You don't like him?'

'I don't even know him.' Sheridan eyed him thoughtfully. 'But they say he's a hero, so I suppose that'll have to do.'

Drummond stirred in his bridge chair and thrust both hands deeper into his duffel-coat pockets. It was almost midnight, and the breeze across the bridge screen contained a chill, despite the day's sunlight.

Around and below his chair *Warlock*'s life went on, measured, routine. Figures eased themselves into gun-mountings and look-out positions, voices murmured through pipes and handsets. One more watch taking over.

It had been an uneventful if tense run down the Channel, he thought. No moon, but the sky was very clear, so perhaps the E-boats had taken their business up the east coast instead. The W/T office had brought him all the latest news from that other war. Families who were now crouching beneath their stairs or in comfortless air-raid shelters, would be listening to the drone of bombers, the sporadic clatter of anti-aircraft guns. Tomorrow they would emerge, examine what was left in the battered streets, and then go off to their jobs. It was like some huge pretence, and yet if it were stripped of its pathetic bravery a whole nation would collapse. It was strange really. The women were probably so worried about their sons and husbands in uniform to care too much for their own real danger. Yet theirs was often the greater sacrifice. There was an air-raid on across the East End of London right now.

Drummond turned his head to starboard, as if he expected to see something. But it was dark and very peaceful. Just the steady throb of engines, the sluice along the hull from a regular offshore swell.

He heard Sheridan taking over from Rankin, the brief exchange of information. Course, speed, weather. Any cocoa left in the wardroom?

The figures thinned out and settled into their allotted positions for the next four hours.

The voice-pipe intoned, 'Able Seaman Jevers on the wheel, sir. Course two-six-five. One-one-zero revolutions.'

Drummond thought about the quartermaster, Jevers. He had been in the ship for six months. His wife had left him for an American G.I. Mangin had told him about it, and how Jevers

53

scanned the mail like a desperate beggar whenever it came aboard. He seemed unable to accept she had gone for good.

Sheridan crossed the bridge, his figure black against the grey paint.

'Starboard watch closed up at defence stations, sir.'

'Very good.' He tugged out his pipe and jammed it between his teeth. 'Seems quiet enough now. Funny to think that Brighton is abeam. Or should be if Pilot's calculations are correct! In peacetime you'd have seen the lights on the piers and promenades from miles out to sea. Now, it could be the Black Hole of Calcutta.' He watched as Sheridan checked the compass repeater. 'And all the would-be Nelsons of the wartime Navy are over there, too, sleeping and worrying about getting their commissions.'

Sheridan's teeth shone in the gloom. 'Young Keyes was telling me about it. He only left *King Alfred* a month or so ago. Apparently all the lads are sweating with the fear that the war'll be over before they get their bits of gold lace.'

'What do *you* think, Number One?'

In the stillness he could almost hear Sheridan considering the question. Feet grated on steel, and from the open hatch he heard the regular, comforting ping of the Asdic.

'Years yet, sir. I can't really accept that peace will ever come. You, of course, will think that strange, I expect. Regular naval family. A better continuity for assessing this sort of thing.'

Drummond shook his head. 'No. I'm the first in the family, as far as I know. My father was a soldier.'

Sheridan peered at him. 'Really, sir? So was mine, although he was only in it for the Great War.' His voice hardened slightly. 'He used to embarrass me sometimes. I was a bloody fool. Must have been, not to see what he was trying to show to others.'

Drummond watched him. 'Go on.'

Sheridan rubbed his gloved hands along the screen.

'Sounds silly now. We're up here, and the war could explode right beside us. Any minute of the day.' He hesitated. 'Every Armistice Day it was. Dead on eleven. All the buses and cars stopped at the first stroke of the town hall clock. Everyone standing quite still, faces like stone, for the two minutes' silence. It used to thrill me as a boy. Make shivers run up and down my spine.'

'Your father was badly crippled, I believe?'

'That's right, sir. At the Menin Gate. Shrapnel through both legs and spine. Had to live in a sort of wicker chair on wheels. Died just a year ago. I think of him quite a bit now.'

Sub-lieutenant Hillier, who was assistant O.O.W. under Sheridan, called anxiously, 'B-7 buoy abeam to starboard one mile, sir.'

'Thank you, Sub.' Sheridan rubbed his chin. 'Every Armistice Day my old father would wheel himself out of the house in his chair and, well, he just kept going until the silence was over. A bus conductor threatened to overturn his chair once, he was that angry.' He chuckled sadly. 'When my mother used to go on at him about it he used to shout, "What the hell do they know about it, woman? Standing po-faced like a lot of bloody heroes! They should have seen the mud, the lice, and the bloody corpses! At the Menin Gate we couldn't even bury 'em, they were that thick!" Funny thing was, of course, many of the people he was slamming were in the war like him. It was as if he felt more akin to the dead than the survivors.'

'Probably.'

Drummond peered at his watch. A couple of hours' sleep in the hutch behind the wheelhouse. He needed it badly. The two days at Harwich had everybody dashing about like a maniac. Drills and exercises to settle the new men into one company before they sailed for Falmouth. The other destroyers were spaced ahead and astern of *Warlock*, each independent of the rest. He thought of the half-leader and smiled. Except *Warden*, of course. She had Beaumont to contend with.

Yet sharing these small confidences with Sheridan had helped him in some way. He knew little or nothing of him, but already felt that he had known him for months. Perhaps Frank had not spoken of such personal things. Looking back, he wondered if he had really known Frank as much as he imagined.

Sheridan asked quietly, 'What about your father, sir? Is he still alive?'

'No.'

Drummond thought of his home at Arbroath outside Dundee. The battalion on parade each Sunday and other special occasions. Maybe it had been the Army which had made him insist on being given a chance for Dartmouth. His father had also been in France in the same war which had crippled Sheridan's. And God alone knew how many others. Nobody had ever discovered what had happened. He had gone out with a night wiring party. Into that stark moonscape of drifting flares, shell-holes and barbed wire. Neither he nor any of his men were seen again. Drummond, of course, had never known him, and his mother rarely seemed ready to talk about him. He could not really blame her. She had remarried after the war. Another officer in the same regiment. Drummond had never been able to get on with him, although his stepfather had tried hard enough. A big, jolly man in khaki tunic and impeccable kilt. Perhaps he had been trying to see his real father behind all the laughter and offers of friendship.

He added slowly, 'He was killed in France.'

He fell silent, and heard Sheridan move away to the other side of the bridge to consult with Hillier.

Drummond often brooded about it. Maybe that was why he had told Helen he would never get married in wartime. Because of his own father. A grave-faced lieutenant in a browning photograph which he had discovered in his mother's desk drawer.

Across the water he heard the dismal clang of a bell-buoy. There was a wreck nearby. A destroyer which had hit a mine some months back. He hoped Hillier was taking full advantage of a quiet passage to learn all he could. He seemed very pleasant.

He heard Sheridan say, 'I'm just going to the Asdic compartment, Sub. Take over.'

Hillier muttered something and then strode to the forepart of the bridge. Drummond turned slightly to watch him. The quick way he moved his head from bow to bow, as if expecting a sudden disaster.

'How does it feel, Sub?'

Hillier tried to relax. 'Fine, sir.' He looked aft towards the little steel shack at the rear of the bridge. Above it the radar lantern swayed gently to the ship's easy roll, and below it Sheridan had already been swallowed up by a steel door which led directly to the cramped Asdic compartment. He added, 'Feels a *bit* dodgy, sir.' He grinned. 'But I guess I can ask you for help if I need it, sir?'

Drummond smiled. This New Zealander was quite unlike the other sub-lieutenant, Tyson. Originally he had thought Tyson's manner was part of some inner grief over his missing brother. Now he was equally certain it was not. He was arrogant and unyielding to his subordinates, argumentative with his equals, and sullenly silent whenever he was choked off by the lieutenants.

'I expect so. You're from Dunedin, I'm told?'

'That's right, sir. My father's a doctor there. I think he hoped I'd be one, too, given the time. But I like the sea, always have. When this lot's over I think I'll try and stay in the Navy. If not, I'll go for the merchant service.' His voice broke in a quiet chuckle. 'You know, sir, some big liner, with all the girls chasing the officers!'

Sheridan came back and snapped, 'Tell the quartermaster to watch his head, Sub! He's wandering a degree or so all the time!'

Hillier hurried to the voice-pipe and almost fell on some unseen grating or bracket.

Drummond said quietly, 'My fault, Number One. Sorry about that.'

Sheridan lifted his night glasses to study a large flurry of spray on the port beam. A leaping fish? Sea birds taking off? It was nothing.

He said, 'My old captain used to catch me out, sir.' He lowered the glasses. 'If I didn't bottle my assistant, the captain'd say, "It's *your* watch, Number One. Don't mind me."' He sighed. 'I got on well with him.'

Drummond bit hard on the unlit pipe. There it was again. He was still worrying about the captain who had killed himself after the enquiry into *Conqueror's* loss.

'Maybe he just didn't know how to overcome the real challenge when it came, Number One. I think your father would have understood him. Probably more than most. It takes a man who has lived through hell to help another who is suffering one of his own.'

A bosun's mate was murmuring into a voice-pipe. Then he said, 'From W/T office, sir. "All Clear" over London now. No enemy aircraft being engaged.'

'Thank you.'

Drummond pictured the bombers heading out across the Channel and North Sea to bases in France, Holland or Germany. A lot of *Warlock's* company came from the south-east. It was to be hoped that no signals would be waiting in Falmouth. *Come home. Your family was bombed last night.*

Sheridan said suddenly, 'This new role, sir. Do you think it's anything to do with an invasion?'

'Indirectly. I imagine so. We'll probably invade through the Med first and then into northern Europe.' He smiled wearily. 'That's what it said in the newspaper the other day. But where *we*, as opposed to the whole Allied invasion force, fit in, is beyond me as yet.'

He slid from the chair and stretched his arms.

'Call me if in any sort of doubt. I'm going to turn in.'

He walked stiffly towards the hatchway, seeing Hillier's pale face watching him as he passed. He groped his way beside a dim police light to the door of his sea cabin. From the wheelhouse he could hear the clatter of loose gear, someone humming quietly and the occasional stammer of morse from the W/T office on the deck below. The bridge was like a tight little steel hive, he thought. Connected up to the rest of the vessel by wires and pipes, which in return relayed information and observations to him. His brain.

He closed the door and threw his cap on to the bookshelf. There was barely room to move, and with the deadlight screwed shut, the air which came through the deckhead vent tasted dirty and over-used. He laid down and closed his eyes. Thinking of Beaumont. Of Frank. Of the ship which trembled through the mattress on his bunk.

The telephone above the reading light buzzed and he snatched it from its hook in one quick movement.

'Captain?'

'Number One speaking, sir. Time to alter course in two minutes.' He sounded surprised.

Drummond peered at his watch and grimaced. He must have fallen asleep after all. And he felt like death.

'I'll come up.'

'I can manage, sir, if—'

'I'll come up.'

He dropped the telephone on its hook and rubbed his eyes violently. This was the part which wore you down. Really wore you down.

He stared at the phone and stood up, adjusting automatically

58

to the ship's uneven motion. Sharper swell. That would be a throwback from Selsey Bill, his mind told him.

But the telephone in the night. That, you never got used to. You woke up with your guts in knots. Your mind cringing. He remembered another captain from the past. He, too, had awakened in his cabin to the call of the bridge telephone. As he had seized it, the door had burst open and the sea had flooded the cabin. The ship had already been plunging to the bottom, yet he had heard nothing of the explosion. Only the telephone. It had taken minutes, but the whole nightmare had been compressed into one tiny fraction of time. He had survived. For six months anyway.

He jammed on his cap and slung the glasses around his neck. As he stepped from the cabin he saw a bosun's mate carrying a tin of milk towards the bridge ladder.

The man froze and said quickly, ' 'Mornin', sir. Bit fresh up top still.' He held the tin behind his back.

Drummond smiled gravely. 'Good morning, Toogood. Rustle up some cocoa, if you can.'

He groped for the ladder to the upper bridge. It was funny when you thought about it. The bosun's mate was taking milk for the ship's cat, Badger. Everyone knew about the cat, but its presence was carefully never mentioned. The previous Captain (D) had had a thing about pets in his flotilla. Likewise, Badger carefully ignored most of the ship's company. Except for the members of the stokers' mess where he slept, and those entrusted to bring his milk.

The air was still sharp, and he saw Sheridan waiting beside the gyro repeater.

'Keeping quiet, Number One?'

He eased his body into the chair. Its arms were damp and ice-cold.

'Nothing much, sir. Report of a freighter sinking off Wolf Rock. Not quite clear why. Mine, I expect. We're due to pass an east-bound coastal convoy before 0400, and there are some sweepers heading our way from Portland. Otherwise, pretty slack.'

Feet scraped across the gratings and the bosun's mate handed him a mug of steaming cocoa.

'Kye up, sir.'

Drummond watched him over the rim, cradling the hot mug between his hands.

'Get rid of the milk all right?'

The seaman grinned. 'Yessir.'

Sheridan was at the compass. 'Port fifteen.' He glanced down at Hillier. 'Check with the plot, Sub. Can't afford to be off course again.' He bent to the glowing compass repeater. 'Midships. Steady. Steer two-three-five.'

Far inland a fire glowed redly in the night, but there were no clouds to reflect or measure its distance and intensity.

Sheridan said, 'Bomb with a time fuse probably. The poor devils will be able to get to bed now.'

'Radar—Bridge.'

Sheridan snatched up a handset. 'Bridge.'

'Some faint echoes at Green oh-two-five, sir. Probably the sweepers coming round the Isle of Wight from Portland.'

'Good, thank you, Yates. Carry on with the sweep.' To the bridge lookouts he added, 'You heard that. Keep your eyes peeled.'

Drummond swallowed the thick, sickly cocoa, feeling it exploring his empty stomach. That was good. Sheridan had even got to know the leading radar operator by name. It helped confidence, broke down the uncertainty of strangers on a night watch. Doubt, fear of rebuke from a faceless voice-pipe or handset often took valuable seconds. It was sometimes fatal.

A light blinked briefly across the heaving water, and a reply was shuttered back just as quickly by the waiting signalman.

Drummond relaxed. It was going well. And the sooner they reached Falmouth, the better he would be pleased.

Sheridan paused to peer at the chart table beneath its canvas hood, and when he looked again he saw that Drummond's head was lolling in time with the ship's motion. He smiled grimly. At least he trusts me, he thought. The smile faded as he looked slowly around the darkened bridge. I could have had one like this. Could be the one using his brain and mind, making decisions instead of taking orders.

The bosun's mate said, 'The plot 'as just called, sir. Says 'e's 'avin' a bit of bother with the new chart.' He fell silent, uninvolved, his duty done.

Sheridan nodded. 'Very well. Go down, Sub. Use some of that

60

magic they taught you. Give the plot table a kick if all else fails.'

At five minutes to four Wingate appeared on the bridge to take over the morning watch.

Course, speed and weather. Any cocoa left in the wardroom?

The relieved watchkeepers scrambled down to their cabins and messdecks, groping for somewhere to snatch a couple of hours' sleep before another day was upon them. On mess tables and narrow benches, in overcrowded compartments where they shared their blankets with tinned food or ammunition. Hammocks were not supposed to be slung at sea, but many were, and the luckier men swung together like creatures in warm pods, their lifebelts and sea boots handy should the alarm bells tear at their hearts again.

Hillier lay in a camp bed below a bunk where Lieutenant Rankin snored in regal splendour, and stared up at the darkness. Thinking of Dunedin and the girl who had promised to wait for him. He could hardly remember her face, which was very strange, as he had grown up with her.

In his white-painted cot near the sick bay the doctor was also awake, his stomach queasy from the sluggish motion, the sealed stenches of oil and cabbage water, the sharper tangs of his own department. Outside his own little cabin he could hear his leading sickbay attendant, Froud, groaning in his sleep. Dreaming of a conquest somewhere, or a defeat. Surgeon Lieutenant Adrian Vaughan switched on his reading lamp and groped for his glasses. He would read for a bit. Take his mind off things.

The S.B.A. turned over in his bunk as a shaft of light probed through the slit of the doctor's door. Froud groaned and pulled his pyjamas more tightly about his body. He had been dreaming. Violently. The ship had been going down, and he had been trapped. But he had been about to be rescued, by a tall, handsome sailor. It would be, of course. Froud hated all women to a point of torment.

But the dream had gone with the click of Vaughan's reading lamp. Froud glared at the deckhead and swore savagely.

In the brightly lit tunnel of the engine room the chief stoker, 'Soapy' Hudson, was singing at the top of his voice as he moved slowly amidst the glittering machinery and vibrating catwalks. Only his lips gave any hint of sound, the words being lost in the din, the unending roar of the destroyer's engines and fans. A few boiler-suited figures crouched or ducked around the gleaming confusion, speaking to each other by sign and touch. A good bunch, Hudson decided. Most of them had given him a tot on his birthday. The chief had even slipped him half a bottle of gin from the wardroom.

He sighed and picked up his check board. Presents or not, old Galbraith would tear him off a strip if anything was wrong when he arrived for his pre-breakfast rounds.

From the captain, dozing in his bridge chair, to Badger, the cat, who was deeply sleeping, nose in tail, in his own special hammock on the stokers' messdeck, *Warlock* carried them all. Indifferent to their personal hopes and disappointments, needing them only as servants to her own particular skills.

She had had her rest. Now it was time to pick up where she had left off.

4

Bait

SHERIDAN stepped into the day cabin and said quickly, 'You wanted me, sir? Sorry I didn't come earlier. I've been ashore.' He noticed with sudden annoyance that Wingate was already in the cabin, leaning back in a chair, one leg crossed over the other.

Drummond smiled. 'Not to worry, Number One. Take a seat.' He gestured to the table. 'Help yourself to a drink if you like.'

Sheridan shook his head. 'Not just now.'

Wingate grinned. 'Well, you will in a minute when you hear what we've been given!'

'Orders?' Sheridan could not keep the edge from the question.

They had been in Falmouth for two days, and had been joined by the other half of the flotilla. Although how seven more destroyers had managed to find moorings amidst the mass of escorts, trawlers, supply vessels and a collection of new landing craft was little less than a miracle. Nevertheless, while the commanding officers and base staff had been busy with comings and goings between ships and shore headquarters, the companies of the destroyers had taken time off to enjoy their surroundings. Not even the crowded moorings, the port's heavy defences and the impressive troop movements ashore could spoil this almost detached existence. Green hills behind the harbour, the friendly little houses which lay comfortably on the slopes or beside the gentle Helford River, all were as remote from grey skies and barrage balloons, air-raid warnings and east coast convoys as Cornish cream differed from powdered eggs.

Sheridan had been ashore for most of the afternoon. Just walking, getting the air into his lungs and enjoying the sunshine. Orders would soon arrive, a plan, probably conceived in a dusty Admiralty bunker, would be produced to be put into effect *without delay*. They always said that. Sheridan thought it was because someone high-up feared that flaws in his plan might be laid bare if too much time was allowed.

And yet, like most young men in war, Sheridan was able to put it off, knowing that when the time came he would somehow manage to cope. Or, if his number came up, that was it anyway.

The sight of Wingate lounging in the chair, grinning at him, obviously fully informed of the orders' content, was like a petty disappointment. Like a child hearing a teacher speaking disparagingly of him behind his back, when until that time he has worshipped that same teacher.

His glance passed quickly over Wingate's sleeve. Perhaps that was it after all. The regulars against the amateurs.

Drummond was saying, 'We will be sailing at midnight. Make sure that all libertymen are accounted for by 2100. We're going out in a group of four. *Warlock*, *Whirlpool*, *Waxwing* and *Ventnor*.' He smiled gravely. 'That makes us the senior ship.'

Wingate groaned. 'It also means that Captain (D) will be coming aboard for the trip.'

Sheridan asked quietly, 'May I enquire *where* we are going?'

Drummond eyed him curiously. 'Pilot and I have just been going over the charts. Officially we are sailing as additional covering escort for a convoy to Gibraltar. *Officially*. This is all very top-secret stuff, Number One.'

I was beginning to wonder. He controlled himself and asked, 'And the rest of the flotilla?'

'Oh, they're pushing off under the half-leader to do some exercises with the Army in the Bristol Channel. We, on the other hand, are going after live game.' Drummond paused to put a match to his pipe. 'The Germans are showing great interest in all convoys making for the Med. With a possible invasion in the wind, they are trying to get every piece of information about ships and equipment, vehicles and troop movements. In fact, *anything*. Convoy stragglers, damaged ships, any vessel which gets separated on the last run south, is in real danger. The intelligence people are getting worried. Over the last few weeks several ships have been sunk fairly close to neutral waters.' He spread out a chart of the Bay of Biscay. 'Here, near the north-west corner of Spain. And sometimes further south, closer to Gib itself.'

Sheridan said, 'And the ships in question are always alone?'

Despite his resentment he could not fail to see the point of Drummond's remarks.

'More or less. One or two had got left behind by fast convoys and were keeping inshore for safety's sake. One was having engine trouble and ran for shelter when a storm got up.'

Wingate said, 'Well, there's no mystery then. A U-boat bagged them. Or maybe a drifting mine or two.'

Sheridan answered, 'I can't agree. Once perhaps, but so close to neutral waters it's too much of a coincidence. We'd have heard something.'

Wingate laughed. 'You call Spain *neutral*?'

'Officially.' Drummond interrupted quickly as if he had sensed something between them. 'But there is one bit of news, two if you like, which cannot be coincidence. On several of these instances a Spanish freighter has been in the vicinity. Our agents have checked her out, and know her as the *Aragon*. She trades the coastal routes, and has turned up as far north as Ireland. She's Spanish all right, but her present ownership is a bit vague, and nobody's talking very much about her.'

Sheridan said, 'You suggested there were *two* bits of news, sir.'

'Yes.' His pipe smoke floated to the deckhead and was immediately plucked into a fan. 'On every known occasion these attacks have been in perfect weather. Other ships in similar circumstances have got to Gib safely whenever it has been blowing up, or there has been a stiff sea running.'

Wingate nodded gloomily. 'That does seem to rule out U-boats. These days they don't give a damn about the weather once they've got a ship in their sights. And mines are out, too. Even the Spanish government would object to Jerry dropping them near their coast.' He winked at Sheridan. 'You were right again, Number One. No wonder I had such a sweat to pass my exams!'

Sheridan returned the smile. Wingate's cheerful acceptance made him ashamed. 'Guessing.'

'Guessing or not, we're going to try and cut out that Spaniard if he shows any sign at all of interfering with our ships.'

Sheridan stared at him. 'Isn't that asking for trouble?'

'We are already at war, Number One.' Drummond watched him calmly. 'That's trouble enough for me. But seriously, we must find out what is happening. Captain (D) informs me that a suitable "bait" has been prepared. The rest is up to the weather, luck and'—he shrugged—'*us*.'

Wingate smiled. 'I said you'd need a drink, Number One!'

'Do you want me to tell the wardroom about it, sir?'

'Tell them nothing. Not until we're committed. If things go wrong, or intelligence have made a mistake,' he smiled briefly, 'I almost said *again*, our people might as well still believe we are merely engaged as additional escort support. But the signs are good, for apart from a large forty-ship convoy from Halifax to Liverpool, and another big one from U.K. down to Freetown, there'll be plenty to keep the U-boat packs busy and interested. Our particular "bait" will be detached from a fast convoy of Liberty ships. That's all I can tell you at present.' He nodded 'So let's get cracking, shall we?'

Wingate stood up and carefully folded his charts. 'I'm going to lock myself in and do some work on these.'

Sheridan asked, 'Will Captain Beaumont be aboard soon?'

'After sunset. And as soon as it's dark I want you to have our pendant numbers painted out. The other three destroyers will do likewise. There are enough busybodies about without adding to the risk of recognition at a later date.'

Sheridan started. 'You mean this sort of operation may become our permanent role, sir?'

Drummond faced him and replied evenly, 'I said nothing of the sort.'

Sheridan picked up his cap and followed Wingate from the cabin.

Wingate said casually, 'Hell of a responsibility, isn't it?'

Sheridan looked at him, realising what he meant for the first time. He had not thought of Drummond as a young man of twenty-eight, but as the captain.

Wingate added, 'I think this has got him rattled.' He grinned. 'Poor bastard. I'm glad it's his decision and not mine!' He strode towards his cabin whistling softly.

In his cabin Drummond had moved to an open scuttle. He stared fixedly at the sloping hill nearest to the anchorage, the tiny sheep dotted about, pale against the lush green. People, too, made aimless by distance, like ants. But if you watched carefully enough, each took on direction. And purpose. He found he was clenching his fists until it was almost painful. He had a sudden yearning, a craving to tramp through grass like that on the hillside. To rest his hands on bricks and stone walls, warm in the sunlight. To know that somebody would be glad to see him.

The door opened behind him and Owles said, 'Gib then, sir.'

Drummond did not turn. 'It's supposed to be secret. How did you know?'

Not that it mattered. Owles seemed to have unfailing information.

Owles considered the question. 'Well, I mean, sir, it stands to reason, don't it? Where else?'

He pattered across the carpet, laying a place for tea on the table.

Drummond sighed, thinking of the next hours and days. Vigilance and waiting for the right moment. Commander Duvall must either have upset Beaumont on passage from Harwich or was now considered too valuable to use for flushing out a Spanish spy-ship, or whatever she was. Beaumont obviously considered it a good risk. Otherwise he would have stayed clear.

Owles asked, 'Will the other gentleman be bedding down in here with Cap'n (D), sir?'

Drummond turned. '*Other* gentleman?'

Owles regarded him passively. 'I thought you knew, sir. He'll be from the Ministry of Information, an important gent, I expect, sir.'

Drummond stared at him. God, that's all we need now. A bloody war-correspondent along for the ride. To get a bit of material for one of those sickening programmes. *I'm speaking to you tonight from the front line.* Or, *Within yards of where I am sitting, the enemy are about to launch an attack.* It always sounded as if the speaker was totally alone at the time.

He replied, 'Well, I know *now*! Yes, put him down here. Keep him from getting in my way.'

Owles pattered back to his pantry, considering the captain's sudden anger.

He liked Drummond, although he considered him too serious for one so young. And available. He thought of his sister in Rochester. Pity she couldn't get her hands on the captain, he thought. But she had two blokes already. A petty officer off the

Waxwing, and a Canadian sergeant who was based over in Wales. Christ help her if those two ever got leaf on the same day!

On deck, Sheridan sought out the chief boatswain's mate to tell him about detailing hands for painting over the ship's numbers. He saw the coxswain blinking in the late sunlight and trying to appear interested in what a seaman was asking him. Mangin took things easy in harbour and rarely went ashore. unless night leave was granted. He was wearing his usual off duty rig, old jacket, patched trousers and carpet slippers. As the seaman turned away, Sheridan saw that it was the quartermaster, Jevers. The one whose wife had gone off with a Yank.

Mangin sighed. 'Th' usual, sir. Askin' about mail. Never gets one from 'er, poor sod.' He dismissed it from his mind. 'Lookin' for the Buffer, sir? I'll get 'im for you. Got 'is 'ead down in the P.O.s' mess, if I know Arthur Vickery.'

Sheridan leaned on the guardrail and stared down at the current swirling against the side. They knew everything. Security was a joke.

The seaman, Jevers, walked slowly towards the break in the forecastle and the main messdeck. At first it had been difficult, even frightening. Now, he could stand back and watch it all happening. Like being a spectator at a well-acted play.

Poor old Tommy Mangin, the coxswain. He shivered with that same fierce excitement. What would he say if he knew? *Really knew.* That his wife Janice was not having a fine old time with her Yank, but buried under a house in Hackney in East London. Even that memory had a new perfection. The roar of the exploding bombs, the crumbling walls changing shape in leaping shadows as incendiaries took hold and explored the wood and blazing curtains. And her mouth wide open like a black hole. She had been screaming, but he had heard nothing. Felt nothing, but the sickening crunch as he had brought the brick down on her skull. Over and over again. If she was finally discovered she would have been buried by now, with all the rest of those charred bodies. Merely another incident. One more air-raid. He would have heard by now if anyone had connected her remains with his bloody Janice. He screwed up his fists and tried not to speak her name. The rotten, stinking cow!

Leading Seaman Rumsey, the chief quartermaster, clattered

down a ladder from the forecastle deck, a towel and swimming trunks over his arm.

He saw Jevers and asked, 'All right, mate?'

Jevers nodded, watching his own expression as he replied dully, 'Yes, thanks, Harry. Just been to see if there's any mail come aboard.'

He saw the way Rumsey's eyes clouded over as he spoke. He turned away. It never failed. He was as safe as the crown jewels.

Sub-lieutenant Victor Tyson was walking along the other side of the ship, aft towards the quarterdeck. He was twenty-two, but already had the set lines around his eyes and mouth of a much older man. Apart from a general appearance of ill-humour, there was little to mark him out of the ordinary. His uniform, on the other hand, was always perfect, and his cap, minus grommet, was worn with a floppy, devil-may-care indifference which was quite at odds with the wearer. In fact, someone had jokingly remarked after the passing-out parade at the officers' training establishment, '*I say, who is that uniform which is wearing some sort of man!*'. It had been meant in fun. Tyson had been almost sick with fury and humiliation.

He had just come from the forecastle after checking the cable which held them to the forward buoy. Some seamen had been lounging in their swimming trunks, spread about like a lot of louts at Southend on a factory outing. He had put them squarely in their place, and he had enjoyed it.

He heard splashing alongside and paused to watch the swimmers who were flailing about close to the ship and a safety-boat nearby. He stiffened as he saw Midshipman Keyes bursting to the surface, shaking water from his hair before hurling a rubber ball to some of the other swimmers. It made Tyson feel sick. Keyes did not know he was born. Spoiled all his life, and came from a well-to-do family, from what he could discover, and yet he had no more idea of acting like an officer than the bloody gunner (T). At least Noakes knew about discipline, even if he was incapable of putting two words together in proper English.

Tyson leaned on the guardrail. 'Mr. Keyes!'

Keyes turned and trod water, his eyes red-rimmed from salt as he peered up at Tyson's silhouette.

'Yes?'

'Yes, *sir*! I'm officer of the day, remember?'

The other swimmers idled away, apparently very engrossed in the rubber ball.

Tyson shouted, 'The swimming party is for the ratings, in case you did not know it?'

Keyes stared at him blankly. 'I thought it was all right . . .'

It made Tyson angrier. This stupid innocence. He wanted to drag Keyes across the deck and kick his naked body until he did understand.

'Well, it's *not*!'

'You the O.O.D.?'

Tyson swung round, fuming at this new interruption. Then he stared at the lieutenant-commander whom he vaguely recognised as an operations officer from the base.

'Yes. I mean, yes, sir.'

'I was beginning to wonder.' The officer's eyes were without mercy. 'I thought for a moment I had stumbled into an ENSA show!'

Tyson could not speak. He could feel the blood rushing to his head, blinding him, choking him, as if his collar had shrunk in size.

The staff officer added curtly, 'When I come aboard I expect the O.O.D. to find *me*, not the other way about!'

He strode aft towards the lobby without another glance.

Tyson turned towards the sea, his mind reeling.

'Clear the water! Swimmers return inboard!' It was all he could think of.

But when he looked again he saw that the swimmers, including Keyes, had vanished.

Only Leading Seaman Rumsey remained, and he was squatting on the safety-boat's stemhead.

He looked up at Tyson's crimson face and remarked calmly, ' 'Ot, annit, sir?'

Tyson retreated.

Down in the day cabin the staff officer shook hands with Drummond and grinned.

'That's a right little bastard you've got up there, Keith.' He became serious again. 'Now, this is the final briefing.'

Drummond nodded, unable to keep his eyes off the thick envelope which the other man seemed to be taking an age to unfasten.

Bastard or not, when the crunch came it would be Tyson and all the rest of *Warlock*'s company who would have to face up to it, he thought bitterly.

Drummond sat well back in his tall chair and wedged his sea boots between the voice-pipes. *Warlock* was pushing along at an economical cruising speed of twelve knots, and her narrow hull was finding the going uncomfortable in a beam sea. It was evening, with barely a breath of wind to ease the oppressive heat which seemed to cling to the steel plates and bridge fittings, and to Drummond it felt as if they had been steaming in this same, slow way for an eternity. In fact, it was three days since they had left Falmouth in company with their consorts, three long days of working clear of coastal patrols and convoy routes, heading west and then south towards the fringe of Biscay. The first two days had been like a circus, with Captain Beaumont up on the bridge for most of the time, making signals to the group, getting each captain to change position, abeam, astern, and on one nightmare occasion having all four ships criss-crossing through each other's wakes like gun-carriages of the King's Horse Artillery.

Now, the other three ships were somewhere out of sight off the starboard bow. He hoped that the radar would not choose this moment to break down and sever their only contact.

He heard voices below the bridge on the port wing, and recognised one to be that of Miles Salter, Beaumont's companion for the operation. It was still not quite clear what Salter was here for. To report if the job went well, or merely to collect material for the Ministry of Information? Or perhaps he was merely interested in Beaumont's role? The latter would certainly explain Beaumont's eagerness to put his ships through their paces. Drummond had been unable to to control his own excitement, his pleasure at seeing the four destroyers charging through the Atlantic swell, much as they had been designed to do for the old Grand Fleet.

But all that was over, and *Warlock* moved like one discarded by the rest of the living world. And how different was the sea's face now. Not even a cat's-paw to break the unending procession of long, even swells. *Warlock* would lean irritably on to one beam, hang there for what seemed like minutes, before sliding her pitted flanks up and over to await the next challenge, her lower hull shaking violently as first one and then the second screw came close to the surface. It was even worse than the North Sea 'corkscrew'. Drummond had seen more than one luckless seaman dash from below decks to vomit over the guardrails.

'All right to come up, Captain?'

Drummond nodded without turning his head. 'Help yourself.'

Miles Salter was short and overweight, his shape made stubbier by a windcheater, beneath which he always wore a lifejacket. He could be any age from thirty to forty, and had a way of screwing up his eyes when he was talking, so that you could never really see what he was thinking.

Salter climbed up on to the gratings and gripped some voice-pipes as the hull leaned over once more.

'God, I don't fancy eating much tonight!'

Drummond heard Sheridan, who had the watch, speaking to Hillier, but kept his eyes towards where the horizon should be. The sky was hidden in pale cloud and low-lying mist, so that the array of rollers seemed to be marching straight out of the filtered sunlight.

Salter said, 'I just wondered how things were coming along?'

Drummond turned slightly in the chair. He had deliberately kept silent. Leaving it to Salter. If this was just one of his usual aimless visits to the bridge he would have been pestering Sheridan or Hillier by now.

Salter added quickly, 'Captain Beaumont has put me in the picture, of course.'

Of course.

Drummond replied, 'We are now steering almost due south.' He raised one hand above the salt-dappled screen. 'Over there, about one hundred and seventy miles off the port bow, is Cape Finisterre, the tip of Spain. All the rest is the Bay of Biscay.'

Salter said vaguely, 'I thought it was always rough in the Bay?'

'Like the song, you mean?'

He tried to relax, to pass the time with Salter until dusk, or whenever he chose to leave. But this expanse of sea, this silence, seemed to make a mockery of plans and secret arrangements hatched in high places.

Hour by hour they had kept a more than usually careful listening watch. Distress calls, sighting reports, coded signals from friend and enemy alike had kept the W/T staff going without respite. A west-bound convoy had been attacked three days out from Liverpool. Elsewhere, a freighter had collided with an escort while trying to pass wounded men across for medical aid. Nothing out of the ordinary.

Beaumont had called the bridge from his quarters aft with ever-growing impatience, as if even he was beginning to think somebody had slipped up.

He relented and said, 'We are still waiting for a confirming signal from the Admiralty. If it comes before dawn, then it will be time to get moving. If not, well, we'll just have to try again, or forget the whole idea.'

Salter said nothing, so he continued, 'A decoy ship has been detached from a Gibraltar convoy, acting as if she is in trouble. She should be somewhere ahead of us right now.'

Or lying on the bottom, he thought grimly.

'A deep-sea tug has been despatched from Gib to give her assistance, take her in tow.'

'I see.' Salter's eyes had vanished into a mass of crow's-feet. 'So it's up to the enemy.'

'Something like that.' He turned in his chair. 'Sub, check with radar again.'

Hillier said, 'I just did, sir.'

'*Do it again.*' He was irritated at the sharpness in his voice, at the way his mood was being noted by Salter. 'The tug will have been careful to make a bit of a show. There's no shortage of spies around the Rock. I'll bet the enemy have guessed what's happening by now.'

'But won't they be a bit suspicious, Captain? I mean, the decoy having no escort.'

Drummond watched him gravely. *Where have you been all these months and years?*

'It was a fast convoy. We just don't have enough escorts to allow them to hang around. You either abandon a straggler, or you take off her people and put her down yourself. It's a sort of two-way trust we share between Navy and merchantman. It's all we've got, most of the time.'

Salter's lips curled slightly. 'You sound bitter.'

'I've a right to that.' He looked abeam. 'I've seen too many

73

good ships go under because we simply couldn't protect them. In peacetime, people aren't interested. In war, they expect a bloody miracle.' He saw Hillier's shadow against the steel and asked, 'Anything?'

'No, sir.'

Sheridan called, 'Bosun's mate! Pipe the port watch to defence stations!'

Drummond said, 'Strange to think that out there in Spain and Portugal there are lights in the streets. No worries if you're going to wake up in the morning.'

Salter said in a solemn tone, 'Ah, Spain. I was there, you know. In the Civil War. Terrible tragedy.'

'Yes. I was there, too.'

Several people shuffled to attention as Beaumont strode into the bridge, his oak-leaved cap tilted rakishly over his eyes. He had a pure silk scarf around his neck, and against the weary watchkeepers looked as if he was about to take over a major role in an action film.

He nodded to Drummond. 'Don't get up, Keith. We'll need all your energy later, eh?' He smiled at Salter. 'What it is to be young!'

Drummond watched them both curiously. The use of his first name. Was it really Beaumont's intention to dispense with the usual formality, or merely to impress Salter, and anyone else who might be listening?

Hillier's eyes were like saucers. He was probably already planning another letter to Dunedin. *Today Captain Beaumont told us how it was done.*

Salter leaned forward to watch as the crew on B gun was relieved in seconds. When the other crew had vanished below for their evening meal it was impossible to tell that there had been any change at all.

He said, 'The C.O. doesn't seem to have much faith in this operation.'

Beaumont looked at Drummond and shot him a ready grin. 'Really? Cold feet?'

Drummond removed his cap and ran his fingers through his hair. It felt matted with salt.

'Not my words, sir.' He glanced at Salter's back. 'Ask me about the way it'll be reported. That's something else again.'

The grin broadened. '*Touché*, Miles! You shouldn't play with this one, you know!'

Feet clattered on a ladder and Midshipman Keyes appeared breathless below Drummond's chair.

'Signal from Admiralty, sir. I've been helping with the decoding.' He saw Beaumont for the first time and flushed. 'I—I'm sorry, sir.'

Drummond snapped, 'Read it.'

'It says, sir, that the Spanish ship, S.S. *Aragon*, was reported as leaving Bilbao yesterday. Heading west.' He sounded mystified.

Beaumont clapped him on the shoulder but kept his eyes on Drummond.

'See? The bastards have taken the bait! Provided our decoy gets here on time, I think we're in business.'

Drummond smiled. 'She must be a communications ship of some sort. If we can pick up one transmission, to show she's aiding the enemy, we'll take her.'

Salter laughed. 'Sounds exciting!' He looked uneasy.

Beaumont eyed him fiercely. 'It's time for a bit of hitting back, Miles! Good for the country, and good for your programmes, eh?' It seemed to amuse him.

Sheridan saluted. 'Port watch closed up at defence stations, sir. I'll hang on until Pilot comes up from the W/T office.'

There was a question in his eyes, and Drummond said, 'All right, Number One, you can pass the word round now. Tell everyone what we're doing, or hope to do. Then go round the ship yourself and check that nothing has been overlooked.' He glanced at his watch. 'Action stations from midnight, I'm afraid, but see that there's a regular supply of cocoa and sandwiches for gun crews and watchkeepers.'

'Aye, aye, sir.' Sheridan touched the midshipman's arm and said quietly, 'Don't *stare*, laddy, it's rude.'

Keyes grinned and followed him towards the hatch.

Drummond thrust his hands into his pockets and frowned. Another letter home. *Today I carried the signal which came from London. I decoded it and gave it to Captain Beaumont.* Drummond glanced at Beaumont's profile. He certainly seemed to be enjoying it.

'Radar—Bridge!'

Sheridan snatched up the handset. 'Forebridge.'

'Getting a strong echo at Red oh-three-five. Range twelve thousand yards.'

Drummond was out of his chair and across to the small radar repeater which had appeared on the bridge during a boiler-clean in Chatham.

It took time, as it always did. After hours of sitting and staring at the sea it was hard to adjust to the dim picture in the small, enclosed screen. Echoes and writhing outlines moved with the radar's probing eye like weed on the sea-bed. And then he saw it, a bright, solid blip. A ship, with another, smaller drip of green light close against it.

To confirm his thoughts he heard Sheridan say, 'Radar reports a second echo, sir. Must be the tug. Nothing else around.'

Beaumont rubbed his hands. 'Soon will be!'

Drummond straightened his back and returned to the chair, his mind calculating and discarding.

'Take a look, Number One.' He saw Wingate's head rising over the hatch coaming. 'Check with radar, Pilot. Then lay off a course to intercept. Get the chief for me. I'll want maximum revolutions in a moment.

He knew Salter was staring at him, memorising every detail, like someone watching a piece of hoarded machinery coming alive again.

'Chief, sir.'

He snatched the handset.

'Chief? This is the captain. Decoy in radar contact. Stand by for full revs.'

Galbraith sounded very calm. 'Aye, sir. Expecting trouble, are we?'

'God knows.' He saw Wingate at the table, his dividers busy. 'Well?'

'Course to steer is one-three-zero, sir.'

'Good. Bring her round.' To Beaumont he said, 'Decoy will be in sight well before sunset, sir. Would be now but for this mist.'

Wingate glanced at Sheridan and winked. 'Tally bloody-ho!'

Then he said into the voice-pipe, 'Port fifteen.'

'Fifteen of port wheel on.' Even through the pipe it was obvious that the helmsman had his mouth full of sandwich or chocolate.

'Midships. Steady. Steer one-three-zero.'

Drummond looked up at the tallest funnel, the sudden strengthening of vapour above its stained lip.

'Full ahead together.'

As if she, too, had been waiting and gathering her energy for this moment, *Warlock* dug her stem into the swell and cut across it like a ploughshare. With every mounting revolution the bow wave grew higher, higher, until the creaming water rose level with the iron deck as she thrust her way through the water. Below, and throughout the ship, every plate and rivet seemed to be vibrating in protest or approval, and in the crowded messdecks the relieved watchkeepers braced themselves against the tables and tried to stomach their evening meal. Few spoke or even looked at each other. A glance could be a question. And the answer might be too grim to contemplate.

Sheridan, on his way aft to the wardroom, clung to a stanchion and paused to watch the great surge of sea and spray alongside. He was still thinking of Drummond, seeing him come alive, the doubt and anxiety slipping from his face like an unwanted mask. And he had thought he had begun to know him. He had looked like a stranger. A fighter.

He saw Mangin and the chief stoker standing below the pom-pom mounting contemplating the glistening bow wave with grave interest.

'Suit you, 'Swain?'

Mangin shrugged. 'Poor old cow'll shake 'erself apart one o' these days!' He grinned. 'Sir.'

They all looked up at the tall bridge as a signal lamp clattered shortly.

Mangin remarked, 'Sighted 'er then.'

Sheridan watched the signalman's black silhouette as he shuttered off another brief acknowledgement. No need to pass the word. Everyone knew they were going to have a crack at something. The rights and wrongs of it were nobody's concern but the skipper's, apparently.

As if to confirm Mangin's words, the great bow wave began to sigh away, falling and smoothing until *Warlock*'s speed had dropped to even less than her original one. Only the great, seething white wake, spreading and intermingling with the swell like a pale arrowhead, gave a hint of her momentary return to her true glory.

Sheridan continued aft. Now, all they had to do was hold the other ship on the radar, listen for some hint of a sighting signal from the Spaniard, and then, as Wingate had wryly remarked, it would be tally bloody-ho indeed.

At the rear of the bridge Drummond saw Sheridan walking towards the quarterdeck, but his mind was elsewhere. That momentary contact with the other ship had been like a trust. The brief stab of signal lights from the elderly destroyer and from that murky outline of the decoy meant that time for supposition and doubt was almost over.

It would probably be a solitary U-boat to which any sort of sighting signal would be made. The Germans were unlikely to deploy more than one boat for possible stragglers, no matter how desperately they needed information about convoys and their contents. The other three destroyers would be close by to catch the submarine when the time came. It would be up to *Warlock* to corner the spy-ship.

But to those unknown men aboard the decoy one thing was certain. They were a deliberate target, and that quick exchange of signals was their only hope of survival.

Beaumont said, 'Seems quiet enough. No wind to speak of. Easy swell.' He nodded, apparently satisfied. 'Think I'll take some supper.'

He left the bridge, and Salter said fervently, 'God, what a man, eh? No wonder people look up to him.'

Drummond moved from his chair again. It was hopeless trying to think with Salter chattering all the time. He probably meant well, and in any case he was quite likely feeling a bit apprehensive now that there was some likelihood of trouble.

But Drummond needed to be alone. To think, to try and discover what was troubling him. Everything was going like a clock, just as Beaumont had predicted and planned. And yet there was something. Some flaw, like a false echo on a radar screen, or on an incomplete painting.

He said, 'I'll be in my sea cabin, Pilot. Have a sandwich or something sent up, will you?'

As he left the bridge Salter said, 'I suppose he has to try and copy Captain Beaumont's coolness.' He shook his head. 'Must be a bit of a challenge to have a public hero as your boss.'

Wingate studied him gravely. 'We must all try and live up to it.'

Salter glared at him as the lieutenant started to chuckle. 'I'm going below!' He was still muttering angrily as he clambered off the bridge.

Wingate wiped his night glasses with a piece of tissue before peering along the bearing where the decoy ship would be, if only she was visible again. Pompous bastard, he thought cheerfully. He felt the deck begin to roll in another series of uncomfortable troughs. Salter would get a shock when he reached the wardroom, or rather his guts would. Greasy sausages and overcooked potatoes. Just the job for the likes of him.

He saw Keyes hovering by the voice-pipes and said, 'Now, Mid, I'll tell you how it was when *I* joined, how about that?'

Keyes came out of his trance. He had been thinking of the signal, of Beaumont's hand on his shoulder. Friendly. Like an equal. He liked the navigating officer, even if he was a bit crude at times. But it was wrong to make fun of Salter in front of the other watchkeepers. It was like hitting at Beaumont.

He sighed and said, 'You've already told me.'

Wingate shook his head. 'Bother.'

'Object in the water! Green four-five!' The lookout was crouching against the darkening sky like a carving on a church tower.

Wingate pushed past him, his glasses already trained above the screen.

Keyes called excitedly, 'I can see it!' Then he added, 'Oh, it's only a piece of wood.'

Wingate walked deliberately along the gratings at the side of the bridge, his eyes never leaving the small, bobbing fragment until it was overturned and lost in *Warlock*'s wake. Part of a boat's keel.

He swung round and said harshly, 'Only a piece of wood, was it?' He saw Keyes recoil, surprised and hurt. 'Well, it was a bloody lifeboat once!'

The other watchkeepers shifted uneasily and kept their eyes trained outboard. Only Parvin, the leading signalman, who had been in the ship when Wingate had first joined her, understood and felt something like pity for him.

He said quietly, 'I'd call down to the wardroom, if I was you, Mr. Keyes, and check up with Owles about the skipper's sandwiches. Just in case the old bugger shuts up the pantry for the night.' He saw Keyes nodding, still confused at Wingate's anger.

Parvin returned to his thoughts. There was no point in trying to explain to Keyes. He would learn soon enough. Or go under, like the last Number One had done.

He knew quite a bit about Wingate. Gossip soon got round in small ships. He had been navigating officer in a sloop in Western Approaches. The ship had been torpedoed in a snow-squall, four hundred miles out in the Atlantic. Most of the survivors were picked up by another escort, but somehow they missed Wingate's little boat. When a destroyer had found them four days later there were only half of the original ten men still alive. One had been frozen bodily against Wingate's oilskin. It was said that it had been his best friend and had died soon after rescue.

Parvin heard him exclaim bitterly, 'Don't talk to me about heroes. I've seen too many of them.'

When Drummond returned to the bridge just before midnight the sea felt calmer, flatter, and through a high bank of fleecy clouds he caught occasional glimpses of the moon. He shivered slightly. A good night for it.

'Ready when you are, sir.'

He glanced at Wingate, noting the dullness in his voice. Equally the lingering tension around the bridge. An argument. Assertion of discipline. Keyes making a mess of something.

He dismissed it from his thoughts. It did not matter now.

'Yes. Sound action stations, please.'

5

A Great Find

DRUMMOND rested his elbows against the bridge screen and trained his powerful glasses beyond the port bow. It took steady concentration with the ship moving so sluggishly, and after a slow examination of the faint horizon he returned to his place beside the chart table.

Beaumont had taken over the bridge chair, and appeared to be sitting very erect, listening. In fact, the whole ship was like that.

It was nearly four in the morning, with the moon still playing tricks between the thin clouds and touching the crests of the long swells with silver, so that the troughs seemed far deeper than they actually were. The motion was sickening, for with her engines stopped, her fans almost stilled, *Warlock* idled and swayed over each low swell with all the intensity of a quarter-sea.

An hour earlier the lookouts had sighted a light, far away on the eastern horizon. It had moved slowly and then vanished. Radar had reported it as a ship, and it had seemed likely that the light had been the illuminated hull of a neutral. The *Aragon*, Beaumont had insisted forcefully. Now nobody was certain of anything, except that their own ship was drifting uneasily in moonlight which could make her a fine target.

Drummond asked, 'How is the decoy?'

More murmurings, a clink of metal as a lookout's belt scraped against a locker. In the silence it sounded like the crash of an oven door.

'In position, sir. Now almost dead ahead. Range six thousand yards.'

'*Damn!*' Beaumont wriggled round in the chair, his face square against the sky. 'We can't crack on any speed or we'll be up to her in no time.' He was calculating aloud. 'That other bugger is probably listening or watching from somewhere. Waiting to see if the decoy stops or retraces his course.'

Drummond said nothing. If there *was* a spy-ship out there, her captain was cunning all right. *Warlock* could do little but wait. In the morning they would be too close to Spanish waters to take decisive action. And the trap might be sprung against them.

'Check with the W/T office.'

Drummond heard Hillier muttering into the voice-pipe at the rear of the bridge.

'Nothing, sir.'

Drummond groped for his pipe and put it between his teeth. He could see Wingate lolling against the chart table, the portly outline of Tucker, the yeoman of signals, at his elbow. Lookouts and bosun's mates, and Sheridan on the opposite side of the bridge. In action he would be elsewhere with the damage control parties, but in this peculiar situation he might be required right here.

Wingate asked, 'I wonder where the other destroyers are?'

Beaumont snapped, 'Laughing their bloody heads off, I expect!'

Miles Salter edged around the compass platform, his hands groping before him like a blind man.

'Maybe they'll try again later?'

Beaumont looked down at him. 'Perhaps. But we will have to close with the decoy and get her out of it. She's got a list, which her crew created by flooding. She looks the part, but it could be difficult to put her to rights for the next leg to Gib.'

He swung round in the chair. 'Who has the nearest patrol area?'

'*Ventnor*, sir.' Wingate did not consult his notes. 'Her captain is Lieutenant-Commander Selkirk.'

'I see.' Beaumont peered down, searching for Drummond. 'Remember him at the conference? Bloody troublemaker, if I ever saw one.'

Salter asked mildly, 'A reservist, I believe?'

Beaumont looked away. 'Yes.'

'Radar—Bridge.'

Sheridan was there. 'Forebridge.'

'Firm echo at Red four-five, sir. Range seven thousand yards.'

'Ask him why the bloody *hell* he didn't get it earlier!' Beaumont sounded savage.

The radar operator must have heard him and said, 'Been having a lot of back-echoes, sir. Or it may have been some kind of jamming. Can't tell under these conditions.'

'Light on the port bow, sir.'

Drummond stepped quickly on to the gratings behind the chair. He saw the blurred glow as before, a touch of red, like a painted emblem.

The lookout added, 'Moving away, sir.'

'Must have smelt a rat.' Salter sounded vaguely relieved. 'Off like a shot!'

The explosion when it reached the ship was like a thunderclap. But seconds before, a great scalding tower of flame shot skyward with such fierce intensity Drummond could imagine the heat against his face. Then came the bang, rattling the bridge and making several of the men cry out with alarm.

'Christ! The decoy has been torpedoed!'

Beaumont stood and seized the screen with both hands, his head and shoulders clearly outlined by the distant fire.

'Full ahead together!' Drummond ignored the shouts and questions on every side. 'Stand by B gun with star-shell!'

Telegraphs clanged, and with an urgent roar of screws and fans *Warlock* lunged ahead towards the blazing ship.

Drummond stood up beside Beaumont, his glasses quivering to the increasing beat of machinery.

'It's the tug, not the decoy, sir.' He waited for Beaumont's mind to clear. 'Look, you can see her broaching-to!' He turned slightly. 'Tell Guns to put a star-shell at Green four-five. There must be a U-boat on the surface.'

'Asdic have had no contact, sir.' Sheridan kept his voice steady.

Beaumont shouted, 'I don't give a bugger about that! That fool Selkirk must have let the Jerry slip right under his nose!' He winced as B gun exploded below the bridge.

Drummond waited, counting seconds, feeling his ship tearing through the water beneath him, the clatter of a shell-case as the gun crew opened their breech.

The star-shell burst far abeam of the two ships, lighting up the sea in a pitiless white glare which made the moon and even the spurting flames seem dull.

Nothing.

Drummond shifted his glasses, trying not to look at the dying tug, the way the fires were spreading now across the water and engulfing the listing decoy. Nothing. No U-boat on radar, or detected submerged by Asdic. Yet a ship had just been blown up before their eyes, and out there men were burning and dying.

He snapped, 'Pass the word. Collision mats forrard, starboard side.' He touched his cheek as if to confirm the direction of the breeze. 'Tell the doctor to get up there. There'll not be much time.'

Beaumont staggered across the gratings and said sharply, 'Get after that bloody Spaniard!'

'There are men dying. We may save a few.' He thought he saw the conflict on Beaumont's face, his eyes shining like stones in the drifting flare. 'If we grapple with a neutral, with no evidence she was acting unlawfully, we will have wasted time and lives for nothing.'

He turned away. 'Number One, get down to the fo'c'sle. Fire parties and damage control sections, too.' His voice checked him as he ran for the ladder. 'I'll drop the motor boat as we make our run-in, so make sure she has a good crew.'

A dull explosion rattled the glass screen and threw a ragged smoke-stain across the moon. Some of the fire disappeared, and Drummond guessed the tug had plunged under. She would be big, with a sizeable crew.

Faintly above the din of fans and surging water alongside he heard the cry, 'Away motor boat's crew! Lowering party at the double!'

He could imagine the startled confusion aboard the other destroyers waiting out there beyond the flare and the glittering reflections of a dying ship. They would come rushing to give assistance, no doubt blaming *Warlock* for failing to detect the U-boat, even now after the savage attack.

Feet hammered along the iron deck, and on the forecastle he saw the chief bosun's mate and a dozen hands working feverishly to lash fenders and collision mats, hammocks and anything else which might cushion the impact as they swept alongside.

Salter was saying, 'God Almighty. God, look at her burn.' Over and over again.

More explosions echoed across the swell, the surface of which shone with red and orange, for as the flare died away *Warlock*'s company found they were staring into the very heart of an inferno.

Beaumont said tightly, 'You're taking a chance.'

'I know, sir.' He leaned sideways above the voice-pipe. 'Slow ahead together. Stand by the motor boat.' To Beaumont he added, 'No choice.'

'Ready to drop the boat, sir.'

'Very well. Stop both engines.' He felt *Warlock* sighing ahead on her fading bow wave, the shout from below the bridge, 'Out pins! *Slip!*' The rattling splutter as the motor boat veered away like a mad thing before coming under the command of its own engine.

'Half ahead together.' He heard Mangin's acknowledgement. Stiff, every fibre concentrated on the ball of fire directly ahead. 'Starboard side to, Cox'n. Easy as you can.'

Mangin replied, 'I'll try not to score the paint, sir.'

Drummond peered down at the deck again. The figures touched with cruel reflections now, the air around them tinged with smoke and ash. He saw the doctor in his white coat, Froud, his effeminate S.B.A., close behind him, a satchel bouncing on one hip. All available hands. Extra stokers, cooks and stewards, the supply assistant, and anyone else who was not employed on the guns. And what a target they would present to any stalking submarine. Slowing down, black against the flames, a perfect shot.

Drummond bit so hard on the unlit pipe he almost broke it. There *was* no U-boat! So how the hell had it happened?

He turned to Hillier, 'Warn depth-charge crews to stand by. Shallow pattern.'

He swung back to the screen. *Just in case.*

The decoy ship was looming high above the starboard bow now, less than a cable clear. She had been one of the hastily built Liberty ships but had broken her back in a storm off Miami the previous year. Repaired with no particular use in mind, she was now dying as bravely as any ship could be expected to do.

'Slow ahead.'

He could feel the heat, taste the stench of burning paint and woodwork, as well as the seeping oil which was trickling in an angry flood away from the sinking ship, like lava from a volcano.

He saw men, too, very small against the fires, creeping or darting from one place to another, their shouts lost in the pandemonium of leaping flames and escaping steam.

Something heavy grated through a bulkhead, and a wild column of sparks burst out of the after well-deck, hurling several tiny figures over the side.

When he glanced abeam he saw the *Warlock*'s small motor boat chugging steadily towards the flames, her crew standing like bronze statues in the reflected glare.

'Stop together.'

He tried not to drag himself up to the top of the screen to watch. He could almost feel the other ship's hull getting closer, his stomach muscles contracting as if they and not *Warlock*'s bow were going to take the collision.

Someone jumped outward and down, and Drummond heard Hillier retching helplessly as *Warlock* pushed firmly under the decoy's quarter. The wretched sailor must have been pulped between the hulls like fruit.

'Slow astern together!'

He gritted his teeth, imagining Galbraith in his private world of noise, watching the dials, with nothing between him and his men but thin steel plates. And his trust in those on the bridge.

The screws beat the sea into another frenzy even as the flared forecastle lurched drunkenly against the other vessel, ropes, fenders and makeshift mats all splitting and flying like live things as steel carved through them, bringing the hulls together with one resounding boom.

'Slow ahead port. Stop starboard.'

Drummond squinted against the fierce glare, feeling the heat on his face and mouth, sensing that the other ship's foremast and derricks had already gone smashing over the side. She was burning fiercely within, but would not sink just yet because of her extra buoyancy of packed timber. Better if she plunged down right now after the tug. It would at least spare some of those trapped between decks.

Faint cries floated up from the forecastle, and heaving lines lifted or fell across the fires like crazy serpents. Some of *War-*

lock's men were retreating from the heat now. Others lay like corpses, overcome by the roaring inferno alongside.

Beaumont shouted hoarsely, 'Not many of them left!'

Drummond wiped his streaming face. A mere handful, and some of those had probably dropped between the two hulls.

Sheridan was signalling with his torch from the top of A gun. 'Cast off forrard.'

Drummond stood with his chest against the screen, making himself watch the last agonies. Then he saw two figures, isolated from the decoy's poop by some fifty feet of solid fire. How they had survived this long he could not explain. Or accept. It was suddenly important that they should be saved. That they should not see *Warlock* sliding away in those last agonising minutes.

'Fire parties!' He gestured over the screen. 'Get some hoses on those men!'

He watched narrowly as more flames darted through the fractured poop, some licking eagerly towards the *Warlock*'s forecastle and making the men scatter like skittles. But one hose found and held on to the two staggering survivors. Even in all this bedlam it was possible to see the steam rising from their clothing as they fought their way aft. There was Vickery, the chief bosun's mate, and a cook still wearing his apron, clinging to the bucking hose as they guided them to safety.

Hillier yelled, 'They're inboard!' He sounded close to sobbing.

'Slow astern together!' Drummond thrust his hands into his pockets. Every limb was convulsing as if he had a terrible fever. 'Hard a-port!'

Sheridan came to the bridge, coughing and gasping.

'Fifteen survivors, sir. Some may be from the tug, of course.'

He leaned on the chart table, and Wingate said quietly, 'Well done, old son.'

Drummond walked to the port side again, watching the spreading lake of fire, dark red like blood against the paling sky.

'Stop together. Wheel amidships. Can anyone see the motor boat?'

He heard himself ask flatly, 'Those last two. Are they all right?'

Sheridan stared at him. 'One might make it, sir.' He looked away. 'The other has lost most of his face.'

'Motor boat on starboard beam, sir.' A pause. 'Her cox'n is semaphoring. Six picked up.'

'Recall the boat.' He threw his cap on the chart table and took several deep breaths. 'Twenty-one all told.'

Salter said thickly, 'I'd never have thought it possible. Bloody marvellous.'

Beaumont turned on him. 'Bloody disastrous, you mean!' He spoke in a fierce whisper. 'We've gained nothing! *And* lost two bloody ships!'

Hillier was dabbing his eyes and peering down at the motor boat as it moved very slowly towards the ship. In the paling light and the angry glow from the distant decoy it was easy to see the oil-sodden figures, the way they coughed and wheezed against their rescuers. He stood very still, quite unable to move. He knew Beaumont and Salter were arguing about something, that Drummond alone seemed to be in command of the ship and all about it. The rest were like parts of an intricate machine. Momentarily disturbed, but now returned to order and purpose.

Still he stood quite rigid. Frozen as he watched something drifting away into the shadows.

Drummond was also watching the motor boat when Hillier exclaimed in a shaky voice, 'Down there, sir. In the sea.'

He strode quickly to his side and gripped his arm. Through the duffel coat and reefer he could feel Hillier's body shaking violently.

'What is it, Sub?' He leaned over the rough metal, keeping his hold on Hillier's arm.

Hillier said huskily, 'Gone, sir. But I—I was almost sure . . .' He turned, his face like that of an old man. 'Like a torpedo, sir.'

Drummond retained his grip, his voice very even as he said, 'Signal the boat. Pass the word to guns and depth-charge parties.'

Hillier shook his head, oblivious to the sudden rush of feet all around him. 'I was mistaken. It was just floating. Must have been—'

'*Sir!*' The yeoman was waving his fist towards the sea. 'The boat's sighted something!'

Beaumont said quickly, 'I'd get going, if I were you, Keith.' He was very cool. Detached.

Drummond replied, 'It would have attacked by now, sir.'

He watched fixedly as the motor boat lifted and dipped over a long, easy swell. A torch was being trained carefully into the water. Something black, like a dead dolphin, swam into the brief beam of yellow light.

Hillier murmured, 'It *was* there.'

The yeoman said, 'Bloody hell!'

Another voice, sane, almost matter-of-fact after what they had just seen and done, said, 'Radar report, lost contact with Spaniard, sir.'

Salter said to the bridge at large, 'God, the Spaniards will make capital of this!'

Drummond was still watching the thing in the water.

'They won't, you know. Not after we get this back to base.' He released his hold on Hillier's arm. 'You did well. Now go aft and tell the gunner (T) to rig one of his depth-charge hoists. We'll get that thing aboard if it's safe.'

Salter jumped with alarm. 'It might explode, surely?'

Beaumont cleared his throat. 'He has a point, Keith.'

Drummond brushed past him to peer down at the iron deck. 'I believe that this is what you came to get, sir.' He glanced bitterly at the dying flames on the water. 'Even if we did not know what we were looking for at the time.'

Sheridan said, 'Radar has contact with the other destroyers, sir. Now closing to six thousand yards.'

'As soon as we get under way again, they'll know it's over. The fewer signals made today, the better.' He glanced at Beaumont. 'Right, sir?'

The other man nodded slowly. 'Yes. We will return to Falmouth.' He seemed to shake himself from his inner doubts. 'With the catch.'

'Decoy's going under, sir!'

With a great hissing roar the burning ship rolled over and slid beneath the surface in a welter of bubbles and corkscrewing flotsam. It was suddenly very quiet.

Beaumont said, 'You can go aft if you wish, Keith. I'll take over while you assess the situation, eh?' He forced a grin. 'You've earned a break from all this.'

Drummond nodded to Sheridan. 'When I pass the word, get under way. Course and speed to rejoin the others by dawn.'

He lowered himself down one of the outer ladders, past a hooded Oerlikon gunner, and further still until he reached the iron deck and the empty motor boat davits.

Figures passed this way and that, and he saw the S.B.A. gently putting a dressing on a man's face. There was a stench of burned oil, of vomit, of survival.

The thing was already alongside the quarterdeck, held clear by some spare fenders which Noakes must have been saving for his own part of the ship. It looked very much like a torpedo, except now that it was just below his feet, Drummond could see it contained a small perspex dome, rather like the ones they used to cover pies and sandwiches in railway buffets.

Noakes flashed his torch carefully along the rounded shape as the hastily rigged tackles took the strain.

Drummond looked at the dome again. It contained a staring, petrified face, the head of which was covered by a sort of rubber helmet.

He said quietly, 'Midget submarine. No wonder we got no contact.'

'Hoist away!' Noakes stood back as the seamen laid on to the tackles. 'Take up the slack!'

As the strange, torpedo-shaped cylinder rose above deck level it tilted to *Warlock*'s swaying motion. Inside the little dome the helmeted head lolled, and Drummond saw water slopping from its mouth.

Noakes muttered, 'Rum do, sir.'

'Yes.' Behind him he heard a man scream with sudden agony. 'I only hope it's worth all this.'

'Sorry to have kept you waiting, gentlemen.' A marine sergeant held open the door. 'They are waiting for you now.'

Beaumont threw his cigarette into a white-painted tin and snapped, 'About bloody time!'

Drummond followed him from the tiled waiting room and into a long passageway. His body felt chilled to the bone, although whether it was the actual building or the fact he had hardly snatched more than two consecutive hours' sleep for six days, he was not sure.

Warlock had tied up in Falmouth that afternoon, and he had been surprised at the reception committee which had swamped the upper deck, whisking away their strange capture on a carefully disguised trailer, with a full escort of marine and military police.

Drummond had waited aboard to see the decoy's survivors safely into the waiting ambulances, a small, silent procession of bandaged, limping men, the less fortunate being carried on stretchers. The man who had had most of his face burned away had not survived after all.

Drummond thought of Frank, the accusation in Helen's eyes. Perhaps it was just as well that one so mutilated should have been saved the embarrassment of living.

The immediate aftermath of their attempt to lure the spy-ship into betraying itself, the horror of the two burning vessels, and the totally unexpected discovery of the midget submarine had been further livened by an air attack as they had altered course for the last approach to Falmouth.

A German bomber had come across them almost by accident, it seemed. The pilot had probably been making a quick hit-and-run raid along the coastline, when diving out of low cloud had sighted *Warlock* and the other three destroyers immediately in his path.

At any other time, and especially with a ship's company comprising largely of new and inexperienced hands, it could have been a disaster. It was a known fact that many sinkings were caused on the way home after a mission or patrol, with gun crews thinking more of wives and girl friends than of watching the sea and sky around them.

Perhaps *Warlock*'s company were still shocked, still smouldering at seeing the nearness of death, at having the gasping, burned survivors living amongst them for the passage back to Falmouth. Whatever it was, Drummond had been surprised at the ferocity of the barrage from pom-poms and Oerlikons, the accuracy of the very first time which his new company had fought together in earnest.

They might have clipped the German's wings, or equally they might have missed him altogether. That did not matter. Just seeing the bomber speeding away within feet of the sea, pursued by occasional shots from the other destroyers' main armament, had been something like a tonic.

Beaumont had gone ashore immediately, having been picked

up on the jetty by an imposing Humber staff car. That, Drummond had thought, was the end of it. He had gone around the ship, speaking with the men who had suffered burns when *Warlock* had grappled with the blazing decoy, examining the damage, telling Sheridan his plans for repainting the blackened scar along the starboard side of the forecastle.

He knew now that Vaughan, the doctor, had been right when he had insisted, 'You should be resting, sir. It seems to me, you've done far too much of this sort of thing.'

Vaughan was a strange fish, he thought. Distant, very cool. Impossible to measure. Inexperienced or not, he had proved he was good at his work. The fact that only one of his charges had died spoke volumes. He had also been very right about Drummond.

At the end of his inspection he had been about to go aft for a bath and change of clothing, when a messenger had hurried aboard with a summons to the local mortuary, which had apparently been commandeered by the military.

Now, as he followed Beaumont beneath one enamel-shaded lamp after another, he was aware that the other man was none too pleased at being kept at arm's-length while experts examined their catch.

'Bloody eggheads! What do they know of new weapons?'

It was an illogical comment, but Drummond could appreciate his feelings.

The marine threw open a door and they walked into what had once been the room where post-mortems were carried out. In the centre, propped on stout trestles, the midget submarine looked even larger in this confined space. Close by, naked under powerful lights, lay the corpse of its luckless commander. On another table, his rubber suit, helmet and various pieces of equipment were displayed in neat rows, like exhibits in a museum. There was a strong stench of disinfectant, which refused to merge with the other smells of oil and death.

There were about two dozen people present. Some in army battledress, and several naval officers of various ranks and ages. Two grave-eyed men in white coats were walking around the miniature submarine, followed at a discreet distance by a plain-looking girl in A.T.S. uniform who was taking down notes in shorthand.

The taller of the two white coats said, 'Ah, here you are then.'

He shook hands warmly with Beaumont and nodded to Drummond. Across the room Drummond saw himself in a mirror, above which were the words, *Wash your hands afterwards*. Afterwards.

No wonder the man in the white coat had all but ignored him. Once more, Beaumont's elegant appearance had made him look like another survivor.

'Please find yourselves some seats.'

The white coat was obviously important, and all the people in the room were sitting down in seconds. The girl sat, with legs crossed, her back against the table within inches of the corpse, her face completely expressionless, even bored.

'This must all be kept as top secret, naturally.' The white coat darted a searching glance around the room. 'It is a great find. A discovery which will certainly disturb a few brains in Whitehall.'

'Didn't know there were any!'

The second white coat was obviously the light relief, Drummond thought wearily. Several people laughed.

'To continue. We know that there has been quite a deal of success with two-man torpedoes in the past, by us, and, of course, the Italians. The "chariots", however, differ greatly from *this*.' He paused to lay his hand on the black metal. 'Inasmuch as they were used to carry a warhead, which could then be attached to an anchored vessel's bilge keel or other underwater protrusion, inside an enemy's harbour. A time fuse would be set, and the remaining part of the chariot would carry the two, er, *riders* back to a rendezvous with a conventional submarine.'

Several people shuffled their feet, and when Drummond looked at Beaumont he saw that he was sitting exactly upright, fingers tucked between his reefer buttons. He could have been thinking about anything.

The white coat dropped his voice. 'This midget submarine is designed to carry a normal type of torpedo slung beneath it. Observe the brackets.' He tapped the rearmost ones like a schoolmaster. 'The torpedo was released, fired if you prefer, at a target *while at sea*.' He looked impassively at Beaumont. 'As you will know better than any of us.'

Beaumont did not blink. 'Quite so.'

'We will know more once we can move all this to our proper location.'

Drummond recalled his own uncertainty before the attack, his need to get away from Salter's questions. To think. It had all been there for everyone to see. The sequence of past attacks, the pattern. Fine weather. Calm sea and good night visibility. He looked at the corpse. The skin was gleaming in the lights like wax. He had seen plenty of dead men. Too many of his own sort. This one should have left him unmoved, so what was the matter? Embarrassment? It could not surely be pity for a man who had burned so many, and had probably killed himself by accident? But it was wrong. The way they were staring at the body. Bored, disinterested beyond a piece of factual evidence. Even the girl, who had risen to follow the white coat to the table, was looking at the corpse as she might at a piece of dead fish.

'Note the man's arms.'

The voice brought them closer. Drummond saw that the corpse had several garish tattoos on either forearm. His eyes were slitted half open, as if he were listening.

'A ranker, I would think. No German officer would consider tattoos quite the thing.'

Someone else laughed.

Beaumont murmured savagely, 'Stupid sod.'

The white coat wheeled round. 'But an important point! Only *one* man needed to navigate and steer, to aim and fire the torpedo. And not even an officer! Just imagine what the enemy will achieve with these weapons, if they can manufacture and perfect them by the hundred!'

A voice asked, 'No other identification, I suppose?' He was turning over the rubber suit with a pencil.

'None.'

Beaumont asked shortly, 'Where do *we* come in?'

'We?' The man smiled politely.

Beaumont gestured with his free hand. 'Lieutenant-Commander Drummond commands the ship which carried out the operation. I expect he'd like to know, too.' He did not hide the sarcasm.

'In due course I am sure that the proper authority will be requiring further reports on what you saw at the time.' He looked

94

blandly at Drummond. 'Your surgeon was sensible to keep the body intact in its cockpit. The photographs which have just been taken will be helpful. It would appear that the torpedo was released too close to the target. Panic, probably.'

Drummond walked slowly towards the table, feeling the on-lookers, senior and junior alike, falling back to let him through. He stood looking down at the dead face. Young, tanned by off-duty hours aboard his base ship.

He said quietly, 'The wind had shifted slightly.' He recalled the feel of it on his cheek, the roar of fans as *Warlock* had charged to the rescue.

Around him there was complete silence, as if they were afraid to disrupt the picture he was creating.

'I noticed how the swell was getting up. I had to watch it be-cause of dropping a boat. I couldn't risk it capsizing. This man must already have been well away from his base ship. Alone in this little pod, a floating test-bed, in all probability. It looks big enough in here. Try and picture it at sea, *yourselves at the helm*.' His voice had grown harder. 'I expect you were right, sir. He did fire too close, in that swell, and with the little dome only a foot or so out of the water, he would be nearly blind. He tried a bow shot, but hit the tug instead. The explosion probably rup-tured the casing and flooded his cockpit.' He reached out and dragged a soiled sheet over the man's nakedness. 'But panic? I don't see that at all.'

They were staring at him, as if he had just shouted some ter-rible oath or obscenity.

• *They don't understand a bloody word*. How can they? Their minds were suited to detection, and discounted the human ele-ment completely. It was totally alien to his own world. He had seen the flaw even though he had not the experience to recog-nise it. But once it was in his mind, it would not shift. Observa-tion—Conclusion—Method. He would be ready if there was a next time.

The white coat said quietly, 'Thank you, Commander Drum-mond. You must be very tired.'

Beaumont looked at his watch. 'Of course he isn't tired. My commanding officers are ready at all times.' He touched Drum-mond's arm, a bright grin on his face. 'Right, Keith?'

He nodded, angry with himself at his outburst. Maybe he was

not as fit as he had imagined. Bomb-happy. Round the bend. It had happened to plenty of people.

Beaumont replaced his cap at a rakish angle. 'I'll be in touch, gentlemen.' As the door swung behind them he added, 'Sooner than they bloody well think!'

Drummond saw Salter lounging by a small telephone booth, an angry-faced military police sergeant glaring at him. Salter held out the telephone, ignoring the redcap.

'Got him for you, just like you said.' He yawned. 'Cut through all the red tape and, er, caps.'

Beaumont stared at his reflection in the glazed tiles.

'Beaumont speaking. Ah, yes, sir. Yes, I agree. A damn good show all round, I thought. Went like a Swiss watch!' He winked at Salter. 'Tomorrow then. Look forward to it.' He put down the telephone.

To Drummond he said calmly, 'I'll come back to the ship with you. I feel like a very large drink, on you.'

Drummond fell in step beside him, while Salter slouched along in the rear.

'We are going to London, Keith.' He threw up a snappy salute to two sentries. 'To *get things moving.*'

Salter called, 'I've laid my bit on.'

Beaumont did not seem to hear him. 'Tattoos, ranker, what the hell do they know! I'd like to see them get those poor devils off a burning ship like we did, eh?' He sounded angry.

Drummond smiled, despite his tiredness. 'Yes, sir.'

Beaumont quickened his pace. 'We'll show 'em.'

Behind him, Drummond heard Salter mutter, 'What a way to fight a war.'

He was inclined to agree.

6

Not What They Were

THE map room, which was situated in a concrete bunker below the Admiralty buildings, felt almost as cold as the Falmouth mortuary. While he was waiting to be introduced by Beaumont, Drummond let his gaze move slowly around the spartan interior, noting the many wall charts and plans, the few personnel who seemed to be needed in this very special place. He and Beaumont had been driven by a madcap marine all the way from Falmouth, pausing only for a brief lunch at a small inn before charging on again for London. And now, after a series of checks, murmured acknowledgements over telephones and further examination of passes, they were in the hub of the Navy's special operations. He had lost count of the stairways and lifts, and could not begin to guess how far they were below the other living world. A world of shabby buildings scarred by bombs, yet cheerfully determined to be 'Open as Usual'. Streets thronged with people, most of whom were in uniform. Poles and Free French, Americans by the hundred, Norwegians and Danes, and plenty of British from all three services. It had given a better indication of Germany's conquests than this noiseless bunker gave of any sort of Allied gains.

He realised that Beaumont was saying, 'This is Drummond, sir.'

A slight figure in a creased grey suit stepped from the group and held out one hand. Like the man, it was small and wizened.

Beaumont said, 'Vice-Admiral Brooks.'

Drummond returned the handshake. It was surprisingly strong. Vice-Admiral Brooks. 'Nick.' It was hard to picture him in a flag officer's uniform with all its gold lace. Maybe that was why he wore a suit. The other would swamp him completely.

Brooks said crisply, 'Good to see you. I shall have to tell you a lot more than I intended at this stage. However . . .' He did not go on, but produced a cigarette from his pocket and waited for one of the duty officers to light it. He took several long pulls, displaying his upper teeth, which were very large and ugly.

'Ready, sir.' Another officer spoke from one of the maps. His voice was hushed, as if in church.

Brooks sat down on a table and swung one leg carelessly above a waste-paper basket.

'I've been hearing all about your capture. Seen the photographs which my people took in Falmouth.' He had a quick, darting way of speaking and moving. A compressed bundle of energy, Drummond thought. 'We guessed that the Germans were up to something, of course, but they have reached a far more advanced stage than I had imagined. I have ordered immediate enquiries elsewhere,' he shot Beaumont a quick glance, 'but there seems little room for doubt.'

Drummond thought of the speed with which things had moved. They had only reached Falmouth yesterday, yet already Admiral Brooks had seen the reports, checked the pictures and intelligence data and was, it appeared, ready to make further decisions.

Brooks said, 'I've been hearing quite a bit about you, too.' He measured Drummond with a lingering stare. 'Record's a good one.' The teeth dipped down like a portcullis. 'Considering you come of an army family!'

Drummond smiled. 'I am trying to live with it, sir.'

The smile, if it was one, vanished. 'Quite. You have served without any real break since the beginning. Convoy escort, anti-submarine work, Mediterranean and Atlantic.' He was ticking off his record like a grocer's list. 'But this may be something more of a challenge.'

He swung round on the corner of the table and stabbed his cigarette towards the nearest chart. It was of Norway. All the long, craggy coastline from the Skagerrak to North Cape.

Brooks said, 'It has been a hard slog. It is impossible to tell just how many valuable warships have been tied down because of Germany's remaining heavy units. *Bismarck* has gone, *Graf Spee* and others either sunk or disabled. But up there, like wolves in their lairs, the greatest menace still remains. *Tirpitz*, with her more successful consort, *Scharnhorst*, can pounce on any Russian convoy they choose. To contain them and their escorts, we in turn must tie down our battleships and cruisers, use them to shadow the Arctic convoys, when they are needed, or soon will be, elsewhere.'

Drummond said quietly, 'To cover an invasion, sir.'

'Yes.' Brooks looked round the room. 'Even the word sounds like a betrayal of a secret.' He laughed shortly. 'But you can't keep a million men and a thousand ships in the dark forever.'

Through a small doorway Drummond heard the muffled rattle of teleprinters, the jingle of phones, and imagined all the information which was coming into this bunker, to this small, remarkable man. It made the actual fighting part seem almost unimportant. For the moment.

Brooks added softly, 'And *your* old friend is about, too.' He watched Beaumont's reaction. 'The one which put *Conqueror* on the bottom with a lot of fine men inside her.'

Beaumont said, 'That is why I'm so glad, no *honoured*, to be part of this, sir.'

Drummond saw his hands opening and shutting, the way he was staring at the great chart.

'Yes.' Brooks continued, 'Last year we made an attempt to cripple *Tirpitz* in her Norwegian fjord by using chariots. Had 'em slung on either side of a fishing boat, the idea being to release them once they were within range of the battleship. It sounds crazy, standing here looking at that chart. I am only moved to realise that men will volunteer for such impossible missions.' The mood passed on. 'Things have prospered since then. We have perfected a midget submarine which will, with luck, be able to penetrate the net defences and get right under the *beast* before releasing its saddle charges. We will be sending several such midgets, and I have no doubt from what I have seen of their crews, that some will be successful. Just a few months is all we need. Put her out of action, and *Scharnhost* will have to come out to make a play for the Russian convoys. And when that happens, gentlemen, our forces will no longer be split into fruitless search parties. We will catch her and put her down, and release our ships in readiness for invasion.'

Drummond said, 'I don't quite see where we come in, sir?'

'You will.' Brooks watched him through his smoke. 'Your "catch" has given me a headache, but in the end it may save us lives and valuable time.' He nodded to a sad-faced staff officer. 'Show him.'

The man lifted a long pointer and laid it on the top of the chart.

Brooks said gravely, 'Tirpitz is up there. To have a snowball's chance in hell of crippling her, making her a stationary target for the R.A.F. to bash at leisure, our midget submarines must have complete freedom to approach.'

He nodded again and the pointer moved down very slightly. 'There, in that adjoining fjord, is the German experimental base for underwater weapons. These small submarines, human torpedoes, call them what you will, are being assembled and tested round the clock. The fact that you have discovered how near to perfection they may be is unsettling. Worse, any attempt by our midgets to slip through Tirpitz's defences could be foiled by the enemy's own exercises in the area. Our boats will have to be towed by conventional submarines almost to the threshold, so to speak. Passage crews will have to be exchanged for the ones who are going to make the attack, and all that on the surface, within range of this damned base.'

Beaumont said, 'I suppose air attack is out of the question?'

'Yes. They're not much of a target, you see.' He looked at Drummond. 'Well?'

'I can see two problems, sir. One, for any proposed underwater attack on Tirpitz, as you have just explained. And secondly, if and when we begin an invasion of Europe, these small subs could play havoc with our heavy landing ships, floating docks and the like.' He bit his lip and returned the admiral's unwinking stare. 'As a destroyer man, I'd say a surface attack into the fjord is the only choice.' He hesitated, waiting for a sign. 'Or call off the British midgets' attack.'

'I see.' Brooks took out another cigarette and waited for a light. 'And you, Captain Beaumont?'

'I agree, sir. Like the attack on Narvik. We did it then. We can do it again.'

'That was at the beginning.' Brooks spoke dryly. 'The Germans have increased their vigilance since then.'

'Perhaps they are too confident, sir.' Drummond stepped forward, his eyes moving along the coastline. 'After all, we would hardly expect a surface attack in the Clyde! It would be madness, of course, but any determined commander could still do one hell of a lot of damage.'

Brooks smiled. 'Another Narvik, eh? Quite apart from the damage you might do, it would work wonders for morale.'

Beaumont said, 'Am I being offered this mission?' He sounded strange. As if he were holding his breath.

'I have to visit the War Room.' Brooks glanced at a clock. 'I must make reports to superiors like everyone else. But remember, not a living soul must learn a word of this. I have passed information for press release that our surface vessels sunk or severely damaged a U-boat near Biscay. That will keep the enemy from knowing we have actually captured one of his midget subs intact. If he knew that, you'd have about as much chance of a surprise attack as a nun would have of saving her honour in the Royal Marine Barracks.'

Drummond asked, 'Won't the Spanish government complain about our being so close to their waters, sir?'

'Would you? After their failure to prevent the enemy from using one of their vessels.' He shook his head. 'No. The next move must be ours, as I see it.' He walked towards the door. 'See you later. I believe there's some sort of press conference being arranged for this evening. Have dinner with me afterwards.'

Beaumont nodded. 'At the Savoy, sir?'

'Where else?' Brooks walked briskly out of the bunker, adding, 'Don't expect too much. Things are not what they were.'

Beaumont looked at Drummond for several long seconds. He was rubbing his palms down his sides and saying, 'By God, eh? By God, how about that then?' He seemed unable to accept what Brooks had said.

Drummond replied, 'Probably nothing will come of it.'

He pictured *Warlock* and the rest of the Scrapyard Flotilla shooting their way into one of those deep fjords, but the more he imagined it, the less impossible it seemed. Brooks was right about one thing. The effect on morale, especially the Norwegians', would be considerable. Their country occupied, resources drained dry to feed the German war machine, their families living in constant fear of punishment or reprisal, it might show they had not after all been forgotten.

They walked out of the bunker, their passes ready for more checking and inspections.

Drummond asked, 'This press conference, sir. Bit unusual, isn't it?'

Beaumont flicked something from one sleeve. 'Oh, I don't know much about that sort of stuff.' He sounded very vague. 'Still, if it keeps the home fires burning, it can't do much harm, what?'

They reached the lift to the surface, and Drummond wondered if the sun would still be shining. It was all like another existence. The bunker, Admiral Brooks. He smiled inwardly. The Savoy, too.

Beaumont certainly seemed at home with it. Within minutes of escaping from the complex of Admiralty corridors and sand-bagged doorways they were both in another staff car and speeding amongst the jostling traffic in a manner born.

As he watched the hurrying figures on the pavements, the shabby clothes of the civilians, the varying uniforms from a dozen nations, he was reminded again of the war he would soon have to rejoin.

Beaumont said abruptly, 'We'll have a drink before we meet the press boys. I expect you know your way around here, eh?'

Drummond glanced at the hotel's shining façade as the car roared past towards their next destination. The one where they would be dining with Nick Brooks.

'Mostly second-hand, I'm afraid. I live on my pay.'

Beaumont's eyebrows lifted slightly. 'Ah well,' was all he said.

The press conference turned out to be quite different from what Drummond had expected. It was held in a room at the rear of yet another ministry building, and the gathering of rather tired-looking journalists bore no relation to their counterparts in the films.

It was obviously for Beaumont's personal benefit. Several flash-pictures were taken, and Drummond saw Miles Salter, as untidy as ever, clearing up points as they arose with his colleagues.

He heard him say, 'You know the idea. *The hero of the* Conqueror *returns. The smile on the face of the tiger.* That sort of thing.'

More bulbs popped, and someone passed around a tray of glasses. They had not apparently noticed Drummond at the end of the room.

'Are you waiting for anyone?'

Drummond turned in his chair and saw a girl looking down at him. She was wearing a green suit, and there was a smudge of ink on one of the cuffs.

'I'm with him.'

He made to stand but she waved one hand.

'It's all right. I'm not used to formal behaviour.'

She sat down wearily and stretched her arms. She had short chestnut hair, dark eyes, and from what he could see through the suit, a very good figure.

'God.' She turned and studied him gravely. 'How do you stand it?'

'It's just a job . . .'

She showed her teeth. 'Not the Navy, I mean *him*, the rest of that lot!'

Drummond looked again at the gathering, the way Beaumont seemed to glow amongst the rumpled suits and jackets.

She added, 'They're so pleased with themselves, it's obscene!'

He replied, 'I've not been to this sort of thing before.'

Her mouth turned down. 'Obviously.'

He turned to face her. 'Look, I don't know what's eating you, but I didn't ask to be here. I don't even know what it's all about.'

She rested her chin on her hand, studying him.

'You're the *Warlock*'s captain.' She added slowly, 'Younger than I'd expected. Are you on the Atlantic run?' She smiled again, but her eyes remained impassive. 'It's all right. I'm *of* the ministry, too. One of the image-makers around here. I expect I know more about the war than you do.'

He said, 'Well, I'm not on the Atlantic run, as it happens.' She made him angry, out of his depth.

'No matter. But if you were . . .' She raised one knee. 'I thought you could get me some proper stockings from the Yanks. My ladders are getting ladders now.'

He watched her while she had her eyes lowered. She was very attractive, despite her irritating way of getting under his guard. About twenty-five.

He asked, 'Can you tell me what all this is for?'

The eyes lifted to his face again. 'Your boss, Captain Beaumont, has influence. Read the newspapers tomorrow.' One hand moved through the air as if feeling the words. '*Conqueror*'s only officer-survivor returns to even the score! U-boat dies at his command, etc., etc.' She gestured to the crowd, which was getting noisier. 'With a picture of him like that, you can't miss.'

'I gather you don't approve?'

She ignored the question. 'It was an accident really, wasn't it?' When he stayed silent she added, 'I thought so. Beaumont seems to have a knack with accidents.' She stood up. Quickly, angrily. 'I may see you around.'

Drummond was still staring after her when Miles Salter touched his arm and said cheerfully, 'All for now. Let's go and share some civilised company.' He followed Drummond's gaze. 'That was our Sarah. Quite a girl. Don't be put off by her attitude, she's very good at this sort of thing.'

'She doesn't seem to like Beaumont.'

It just slipped out, and he saw the guard drop in Salter's eyes like a shutter.

He snapped, 'Her brother was in the *Conqueror*. She probably feels bitter. None of our concern right now.'

'What is exactly?'

Salter gripped his arm. 'Look. I know you're a good destroyer captain, otherwise you wouldn't be here, believe me. You probably think that the only way to win wars is to go out and kill somebody, or blow up a few ships. Well, my friend, there's a helluva lot more to it than that.' He glanced at Beaumont. 'But it all adds up.'

Drummond thought of the girl's quiet hostility. *One of the image-makers.*

Beaumont strode across the room, his face shining, eyes questioning. 'Went well, I thought.'

'Yes.' Salter looked at Drummond guardedly.

Beaumont nodded. 'Nick Brooks seemed pleased with things, too. All helps.' He smiled warmly at Drummond. 'You're in luck, you know. It needn't have been your ship. I can see big things for you.' He seemed to recognise something in Salter's glance and added hastily, 'Still, early days, eh?'

Salter said dourly, 'He was speaking with our Sarah.'

'I see.' Beaumont waved cheerfully to a departing journalist. 'Well, I'd not waste your time there, Keith. Good at her work, but . . .'

'Anyway, she's married.' Salter was showing impatience. 'Though, God knows, you'd not think it, the way she carries on. I ought to see about getting her moved to another sectio...

Beaumont clapped him on the shoulder. 'Rubbish. Just because you haven't made any progress in her direction! Anyway, I like a bit of opposition in a girl. So take it off your back, Miles, for God's sake!'

'I've got to go and make a few phone calls.' Salter studied his watch. 'Meet you in an hour.'

Beaumont watched him go and then walked with Drummond out into the fading light. People were hurrying past, on their way from offices and shops, trying to get to their homes before the sirens wailed again.

Beaumont paused and stared up at a solitary barrage balloon which was lying motionless against the sky, holding on to the hidden sun like a sleeping whale.

'What times to be living in. It makes you feel grateful. Humble in some ways, too.'

Drummond watched his profile, recalling the burning ships, and all those other days and nights. Beaumont was either trying to forget that part of it, or else he really believed what he was saying.

He heard himself ask, 'That girl's brother. Did you know much about him?'

'What girl?' Beaumont turned sharply, the mood broken. 'Oh, yes, I knew him vaguely. Not much bottle really.' He gave a huge sigh. 'But he's back there with the rest of the poor devils now, good or bad.'

Drummond fell in step beside him. Just for those few seconds he had caught a glimpse of another Beaumont. Unsure, even guilty. It had been there as plain as the look in Helen's eyes.

Beaumont added, 'But we'll make the bastards pay for what they did to my ship, and all the others, too.' He smiled. 'I can hardly wait.'

Lieutenant David Sheridan sat with his feet on the leather-topped fender and leafed through an old copy of *Lilliput*. He was conscious of a great sense of peace and laziness, brought about partly by the sunshine which played through the scuttle, and by several drinks, one of which was close by his elbow.

Apart from an occasional squeak from the pantry hatch, where a steward was patiently waiting to lock up the drinks until evening, Sheridan felt he had the *Warlock*, indeed the whole of Falmouth anchorage, to himself. Since Drummond had dashed off to London with Captain (D), the moored destroyers had enjoyed a complete rest. Other vessels moved fussily in and out of port, patrols slipped alongside oilers, took on fuel and put out to sea again, but the seven destroyers of Beaumont's command remained happily idle. War quickly took an edge off guilt, and few of the destroyers' companies cared much that others were working while they enjoyed shore leave and whatever else Falmouth had to offer. As Mangin had remarked more than once, 'I reckon we've done our bloody share. Let some bugger-else take the strain for a bit.'

Sheridan heard footsteps moving along the quarterdeck and smiled. That was Sub-lieutenant Tyson, the O.O.D. Like the rest of the wardroom, Sheridan found it extremely easy to dislike Tyson, but as first lieutenant he had to find some way of concealing the fact. He reached out and sipped his gin. A long afternoon, with nothing much to do but check on the duty part of the watch which remained aboard. They were completing the new paintwork on the forecastle, their brushes usually working only half-heartedly as they sat almost naked in the bright sunlight, their skins browning while they peered hungrily at the shore.

It was strange about Drummond, he thought. It was four days since he had gone, and apart from the daily call from London, and that was made by some bored-sounding staff officer, there was no contact between them.

Local leave was to be allowed, and as often as possible, but apart from that the flotilla was on the shelf.

Sheridan had met several of his opposite numbers in the other ships, and a few of the commanding officers as well. Some, he suspected, were resentful that Beaumont had taken *Warlock*'s captain to London, even though this ship had been the one to capture the midget submarine. Everyone had been threatened with a fate worse than death if that particular secret leaked out, although if the ships remained in harbour much longer, Sheridan did not know how it could be prevented.

Tyson bustled into the wardroom, his face creased into a frown.

'Signal from the pier, sir.' He looked at the half-empty glass, his eyes disapproving. 'A visitor requesting to come aboard. Officer of the guard verifies that it is in order.'

Sheridan looked at him thoughtfully. Tyson was all wrong. His attitude, his inability to lose an argument without his temper going as well, and most of all the fact that he seemed to make people turn against him.

'Better send the motor boat then.' He waited, seeing Tyson's frown growing. 'Well?'

'It's a woman, sir.'

Sheridan dropped his legs and walked to a scuttle. 'Is it, by God?'

'Yes. A Mrs. Kemp from the Ministry of Information.'

Sheridan shaded his eyes against the glare. 'Mrs., eh? Still . . .'

'I don't think it's right to allow women aboard. Not in wartime.'

Sheridan regarded him sadly. You wouldn't. He said, 'You've a lot to learn, Sub. Now whistle up the boat before the cox'n succumbs to his rum ration.' He walked to the pantry hatch. 'Get some fresh glasses, Napier. I might want some sandwiches, too.'

The face in the pantry hatch was expressionless. 'Well past time, sir. I've washed up all the lunch crocks.'

'Relax, Napier. I'll take the responsibility.'

Sheridan walked to a mirror and straightened his tie. These four days had given him an even better idea of what a command could be like. Dealing with visitors from the shipyard or naval stores. Entertaining other officers, who like himself had been left stranded by their captains for various reasons. He had even been in Drummond's day cabin to check the mail and the daily flow of signals. It was childish, and he knew he should have known better.

He heard the motor boat spluttering away from the side and wondered what this Mrs. Kemp would be like. Probably an intense investigator gathering more information about the war at sea. He would have to put her off, unless her authority forced a decision on him. He recalled the excitement when they had entered harbour, the awe on the faces of the working party which had been sent to offload their strange capture. As it had been swayed out to waiting transport he had seen the dead German staring out of his little cockpit, as if he, too, was amazed at all the fuss. But after taking on oil, *Warlock* had moved out to her buoy again, and had remained there. All her officers and ship's company, apart from the usual handful, were ashore, and this unexpected visitor might help, if only in part, to explain their isolation from outside events.

He heard more feet overhead, and guessed that the quartermaster had roused himself to welcome the returning boat.

Sheridan picked up his cap and ran quickly up the ladder and into bright sunlight.

The motor boat was already lurching against the gangway, the bowman's face flushed as he made two attempts at hooking on. Then he saw the visitor, the respectful way the motor boat's coxswain helped her on to the short ladder, his eyes never leaving her legs. She was wearing a plain blue dress which left her arms completely bare, and carried only a small bag and what looked like a camera. The latter was interesting, he thought. She must have a lot of pull to be allowed to bring it into a restricted anchorage. He forgot all about the camera as she reached the deck and stood looking around her, as if searching for something familiar.

'I'm David Sheridan.' He held out his hand. 'I don't know why you're here, but it's good to see you.'

She smiled at him. Her mouth was the only part of her face which moved, for her eyes were completely hidden by a pair of dark sunglasses. She had a good handshake, but her skin was hot and moist, and for that brief moment he imagined the blue dress clinging to the supple body underneath.

She asked calmly, 'Do you approve?'

'Sorry.' He grinned. 'I'm a bit out of practice.'

'I can imagine.' She brushed some of the hair from her forehead. It was the colour of polished chestnut. She added, 'You're the first lieutenant.'

'How did you know that?' He did not really care, and was glad of the chance to make up for the first opening.

'I know everything.' Her mouth lifted slightly. It was moist, and he could see tiny droplets of perspiration below her hairline.

'Well, come below and have a drink or something.'

She tilted the glasses down her nose, just long enough for him to see her eyes. They were dark brown.

She grimaced. 'I'll take the *drink*, if there's a choice.'

In the wardroom Sheridan was relieved to see that Napier had arranged some clean glasses on a tray, and some small, neatly cut sandwiches were close by.

'Gin and?'

He watched her as she moved slowly around the wardroom. She had a perfect figure, and he liked the way she reached out to touch things. Like a child.

'Anything.' She turned and removed the glasses. 'So long as it's cool.'

When he had finished preparing the drinks he saw that she was sitting in one of the battered chairs, her legs crossed, her eyes watching him thoughtfully.

'Now, er, Mrs. Kemp. What can I do for you? The captain's away, I'm afraid, so . . .'

'Yes. I met him. In London.' Again that slow smile. 'I'll bet he's having a fine old time right now.'

Sheridan forced a grin. 'He's earned it.'

She raised the glass. 'Cheers.'

Even that touched Sheridan's guard. It was what Drummond always said. Without thought. Like part of an old joke which Sheridan did not share.

'I can see that you're sincere.' She touched her upper lip with her tongue. 'What did you put with this gin? *More* gin?' She waved him away. 'It's all right. I'll live.'

'Are you living around here?'

'In an hotel. I only arrived last night. Off again shortly.' She leaned back on the worn leather. 'Now, about you. I understand that you were mixed up in that convoy when the battleship *Conqueror* was sunk?'

Sheridan stared at her. If she had told him she had just been assaulted by the port admiral he could not have been more surprised.

She said, 'Your old captain was the escort commander, right?'

He replied tightly, 'It's well known.'

'I know it is. He killed himself after the enquiry.'

'Look.' Sheridan found he was on his feet. 'I don't know if this sort of thing is allowed or not. All I know is I'm sick of people dragging that man's name through the mud. They weren't there, he was. He'd seen and done more than their sort will ever know—'

She said, '*Easy!* Don't get so touchy!'

'It's just that I'm fed up—'

'You told me.' She was very calm. 'Sit down. Please.' She put her glass on the deck. 'The point is, you were there, too. You must have thought the orders all wrong, misguided?' She leaned forward, her eyes unwavering. 'Tell me. It will go no further. It wouldn't be allowed anyway.' Her mouth tightened and she added bitterly, 'But I've pulled strings to see you and I'd like an answer.'

Sheridan grew calmer. The tone of her voice, that brief moment when he had seen her despair, had changed things. She had come from London to see him.

He said quietly, 'Well, let's make a bargain. You tell me *why.*'

'My brother was aboard the *Conqueror*, he was a quarters officer, whatever that means.'

'Oh, I'm sorry. I didn't know.'

She picked up the glass. 'That's what everyone says. *I didn't know.* Why *should* you, for God's sake?'

Sheridan smiled. 'You're right, of course. People always do say that.' He looked away. 'I once saw a man burn to death. Couldn't get near him because of the blazing fuel. I told an officer at the base about it afterwards. He said, "If he had to die, it was a fine way to go." ' He looked at her again and saw a new brightness in her eyes. 'Can you imagine that?'

She nodded. 'Now I can.' She stood up and moved restlessly to the open scuttle. 'My brother used to tell me about your Captain Beaumont. He was a commander then. On the admiral's staff.'

Sheridan said quietly, '*Conqueror* was the flagship.'

'Yes.' She sounded distant. 'Well, he's changed. He's altogether different. I can't understand it.'

'In what way?'

She shrugged. 'Tim, my brother, used to tell me what a bastard he was. Sarcastic. Always riding everyone, and never in the wrong himself. I grew to loathe him, just listening about him.' She turned swiftly, her eyes in shadow. 'Does that make sense to you?'

He shook his head. 'Perhaps your brother was wrong. It can happen.'

'I don't think so. He wasn't like that.'

'When did you meet Beaumont?'

'Shortly after the disaster. He came to the Admiralty for a private press conference.' She shuddered. 'It was like seeing someone else. He was nothing like Tim's Beaumont. Charming. Tragic, if you can understand, and full of humanity. But as I've got to know him, I'm beginning to think it's all sham. That Beaumont is empty inside. It's why I wanted to hear your part of it. The mechanics of naval warfare are beyond me.'

'Did you ask my skipper about him? He was with Beaumont before the war.'

Her eyes widened. 'I didn't think of checking back. What does he say about him?'

Sheridan smiled. 'You've met Drummond. Do you think he's the sort who gossips?'

She grimaced. 'I didn't really get a good look at him. I was angry at the time.'

'He's a career officer. A very competent Scot. I've watched him at work. I've not seen ship-handling like his before.'

'What about him? The *man*?'

He looked down. 'I'm not certain I know him. Does that sound disloyal?'

'It sounds honest.'

He smiled at her. 'How about having a meal with me tonight?'

'All right. If you like. Can you get away?'

He nodded. 'The skipper will not be back today.'

'No.' She picked up her sunglasses. 'He's returning tomorrow afternoon.' She looked at him impassively. 'I told you. I know everything. Almost.'

He followed her from the wardroom to the ladder, and could feel her warmth as she brushed against his arm. He wanted to reach out and hold her, here and now. But she was not that sort of girl. Apart from being married, she obviously knew how to deal with casual encounters.

The messman pattered into the empty wardroom and studied the uneaten sandwiches with disdain.

'Bloody officers!'

Sheridan watched the motor boat curving away towards the shore and shaded his eyes to look for the girl in the cockpit. But she was looking away and did not turn to wave back at the ship.

Tyson said stiffly, 'A pretty woman, I thought, Number One.'

Sheridan was miles away. A proper meal in some local hotel. Get behind her guard, as she had his. He could not really help her about Beaumont, for there did not seem any more to say on the subject. But if that was all it needed.

He asked, 'What did you say?' But Tyson had gone.

Vice-Admiral Brooks dabbed his mouth and reached across the table for his cigarettes. An elderly waiter waited just by his shoulder, matches ready, his face lined with concentration.

He asked, 'Enjoy your dinner, sir?'

Brooks nodded curtly. 'Fair.' He drew in on the smoke and said to the others, 'But still...'

Drummond sipped the wine and watched the crowded tables all around him. Every sort of uniform, and the buzz of conversation and clatter of cutlery was more than a match for some violin music which was filtering from somewhere in the hotel.

He knew Brooks was discussing something with Beaumont, and that Salter was close to being drunk, but he was able to detach himself from all of them.

Fair, Brooks had said. Yet he had just enjoyed some minced pheasant with asparagus tips and Madeira sauce, and was now washing it down with some 1928 Château Yquem. It was incredible. Drummond thought back over the last months, the food he had eaten in his sea cabin after its perilous journey along the upper deck. Even the loyal Owles could not keep a certain amount of salt spray from reaching under his dish cover. Spam. Tinned sausages. And, if you were lucky, the occasional wedge of tough beef. He watched the waiter lay a dish of ice cream before him and smiled. *Fair.*

He thought suddenly of the girl. Sarah. A nice name. How good it would have been to be with her across the table from him. Make all those red-tabbed staff officers turn and stare. He frowned. But she probably came to places like the Savoy every week.

The head waiter came to the table.

'An air-raid warning has just been sounded, sir.' It was almost an apology.

Brooks grunted. 'I see. We'll go round to my club and talk for a while, if that suits, gentlemen?'

The head waiter looked at Salter, whose head was lolling. There was wine slopped over his shirt-front.

'Perhaps a taxi for the gentleman, sir?'

Beaumont flashed a grin. 'Just the thing.'

They left the table with Salter still dozing to await his transport.

The elderly waiter waited for Brooks and Beaumont to leave the grill room and then asked timidly, 'You're Commander Drummond, sir?' He was bent, and looked as if he rarely slept.

'Yes.' Drummond felt some of the other diners staring at him. 'Is something wrong?'

'My boy, sir. He served with you . . .' He faltered, his hands winding and unwinding his napkin. 'I saw you afterwards. At the funeral.'

Drummond looked at him and then touched his arm. 'What was his name?'

'Jelkes, sir. He was a—'

'I remember.' It pushed across the faces and the gleaming tables like a screen. A round-faced youth, full of fun. Could he really have been this man's son? 'Leading Telegraphist. And a good one. I'm very sorry.' Another picture. The bomb bursting in the sea close against *Warlock*'s hull. The screaming splinters scything through the frail plating. The old waiter's son had almost been cut in half.

The man said, 'He always spoke very kindly of you, sir.'

Beaumont's voice was coming back, and Drummond said, 'I'm glad you told me.'

'Did you enjoy your meal, sir?'

Their eyes held.

'Bloody good. I hope I can come again soon.'

The waiter watched him go. He would tell her about this when he got home in the early hours.

A red-faced group captain asked sharply, 'Who was that, Jelkes?'

The waiter regarded him impassively. 'A gentleman, sir. Just a gentleman.'

7

During the Night

'JUST tell me this, Keith.' Beaumont leaned back comfortably in the neat canvas chair and tucked a napkin into the front of his jacket. 'Do you believe in fate?'

Drummond pushed a persistent fly away from his face and tried to regain a sense of reality. The staff car in which he and Beaumont had driven from London was partly hidden beneath the shade of two great oaks, and as far as the eye could see there appeared to be nothing but open fields, neat green hedgerows and occasional clumps of trees. Beyond the nearest hedge he heard the irregular growl of heavy transport, the rarer note of a car. Otherwise there was nothing to show the closeness of the main road which headed to the West Country.

The marine driver had the car boot open and was carefully placing sandwiches on paper plates, and Drummond could see a bottle of something glistening in a silver bucket.

'Sometimes.'

Beaumont regarded him with amusement. 'You're too canny. That's your trouble by half.'

Drummond smiled. Beaumont was obviously very pleased with himself and all that had happened in London.

He was saying, 'I thought this would be a good place to stop for a bite. Almost halfway to Falmouth. I used to own quite a piece of land hereabouts, but had to let it all go for the war effort.' He grinned. 'At a fair price, of course.'

The marine said, 'Shall I open the bottle, sir?'

'Unless you want me to do it with my teeth.' Beaumont added sarcastically, 'Be careful with it, man. The way you drive won't have done it much good.'

Drummond watched the man's back as he stooped over the bottle. He could almost feel his resentment.

Beaumont was unconcerned. 'Strange how things work out.

Between ourselves for the moment, but you'll have to know sooner or later.' He glanced across at the perspiring marine and lowered his voice. 'Nick Brooks has certainly been looking into things since we brought our catch to Falmouth. It seems there are more reasons than we imagined for mounting an attack on that Norwegian fjord.'

'I guessed as much.'

Drummond saw the merest twitch of annoyance on Beaumont's smooth features. Like a child whose secret has come to light too soon. But it passed just as quickly.

'With the better weather on the Russian front, and Ivan trying to get his own back against the Germans, the enemy's need of fuel is more desperate than ever. Hitler, after all, is an army man, and sees more sense in giving priority to tanks and transport than to costly, and in his eyes useless, capital ships.'

He paused as the marine handed them the plates and placed glasses on a small folding table.

Drummond asked quietly, 'The big German ships are being kept at anchor because of a fuel shortage?'

It sounded like just one more myth. Wooden tanks the Germans were said to have had when their army slammed into Poland. They had turned out to be very strong indeed. Only a handful of submarines, none of which could operate deep into the Atlantic, and so on. He wondered if it had been men like Miles Salter whose optimism and lies had caused so many losses and deaths in those early days of war.

Beaumont lifted the corner of a sandwich and nodded. 'Smoked salmon. A word in the right place still has some value, it seems.' He looked up again. 'I know what you're thinking, but this time it's true. Our intelligence people and the Norwegian underground have left no doubt that the Germans are in a bad way for fuel until the winter closes down again. The big ships can still come out for something worthwhile, of course. A nice, fat, Russian-bound convoy, for instance. But the fuel will not be squandered, you can rely on that!'

The bright sunlight lanced through the wine as the marine poured it carefully into their glasses. Drummond watched Beaumont's face as he tested it with a careful sip. What would he do, he wondered, if it didn't suit? Send the poor marine all the way back to London for another bottle probably. But it was good to enjoy the drowsy heat, the sounds of insects and birds, and the distant rattle of a tractor. The sky was an open blue, and there was nothing, not even a vapour trail, to give any stain of the war. Just two naval officers sitting in a field, eating smoked salmon and drinking hock. He grinned, despite his normal reserve. Some war.

'That's more like it.' Beaumont nodded at him. 'Relax a bit. Take it off your back. We've earned a break.' He looked across at the car where the marine was opening his Thermos and a packet of cheese rolls. 'The German Navy has got a fuel dump in the same fjord as the midget submarine school.'

Just like that. Drummond stared at him, a sandwich halfway to his lips. The sun and sky, the clicking insects and cheerful birds seemed to fade away before Beaumont's simple comment. Peace and escape, *they* were the myth.

He heard himself say, 'And we're going for the lot, sir?'

Even as he spoke he could picture it, or most of it anyway. He had been at the second battle of Narvik at the start of the war. When the British were merely prolonging what could only end in retreat. But it had been a great moment. The battleship *Warspite*, like a pale grey berg against the sides of the fjord, the throwback from her great guns rendering speech and thought almost impossible. And the destroyers, dashing in around her like maddened terriers. But that had been three years back. In war that was an eternity.

'The lot.' Beaumont took a long sip at his glass. 'Won't be easy, but it can be done.' He lowered the glass, his face suddenly grim. 'It *will* be done, by God!'

'You want my opinion, sir?'

'Not necessarily.' Beaumont smiled, but his eyes did not flicker. 'Shoot.'

'We'd never get the scheme off the ground. Admiral Brooks said that to give maximum help to the Russians and pave the way for our invasion of Europe we'd have to have a crack at the major German warships along the Norwegian coast. By the time the autumn comes the pace will have slowed, the Germans will be up and fighting-fit all over again. It'll be too late for us, or any other force, to help.'

'I agree entirely, old chap.' He held the bottle above the glasses. 'Couldn't have put it better myself. In fact, I said much the same to Nick Brooks. Which is why'—he looked steadily into Drummond's eyes—'we're not waiting at all.' He could not hide his excitement. 'We're going to prepare for the attack as soon as we get back!'

Drummond dragged his pipe from his pocket and held it with both hands. It helped to steady him.

'In bad weather it would be a less than fifty-fifty chance.' He glanced at the sky, remembering the great, unbroken swells in the far north, the bombers coming out of an Arctic sun. The convoys must have looked like helpless insects pinned down to await their fate. He continued in the same flat voice, 'But at this time of year it would be suicide.'

Beaumont said dryly, 'Thanks for your encouragement. But I'd rather have your attitude than the stupid buggers who agree with everything I say.' He consulted his watch. 'Better get going. Lot to do.'

He relented slightly and laid one hand on Drummond's shoulder.

'Not to worry too much. Nick Brooks has fingers in all sorts of pies. If he says he is going to back this operation, then back it he will. Right down the line.'

Drummond held a match above the pipe and watched the smoke floating above the hedgerow. It had taken less than a few minutes, and yet he could accept it. It must be like that when you are condemned to death, he thought. He shook himself with sudden anger. There was far more at stake than his own uncertainty.

He said abruptly, 'If it came off, it'd be the biggest raid of all time.'

Beaumont smiled gravely. 'That's more like it. The old destroyer spirit. Bash on regardless!'

Drummond followed him towards the car where the marine was repacking the glasses and canvas chairs. As he climbed into the rear seat he paused and looked back at the little clearing by the hedgerow. A bird was hopping in the lush grass, probably enjoying some fragment of smoked salmon sandwich. There was nothing at all to show any human had been there, and the realisation disturbed him almost more than Beaumont's crazy plan.

Was that how it went? Not even a shadow to remind others you had once been here.

Beaumont settled back in the seat and remarked casually, 'After this little lot's over and done with, I suggest you take a spot of leave. I hadn't realised how much strain you'd been under.'

'I'm all right.' He shrugged. 'As much as anyone.'

The car jolted off the grass verge and fell in behind a lorry full of singing airmen. He looked back again but the hedge hid even the two oaks from view. Beaumont was already asleep, his pale manicured fingers interlaced across his stomach. He wore an expression of complete peace, like a man who has just come face to face with truth for the first time.

Drummond relaxed and stared at the swaying lorry ahead of the staff car. Here we go again. Or, as Beaumont had said, *right down the line.*

Leading Writer Pickerell removed the last folder and said, 'That's the lot, sir. I've put the other signals over here.'

Drummond leafed through the clip. He had seen all the important ones as soon as he had come aboard, but there had been nothing, secret or otherwise, which bore any relationship to either Beaumont's battle plan or the dead German in the Falmouth mortuary. Back aboard his own ship, with all of *Warlock*'s familiar smells and sounds around him, it was hard even to believe that all the rest had happened. Brooks, the Savoy, Beaumont and his smoked salmon. He sighed and then held one signal flimsy away from the rest.

'What's all this about?'

Pickerell leaned forward from the waist. The schoolmaster again, checking somebody's essay.

'Ordinary Seaman Davis, sir. The one who went adrift before we sailed.'

Drummond stared at him. 'I *know* that. But it says here that he's in custody, awaiting escort, etc., for desertion.' He paused, feeling the same unreasoning anger again. '*Well?*'

Pickerell smiled thinly. 'First lieutenant handled it, sir. The shore patrol picked up Davis near his home in Gillingham. He was sent here direct, in view of our, er, special orders.' He sucked his teeth.

'All right, Pickerell.' Drummond sighed. The leading writer knew well enough, but it was out of his province. 'Who was

O.O.D. when this rating was brought aboard?' He lifted his pad. 'Oh, I see it was Number One.'

Pickerell watched a point somewhere above Drummond's left shoulder.

'Well, as it happens, no, sir. That is, Sub-lieutenant Tyson was *acting*, so to speak.'

'Yes. I see.' He looked at the bulkhead clock. 'Ring for Owles.'

The door opened. 'Ah, sir.' Owles beamed at him with obvious pleasure. 'You're back then, sir. Good *leaf*?'

'I wasn't on—' He shook his head. 'Never mind. Get me a large drink, and find the first lieutenant.'

Pickerell said, 'I think he's across in *Waxwing*. You weren't expected for another hour yet.'

Drummond thought of the way Beaumont had goaded the marine to drive faster and still faster. It was a wonder he had arrived at all.

Pickerell was still by the desk, his folder under his arm. He looked meaningly at the one remaining book.

'You've not seen that one yet, sir.'

Drummond rubbed his forehead. Perhaps they had all been going round the bend for months without realising it.

'The *visitor's* book?'

He opened it, nevertheless, and flipped over the worn pages, seeing scrawled signatures. Moments of warmth or drunkenness made small pictures swim from each page. Old friends now at the other ends of the earth. In other ships, prisoners of war, discharged wounded or unfit. Dead. There were all the signatures when Frank and Helen had got married. It had been quite a party. The last page stiffened in his grasp.

He said sharply, 'Mrs. Sarah Kemp? Aboard this ship?'

Pickerell said nothing. There was no point in adding more fuel now.

Owles came in with a decanter and a glass, still smiling.

'I've passed the word for the first lieutenant.' He busied himself at the table. 'Won't be long.'

Somewhere overhead the tannoy intoned, 'Stand easy. Senior hands of messes muster for mail.'

Drummond stood up and walked to an open scuttle, letting the sea air play across his damp forehead. The land was shimmering in haze, and below the headland he could see a slow procession of small fishing boats making their way into harbour. Peace or war, fog or gale, it made no difference.

She had been in this ship. His ship. Knowing he was in London. Why? It shouldn't matter. He did not even care. He swallowed the drink and almost choked. But it did matter. Now more than ever.

There was a tap at the door and Sheridan stepped over the coaming.

'I was in *Waxwing*, sir.' He watched him curiously, his features in shadow. 'I'm sorry I didn't meet you at the gangway.'

Drummond said, 'Ordinary Seaman Davis.' Even as he spoke he saw something else on Sheridan's face. Surprise, and perhaps relief. He continued, 'What the hell has been going on?'

'Oh, Davis. They caught him in civilian clothes apparently. Obviously trying to desert. Tyson sent a party ashore to collect him from the provost boys. He's in his mess under close arrest if you want—'

'Is that all?'

'Yes.' Sheridan stepped nearer. 'All I can think of.'

'Did it never occur to you that once off this ship and out of his usual surroundings, Davis might very well start shooting his mouth off? About what we've been doing, and might be training for in the very near future?'

'Tyson said—'

Drummond could feel his hands shaking and he thrust one into a pocket and gripped the empty glass with the other.

'I'm not talking about Tyson! I want to know what the hell you were thinking of to treat this matter so lightly? Don't you realise even now that men's lives depend on security? Not keeping mum and all that rubbish, but trusting their officers' judgement even if they hate their guts!'

Sheridan said quickly, 'Look, sir, I'm not sure what I've done, but if you would explain, then I'll try and put it right.'

'Yes.' He placed the glass on the table. 'You *will* put it right, Number One. I want Ordinary Seaman Davis charged with overstaying his leave, being drunk, being beaten senseless by enemy paratroopers if you like, but I want him kept in this ship, *do you understand?*' He could sense Sheridan's shocked surprise at his anger, just as he could imagine Owles listening behind the door.

Sheridan said stubbornly, 'He had every intention of deserting.'

'Perhaps. Although I always thought he was a good man. Either way, I want his yardarm cleared as of today. This ship is not on the bread-run, nor is she in Falmouth for all time. She is detailed for special duty, work which might well kill the whole damn lot of us, right?'

'Right, sir.' Sheridan's features were like stone. 'Is that all?'

'Carry on.' He waited until he had reached the door. 'Why were you ashore when all this happened?'

Sheridan opened his mouth to reply and then saw the open visitors' book on the desk. He said shortly, 'I think you know that, too, sir.'

As the door closed the other opened and Owles hurried to the decanter.

'All done, sir. Now you can settle down again.'

Drummond looked away. 'If one word gets beyond this cabin . . .'

Owles regarded him sadly. 'What a thought, sir.' He sounded hurt. 'As if it would.'

He left the cabin, and for a long while Drummond sat by the desk, seeing nothing, remembering only his anger against Sheridan. He should have leaned on him, but there had been no need to make him eat dirt like that. Had it been because of her, or because he was really beginning to crack wide open? He would have to watch himself with no less care than his subordinates, for his was the greater responsibility.

Two hours later Lieutenant Rankin came to the cabin, his blank features guarded as he stood in the dead centre of the shabby carpet.

'Ordinary Seaman Davis, sir.' His sleek head shone in the reflected light. 'Had a word with him. In my division, after all, quite a foolish thing to do, but . . .'

Drummond nodded. He had hoped Sheridan would return. Together they might have sealed the sudden rift.

Rankin added crisply, 'Had some mad idea he was going to overstay his leave with a woman he'd met.'

'Didn't intend to *desert*?'

Just for a moment Rankin came out of his trance. 'No, sir. I explained things to him.' His mouth lifted slightly. 'Forcefully. I've put him in the first lieutenant's report.'

'Thank you, Guns. I'll have a word with the young idiot later. But thanks.'

The gunnery officer touched his centre parting with one finger as if to test its straightness.

'I'll give Davis so much to do he won't have time to worry about anything.'

There was another tap on the door, but it was Wingate, the O.O.D.

'Sorry to interrupt, sir. But there's been a signal from Captain (D). All commanding officers to report aboard the *Warden* in two hours' time.' His gipsy face split into a grin. 'Action at last, sir?'

Drummond felt the tension easing away. 'A choking off more likely.' In his heart he knew Wingate's guess was close to the mark.

Beaumont would be telling the others aboard the half-leader what he had already heard in London and by that quiet roadside. He was that eager to get things moving.

He waited until they had both left the cabin and then poured another drink. Wingate was like a rock when things got difficult, and Rankin, whose imagination was limited almost to the length of a gun barrel, had not hesitated to make the unfortunate Davis believe he had intended to return to the ship. Eventually. Rankin was a book man through and through, and it must have cost him dearly to expand a lie for Drummond's benefit. He thought of Sheridan, and how Frank might have handled it, and then forced them both from his mind.

On the opposite bulkhead was a miniature of the ship's crest. *Who touches me dies.*

Whoever had thought that one up must have had Beaumont in mind.

Two days after Drummond's return to Falmouth the first stage of Beaumont's plan had gone into motion. Drummond had watched Sheridan's and Wingate's expressions as he had told them the news.

Wingate had spoken first. 'Iceland, sir? And I was just getting used to this place.' But behind his eyes his mind had already been busy with his charts. Courses and currents, speed and distance to be made good. It never ended for the navigating officer.

Sheridan had asked, 'And then? Or is it too early yet to know the whole plan?'

They had barely spoken beyond the requirements of duty. Defaulters and requestmen, inspections and the like.

Drummond had opened his great wad of orders. 'Stage by stage. This is all I can tell you. It may come to nothing anyway.'

But it had all begun on time, just as Beaumont had predicted. Without fuss he had left Falmouth aboard *Waxwing* and in company with two other destroyers, *Victor* and *Ventnor*. They would return to Harwich, join forces with the now repaired *Lomond*, Beaumont's own ship, and make their way north to Iceland.

A day later, with *Warden*, the half-leader, in command, the other four had slipped quietly out of harbour. It had all gone remarkably well. No more deserters, no last-minute news from the intelligence officers at the Admiralty to say that the enemy had got wind of this new, if elderly, force of destroyers. Nothing. Going like a clock.

They had had one brief commanding officers' conference before slipping from their buoys. Just the bare facts relating to recognition signals, R/T procedure, met reports. Nothing startling.

Commander Hector Duvall, the flotilla's second-in-command, and *Warden*'s captain, did not beat about the bush. When he had got rid of the other two captains he had said to Drummond, 'One for the road.' As he had slopped gin into their glasses he had said in his thick, fruity voice, 'Don't like this cloak-and-dagger stuff. Never have. What with the commando, combined ops, the S.O.E. and the Special Boat Squadron all fighting their own private wars, *and* the Americans doing the same, I only hope we all arrive at the same bloody victory in the end!'

He was in his early thirties, but with his thick beard, already tinted with flecks of grey, and his heavy frame, he looked years older.

Drummond had said, 'This job is just that bit more crazy. It might come off. You never know.'

'It's not that.' Slop, slop. More gin into the glasses. 'It's Captain (D). I can't get his measure. You know him better maybe. How d'you rate him? I mean, actually in combat?'

You were not supposed to discuss a superior in this way. Equally, everyone did.

Drummond had replied, 'He was with me when we went alongside the decoy ship. Seemed cool enough. But he was that eager to get after the Spaniard I had a hard time for a moment or two.'

'I'd heard he was a callous bastard.'

A small signal had sparked off an alarm. 'Who from?'

Duvall had seemed momentarily off guard. 'A couple of nights ago. I forget exactly when. I was ashore at that nice hotel. Met up with your number one. He had a real charmer with him. I could have done her some damage myself.' He had frowned. 'Where was I?'

'The hotel. You heard something.'

It was all Drummond had been able to do to hide his bitterness. It was stupid. He kept telling himself so. It still did not help.

'Yes. Your number one got the conversation round to the *Conqueror*.' He had looked awkward. 'You know. Beaumont. The only three survivors.'

'Yes.'

'Somebody said that Beaumont was the same aboard that old battleship. Didn't give a toss for anyone but himself. A glory boy. I don't know what to believe.'

But all that had been back in Falmouth. Now, as Drummond sat lolling from arm to arm in his bridge chair, he could imagine Duvall on his own bridge away out ahead in the pitch darkness. Three days out of harbour, four old destroyers in the North Atlantic. It sounded like the start of a poem, he thought vaguely. He lifted his watch level with his eyes. Nearly one o'clock in the morning, and the motion so sickening that he was glad he had decided not to turn into his bunk. He heard the watchkeepers moving around the open bridge, the occasional murmur of voices over handsets and pipes as the ships played follow-my-leader across an empty ocean.

At the slow, economical speed, with a deep quarter swell, *Warlock* was taking it badly. She had the advantage over her three consorts, however, for being last in line she had little fear of being run down from astern. All the watchkeeping officers had to do was hold on to the next ahead. *Up two turns. Down two turns.* It was an eye-aching job, with the *Whirlpool's* narrow stern rising up in a welter of spray and propeller froth, seemingly within feet of *Warlock*'s stem, and at the frantic adjustment of revs, fading just as quickly into the curtain of sea and sky.

Wingate was officer of the watch, and Drummond could see his buttocks and legs protruding from beneath the chart table's canvas hood where he was checking his calculations, enjoying a moment of privacy under the tiny electric bulb.

Hillier was on the starboard gratings, his binoculars trained above the screen. He had settled in well. Even the way his legs and body were adjusting to the slow, prolonged rolls was that of a seasoned watchkeeper.

Wingate reappeared at the side of the chair. 'Quiet enough, sir.' He darted a quick glance at the bridge lookouts. 'Doc will have a few down with seasickness tomorrow, I'm thinking.'

Drummond gripped his pipe between his teeth, counting seconds as *Warlock*'s stern came up yet again and the bridge tilted out and over. He could hear the structure protesting, the clatter of steel from the Oerlikon guns as they jerked on their mountings. A man slipped and fell, cursing obscenely in the darkness. Another called, 'Roll on my twelve and get me off this bucket!'

Wingate grinned, his teeth white against the sky. 'They don't change, do they?'

Drummond shook his head. 'I'm relying on that!'

A bosun's mate said something into a voice-pipe and then called, 'Captain, sir. W/T have convoy information from Admiralty.'

'Very well.' He looked at Wingate. 'Better go down yourself. Check it against our signals.'

Wingate nodded. 'That'll be the north-bound to Reykjavik. Fairly fast convoy, to all accounts. Shouldn't bother us.' He paused beside Hillier and said, 'All yours again.'

Hillier moved cautiously across the gratings, feeling his way. Drummond asked, 'Got the feel of her now, Sub?'

'Getting better, I *think*, sir.' He gestured vaguely abeam. 'It was something Pilot just said when we were working on the chart. The nearest land are the Faroes, and they're about two hundred miles to the east of us.'

He fell silent, and the regular ping of the Asdic echoed around the bridge as if to give weight to his words.

'Yes. This is a bad place. The start of the killing-ground.'

They did not speak again until Wingate returned.

He said, 'I was right, sir. The north-bound is steering three-four-zero. About forty miles ahead of us.' He sucked his pencil. 'Ten knots.'

'I thought it was supposed to be fast?' Drummond peered at him. 'Fifteen at least, surely?'

'Signal states that convoy had a bit of bother. Attacked by two U-boats. One ship sunk, another damaged. So they're probably slowing down to stay together.'

There was a long pause and Wingate added slowly, 'The convoy commander must be a good bloke. It's a bloody awful place to be left on your jack.'

Drummond looked away. Wingate was probably remembering. It could never be far from his thoughts. When he had been left behind. His friend frozen to his oilskin. Dying within touch of safety. But he never showed it. Time after time, as *Warlock* had driven through sleet and snow, he must have looked outboard. Watching. Listening. Waiting for that terrible explosion.

Drummond said, 'They'll get air-cover tomorrow if the cloud lifts.'

Wingate muttered, 'Like searching for a . . .' He did not finish.

The bosun's mate called, 'W/T again, sir. They have *Warden* for you.'

Drummond slid off the chair and waited for the deck to sway upright again. Duvall was using the short-range radio-telephone, which was unusual. Probably wanted to discuss the convoy report. He reached the little steel shack below the radar platform and lurched through the door. As the light automatically came on again he saw the crouching figure of the Asdic operator, a man pouring cocoa into a line of chipped cups, another fumbling with a lifejacket. He jerked the handset from its case.

'This is *Yoke Seven*.' He waited, imagining Duvall's beard on the other end of the sound-wave. 'Come in *Yoke One*'

A hissing roar of static, and a clatter of mugs from elsewhere as *Warlock*'s hull tilted savagely into another trough.

Then Duvall's voice, surprisingly clear. 'This is *Yoke One*. I will be brief. I have a strong radar echo, directly ahead of us. Eight miles. Same course and speed.'

Drummond licked his lips. The radar sets supplied to these

old ships were a tremendous advance on nothing. But compared with all the latest equipment they were already well out of date. Eight miles. It was about the maximum range in this sort of weather.

Duvall added, 'Too small for a straggler.' He was thinking aloud. 'Too far astern for Tail-end Charlie.'

Drummond waited, feeling his stomach dragging violently as the deck fell into another abyss. 'Submarine.'

'Yes.'

Drummond looked over his shoulder, seeing the Asdic operator's eyes glowing above his screen and dials like twin marbles.

'Get the first lieutenant up here. Chop chop!' To the handset he said, 'We will have to stay clear. Disregard.'

He could imagine Duvall's agony of mind. To increase speed in the hope of stalking a possible U-boat, or to stay within the letter of his orders and keep out of trouble until otherwise instructed. To signal the Admiralty and get them to pass the information to the convoy commander, or remain mute and allow men to be slaughtered.

Duvall's voice again. 'This is *Yoke One*. Over and out.'

'You want me, sir?' Sheridan was forcing himself through the tight mass of equipment and people.

'Yes. Get your best radar and Asdic teams closed up.' He looked past him. '*Warden*'s got a firm blip. Same course and speed. Range eight miles.'

He heard Sheridan's stubble rasp against his collar.

He said, 'Sorry to drag you out, Number One.' It was almost the first contact they had made.

Sheridan shrugged. 'I have the morning watch anyway.' He smiled. 'Could do with a hot drink.'

'I'll lay it on while you get your people moving.' He dragged open the door, seeing the dials glowing like eyes as the main lighting went out. 'I'll be on the bridge until . . .' He did not have to end it.

Wingate was waiting for him. 'A kraut, sir?'

'Looks like it.' He thrust his head under the chart hood and peered at the neat pencilled lines and bearings. 'What is the convoy escort? Do we know?'

Wingate joined him under the screen. He smelled of salt and oil.

'Four corvettes and an Asdic trawler.'

They glanced at each other.

Drummond said flatly, 'Not too much. I'll bet that bastard is following them, homing the rest of the pack to intercept at first light.' He groped for his watch. 'Not long now.'

Feet skated across the metal decks and voices murmured outside the screen. Muffled, but obvious in their discontent. 'What the hell's wrong now?' 'Can't a bloke get any kip when he's off watch?' Another voice, more hushed. 'Careful. The old man's under the screen.' Then silence again.

Clang. Like a wreck buoy's bell as someone carried a heavy fanny of cocoa across the bridge, pausing between the sickening rolls.

Hillier's voice. 'Our radar has nothing yet, sir.'

Drummond thought of the three ships in direct line ahead. It was not surprising. He was sorry for Duvall. His was the only useful radar. His the only information available.

He ducked out from the chart table and waited for his vision to return.

Sheridan said, 'Senior operators closed up, sir.' He tapped the voice-pipe at his elbow. 'Cox'n's on the wheel, too. He has a nose for trouble.'

They sipped at the thick, sickly cocoa. Gathering time. Waiting.

'W/T office reports that *Warden* is still in contact, sir. Course and range constant.'

'Very well.'

Drummond walked to the forepart of the bridge and gripped the teak rail below the screen. By the time they had worked up to full speed it would take twenty minutes to get within useful range. He raised himself on his toes and peered down at the square outline of the nearest gun. *Star-shell. U-boat on the surface. Rapid fire.* But suppose . . . ? He shook himself and staggered back to his chair. Duvall would never break his cover. No matter what he might be feeling. He was too professional. Too hardened by past events.

A telephone buzzed like a trapped wasp.

'Forebridge?' Hillier sounded very tense. 'It's the chief calling from the wardroom, sir.'

Off the chair again, half wondering what Galbraith was doing out of his bunk.

'Captain.'

'Chief here, sir. I was wondering . . .'

'Thanks, Chief. I'd appreciate a bit of weight in the engine room just now.'

He replaced the handset, knowing Hillier was staring at him, mystified. And he could tell him nothing. Like the coxswain and some of the others, Galbraith just *knew*. There was no proper explanation.

He peered through the stained glass screen, seeing the faint white blur of *Whirlpool*'s wake. The other destroyers would have been listening, too, and wondering.

'Captain, sir. *Warden* is calling you up again.'

He knew what Duvall was going to say even before he had reached the Asdic compartment and the handset which was connected to the W/T office below.

'This is *Yoke One*. Are you receiving me, *Yoke Seven*?'

Drummond replied, 'Loud and clear.'

'You will assume lead. Retain course and speed. Acknowledge.'

Drummond could picture the others listening to his voice.

'Acknowledged and understood.' A pause. 'Over.'

'Am engaging. Over and out.'

He stared at the handset and then replaced it very slowly. Bloody, stubborn, brave fool.

The air seemed much colder when he regained the bridge chair.

He said, 'Stand by to increase revolutions. We will pass the other ships to starboard. Inform the engine room and wheelhouse.'

'We're going to attack, sir?' Wingate sounded hoarse.

'We are assuming the leader's position, Pilot.'

'Radar to bridge. *Warden*'s increasing speed, sir.'

'Thank you.'

They were all looking at him.

He said, 'Commander Duvall is going after the submarine. It is his decision.'

Wingate called, 'Ready, sir.'

'Very good. Port ten.' He saw the other ship's wash easing away to starboard. 'Midships.' How quiet it seemed. There should be the sound of *Warden*'s engines, a background chorus like they had in films. 'Starboard ten. Meet her. Steer three-four-zero. Increase to one-one-zero revolutions.'

The deck vibrated more insistently and steadied against the thrust of screws and rudder. *Whirlpool*'s lithe shape was already sliding abeam, her length shown only by her sluggish bow wave and steep rolling. And there up ahead was the other one, *Whiplash*, the blackness of her funnel smoke making a long streak against the clouds. Or perhaps it was getting lighter already?

'How long is it now?'

'Fifteen minutes, sir.' Sheridan cleared his throat. 'I don't see that Duvall should be left to cope on his own.' It sounded like an accusation.

'He's left *us*, by the sound of it.' Rankin's voice.

So he's come up, too. Drummond replied quietly, 'That's enough!'

'Radar—Bridge.' The call echoed tinnily from the little microphone at the rear of the compass platform.

'Bridge.' Wingate had the handset almost against his lips.

'Have picked up the echo now, sir. About eight miles.'

Drummond crossed to his side and took the handset. To Wingate he said, 'Bring her round ahead of *Whiplash* and resume course and speed.' To the handset he said, 'This is the captain. How is *Warden* getting on?'

'Closing very fast, sir. Approximate range is oh-eight-five.'

'Very well.'

He tried to clear his mind, wipe it clean of despair and doubt. It was not unknown to catch a U-boat on the surface. One so intent on following a convoy that its lookouts failed to watch astern.

He heard Sheridan breathing heavily beside him. He sounded bitter as he said, 'I wish to God we were with him!'

A pinpoint of bright orange flickered across the sea's face, parting the horizon and then fanning out into one great fiery ball. Seconds later came the explosion, sighing and then thundering against the hull like a solid thing, making the steel jerk violently in protest.

'Got it!' Hillier yelled wildly. '*He got it!*'

'Asdic—Bridge.' The merest quiver in his normally steady voice. 'Ship breaking up. Dead ahead.'

Drummond brushed past Sheridan and someone else he did not even see.

'Bridge—Radar. This is the captain. Is the first echo still there?'

'Yes, sir. But fading.' Somebody in the radar compartment let out a long sigh. 'Target is diving, sir.'

'Very well.' He handed the instrument to the bosun's mate.

The U-boat must have timed it perfectly. Her commander had realised that he was being stalked, might even have picked up *Warden*'s radar on his reflector. One, or perhaps two, torpedoes fired from the stern tubes. At her maximum speed, her old hull straining to full power, *Warden* would plunge headlong for the bottom, breaking up as she went.

'Asdic reports no contact, sir.'

In the twinkling of an eye.

He put his hand in his pocket and felt for his pipe. It had been snapped in two, yet he had not felt himself doing it.

He said, 'Keep a good lookout for lifejacket lights and wreckage. Pass the word to the doctor.'

Drummond could feel his limbs shaking badly, although when he touched his thighs they felt like metal, cold and unmoving.

Sheridan said in a tight voice, 'And for *what*?'

Drummond regarded him for several seconds. 'For a gesture, Number One. I suggest you remember it.'

Sheridan walked unsteadily towards the bridge ladder. 'I will, sir. I'll never forget tonight, of that I'm certain.'

Rankin gripped the screen and said dully, 'Bloody bad luck.' He looked sideways at Drummond and added, 'Makes us the half-leader though.'

He walked away, his mind already grappling with whatever new duties would now come his way.

Drummond could barely breathe. Perhaps it was better to be like Rankin. Without imagination there could be no pain. And no guilt.

8

Missing Persons

GALBRAITH climbed to the upper bridge and waited until he had caught Drummond's attention.

'Oil intake complete, sir.' He gestured to the rust-streaked tanker alongside where some stokers were already grappling with the great dripping hoses. '*Whirlpool*'s next.'

Drummond nodded and glanced at the sky. It was still cloudy, but there was a hint of sunshine which was already feeling its way across the houses by the harbour and the strange, pink-coloured landscape beyond. The quaint houses with their Scandinavian-style windows and coloured, corrugated-iron roofs were as different from Falmouth as they could be. But the harbour could have been almost anywhere. Reykjavik was jammed with all the usual mixture of minor war vessels, trawlers and motor gunboats, armed drifters and corvettes. The latter were the escort from the convoy. He glanced across the tanker's littered deck at the busy jetty. Ambulances had been and gone. It had probably been a familiar job for them.

They had picked up thirty survivors all told. Gasping, shocked and half choked by the filthy oil. Some had been so badly scalded by escaping steam it was a miracle they had got this far. Now they were somewhere beyond the town, in the naval camp or at the R.A.F. hospital. He had sent Vaughan with them. It was all he could do.

At the time he had been almost grateful to have picked up as many as he had. While the other two ships had kept a constant watch for submarines, *Warlock* had made a slow and careful search. The great patch of oil had been their marker. It usually was. Corpses in various attitudes of restful abandon. The living splashing feebly like dying fish, obscene in their skin of black oil.

But now in harbour, with normality and efficiency on every hand, it did not seem so many. Thirty out of a whole company.

Over a hundred gone. There had been only one officer survivor. The ship's eighteen-year-old midshipman. He had been in the wheelhouse with the plot operator. He had heard the coxswain shouting something, then felt a great pain in his back. The latter must have been caused by his hitting the sea as the ship turned turtle and exploded like a bomb in their midst. The torpedoes, the actual sinking, the horror of total destruction was mercifully wiped from his memory.

Sheridan clattered up the bridge ladder and saluted formally.

'Ready to move ship, sir.' His face looked dark with stubble, and his eyes were like dull stones.

'Yes. We will tie up ahead of the oiler.'

Drummond was so desperately tired he felt he could not move from the gratings. They had arrived in the first light, having been too late to make an entrance earlier. The search for survivors, the need to allow the convoy to reach port ahead of them and disperse. It had all taken time.

He heard Hillier say, 'I thought it would be all snow and ice.'

Galbraith wiped his forehead with one gloved hand and left another streak of grease on it.

He said, 'Stay here a wee while, Sub, and you'll get all the snow you want. They've only got two seasons in Iceland. July and winter!'

Tucker, the yeoman of signals, who was examining the halliards above the bridge, snorted, 'Bloody Icelanders. They'd rather have the Jerries here than us!'

Drummond felt for his pipe, touching the broken stem with his thumb.

'I see that *Lomond* and the others beat us to it.'

He had already exchanged signals with Beaumont's ship, which in her new dazzle paint lay across the harbour at the best mooring. Ten minutes' walk from the officers' club.

Sheridan said awkwardly, 'Shall I take over, sir?'

Drummond nodded, fighting back a yawn. 'Yes. Warp her forrard when you get the go-ahead from the dock party. They've a little engine on rails. You just pass them the warps and they do the rest.'

He touched his cap to Galbraith and the others, his mind already on his report. What he would say. How he would say it.

Galbraith thrust his hands inside his flapping white boiler suit and muttered, 'He feels it badly.'

Sheridan stared at him. 'What about *Warden*'s people?'

'I'm an engineer, Number One. I told you that. I admire a brave man, but I canna abide a fool. *Warden*'s gone west, an' a hundred of her lads with her. *That* we know for certain.' He looked up at some circling gulls, hopefully watching the new-comers. 'We'll never know if that U-boat was any real menace to the convoy. So in my book Duvall was a bloody fool.' He strode to the ladder, adding tersely, 'You do things properly, or you don't do 'em at all. That's the law of the engine room. It should be the same on th' bloody bridge!'

Wingate whistled. 'The old chief's getting steam up again.'

Sheridan looked at him bitterly. 'What the hell's the matter with everyone? Don't you care either?'

'Of course I care.' Wingate was pulling his charts from the ready-use table with quick, savage motions. 'But what good does it do to show it, eh? I care that a ship, and all the other ships I've seen go to hell, are lying on the bottom! I care that the chief gunner's mate's wife and daughter were killed last night in an air-raid on Chatham, and nobody's been able to tell him yet. I care about all these things, and a lot more, Number One, but I know that I don't have to *do* a damn thing about them.' He gestured angrily at the empty ladder. 'He will though!'

Feet clattered through the other gate and broke the sudden stillness like an explosion. Sheridan stared at the petty officer who was watching all of them with tired resignation. It was the chief gunner's mate.

He said, 'Beg pardon, sir, but the dock party is ready to take our wires. I've mustered the duty watch for you.'

Sheridan swallowed hard. 'Thank you, Abbott.'

Wingate said harshly, 'Haven't you forgotten something, Number One?'

Sheridan said, 'Go and see the captain, will you, Abbott.' He saw the man's face growing pale. 'Quick as you can.'

As the petty officer hurried away Wingate said softly, 'See? All you have to do is pass the buck.' He walked past him, his eyes cold. 'Just don't ask if I *care*, that's all.'

Fitzroy, the petty officer telegraphist, appeared from the rear of the bridge.

'Captain (D) wants the skipper over aboard *Lomond*, Yeo.' He saw Sheridan and added, 'Sorry, sir. I thought you were down aft.'

'I'll tell him. Thank you.' He moved very slowly to the ladder. 'He's seeing Petty Officer Abbott at the moment.'

Fitzroy and Tucker exchanged quick glances. Then the bearded yeoman said, 'We'll take him ashore tonight, eh, Maurice? Fetch a jar of neaters with us, too.'

Fitzroy nodded, his eyes suddenly very bright. 'Poor old bastard. Couldn't believe it when I was taking down the signal.'

Sheridan left the bridge, his mind reeling. It was like part of a nightmare. The swiftsure touch of death. The way everyone tried to face up to it. Above all was the unnerving pattern of events which had ended with *Warden*'s sudden destruction. The distorted voice on the R/T, Drummond's impassive acceptance, the way they had held back and let a ship die. It was like the *Conqueror* all over again. The destroyers holding off. *By order.*

He found Mr. Noakes and the chief boatswain's mate, and the weary-looking duty watch waiting with wires and fenders again.

He said, 'Ready when you are.'

Noakes said, 'Look at 'em. All gapin' at the bloody shore. Can't wait to put their fancy gear on and go chasin' the tarts. They'll be lucky, I don't think!'

Vickery, the chief boatswain's mate, turned as Abbott hurried past along the iron deck.

'See you in the mess, Ted. When we get the old girl snugged down.'

Abbott strode on without a word.

Vickery looked at Sheridan and exclaimed, 'What the hell's got into him?' Then he said slowly, 'Jesus, *not his family?*' He swung away, his voice harsh. 'Come on then, jump about! Take up them bloody wires and try an' *look* like seamen!'

In his sleeping cabin Drummond stripped off his sweater and threw it on a chair. For a while he looked at the rusty plates of the oiler alongside, waiting until they began to move slowly and steadily past the scuttle, and then he turned to his mirror. Perhaps a good shave would help. Owles had laid out a crisp new shirt and best uniform. He was doing his best. He heard wires scraping along the deck above and Noakes bellowing at some unfortunate rating or other. He had never allowed anyone else to move the ship like this, even though it was perfectly simple with the dockside engine in control. But he knew he could not have stood a moment longer on that bridge. He would either have smashed Sheridan in the face, or burst into tears. Neither would have changed anything.

Perhaps his last conversation with Sheridan had been on Duvall's mind even at the moment of death. That Beaumont was in some way responsible for all that had happened. The *Conqueror*, the men who had died in the burning decoy, and the *Warden* herself as she split asunder and painted the sea and sky with bright orange fire.

It got just that bit worse each time. Everyone who was in combat said the same. If he was honest. At Harwich, Drummond had known a lot of the fighter pilots at the nearby base. Not unlike destroyer men, in their way. Young, reckless, yet so full of life. Some of them had told him of their own fears. The first kill in the sky, the terror giving way to exultation. Not at killing an enemy pilot, but winning a single-handed battle. The next times were easier, and then they seemed to reach a peak, after which things got more tense, minds became edgier, less tolerant of minor faults in planes and other pilots. After that, they usually died.

In ships, especially small ones, it took longer. For the sense of permanence and indestructibility was always with you. You carried your home wherever you went. Little else mattered beyond the steel shell. But the strain mounted, nevertheless. And he was seeing it now in his own face. As he had watched it on Wingate's and Galbraith's. As he had seen it when Duvall had been asking about Beaumont. *I can't get his measure.* Nor would he, now.

He thought, too, of Petty Officer Abbott, as he had looked when he had told him about the signal. A very tough man was Abbott. He had been wounded twice, and had been in the Navy since he was a boy. He had stood by the desk, not looking at Drummond but at the signal in his hands.

He had said, 'Not *them*, sir! Not *them*!'

Drummond had poured out a glass of brandy. 'Drink this.'

He had wanted so much to know the words. The right way to say them. At the same time he knew there were none.

Abbott had exclaimed brokenly, 'What'll I do, sir?'

'I'll have you flown home immediately. Someone else can take over until . . .'

Abbott had said emptily, 'But *they* was my home, sir.'

The glass of brandy stood untouched on the desk in the other cabin.

Drummond laid down the razor and touched his face. The bulkhead telephone buzzed and he took it as he was about to slip on the clean shirt.

'First lieutenant here, sir. There was a signal from *Lomond*.'

'For me to go across?'

'Yes, sir.'

'Thank you.' He leaned against the cool metal bulkhead, the picture of the neat bunk behind him looming like a spoiled dream. 'He doesn't waste much time.'

'Ship is securing now, sir. *Whirlpool* will be coming along the port side when she finishes oiling.'

'Good. Send the duty watch to breakfast while they're waiting.'

Sheridan seemed to be hesitating. Then he said, 'Sorry I got worked up about *Warden*, sir.'

'Forget it.' He saw the brandy on the desk. 'It happens.'

Sheridan said, 'I'll carry on then, sir.'

'Yes.' He thought of the girl and Sheridan at the hotel. 'You know where I am if you need me.' He replaced the telephone and walked to the desk.

Then he gave a great sigh and pushed the glass away.

'No. I'll drink *his* bloody brandy for a change!'

Through the door Owles listened and gave a satisfied nod. The skipper was getting over it. Just one more time. He busied himself brushing Drummond's cap. It was the only way to manage things, he thought.

Beaumont sat in a new leather armchair and regarded Drummond thoughtfully. His quarters smelled of fresh paint and had an air of unusual comfort.

He said at length, 'I read your report. My number one is adding a few touches for my benefit, otherwise it seems fine.'

Drummond felt the drowsiness coming back and concentrated his gaze on a swaying harbour crane which he could see through one of the polished scuttles.

Beaumont continued, 'Pity about Hector Duvall, of course. But you can't play God without some risk. In his case he went too far, that's all.'

'Would it have made that much difference if the rest of us *had* followed, d'you think, sir?'

Beaumont wagged one finger. 'Now, you must not ask *me*, Keith. I was not there, was I? You've made it all clear in the report. You weighed up the situation and decided. I don't think anyone can blame you for what happened.'

Drummond stared at him. 'Blame me? I was obeying your orders, sir.'

Beaumont picked something from his sleeve and smiled gently. 'Of course.'

'Look, sir, if you think I should have acted as my *instinct* dictated, then I'd like to hear it.'

'Easy, Keith!' He was still smiling. 'It's over and done with. I'm not condoning Duvall's actions for a single second. By charging in like a bull in a china shop he might have brought all hell down on our heads. That convoy arrived almost intact. But even if it had been wiped out, Duvall's four destroyers *did not exist* as far as the convoy's escort commander was concerned. When the convoy weighed anchor it had four corvettes and a trawler to protect it. If their lordships thought them insufficient they should have acted accordingly. Nobody relies on miracles all the time. Especially me.'

He stood up and walked to the nearest scuttle, his face smooth and pink in the reflected light.

'I was only saying that I did not know how I might have reacted in your position once Duvall had gone off at half-cock.' He turned, smiling broadly. 'No traps, Keith. No false motives.'

His P.O. steward peered round a curtain.

'Shall I lay out the glasses yet, sir?'

'In a moment.' Beaumont flicked up one white cuff and examined his watch. 'They'll be aboard in about fifteen minutes. Better not have a drink until then, eh?'

The steward withdrew.

'Visitors?'

The thought of shaking more hands, or facing either friendship or hostility, was more than Drummond could bear.

'Didn't I tell you?' Beaumont tugged his jacket into place. 'Miles Salter and his lot are here, too. Flew up from U.K. to oil the wheels, so to speak.'

He tried to see where it was all leading. 'Anyone else I know?'

'Miles's pet worry, Sarah Kemp. She should be very decorative. The Icelandic girls have been told to stay away from Jolly Jack. They're not too keen on us locally.'

'Won't all this fuss draw attention to what we're doing?' But he was seeing her face as he asked. *One of the image-makers.*

'They're used to the information and propaganda people here. The admiral seems quite taken with the idea.' Beaumont frowned. 'But I agree we must be careful. Too much at stake to risk anything. This operation must be perfect.'

Feet moved overhead, and Drummond heard the O.O.D. hurrying to the gangway to greet the visitors.

Beaumont turned to face the door, arranging himself. Like an actor waiting for the curtain to go up.

Miles Salter came in first. He was as crumpled as ever, but seemed in good spirits.

He shook hands with Beaumont and smiled to Drummond, remarking, 'So you're still with us, Commander. That's the ticket.'

There were two other men in suits which looked as if they had been slept in, one of whom carried a large and very expensive camera.

Sarah Kemp walked across the cabin, smiled at Beaumont and then stopped directly in front of Drummond. She thrust out her hand, her eyes never leaving his face.

'Hello, yourself.' She did not smile. 'I'm glad you're all right.' She tightened her grip. 'Really.'

He said, 'You've heard all about it.'

'I'm sorry. It sounded like bragging, I expect.'

'No. It's just that I'm not used to it.'

She sat down beside his chair, crossing her legs and smoothing her skirt in two quick movements.

'Well, talking about events is easier than enacting them.' She watched him gravely. 'Have they been giving you a hard time?'

'Just the usual.' He forced a smile. 'I heard you were in Falmouth.'

She touched her lower lip with the tip of her tongue. 'You make it sound worse than it was.'

'I'm sorry.' He looked away. 'None of my business anyway.'

'When you say it like that, it means you think it *is* your business.'

Beaumont called brightly, 'How about a drink?'

She laughed. 'I thought you'd never ask. Honestly, this country!' She looked at the others. 'Nothing to drink, the streets full of potty-looking men and beautiful girls, it's not fair!'

The stewards were moving in, the petty officer watching the girl's knees as he deftly arranged the glasses.

Drummond took out his spare pipe. He did not feel like a smoke or a drink, but it would give him time. He watched her as she threw quick remarks amongst the others. She had their attention most of the time, and knew it. And yet it was more like a game, he decided. An act to hide something else. He thought of Sheridan holding her. Feeling her lithe body. Enjoying her, and she him.

'Drink, sir?' The steward watched him.

'Horse's neck, please.'

She swung round. 'You should be in the cavalry!'

More people arrived, including some senior officers from the Area Combined H.Q., Navy and R.A.F. The admiral, it seemed, could not come, but would see them later. It was getting very noisy and jolly, and he could see her being hedged away from him, swallowed up by dark and pale blue uniforms.

Beaumont's voice seemed to carry above all the rest. Like a trumpet. 'So I said to this bloody woman in Oxford Street, how much for the night? And she had the damn nerve to reply, five quid! I mean, I *know* things have gone up in wartime!'

A tall group captain asked, 'What did you say?'

'I told her, by God.' He grinned. 'I want to hire the bloody thing, not *buy* it!'

Drummond turned and found she was beside him again.

'He really is a card, don't you think?' She grimaced and rolled her eyes. 'A man's man from the socks up!'

'I gather you were talking about the *Conqueror* with my number one?'

She studied him curiously. 'You come out with it, don't you? No messing about.' But she did not make a joke of it. 'Yes, I was. I was trying to find out about my brother. Things like that.'

'I heard something of the sort.'

'You heard what you wanted to hear.' She moved closer and dropped her voice. 'And most of it was wrong, I'll bet.'

He had to lower his head to hear above the din of voices and clattering glasses. He could smell her hair. Her skin.

She said, 'I didn't go to bed with him, by the way.' She looked him straight in the eyes. 'There, how's that for directness? Your move.'

He said, 'I never thought—'

'Oh, come *on*!' She was smiling again, showing her perfect teeth. 'Now who's kidding who? It's written all over your face! I'll not say it wasn't a battle at one time, but I'm stronger than I look. I have to be!'

He tried to appear calm. 'I was wondering...'

'There you go again!' She touched his sleeve. 'I've been waiting for you to ask me. And the answer's yes.' She smiled at his confusion. 'When you're free, give me a call. I'm at that special hotel for women, a cross between a convent and a prison. Like Worthing on a wet September Sunday!'

Salter was calling her name, waiting, his face already flushed with drink, to introduce her to the latest arrivals.

She said, 'I'd like to talk. Soon.'

He replied, 'Yes. I'll see what I can arrange.' He smiled. 'And thanks.'

'You should smile more often, Commander.' She stood back and eyed him critically. 'It makes you almost human.'

She was swallowed up in the crush, and her slight figure was replaced instantly by a grave-faced captain, who introduced himself as being on the staff at A.C.H.Q. *On a temporary basis.* Neither he nor Drummond mentioned it, but he was quite obviously Nick Brooks's man in Iceland. Until the raid was mounted. Or dropped.

He sipped a large pink gin and said, 'Fine-looking girl. Married, eh?'

'Yes.' Funny that it did not seem to matter. Until now. 'I don't know her very well.'

The captain signalled to a steward. 'Someone was saying that her brother was in the same ship as Beaumont. Don't know the truth of it.'

Drummond watched him and smiled grimly. *Not much, you don't.* Aloud he said, 'I heard something like that, too, sir.'

The captain saw another face across the crammed cabin. 'I must be off. I'll see you at A.C.H.Q. quite soon.' His gaze was very firm. 'It's on, by the way. Thought you should know, in view of what you've just gone through.'

'Thank you, sir.' For what? For the chance of being blown to pieces? 'I'll keep it to myself.'

'I should hope so.' He smiled shortly. 'I expect Duvall will get a medal. Looks good.' His gaze seemed to shift momentarily towards Beaumont. 'Don't care much for heroes of that sort.'

Drummond waited. Who did he mean, Duvall or Beaumont? Both?

The captain added, 'Nelson had the right definition, I think. He said a hero was a man who inspired bravery in others. Not one who went out for his own glory.' He sighed. 'But the Admiralty of the day didn't like him much either. Must be a moral in it all somewhere!' He pushed his way into the throng.

'All right, Keith?' Beaumont appeared beside him.

'I think I ought to get back to the ship, sir.'

'Good show.' Beaumont's eyes were moving busily over the people around him. 'What was *he* saying, by the way?'

Drummond shrugged. 'Said we'd be meeting soon.'

'Good. He told you.' Beaumont grinned. 'Nod's as good as a wink, eh?' He followed Drummond to the door. 'You'll get your orders. The flotilla will be going round to a fjord on the east coast. Bit more private.' He was obviously eager to get back in the thick of the guests and added, 'Paint up your stripe on *Warlock*'s funnel. You are officially half-leader.' He seemed to expect a display of emotion and said, 'You should be pleased. Stick with me, and I'll get you something worth while.'

He turned and pushed back into the cabin, his voice reaching ahead like a radar beam.

Drummond returned the salutes from the O.O.D. and side party and walked slowly along the jetty. How seriously could he take her? And was it fair anyway, with the raid becoming a grim reality?

An American jeep, with U.S.A.A.F. painted on the side, was parked by some Nissen huts, and he saw a lean sergeant sitting inside it, a cigar sticking dead centre of his mouth, like a gun. As he got nearer, the American climbed down and watched him thoughtfully, as if trying to decide something. He wore heavy flying boots over his uniform trousers, and on his head he had a fur-lined hat, the flaps of which were tied over the top like an Alsatian's ears. He was very tall and tough-looking.

He said, 'Can I ask you something?' The cigar moved slightly. 'Sir?'

Drummond nodded. 'Try me.'

The man grinned. 'I never know where I am with Lime— I mean, the British, sir.' He became serious. 'Sergeant Matthew Wagner. I was in H.Q. a while back and saw the name of your ship on the board. You *are* the *Warlock*'s skipper?'

Drummond nodded. 'Yes. What can I do for you?'

The American held out his hand. 'I guess you think I've got one helluva nerve, but I have a problem. A serious one.' He seemed suddenly anxious. 'You have a sailor aboard called Jevers, right?'

'Yes.' Something from the crowded events of *Warlock*'s private world came back to him. 'A quartermaster. You must be the . . . ?'

He nodded ruefully. 'Yeh. I'm the guy who took his wife away from him. But don't be too hard on me, sir. He treated her bad. And Janice is a good kid. I'm taking her back to the States when I get out of this outfit.'

'Well, I'm afraid I can't do much for you. It's not the sort of thing I deal with.'

'I know, sir.' Wagner threw the cigar on the stones and jammed his boot on it. 'I ain't breaking too many secrets when I tell you I fly the milk-run from here to England once a week. I was planning to get Janice moved to an apartment up in Scotland near the field. So she wouldn't have to worry. But when I took some time off to tell her, she wasn't there, at her home.' He sounded as if he still didn't believe it. 'The neighbours ain't seen her, and believe me, they'd tell me. They're nice folk. Jevers wasn't too popular whenever he was around.'

Drummond rubbed his chin. 'There is the police enquiries department, she might have been injured in an air-raid.'

'She never went out in raids, sir. I've checked every goddamn thing. Our provost, yours, the police, the town hall. I've been going out of my mind, believe me.'

'Did she write to you?'

'All the time. The letters stopped at the same time she disappeared.'

'And you want to see her husband, is that it?'

'I'm not certain, sir. I might spoil the whole deal. And this is the thing which worries me most. He was seen near the house. Leastways, a railway porter swears it was him.' He looked very worried. 'Am I getting out of line, sir?'

Drummond eyed him gravely. 'Leave it with me. I expect she's gone away to think things out. It's a bad time for this sort of thing to happen. Women have a lot to put up with in wartime.' He gestured to the warships along the jetty. 'Not like you and me. Taking it easy all the time.' He wrote a number on a piece of paper from his notebook. 'You can reach me through this office, naval security. They'll keep our secret until we've found out something. And if *you* hear first, let me know.'

He strode off, his mind seeing the sad-faced Jevers in an entirely new light.

Behind him the American took out a fresh cigar and lit it. His friend, another sergeant, came out of a Nissen hut carrying a carton of cigarettes.

'Hey, Matt, that a Limey officer you was shooting the breeze with?'

Wagner smiled grimly. 'Quite a guy, too.' He swung his long legs into the jeep. 'Let's go!'

His friend grinned. 'Jeez! So suddenly we're feeling better already!'

Drummond reached the brow which led to *Warlock*'s iron deck and let his gaze move along her side, seeing each dent and scar like a separate memory. One day, probably sooner than he realised, he would have to let her go. The realisation never failed to move him.

Figures wandered slowly along the upper deck and forecastle, and below the triple torpedo tubes he saw Badger, the cat, pause in the business of washing one paw to watch him, yellow eyes without surprise or warmth.

Sheridan was at the head of the brow with the side party, and the silver calls shrilled in salute as Drummond stepped on to the metal deck.

Sheridan asked, 'Everything all right, sir?'

Drummond nodded, watching him and wondering how much he had tried and how much she had resisted.

'Yes. Shore leave for all but the duty part of the watch. Tell the libertymen about careless talk ashore, and the fact that the locals understand more English than they let on. The base recreation officer has all the gen about the cinemas, cafés which are out of bounds, that sort of thing.'

Sheridan asked quickly, 'Will you be going ashore, sir?'

'Probably.' He hesitated by the quartermaster's lobby. 'I saw Mrs. Kemp, by the way. Sends her regards.'

'Oh, thanks.' Sheridan smiled awkwardly. 'Quite a girl.'

Drummond walked through the screen door. She had not lied. It was as clear as day on Sheridan's face.

He whistled quietly as he lowered himself swiftly to the wardroom flat. And it wouldn't do any harm to meet her; he saw Owles peering from his pantry. He was smiling.

'You'll be off ashore then, sir?' He hurried to the cabin. 'Good, good. Just the ticket, sir.' He never listened to anything.

9

A Slight Setback

THE main operations room of Area Combined Headquarters, Iceland, was large and lined with steel cabinets and impressive coloured charts. Looking round, it was hard to believe he was inside yet another large Nissen hut, Drummond thought, and he was aware of the air of tense expectancy which had greeted his arrival and which was present in this room.

He felt vaguely self-conscious in his best shore-going uniform, especially as some of the other commanding officers looked as if they had come straight from their bunks to be here. He had been about to go ashore to discover Sarah Kemp's billet when the shore telephone had summoned him and all the other destroyer captains to an unexpected early briefing.

Beaumont was bending over a chart at the top of the room, murmuring with the operations officer and his staff. Seated against the far wall, puffing a pipe with studied calm, was the captain he had met only that morning aboard *Lomond*. He caught Drummond's glance and gave a brief smile before returning to his expression of detached indifference.

Several of the officers were chatting quietly together, and Drummond tried to ignore his feeling of uncertainty. Perhaps he was more tired and strained than he had believed. And yet as he glanced round at the other familiar faces he felt it again. Like a barrier which had risen between them. They had greeted him well enough. But no more than they would a visitor. A stranger.

He shook himself angrily. He had known most of them since the beginning of the war. Had fought side by side with some of them, used his own ship to defend others damaged in battle while they all prayed for the enemy to fall back, or for a sign of air-cover, or a miracle. Now there was a distinct coolness which seemed to leave him isolated. Maybe they believed he should have tried to support Duvall's lone attack on the U-boat?

Or they resented the fact he had assumed Duvall's role as half-leader as a direct result of *Warden*'s sinking?

Most likely it was the war, just the bloody war, he told himself for the tenth time. Once they were working together again, training in the fjord on the east coast as Beaumont had described, things would all sort themselves out again.

The voices died as Beaumont tapped briskly on the table.

He looked at the captain and said, 'Captain Kimber has something to tell you, gentlemen.'

Drummond found himself sitting rigidly against the chair. The raid was off after all. He did not know if he felt glad or let down.

Captain Kimber stood up slowly and tapped his pipe against one palm.

'I am sorry to bring you here from your ships at so little notice. Most of you will be pretty tired after your run from England. Some,' his eyes moved to Drummond, 'will be needing time to recover from a totally unexpected diversion. However . . .' He looked at Beaumont. 'Time is short.'

Drummond saw Beaumont's expression. Grim but excited.

Kimber continued calmly, 'This morning, the British and American forces in the Mediterranean performed the first part of Operation Husky. The invasion of Sicily.'

Drummond waited, seeing it in his mind. The drifting smoke from the bombarding squadrons, an anonymous flow of khaki as the soldiers swarmed up the beaches and into the tracer.

'You will all be pleased to know that the invasion is being carried out with complete success.'

Kimber smiled warmly. It lit up his face from side to side, as if like everyone else in the room, in every part of the unconquered world, he had been waiting, afraid even to dream, of this very moment.

But nobody spoke, and when Drummond looked at the others he saw their expressions, each man thinking of the cost, of the waiting, of the hopes which had been pinned on this vital part of the road back from all those retreats and setbacks.

Kimber said, 'You do not have to be a master strategist to guess that an invasion of Italy will follow very shortly. After that,' he shrugged, 'it will be up to the Combined Staffs to prepare the real thrust into Europe from the north.'

He had everyone's full attention now.

'You already know that the presence of German heavy naval units in their Norwegian bases is a real menace to our convoys to Russia. The fact they exist at all means that many dearly needed ships and men are being tied down in case they should venture out to follow *Bismarck*'s example. We will need every ship if our future plans are to have a chance of success. I am entrusted to tell you that an attack by our midget submarines is being planned for the autumn. It is a top secret, that goes without saying, of course. The *Tirpitz* in particular is being held in her northern fjord to conserve fuel. Fuel needed by their army to fight against the Russian advances on the Eastern Front. But when winter closes in that battlefront will become a frozen stalemate once more. *Tirpitz* will be free to move out. To put pressure on our supply routes when our forces are required elsewhere.' He gave what might have been a sigh. '*She will not move out.* Our midget submarines must damage her to such an extent that she can be finished off at leisure at some later date.'

Beaumont cleared his throat and said, 'You know of our mission. At the same time we will attack, and if possible cripple the fuel dump which is situated in the same fjord.' His eyes flashed in the dull light. 'These things we will do.'

Drummond realised that Miles Salter was on the other side of the room, speaking softly to one of his assistants. A large camera stood on the ground at his feet. *A record for all times.*

Kimber nodded. 'However.' He looked at each face in turn. 'Intelligence have informed me that the enemy is preparing to move the midget sub school south, to Holland, in the near future. A surface attack on the fjord after that would show the Germans we are more concerned with the fuel dump. Any attempt to put midget submarines through the minefields, nets and God knows what else, would be met with instant disaster!' He looked hard at Beaumont.

The latter breathed out slowly. 'This is a slight setback for us. But it will mean that our attack must be mounted within the next week or so.'

The commanding officers stared at him as if they had all misunderstood what he was saying.

Then one, Cromwell of the *Whiplash*, exclaimed incredulously, 'But, sir, the weather is too perfect for the enemy! Calm seas, good visibility, they'd kill every man-jack before he got within miles of the Norwegian coast!'

There were several murmurs of agreement, and Drummond saw the brief gleam of anxiety in Beaumont's bland expression before he said curtly, 'I am aware of the meteorological disadvantages, thank you, Cromwell.'

Kimber said hurriedly, 'We will give you every available support. The Norwegian underground have been working closely for months with our agents. It is well known that the enemy has removed part of his northern minefield to facilitate the training of the midget submarine crews.'

He was tapping his pipe stem against the chart table as if to emphasise each point.

'A carrier will be laid on to provide air-cover as you withdraw from the combat area. Everything possible will be done to assist you. It is a very dangerous mission, some would say foolhardy. Because of this, however, it will carry the necessary element of surprise, enough to take the enemy aback just long enough for you to hit him where it really counts.'

Beaumont looked round the room challengingly. 'Questions?'

Selkirk of the *Ventnor* said gruffly, 'There are only seven ships in the flotilla.' The merest pause. 'Now.' He gestured to the chart. 'Why not send some more destroyers to support us?'

Beaumont watched him narrowly. 'The enemy intelligence is not without skill.' He could barely hide his dislike for Selkirk. 'Any sudden, additional movement of shipping would give the game away before it had begun. As it is, I am quite certain that the Germans have plenty of agents right here in Iceland. No, we will continue as a flotilla.'

Selkirk remained standing. '*Warlock*'s the half-leader, sir. Is that to be permanent?' He did not look at Drummond.

Beaumont smiled gently. 'A matter of seniority is always a problem. Perhaps I should have mentioned it earlier. Lieutenant-Commander Drummond has been promoted to acting commander.' The smile faded. 'Are you satisfied?'

Selkirk turned to Drummond, his face confused. 'Congratulations, Keith.' But his eyes were angry. Hurt.

Drummond said quietly, 'It is the first I'd heard of it.'

'Ah well.' Beaumont was watching him cheerfully. 'You know the Admiralty.' He wagged one finger. 'Just pray the war doesn't end too quickly, eh? Or you'll drop your new stripe before you've got used to it!'

Drummond saw the others looking at him. It was all there. Pleasure, envy, even disapproval. Promoted over a dead man's head. It was rarely popular.

Kimber said, 'The flotilla will be moving to the east coast in two sections as before. Beginning in three days' time. The base staff will be inspecting each vessel, so have your spares and replacement lists ready. Once the show begins to move there'll be no time for second thoughts.'

Drummond asked, 'Is there any chance of the attack being cancelled, sir?' They had to know. To clear the air.

Kimber shrugged. 'No. It is being given a priority rating.'

He looked meaningly at the clock on the wall. 'I expect you've a good deal to do. Tell your people as little as you can. They will resent it now. Later they may realise that security can save lives.'

They all stood up, shuffling their feet. Each man concerned with his own ship, her role, the odds of survival. For those moments they were all strangers, Drummond thought.

Lieutenant-Commander Mark Kydd, the *Whirlpool*'s captain, touched his arm and grinned. 'Well done. Don't mind the others. You deserve it. And by God, we're going to need you before this little lot's in the history books!'

'We'll need each other.' Drummond looked away. 'But thanks.'

For some reason he kept thinking of Frank. All those miles away in hospital. No legs. Helen visiting him daily. Watching him withdraw from her and the world as they had once known it. *Why him?*

Kydd asked, 'Are you all right?'

He tried to smile. 'Yes. A bit bushed, that's all. But I'm glad something's been decided.'

He tried to imagine what it would be like. The coast. The land reaching out for the elderly destroyers.

Kydd picked up his cap as Beaumont walked towards them. 'Yes. God has spoken.' He strode after the others.

Beaumont smiled. 'Sorry about the little drama, Keith. That bloody man Selkirk really gets up my nose. Had to cut him down to size. These reservists . . .' He glanced at Kimber. 'Sounds a bit slow, but Aubrey Kimber is no slouch. He'll be taking flag-rank before this year's out.' He was thinking aloud. 'Nick Brooks can pick all the winners.' He turned and said suddenly, 'No need to mention all this to Mrs. Kemp if she corners you. You know what women are. She might say something indiscreet. Miles will fill her in on details later.'

'When it's all over?'

Beaumont regarded him thoughtfully. 'Something like that.'

'I don't really understand what Miles Salter is doing here, or anywhere else for that matter.'

'You don't?' Beaumont seemed to find it amusing. 'His ministry is keen on putting events in perspective. Boosting morale. That kind of thing. He used to be a magazine editor before the war. He's brighter than he looks.' He winked. 'Not difficult, eh?'

The man in question slouched across the room and said, 'I've fixed up for the pictures. John will have his camera set up as you go on board your boat.'

Beaumont winced. '*Boat* indeed!'

'Well anyway . . .' Salter looked at Drummond. 'I've arranged for a tailor to see you about some uniforms. Must get the new rank made up, if you're to look right.' He moved away, his face frowning.

'What . . .' Drummond fell silent as Beaumont raised one pale hand.

He said, 'Just take it as it comes, Keith. You are now my second-in-command. I could have had anyone. Nick Brooks said so. What he says goes. I wanted a chap who could *think* before all else. Not a Cromwell who wants to be popular all the time or a bloody moaner like Selkirk. Between ourselves, I was going to have Duvall shifted to another billet. We didn't get on. Death or glory.' He winked again. 'I have no objection to the latter, but I've been too close to my Maker for wishing to make his acquaintance just yet!'

Kimber called, 'Are you finished here, Dudley?' He looked at the clock. 'The admiral is expecting us for drinks before dinner.' He nodded to Drummond. 'I'll have a chat with you later.' He smiled. 'Commander.'

Drummond left the building and walked towards the gates. He paused at the guard hut and asked permission to use a telephone to call the ship. It was a bad line to the harbour and he had to wait for nearly ten minutes before he managed to get an answer. Then Sheridan came to the phone almost immediately. As if he had been waiting for a call.

Drummond said, 'If there's nothing urgent for me I'll be ashore for a while.' Faint voices hummed on the line, and he had a mental picture of several German agents tapping the conversation. 'All right?'

'Yes, sir. All quiet here.' He hesitated. 'Is it true, sir? About the promotion?'

News moved very swiftly. 'Yes.'

'Congratulations, sir.' He seemed to be searching for words. 'It must be quite a feeling.'

Drummond saw a jeep preparing to leave the base and wondered if he could cadge a lift.

He said, 'Tell Able Seaman Jevers I want to see him sometime tomorrow.'

'Jevers?' Sheridan sounded puzzled. 'Is something wrong?'

'Tell you later.'

He dropped the telephone, and with a brief nod to the duty officer, ran out to the jeep.

A R.A.F. officer grinned at him. 'All aboard for the gay lights of Reykjavik! Whalemeat and chips!'

The jeep roared from the base camp, red lava dust spewing from its wheels, while the crowded occupants clung to whatever they could to avoid being hurled on to the track.

Drummond was thinking of Sheridan's remark. It must be quite a feeling. Strange. He felt nothing but a sense of foreboding.

They sat opposite each other across a small square table. The restaurant in the commandeered hotel was gaunt and unwelcoming, and the solitary waitress, who was dressed in an ill-fitting white smock, completed the picture of dingy, temporary occupation.

She said quietly, 'Sorry about this place.' She was watching him gravely. 'It's not exactly the Savoy.'

Her chance remark brought it all back. The staff officers in the Savoy grill, his own thoughts at the time. Wishing she had been with him instead of Beaumont and the others. The old waiter whose son had died in *Warlock*.

He smiled. 'It will have to do.'

She was simply dressed in a green costume, and against the

dull walls and dreary room her face seemed to shine like one in a partly cleaned painting.

She said, 'You are staring again.'

The waitress paused by the table. 'Will you want any coffee?' Drummond nodded and she went away muttering.

The girl whispered, 'Nice to be so welcome!' She leaned forward slightly. 'Miles Salter came by. Told me about your promotion. I'm glad.' She thrust out a little package. 'A present for you.'

He stared at her. 'Because of my promotion?'

She laughed, the sound making two elderly nurses on the other side of the room stare at them with obvious disapproval.

'You are the giddy limit!' Impetuously she reached out and gripped his hand. 'It's your birthday, isn't it?'

He replied, 'I'd forgotten.' He smiled at her, feeling her smooth fingers on his skin. 'Thanks very much.'

She shook her head, the short chestnut hair bouncing across her forehead. 'I was hard put to find out about it. Might have guessed *you'd* forget.'

Drummond felt her hand move away as she said, 'I hope it's the sort you like, if not...'

He opened the parcel and turned the brand new pipe over in his hands.

'You must be a mind-reader, too.' He looked at her again. 'It was very good of you.'

She relaxed. 'I'm glad it suits. Had one helluva job getting it. Don't smoke a pipe myself,' She wrinkled her nose. 'Sorry you had to eat here. I just thought you'd like to get away from all those uniforms for a bit.'

'I'm enjoying myself very much.' He took her hand across the table. 'Believe me.'

She did not take her hand away. 'Good. How was it today? With Dudley Beaumont? Miles seemed to think you were feeling a bit fed up.'

'It was nothing much. Just a feeling.' He looked at the new pipe. It must have cost quite a bit and no little trouble to get. 'I had an idea that some of the other skippers were blaming me for Duvall's death.'

'Well, they would, wouldn't they?' She met his astonishment calmly. 'I should think that is *exactly* what Beaumont intended.'

'Is that what you really think? You hate him that much?'

She smiled sadly. 'You think I'm an idiot. You may be right.'

He asked carefully, 'Your brother? You were pretty close?'

'Yes. Our parents died in an air-raid right at the beginning. Tim was everything to me.'

His fingers moved gently across hers, touching the plain gold ring.

She said, 'My husband? You're wondering about him?'

He said, 'Only if you want to tell me.'

'Nothing much to tell. Tim was away with the Navy, I was a bit wild, I suppose. I met Philip at a party. He was a soldier. Good-looking, witty. Just what I needed with all the bombing which was going on in London.' Her eyes were dreamy, far away. 'Just one leave. It was all we had. I don't think we got out of bed for more than a minute or so. Then off he went.'

Drummond waited, seeing the memories crossing her face.

She said, 'He's in Canada now. Army liaison job in Ottawa.' She looked at him, but her expression was distant. 'He wants his *freedom*. Seems he's nicely fixed up with a fresh Canadian girl.'

'I'm sorry.'

'It's her I'm sorry for.' She took her hand away as the waitress banged the cups on the table. 'Philip has had several others before her. He's the sort of boy we find hard to refuse.' She tried to smile, but it did not come. 'So there you are. The story of Sarah, although not the one that gets spread around usually.'

Drummond said, 'He must have wanted his head examining.'

She looked at him again, her eyes misty. 'That was *nice*. Very nice. Usually when they find out I'm married but *separated* they all think I'm fair game. And the married men are the worst. Pawing you about. One minute telling you about the dear wife at home and all the little toddlers, and the next trying to tear your clothes off.' She shuddered. 'Do you take sugar?'

He grinned. 'Yes.'

She sipped the coffee and then said, 'I suppose all this made Tim's death harder to take.' She hesitated. 'There were two other survivors from the *Conqueror*.'

'I know. A stoker and a seaman.'

She nodded. 'The seaman was called Carson. He was a messenger apparently. Got blasted over the side and found his way to a raft of some sort. I saw some of the reports about it. You can get hold of almost anything in this job. There were about four or five men on the raft. One of them was Beaumont. Carson insisted that one was Tim. But when the neutral ship went looking for survivors there was only Beaumont, Carson and the stoker, who was half mad with shock.' She dropped her eyes. 'Poor devil.'

He asked quietly, 'Just the three?'

'Yes. Carson can't remember a thing now. He's in hospital. I went to see him. He told me that *Tim was alive*.' She traced an invisible line on the table. 'Beaumont denies it. He says that there were two other seamen with him, but although he tried to save them, they died of their wounds and drifted away.'

'Perhaps Carson was mistaken.' He gripped her hand as she looked up at him, her eyes suddenly angry. 'I said *perhaps*! Have you thought about it?'

'I'm sorry. Yes, I have thought about it. But he seemed so sure. So definite that it was Tim.'

The waitress returned and said abruptly, 'This hotel is out of bounds to all males as from ten o'clock.' She sniffed. 'Sir.'

Drummond stood up. 'Thank you.' He took the girl's arm and guided her towards the lobby. 'I have to go now.' He felt her arm stiffen. 'But I'd like to see you again. Tomorrow?'

She looked at him evenly. 'Yes. I'd like it, too.' She reached up and touched his cheek. 'Many happy returns.'

He knew he was staring at her. That he wanted her so badly it hurt.

He said, 'I'm not married, and I won't tell you about the wife at home.'

She watched him. 'I checked on that, too.' Then she smiled. 'Perhaps we could get out, away from the town, climb that damned volcano, or something.'

He forced his voice to stay calm. 'What did Salter tell you?'

'Oh, that the mission is being shelved. I'm not to mention it, but I can't tell you how glad I am for your sake.'

'Yes.' He did not know what else to say.

She walked with him to the door. 'It's funny to see all the lights on. Like it used to be at home.' She shook her head. 'No, I am not going to get morbid. The lights are on here, and . . .' She looked up at him again. 'And I'm very happy at this moment.'

As he walked through the town towards the harbour, past well-lit shops and jostling groups of sailors and soldiers, he kept thinking about Sarah Kemp. It was like seeing life through another dimension, and the realisation left him confused, breathless.

Sheridan was waiting for him as he stepped aboard.

'All quiet, sir. Most of the libertymen are off now. Two are in the rattle ashore. Drunk and disorderly.'

'Normal then.'

He glanced along the deserted iron deck. And she had been the only one to remember his birthday. Even his mother had forgotten.

Sheridan added, 'Good run ashore, sir?'

'Yes.'

He nodded. 'Pilot said he saw you going into the hotel by the square. So I guessed you were dining with Mrs. Kemp.' He fell into step beside Drummond. 'I hope she didn't get on to you about her brother. She tried to get me involved like that. When I wouldn't, she soon put the fence up.'

Drummond turned away. 'I'll see you in the morning, Number One.'

Sheridan watched him as he vanished into the quartermaster's lobby. What the hell had made him speak like that about her? Was it jealousy at Drummond's success? At his promotion? He stirred uneasily. Anyway, it had not been completely untrue.

She had kept pestering him about the bloody *Conqueror*. Then on the landing of the hotel he had turned her round into his arm. Pulling her against him so that she was helpless. He had cupped her breast in his hand, his cheek on her hair, feeling his blood surging like a hot wind.

He gripped the guardrail and stared fixedly at the water alongside. She had asked him quietly to release her, her body stiff against his. But he had felt her breast moving beneath his fingers and had known that she was just playing for time. The pain had come like a stab wound.

As he had fallen back, gasping and holding his groin, she had said shakily, 'Touch me again and I'll *really* do you an injury!'

The humiliation still left him ashamed and furious. With her and himself.

Below his feet, in his cabin, Drummond stood motionless

under a deckhead light, examining the pipe, remembering what she had said. How she had looked. Nothing Sheridan could do or say could take that away from him. He sat down in a chair and began to fill his new pipe.

Surgeon Lieutenant Adrian Vaughan stood beside the desk and watched Drummond examining his daily sick report. It was half-way through the forenoon, and around and above the cabin the ship moved uneasily against her fenders and nudged the destroyer which was moored alongside.

A normal routine day in harbour. Drummond initialled the report, his mind only half attending to the list of ailments. A few bruises from a fight ashore. A stoker who had cracked his thumb. A suspected case of V.D. which Vaughan had packed off to the naval hospital.

Boots clumped overhead, and somewhere further forward he heard a man chipping paint. The endless battle against rust.

Vaughan was wearing rimless glasses which only helped to accentuate his lack of colour. Pale hair and eyes, delicate, almost transparent skin. But Drummond had seen him at work. Knew that behind those glasses was a carefully concealed hardness.

He said, 'Well, Doc, it all seems quiet enough in your department.'

Vaughan examined one scrubbed hand. 'You mentioned Able Seaman Jevers, sir.'

Drummond nodded. Straight to the point. Like a scalpel. 'You know his history.' He pushed a folder across the desk. 'Read this and fill in the details for yourself. I'm worried about him. I've made a few notes at the bottom.'

Vaughan's eyes lit up as he scanned the papers. 'Wife missing? There's no report on that from Welfare. They say she went off with an American.'

'Well, maybe she went off with someone else. But I'm not satisfied. You are in charge of welfare aboard this ship. See what you can find out. Discreetly.'

Vaughan smiled. 'Of course, sir.'

'I don't want him worried. There may be nothing in this idea of mine. In which case it will only cause more trouble.'

It was strange to be sitting here like this. Discussing a seaman's problems. Within a few days they would be moving again. And then . . . he felt his stomach muscles contract as if expecting a blow. Was that why Captain Kimber and his staff had been so frank and open about the proposed submarine attack on *Tirpitz*? To stress the importance of the destroyers' mission, or because there was no hope at all of their surviving it?

Vaughan said, 'I have just signed for an additional amount of surgical stores, sir. My S.B.A. was quite upset about it.' He chuckled. 'Ranting about the sickbay like a bitch on heat trying to find room for everything.' He asked smoothly, 'Any reason, sir? I mean, I carry quite sufficient dressings and drugs for most happenings.'

Drummond looked at him. 'We are under orders. That's all I can say.'

Vaughan shrugged. 'It's enough, sir.'

There was a tap on the door and Galbraith peered in at them. 'What is it, Chief?'

Galbraith wiped his face with a smutty piece of rag. 'Just wanted a chat about spares, sir.'

'Doc's finished now. Come and sit down.'

And so it went on.

A few yards away in the wardroom Sheridan was standing with his back to the unlit fire, while Rankin and Wingate sat nearby, their notebooks open on their knees. The base staff had been aboard since dawn, and were now clambering through the destroyer alongside in search of flaws and makeshift repairs.

Rankin drawled, 'Well, my department is all buttoned up.' He sounded resentful, which he was. 'Bloody men peering through my four-inch guns as if they were looking for contraband!'

Wingate was watching Sheridan. 'It's going to be sooner than we thought then?'

'I guess so.'

Sheridan was thinking about the captain. No sign of anger at what he had said about Sarah Kemp last night. At the defaulters' table, where he had been attending to the two ratings who had been in a brawl ashore, he had seen Drummond speaking with some of the base staff. He seemed quite calm. Remote, even, from any sort of nerves.

The quartermaster peered into the wardroom. 'Base staff 'ave left the ship, sir. They're now aboard *Whirlpool*.'

'Thank you, Jevers.' Sheridan thought the man seemed more intense than usual. Perhaps the captain had already spoken to him.

Jevers asked, 'I ain't seen the Old—I mean, the captain yet, sir.'

He licked his lips. He was a sharp-featured man, a bit like a fox, Sheridan thought.

'Well, I expect he will send for you when he gets a moment.'

Jevers hung in the doorway. 'No idea wot it's about, 'ave you, sir?'

'Have *you*?'

'Well, sir,' he hung his head, 'me wife still ain't written.'

Rankin said, 'If you need any help . . .'

The seaman nodded. 'I know, sir. The Welfare.'

He hurried away to the ladder in the wardroom flat.

Rankin said, 'I don't know, but that chap puts me on edge.'

Wingate grinned. 'How would you feel if a Yank went off with your wife?'

Rankin picked up his notebook. 'I'd give him the price of a meal, I daresay.'

Feet grated on the ladder, and seconds later the probing nose of Lieutenant-Commander Dorian de Pass swung round the door.

Sheridan asked, 'Can I help, sir?'

The Informer examined him suspiciously. 'Your captain. Is he free?'

Wingate stood up. 'I'll check for you. The chief was with him just now.'

Rankin said hurriedly, 'I've got to go, too.'

The *Lomond*'s first lieutenant waited until they had left and remarked coldly, 'What's their rush, I wonder?'

Sheridan shrugged. It was odd that de Pass seemed to be the only one who did not know of his own unpopularity.

He was saying, 'I've brought your orders. A slight change. You will be leaving this afternoon at 1730, *Whirlpool*, *Whiplash* and *Waxwing* in company. Operations have arranged for a repair ship to be standing by in Seydisfjord, in case some lazy bugger has forgotten something.' He sounded on edge.

'That *is* early. Can I ask why?'

'Captain (D) will be remaining here for a day or so with the other three ships. He wants to do some work in A.C.H.Q.' He studied Sheridan meaningly. 'Still, we first lieutenants can't have too many secrets, can we?'

Sheridan was staggered. The Informer must be worried to share his information with him. A reservist at that.

De Pass added, 'You know of the German battlecruiser *Moltke*?' It sounded like *of course*. 'You're not likely to forget her, I imagine.'

Sheridan looked away. Remembering his captain from the past. The one who had killed himself because of the *Conqueror* court of enquiry. *Moltke* had been the one to put the old battle-ship down. It had been so easy for her. So terribly easy.

Sheridan had seen her once, just before the war. 1937, when King George had reviewed the fleet at Spithead. It was like a mad dream now. But at the time it had seemed only right and proper for other nations to send representatives to the greatest review of the greatest navy. *Moltke* had been brand new, barely months from her builder's yard in Wilhelmshaven.

The pleasure boats had had a heyday, surging with carefree trippers past the towering grey ships. *Hood* and the French *Dunquerque*, the American *New York*, and just astern of the German pocket-battleship *Graf Spee*, the *Moltke*. She had lacked much of the lean grace of the *Scharnhorst* and her sister ship, and had not measured up to the later armoured giants like *Tirpitz*. But anyone with half an eye could not fail to recognise her latent power and menace as her impeccable ship's company had lined the guardrails and cheered while the Royal Yacht had steamed past.

He replied quietly, 'I thought she was down south. In the Baltic. Wasn't she supposed to be damaged by our bombing? Out of commission?'

De Pass grunted. 'So they said. Well, she's bloody well not in the Baltic *now*.'

Sheridan stared at him. 'You mean, she's up here?'

'Nobody knows anything. There has been a lot of coastal fog around the Skaggerak and Norwegian coast. Our submarine patrols have not seen her. Nor has anyone else, it seems.'

'But you think—'

'I don't know what to think. All I know is that Captain (D) is like a wild man since he got the news. You can imagine what it means to him. He doesn't say much, but I've got to know quite a lot about his moods over the last few weeks. He's got a complete dossier on the *Moltke*. About her capabilities, even her captain's record, right from the moment he was a naval cadet.'

'I can believe that.' He felt suddenly dry. 'It could make a difference to our position, I suppose?'

'Christ knows.' De Pass's great nose swivelled to the door as Galbraith approached from the opposite side. 'I just hope that somebody in high places is all genned up.'

Galbraith sauntered past him and sat down heavily in a chair.

'Skipper's free now.' He raised one eyebrow as de Pass hurried away. 'Bother?'

'Under advanced orders, Chief. Official.' He smiled grimly. 'You'll be busy again.'

Galbraith sighed. 'Ah well. Nothing lasts forever.'

Right forward on *Warlock's* forecastle Sub-lieutenant Victor Tyson was watching some seamen while they half-heartedly slapped paint on the anchor cables. It was quite warm in the frail sunlight, and across the busy jetty alongside he could see the town, the bright coats of some Icelandic girls who were strolling past the enclosing wire fence.

It was true what they said about the Reykjavik girls. They really were beautiful. He had caught a friendly eye several times during his time ashore the previous evening, but that was all. The local male population obviously intended to keep them all to themselves. It was said that any Icelandic girl caught going round with a British serviceman would be labelled a prostitute. Even with an *officer*. But if they were staying a bit longer he would try his luck.

As if to mock him, the tannoy speaker below the bridge rattled into life.

'D'you hear there! D'you hear there!'

The paint brushes all hovered in mid-air as if to listen.

'There will be *no*, repeat no shore leave today. Hands will go to stations for leaving harbour at 1700.' The speaker went dead.

Tyson gaped at the tannoy with amazement. Leaving harbour? What the hell was going on?

The tannoy intoned in a less despairing voice, 'Up spirits!'

A seaman muttered, 'And stand by, the Holy Ghost!'

Tyson swung on him angrily. 'Hold your noise, damn you! I want all this cable painted before you fall out!'

As he turned away, one of the seamen flicked his brush so that two drops of fresh paint fell neatly down the back of Tyson's trousers.

Midshipman Allan Keyes had just been passing the side of A gun and saw the action with the paint brush. The seaman in question also saw Keyes, and knew he had been seen.

Keyes opened his mouth, but remained silent as Tyson snapped, 'And where the *hell* have you been, for God's sake?' He gestured vaguely around the forecastle. 'I can't carry the whole ship on my own!'

Keyes said, 'Sorry.'

He was glad he had said nothing about the paint, and saw the seaman with the brush watching him with obvious relief.

But for once Keyes did not care about Tyson. Or anything else for that matter. For the first time in the whole of his eighteen years he was in love. Not some panting, breathless escapade with a schoolgirl at a carefully managed party, nor a demure and standoffish daughter of one of his parents' friends, but with a *real, vital woman.*

He watched Tyson as he strode angrily this way and that, and found he could feel even a sort of warmth for him. Almost. Unwittingly, it had been through Tyson that he had met Georgina. Even her name had a magic all of its own, and when he thought about it, it was like speaking it aloud.

Tyson had been told to take a packet of despatches up to A.C.H.Q. It had been 'something a bloody rating should be told to do', according to Tyson. So making an excuse about another duty, he had arranged for Keyes to go instead. The midshipman had not minded at all. He had travelled very little, and just to sit in the back of a naval jeep amid a litter of sealed parcels and despatch boxes had been a small drama. At the H.Q. building he had been treated as something between human and animal by a bored staff officer, and then had been told to take a further envelope over to the Americans at Camp Knox. It seemed that it had arrived in the wrong hands by mistake.

His reception at the American camp had been somewhat different. He had been ushered into a comfortable hut, where coffee was produced, and a variety of rich cream cakes, while a lieutenant had gone off to obtain a signature for the envelope from somebody higher up.

And then, like a vision out of a great film, Georgina had stepped into his life.

Vivacious, very blonde, completely gorgeous in every way, she was, it appeared, an actress, one of a group which had arrived in Iceland to entertain the lonely servicemen. Although she had what seemed to be an American accent, she was, she had informed him in her low, husky voice, a Londoner. She was part of an ENSA show, which had been 'exchanged' for an American USO group on the same sort of mission.

He had listened, spellbound, to her tales of the West End shows, the great names in entertainment, cinema and broadcasting. Another, fantastic world.

She was, he thought, a little older than himself. But not enough to matter. More to the point, she gave him a photograph, signed 'To Allan from Georgina'. She had looked at him and then with a secret smile had added, 'Eternally.'

'That will keep your friends guessing,' she had said.

He looked up as Wingate appeared on the forebridge. The navigating officer had not repeated his rare display of anger against him. In fact, he got on very well with him, although he never got beyond Wingate's outer, joking self. He went to the port ladder and hurried up to the bridge before Tyson could find him another job before lunch.

Wingate was sitting on the captain's wooden chair, smoking a cigarette, and letting the offshore breeze ruffle his dark hair.

He looked at Keyes and nodded. 'All right, Mid?'

'I heard the pipe. We're off again then?'

'Seems that way.' Wingate eyed him curiously. 'What's on your mind?'

'I wanted to get a message to someone. I promised to see her—'

'*Her?*' Wingate swivelled round in the chair. 'You're joking, of course?'

'No.' He shifted under his dark stare. 'I met her yesterday. She's an actress.'

Wingate toyed with the idea of making a joke of it, and then saw Keyes' pleading expression.

'Well, you know the drill, Mid. Security. Nobody ever gets told.'

'But I don't *know* anything to tell her!' He was getting desperate.

Wingate nodded. 'Right. I have to go ashore for last-minute met reports.' He grinned. 'But I see from your face you'd already thought of that!'

Keyes smiled gratefully. 'She's at the women's hotel in Borg Square.'

Wingate remembered seeing the captain going into the same hotel.

He said, 'I'll let her know. Tell her what a good bloke you are.'

'*Please*, Pilot. Don't stir it up for me. It's very important.'

He clapped Keyes on the shoulder. 'Sure. Leave it to me.' He chuckled. 'She might have a friend.' He frowned. 'What's her name?'

'Georgina.' Just saying it aloud was like a betrayal.

'Is that all?' He grinned again. 'Never mind, Mid. I don't suppose there are too many actresses called Georgina in that dump!'

Tyson climbed up on to the bridge.

'Come along, Mid! The upper deck is still in a filthy state!'

Wingate smiled gently. 'What about you then, *Sub*? Got bloody paint all over your trousers. Fine one to talk about filth!'

He watched Tyson and the midshipman leave the bridge quiet and empty again. How he liked it. Tyson, all red-faced and fuming. As usual. The boy, glowing with a sort of aura in his new happiness. He glanced at the empty chart table. Poor little sod. He'd better make the most of it, he thought.

10

Touch and Go

IT was five more days before *Lomond* and her two accompanying destroyers entered Seydisfjord and reunited the flotilla. For Drummond, as for most of the others, it had been a time of tension and concentration. Even the least experienced member of the ship's company was now aware of the growing prospect of action, although no announcement had yet been released.

From Admiral Brooks's deep bunker in Whitehall to the monitoring stations in England and Iceland, a constant watch was being kept for any sign of undue excitement in the enemy's arrangements in Norway. Whenever possible the R.A.F. maintained a careful patrol over harbours and coastal waters, seeking any sign that a familiar ship was missing, or that a new one had arrived. But as hours dragged into days, even the unexpected reports about the *Moltke* faded into the background. She had not been sighted again, and so the earlier references to her movements were now open to doubt.

The real enemy was the weather. The clock came a very close second.

Captain Kimber had sent a brief top-secret signal to the effect that the German training base for midget submarines of the type captured by *Warlock* was showing signs of closing down. The base was still there, and the little submarines, or 'Negroes', as they were apparently called by their creators, had been reported as before, and in the same impressive numbers. But there had been less activity, and the local Norwegian underground had signalled other information which left little doubt that the whole organisation was preparing to move south.

At night, as he lay staring up at the darkness, Drummond had often thought about those nameless agents in occupied Norway, and any other land under the German heel. Hourly they must be risking discovery. The torture and agony which would follow capture, the punishment and destruction even of their families as a frightening example to others, it must all lurk in each man's mind as he drew his sketches of installations and railway sidings with their loads of military stores and troop trains. Whenever he switched on his little transmitter and tried to reach London, or flashed his torch from a fishing boat to some invisible submarine off the coast, he must have held his breath. Waiting for the sharp challenge. The arrest. The beginning of unrelenting, unceasing pain.

But the weather knew of no such problems. As the destroyers lay at their moorings in the great gash of a fjord hacked into Iceland's east coast, they were constantly reminded of the calm which seemed to prevail as far south as Biscay and as far north as Spitzbergen. Washed-out blue skies, damp, listless air which hung in messdecks and cabins and painted everything with a dull, misty finish.

True to his word, Kimber had arranged for a repair ship to be at hand, but as the base engineer officer had been heard to remark, 'The old girls need less attention than brand-new ships.' So there had not even been much work beyond daily routine to keep the men's minds elsewhere.

Drummond had gone aboard *Lomond* within minutes of her arrival at Seydisfjord. After hearing what de Pass had said about the *Moltke*, he had been expecting some sort of a change in Beaumont, although he did not know in what way it might show itself. But, outwardly at least, Beaumont had displayed little but gnawing irritation.

He had said, 'When you are told you can go ahead with something, there's nothing so calculated to get on your wick as stupid, bloody delays!'

He had not even shown much enthusiasm for Miles Salter and his small camera crew, who had been busy for most of the passage round the coast from Reykjavik, and once in the great fjord had used a motor boat for further shots of the waiting destroyers.

And Drummond had thought a good deal about the girl, Sarah Kemp.

Fifteen minutes before their time to leave Reykjavik harbour he had been told by the officer of the guard that he was wanted on the telephone in the dock office. He had known she would see through Salter's deception, although he had hoped it would not be quite so soon.

She had said, 'I won't say much over this line. But I *know*!'

He had tried to imagine her face on the other end of the wire. Resigned, matter-of-fact, anxious for him perhaps.

'I'm sorry. It had to be like this.'

'Yes.' She had remained silent, and for a moment he had imagined she had hung up. 'When you didn't call me. About a date. I knew then, I think.'

'It'll be all right.'

Through the dirty windows of the dock office he had seen his own ship against the jetty, the greasy streamers of smoke from her unmatched funnels, going straight up, smearing the empty sky. No wind. Not a breath, he had thought despairingly. *They'll cut us to pieces.*

'I wish you had something better to remember,' she had given a small laugh, it might have been a sob, 'than a silly old pipe. And all I did was moan about my troubles.' That time he had heard her voice break. 'When you *knew*, while I was talking.'

He had said, 'I'll see you soon. I promise. I'm not letting you get away with it like this. You said you wanted a holiday on a volcano, remember?'

He had heard her sniff, the impatient click of a switchboard operator.

'Yes, I remember.' Another break. 'Take care, Keith.'

The line had gone dead. Only when he was striding back to the brow did he realise she had used his name.

And then, on the afternoon of the eighth day, as he had been sitting in his cabin reading about the continuing successes in Sicily, the summons had arrived. All commanding officers to repair on board flotilla leader forthwith.

Kimber was there, too, and as the destroyers' captains arrived in their various motor boats, the *Lomond*'s wardroom seemed jammed tight with them and his assembled staff.

Beaumont did not intend to waste any more time.

'In a few minutes, gentlemen, the met officer and other interested parties will be filling in the pale patches. But I want to tell you right away that the raid is about to begin.'

He leaned his hands on the table, and in the sudden silence

167

Drummond could even hear his own heart beating. Beaumont must have cleared every steward, every officer not required at the meeting from the wardroom area, for the ship seemed like a grave.

Beaumont was saying in the same steady tone, 'Fog is usually a bad enemy to any sailor. This time it will be our ally. The met chaps can put it into better words for you later, but as far as we are concerned there has been a prevailing bank of fog moving up from the Baltic for several days. It now extends right along the Norwegian coast north of the sixty-fifth parallel, and shows no sign at all of clearing away. It is fairly common at this time of year, but it seems heavier than usual.'

The others nodded and moved their feet.

Drummond watched Kimber as he walked to the table. He showed a certain weariness, and he looked as if he had slept badly. But his voice was the same. Unemotional.

'It is all arranged. The flotilla will leave here tonight and head north-east to a rendezvous point off Bear Island. There you will be met by two oilers and replenish supplies. As explained in your final orders, you will then proceed south again. To your objective.'

There was a pause while the R.A.F. met officer assembled his coloured chart on a little easel, showing all the areas of high and low pressure, and bunches of darting arrows which might mean almost anything.

Drummond was still thinking of Kimber's bare announcement. Up to Bear Island, that bleak hump of land south of Spitzbergen, then over a thousand miles towards their target. All the way there, and all the way back, would total well over six thousand miles. He bit his lip. When it still lay ahead of you, it seemed impossible. An endless nightmare.

Kimber looked above the meteorological chart. 'Carrier support is prepared for your withdrawal. Fuelling facilities are in hand in case either of the oilers we already have are lost or damaged by enemy action.' He tapped his own chart. 'Thanks to the ice-edge falling back to the north, you will be able to keep clear of normal enemy patrol areas. A fast convoy will be passing south of Bear Island *en route* for Murmansk, so that should keep the German spotting planes well occupied and away from you.'

He looked at Drummond. 'Well, Commander, d'you have any points to raise?'

Drummond shook his head. 'If the fog lifts . . .' He began again: 'Can we expect support from the Norwegian agents, sir?'

'That is being arranged as of now. One of our submarines has been patrolling the edge of the enemy minefield for well over a week. You will make contact with her as laid down in your written orders. Up to that moment, and until you receive the final go-ahead from the submarine, you must be prepared to delay the attack.' He turned and sought out Lieutenant-Commander Kydd. 'Your ship is fitted with rails for dropping mines?' It sounded like a statement.

Kydd nodded. 'Yes, sir, *Whirlpool* did a bit of mine-laying last year.'

'Yes, quite so.' Kimber was speaking faster. 'I have arranged for mines to be taken aboard your ship immediately. A tender should be on way to her now.' He studied Kydd's face grimly. 'A precaution. Nothing more.'

Drummond glanced at Kydd and gave a quick grimace. It was bad enough as it was, without carrying a lethal cargo on your quarterdeck.

Kimber looked at Beaumont. 'That's it then.'

Beaumont cleared his throat. 'Return to your ships, gentlemen. You can brief your officers right away. Tell them that this is a raid of maximum importance. Cool heads, steady hands.' He seemed to falter. 'Well, you know the sort of thing.'

They all stood up, wanting to leave, to discuss it and find strength with their officers and men. It was always like this before something big, Drummond thought. Few smiles, not even a handshake. That only happened in films.

Afterwards it would be different.

Beaumont said, 'Just a second, Keith.' He waited until the other captains had trooped out. 'I merely wanted to know how you feel about it.' He studied him meaningly. 'I mean, *really* feel.'

Drummond followed him into his big day cabin. There were charts and folios on every piece of furniture, or so it appeared. He caught sight of himself in the bulkhead mirror, remembering his first meeting with Beaumont as Captain (D). In his hurriedly delivered uniform, with its three bright stripes, he looked younger than ever, he thought.

He said, 'It could work smoothly.'

'*Could?*' Beaumont's forehead was damp with sweat. 'That's not damn well good enough, Keith.'

Drummond looked at him gravely. He had imagined Beaumont was testing him in his new role as second in command of the Scrapyard Flotilla. Measuring him, gauging where the gaps might need to be filled when they were committed to action. But it was not like that at all, and the realisation was unnerving.

'I think that there are too many links, sir. The submarine, the oilers, this gap in the Jerry minefield, the Norwegian underground, the targets, and, of course, *us* at the tag-end of it.' He smiled slightly. 'Quite a few things could go adrift.'

Beaumont nodded, his eyes distant. 'Yes. I see. I see that. But it was your part which interested me. In *yourself*.' His eyes were intense. 'You *feel* we can make a go of it?'

'Yes.' How easy it came. 'I do.'

Beaumont rubbed his palms together. The sound was like paper. 'I'd ask you to have a glass with me. But I've things to do. Aubrey Kimber.' He shrugged vaguely. 'You know the drill.'

Drummond was relieved. He wanted to go. Needed to be on his own and think out the flaws, the faults in the pattern.

Beaumont smiled. 'Good luck then, Keith. Rather have you with me than anyone right at this moment.'

De Pass peered round the door. 'I was wondering, sir—' He got no further.

'What the *bloody hell* d'you mean by interrupting!' His face was almost crimson. 'Can't I do anything without some idiot eavesdropping?'

De Pass seemed to shrink. 'I—I'm sorry, sir.' He fled.

Beaumont prodded Drummond's arm. 'Damn fool. That'll teach him, eh?'

'I think it will.'

Drummond picked up his brand new cap with the gold oak leaves around its peak. Once, promotion had been a dream. Now the reality seemed without any substance at all.

Another glimpse of the hero. Beaumont had really lost control for a few seconds.

They walked from the cabin.

But then, in battle, it only took seconds to wreck everything.

Beaumont said, 'I won't come up, if you don't mind.' He turned and strode back to the chaos of charts.

On deck the air was crisper, but every gun and fitting retained its damp sheen. No wonder Icelanders were said to be chronic T.B. sufferers, he thought vaguely. He glanced at the motor boat which was waiting to collect him. And what a party it's going to be, *right down the line*, as Beaumont had once promised.

The O.O.D. said, 'Your boat's alongside, sir.'

Drummond raised his hand in salute and ran quickly down the short accommodation ladder.

As the motor boat pounded past the *Whirlpool* he saw that the job of swaying the big, ugly mines aboard had already begun. *A precaution. Nothing more.*

Kydd was on deck speaking with his first lieutenant. He had known Kydd longer than anyone. They had been in the same division at Dartmouth. Just boys in uniform. And now? He waved as the boat surged abeam.

Kydd was one of the few who knew how he had felt about Helen before she had married Frank Cowley. She had never even guessed. It all seemed so long ago. An eternity.

They passed under *Whirlpool*'s dented stem and he saw his own ship lying directly ahead. Despite her new paint, she looked tired, he thought. *Like the rest of us.*

The bowman raised his boathook and the boat sighed against the rope fender below the ladder. He adjusted his face to meet the side party and stepped from the boat. It had started.

Drummond settled himself more comfortably in his tall chair and waited while Sheridan completed his conversation on a telephone.

Sheridan said at length, 'Exercise completed, sir.'

'Thanks.'

It was pitch dark, and above the bridge the stars looked tiny and feeble. The flotilla was steaming a steady twelve knots in two parallel lines, with *Lomond* leading the shorter column to starboard. They had been under way for three hours, testing guns, checking everything and then checking it again.

He slid from the chair and waited for the deck to steady in the deep swell which was coming almost abeam.

'Give me the mike.'

He saw Hillier and Wingate by the compass platform, could tell from the stiff shoulders of the bridge lookouts that like everyone else aboard they were waiting for his voice. He snapped down the button.

'This is the captain speaking. Most of you know something of what is expected from us in the next few days. It is quite a lot, but no more than we can manage. In the past we have often been alone, or too late to help our friends and messmates. This time it's different.'

He pictured the other captains preparing the ground in their own way. Beaumont would no doubt make a fine speech. Something memorable. He had an insane thought that Miles's cameraman would be recording every action, even Beaumont having a last meal before battle.

He continued, 'We'll all be together. The old crowd. Whatever we meet with when we reach our objective, I am certain you will do your best for each other, and for the ship. That is all.'

Faintly above the whirr of fans and the sluice of water along the hull he heard someone give a solitary cheer, like the sole supporter of an unpopular team.

Wingate grinned, his teeth very white in the gloom.

'That sounded fine, sir. Just enough.'

Drummond returned to his chair. 'One chap seemed to approve.'

He looked for Sheridan. 'You can fall out action stations. Port watch to defence stations, if you please.'

The pipe trilled over the tannoy, and he heard feet and bodies thudding down ladders and through screen doors as the off-watch men scurried to the warmth of the messdecks.

Not that it was too cold. He looked up at the masthead. It even felt like rain although there was no cloud in sight. They just wanted to get below. To shut out the sea for a bit. Put up their individual barriers as best they could.

'Wheel relieved, sir. Able Seaman Jevers on it now.' Sheridan dropped his voice. 'Is it all right about him yet, sir?'

'I don't know, Number One. I haven't heard anything about Vaughan's handling of the matter.'

Sheridan ducked as some droplets of spray danced over the

screen. 'I'm off then, sir. I've got the morning watch.'

Wingate was saying to Hillier, 'We will alter course in ten minutes. Course to steer zero-three-zero.' He called across, 'It seems peaceful enough.' It was his way of giving a hint.

Drummond smiled. 'Yes. I'll go to my sea cabin for a nap.'

As he left the bridge Wingate relaxed and unbuttoned the throat of his leather jacket. He heard Hillier breathing heavily as he sprawled beneath the canvas hood on the chart table, and grinned. Nice and quiet. Time to think. To put yourself together. He thought suddenly of the girl at the hotel. Georgina. It was a bloody shame really. But then . . .

He crossed the bridge and trained his glasses above the salt-dappled screen. He could just make out the jagged line of *Lomond*'s small bow wave, the darker smudge of her hull riding above it. Right on station. He hoped the ones at the tail-end were keeping a good lookout. Despite all the information and monitoring which had been done, it was still possible for a solitary, sneaky U-boat to be in the area.

Georgina. What a girl. So alive and sensual, and as fluffy as a young kitten. And what a figure. Through her dress he had seen the full curve of her breasts, the restless way she crossed her legs as she had spoken with him. When he had started to tell her what Keyes had said she had sounded puzzled. Then, 'Oh, *him*!' She had leaned forward and laid one hand on his knee. 'Such a sweet boy!' After that, Wingate had known the full extent of her interest in poor Allan Keyes.

She had asked, 'Will you be going home to England soon?'

'Can't tell you that, my love.' He had grinned, feeling the surge of desire running through him. 'Ask me something else.'

She had pretended to scowl. 'This show is going to London next month.' She had given him a small card. 'This is the number to ring.'

He had said bluntly, 'I'd like that.' She had not budged as he had run his fingers up her arm. 'I think we'd be rather good with each other, don't you?'

She had been called away, but had kissed him very quickly on the cheek, her breast brushing his shoulder for just those few extra seconds.

'I think we'd be *perfect*.'

He had returned to the ship, wondering how he was going

to explain the facts of life to Keyes. When he had seen him fidgeting at the top of the gangway, all his resolve had crumbled. After all, he might never make it to London. They could very well get made into mincemeat within the next few days.

He had lied cheerfully, 'She sends her love, Allan. She's a real fine girl.'

It had been worth it to lie. Keyes had looked so pathetically happy.

'She *is*, Pilot! I shall write to her when we get back. Buy her something.'

Aloud Wingate said, 'You do that thing.'

Hillier asked, 'What was that?'

'Nothing. I'm getting bloody old.' He peered at his watch. 'Get ready. The flotilla will be taking up the new course soon. Tell the captain. He'll want to know, although thank God he trusts me.'

'Unlike some, I suppose?'

'You could say that.' Wingate trained his glasses again. 'Some skippers would check the toilet paper used by each watch just to satisfy their officers were not wasteful!'

In the stuffy wheelhouse beneath Wingate's booted feet Able Seaman Jevers leaned on the spokes, the lower half of his face glowing faintly in the compass light. The telegraphsmen lounged nearby, and behind a thick canvas screen he could hear Midshipman Keyes speaking quietly with the navigator's yeoman as they adjusted the vibrating plot table.

What the hell was the doctor up to? Was he trying to discover something about Janice? Or did they think he was so much under strain that he needed special leave? He relaxed slightly, watching the luminous gyro repeater as it ticked a degree off course. That would be a laugh. A nice long leave. He would give a year's pay to see that bloody Yank's face!

'Port ten!' Wingate's voice through the great bell-mouth above his head made him flinch.

'Port ten, sir. Ten of port wheel on.'

'Midships.' He heard feet on the internal ladder. Hot kye for the watchkeepers. 'Steady.'

'Steady, sir. Course zero-three-three.'

'Steer zero-three-zero. And watch your head, Quartermaster!' There was a rasp in Wingate's voice.

'Aye, aye, sir.' Jevers grinned and muttered, 'Bugger you, mate.'

A bosun's mate called, 'Kye up, lads!'

Through the stout canvas curtain Keyes heard the clatter of mugs and tried to keep awake as he stared at the clicking light which marked the ship's course and position on the plot table. Further and further away from land. Like heading out into a desert. He peered at the chart. And God, it was deep. Close on two thousand fathoms. A black, silent, unmoving world. There would be wrecks, too, Right back to—he tried to think what sort of ships would have been in these waters when men first ventured towards the top of the world.

Rigge, the navigator's yeoman, brought two mugs of cocoa from the wheelhouse and smiled to himself as Keyes' head lolled slowly forward on to the chart.

He said, 'I reckon you should go below, sir.'

Keyes shook himself. 'I will. Thanks.'

As he thrust out of the curtain, still holding his mug of cocoa, the yeoman whispered to the bosun's mate, 'Got it bad, Taff. Picked up some party ashore, by the looks of him.'

The other seaman grinned. 'So long as that's all he's picked up, boyo!'

And so with her consorts *Warlock* steamed into the darkness, while within her hull her company slept or stood watch as their roles dictated. Only two were absent, the man who was in hospital for observation, and Badger, the cat. A few minutes before sailing he had been secretly transferred to the repair ship in his basket. He would be waiting for his own ship when they got back. It was safer, everyone agreed. But not to see his belligerent stare from some dark corner or other made more than one sailor feel uneasy.

In his little cabin behind the bridge Drummond sat wedged in his bunk, filling his new pipe and remembering her voice, the touch of her hand. Her husband must be a bloody fool. He rolled over and snatched the phone before it had buzzed for more than two seconds.

'Captain!'

'It's getting light, sir.'

'Already?'

He rubbed his eyes. They felt sore. And they had not even reached Bear Island yet. He yawned.

'I'll come up. Have some coffee brought to the bridge, will you?'

He thrust the pipe into his pocket and stretched his arms. At moments like this he wished he had made the Army his career after all.

11

Side by Side

'SIGNAL from the *Santiago*, sir.' The yeoman of signals had his stocky legs wide apart in order to steady himself and hold his telescope on the nearest oil tanker. '*Come alongside when ready.*'

'Thank you, Yeo.' Drummond watched the *Lomond*'s screws thrashing great gouts of froth as she swung away from the other tanker. 'Acknowledge.'

From first light, when they had taken up their places like customers in a food queue, the destroyers had gone through the tiresome and sometimes dangerous business of fuelling while under way. The two tanker captains were old hands at the game, although their fat, rust-streaked hulls showed plenty of deep scars and dents where naval vessels had found the operation more hazardous than they might have expected.

Drummond lit his pipe and watched Sheridan mustering his men on the forecastle and iron deck below the bridge. It had taken a week to reach this invisible point on the chart, although it felt like a year. It had been hard on nerves and tempers, as rumour followed rumour and all the early excitement of going into action gave way to doubt and open scorn for the far-off planners in Whitehall.

'Port fifteen.'

Drummond heard the halliards squeaking behind him as the signal for oiling shot up to the yard. Like himself, Petty Officer Tucker and his signalmen were glad to be doing something, to see other ships instead of their own tight little group.

Apart from the tankers there was an ugly converted merchantman, described in the manual as a 'fighter catapult ship'. It showed that Admiral Brooks was taking the raid very seriously to provide fighter cover in these early, vital stages. Any prowling Focke-Wulf would have to be seen, caught and shot down before it could radio back to base in Group North that some British naval units were behaving strangely north-west of Bear Island.

'Midships. Steady as you go, Cox'n.'

'Aye, sir.'

Tommy Mangin would be watching the oiler as her length shortened and *Warlock* passed round her broad stern for the approach alongside.

The *Santiago* was heavy and still deep-laden, so that she appeared to be grounded and unmoving, like a detached harbour wall. The uncomfortable swell which was making the slender destroyer lift and plunge without a break, merely rolled along the tanker's fat flank in a continuous wavy line, like the one on Hillier's sleeve as he leaned over the screen, ready to relay any urgent order to the deck.

Seven days of it. Drummond bit his pipe stem and watched the other ship drawing closer. He had almost expected the raid to be cancelled. To hear that for some reason or other their lordships had decided it was no longer even a remote possibility.

'Let her ease off a bit, Cox'n.'

He watched the greasy fenders lowered to take any impact if they got too near, the hoses hoisted on their derricks waiting to be shunted across the narrow strip of water. Too near meant almost certain damage. Too far and the hoses would be torn apart, and valuable time lost in repeating the whole operation. To say nothing of loss of face in front of the other ships.

But the technique was a good one, and had increased the range and use of even the smallest convoy escort from one end of the Atlantic to the other.

He saw the sunlight lying across the hard horizon like bright copper. He shivered, despite his thick coat. It was without warmth, and yet it scored a man's face like hot sand if he stood on watch for too long.

So many miles above the Arctic Circle, so many yet to do before they saw Seydisfjord again. Bear Island was just a blue smudge on the other horizon, a lonely, bitter place which had provided some comfort in the past to beleaguered convoys, or damaged ships trying to rally their strength for the last haul to Murmansk or Archangel. Planes, tanks and supplies for the Russians. It was strange really. They had signed a treaty with

Hitler, had turned their backs on those few who were trying to fight against the Fascism Russia was said to hate. Hitler had invaded their country, none the less, so war dictated that Stalin was to be an ally.

'Slow ahead together.'

He saw a line snaking over from the forecastle, fired by a rifle. That was the chief gunner's mate, P.O. Abbott. If he was still secretly grieving for his dead wife and child, it had not affected his aim.

More cracks, and more lines, until it looked as if a web was growing between the ill-matched hulls.

He was level now with the oiler's ugly bridge and still creeping forward, running a close parallel. One large hose was already rearing up, as if to seek out the stokers without waiting for any guidance.

Spray leapt between the hulls and pattered across the swaying deck plates. In a few more months this area would be gleaming ice again. A place denying shelter when it was most needed. A sea without pity.

The catapult ship would be useless then. For she could only fire off her fighter aircraft. There was no way of getting them back again. The luckless pilot had to wait in his lifejacket after he had jumped from his fighter, and possibly after he had fought with a heavy reconnaissance aircraft, and hope that somebody had seen where he had baled out. And in winter nobody lived in these waters for more than a few minutes.

He glanced quickly at Wingate, and wondered if he was thinking about it. Reliving his own agony in an open boat.

The oiler gave a throaty blast on her siren and both ships settled down side by side, the one rising and plunging across the successive ranks of rollers, the other merely thrusting through them like a battered iron wedge.

Men dashed up and down hauling on tackles, and here and there a more experienced one dashed forward when a junior rating seemed in danger of being hurled over the side into the strip of frothing water as it surged past like a millrace.

Mangin could be relied on to coax the helm whenever it was needed, but a close watch had to be kept on the revolutions.

Drummond had taken on fuel at sea many times, and found that he could think of other things and still not miss any of the sea's little tricks. It was like being cast out of the normal world. The occasional news from Sicily was unreal and did not touch them. The daily inflow of signals relating to everything from U-boat movements to escort rendezvous codes meant nothing at all. They would go on steaming and refuelling forever, and never see land again.

Hillier said, 'The first hose is made fast, sir.' He sounded excited. 'The chief has just given the thumbs-up!'

'Good.'

It was something when the sight of a filthy fuel hose had become more gripping than the real chance of being killed in a Norwegian fjord.

'Coffee, sir?'

Owles had appeared on the bridge, looking out of place in his white coat which he always wore when working in his pantry. He shivered.

'Bit parky.'

He went off again after wedging the pot between some rolled signal flags.

As usual he had put some rum in it. Drummond could feel it in his stomach like fire. What would he do without Owles?

He snapped, 'Tell number one to slack away that forrard line. It's sagging badly on the tanker's hull. It'll carry away otherwise.'

Sheridan would not like being told, but he should have seen it for himself. Just lately he had seemed more withdrawn, less ready to talk about everyday matters. Jealousy? Of the girl, the promotion, or of everything which he still imagined should be his?

He saw Sheridan turn and squint up at the bridge as the message was relayed to him. He waved one gloved hand, but that was all.

A bosun's mate called, 'W/T have a signal from Admiralty, sir.'

'Tell the doc to get it decoded right away.'

Vaughan may have discovered nothing about Jevers, but he had proved very useful with the secret codes. He had the mind for it.

The flotilla leader had her own coding officer, one of Captain (D)'s extra privileges. He was very quick at his job, for within minutes the bosun's mate was saying, 'W/T reports that Captain (D) is calling you up on the radio telephone, sir.'

Drummond gestured at Wingate. 'You speak to him. I'm not going to walk away from this little lot.'

Wingate grinned. 'Trying to catch us out, I expect.'

Drummond watched the great looped fuel hoses. It must be very urgent for Beaumont to get so excited. He knew *Warlock* was taking on fuel, and would never expect her captain to hand over control under any circumstances.

The yeoman of signals pulled the little brass tube up through the pipe from the W/T office. He said, 'Doctor's getting faster, sir.'

Drummond did not turn. 'Read it, Sub. Over here.'

Hillier took the rolled signal and lurched across the unsteady deck where Drummond clung to the voice-pipes.

'From Admiralty, sir. *Intelligence reports that battlecruiser Moltke has been seen in Norwegian port of Trondheim. She has accompanying escort of destroyers, numbers unknown. Aerial reconnaissance terminated by fog. Signal ends, sir.'*

Wingate came back frowning. 'Captain Beaumont wanted to draw your attention to that signal, sir.'

Drummond watched him. 'Well?'

'He said something like, it'll make no difference.' He frowned again, trying to remember the exact words. 'Or, it *can* make no difference.'

'I see.'

He did not. What the hell had got into Beaumont? Perhaps the German ship and what she had done to the *Conqueror* had so affected him, the very fact she was in Norway, and apparently in good shape, was more than he could bear.

'He wants you to call him up when you stop oiling, sir.'

'Very well.'

But when *Warlock* completed her replenishment and idled clear of the heavy tanker, Beaumont was quite normal over the R/T.

'Well, I thought you should give it your attention, too, Keith. We have to think of everything. Don't want that bloody ship coming amongst us without any warning, eh?'

Drummond had already thought about that, although there seemed little reason for more German units coming north. *Un-*

less they knew. And the flotilla would be without radar on the final approach, to cut the chance of detection to a minimum.

Sheridan came to the bridge. 'All secured, sir. No casualties, except one seaman with a cut finger.'

'Good.' He pulled the signal from his pocket. 'Read this.'

Sheridan's features were controlled. 'So she's back, sir.' When he looked up his eyes were hard. 'That bloody *Moltke*!'

'I don't think she'll be anywhere near us. But in case there are some extra destroyers about, we'd better be on our toes. Pass the word to Guns for me.'

'Look, sir.' Sheridan stood closer to the chair, excluding the others on the bridge. 'I've been thinking about this operation. If anything happened . . .'

Drummond asked quietly, 'To me, is that what you mean?'

'Well, yes.' Sheridan looked uncertain. 'Would I have to retain the position of half-leader?'

'No. Don't worry about that, Number One. When we get to grips with the enemy it will be every ship for herself. There's no other way in a close action.'

'I see, sir. I hope you didn't mind my mentioning it.'

'Not at all.' He was seeing him in a different light again. He asked quietly, 'I thought you *wanted* promotion?'

'Yes, I do. But not in the middle of a damned battle, sir!'

He smiled. 'I'll bear it in mind, Number One, believe me!'

The yeoman shouted, '*Ventnor*'s hauled down her pendant, sir! She was the last alongside!'

Drummond stared across at *Lomond*, at the diamond-bright light which winked from her bridge.

Tucker said, '*Take up station as before*, sir.' He was breathing heavily. '*Ships in column form close order.*'

'Acknowledge.' Drummond looked at Sheridan. 'Next stop Norway.'

Sheridan smiled tightly. 'Looks like it, sir.'

Drummond felt the navigating officer watching from the compass platform. 'Take her round, Pilot. Course and speed as directed by leader.'

'Aye, aye, sir.'

Warlock gave a jaunty toot to the two oilers and then swung away in a wide curve, her consorts closing in behind her, their funnel smoke lying on the sea's face like a greasy curtain.

'From *Santiago*, sir.' Tucker lowered his glass. '*Good hunting.*'

'Make.' Drummond watched the signal lamps winking up and down the two small columns. 'To *Santiago*. Will be very, repeat *very* pleased to see you again.'

It was a game. He often wondered if the enemy wasted a similar amount of time with playful signals. Perhaps they took their war more seriously.

'Course is one-seven-five, sir.' The light blinked again. 'Revolutions for fifteen knots.'

'Very well.'

He settled down in the chair and stared at the horizon. It was mistier now. And vaguely menacing.

Part one was over. Part two was about to begin.

'This mist is like nothing I've ever seen, sir.' Wingate's voice was hushed, as if he was afraid someone beyond *Warlock*'s corkscrewing bows might hear.

'Yes.'

Drummond tried to sit back in his chair, to retain an outward show of calm, no matter what he actually felt. In the strange half-light, as the ship moved slowly towards a darker horizon, great patches of mist eddied past the bridge, clinging momentarily to fittings and signal halliards before gliding away astern like demented spirits.

Close on either quarter, two other destroyers, *Waxwing* and *Ventnor*, were still just visible, ghostly shadows, blotted out occasionally by the mist, only to reappear knife-sharp again like watchful guardians.

Out of sight astern *Lomond* and the rest of the group followed discreetly, waiting to give support or cover a retreat if something went wrong.

Drummond heard a voice snap out a reprimand in the gloom as somebody dropped a metal object on the deck. It seemed like a thunderclap. The ship was at action stations, and would be until the operation was over or cancelled.

Wingate added, 'The nearest point of the Norwegian coast is one hundred miles ahead, sir. Give or take a foot.'

'I'm glad to know you are so confident.'

Drummond raised his glasses and swore under his breath as a sharp movement off the port bow showed itself as a tiny cat's-paw along the crest of a deep swell. Once, radar had been a joke. Now, with everything shut down, he realised how much they had all come to depend on it. This was like wearing blinkers.

But it was the moment of decision. When they would know. By dawn they would be hitting the Norwegian fjord, or running like naughty boys for open water and Kimber's air-cover.

Hillier said quickly, 'Asdic reports strong echo at Green four-five, sir!'

Drummond peered at his luminous watch. It was almost midnight.

'Get ready, Yeoman!'

Suppose it was a U-boat?

'Asdic reports submarine surfacing, sir!'

'Object on the starboard bow!' The lookout's voice was cracked.

'Stop engines!'

Even one hundred miles out from the enemy occupied coast it was no time to make unnecessary signals. The destroyers would see *Warlock's* dying wash. It would be all they needed. Unless something had gone wrong, of course, and it was a U-boat.

As the muted engines died away and the sea noise intruded into the open bridge, Drummond heard the muffled roar of compressed air as the submarine blew her main ballast and lurched to the surface.

The yeoman said, 'There it is, sir! The signal!'

'Acknowledge.'

He held his breath as Tucker used a tiny flashlight no bigger than his fist. It was hard to accept that any submarine could be friendly. He still half expected the rattle of cannon fire, or the deafening explosion of a torpedo inside *Warlock's* guts.

'Pass the word. Boat-handling party on the double! And *no noise*!'

Feet padded along the deck, and he thought he heard Sheridan speaking a man's name in the darkness.

It must be worse for the submarine commander, he thought. On the surface in enemy waters, trimmed well up so that he could launch his little dinghy, he might have expected an even greater trap. German patrol ships instead of *Warlock* and her companions.

'Boat approaching to starboard, sir.'

'Very well. Tell the lookouts to keep alert.'

He saw the small dark blob moving up and down across the deep swells, the paddles making white arrowheads as they lunged at the water. A heaving line, hands groping for the scrambling net, and then the dinghy was already heading back to her parent vessel with barely a pause.

More dragging seconds until he heard Sheridan guiding the newcomers into the blacked-out bridge. They groped towards him like blind men.

One said, 'I'm Archer.' He turned and beckoned to his companion. 'Commander Egil Lyngstad, Royal Norwegian Navy.'

They both looked like fishermen, but stank of submarines. Diesel and stale cabbage.

The one called Archer said, 'It's on, sir. Dawn attack. The Norwegian underground are briefed and ready to cripple the local detection unit which might have otherwise interfered. It's not much of a unit, and is connected mainly with the local anti-submarine nets, and has a sizeable R.D.F. set for surface and air cover. The local Jerry commandant relies more on patrols and the two air bases at Tromso and Banak. On the face of it he's sitting pretty, and this will be the first time that the underground has tried anything this big.'

Drummond looked at Wingate. 'Resume course and speed.'

The tall Norwegian said quietly, 'They will succeed, Captain. I have been working with the local group leaders for several months. They have waited and prayed for such a chance to hit the German!'

He spoke excellent English, but sounded drained to a point of exhaustion.

The deck trembled into life again, and the other destroyers faded slightly into the mist. Faintly above the muted fans Drummond heard the dull hiss of inrushing water as the unseen submarine dived back to her proper element.

He said, 'We are in your hands, Commander Lyngstad.' *In more ways than one.* '*Warlock* will lead as arranged. The main group will follow through the channel.'

The Norwegian nodded gravely. 'That is good. I know the channel well, of course. It is a dangerous one, and therefore a double protection for the enemy.' He added harshly, 'Until now.'

Wingate said, 'I've got the chart here, sir. I've marked the arranged approach as far as Vannoy Island and Hammer Fjord, after that . . .'

The tall man laid one hand on his shoulder. 'After *that*, my young friend, it will be up to the enemy, eh?'

'Take him to the chart table, Pilot. No sense in scrabbling about under your damned screen.' He waited until they had left and said, 'He seems a capable character.'

Archer nodded. 'A fine man. The Germans have a price on his head, but he goes back time and time again. He has lost his family. They shot them as part of a reprisal for a German soldier getting killed. Afterwards, the local commandant discovered that the German had killed himself by accident. Drunk probably.' He sounded angry.

'I must call up Captain (D) on the R/T. He'll be itching to know the verdict.'

The man called Archer said, 'Make it brief then. You never know who's about in these waters.'

Drummond hurried to the Asdic cabinet and groped for the handset.

'W/T office. Get me the leader.'

Beaumont must have been hanging on the line. When he heard the codeword, Lipread, he merely said, 'As we planned, Keith. Phase two. You lead.'

Drummond returned to the open bridge, suddenly very alert and on edge. He had anticipated a last-minute change round. Beaumont had hinted at it often enough. *Lomond* in the lead, with *Warlock* covering the entrance and watching over the mine-laden *Whirlpool*. It was probably a right decision. If anything happened to the first ships into the fjord, a change of tactics would be needed, and double quick.

Archer said, 'I'm with Military Intelligence, by the way.' He grinned. 'And am I glad to be in a British ship again!'

'I'll try and keep it that way.' Drummond hesitated. 'If we catch a packet, I hope you've got the right papers?'

Archer patted his jacket. 'Of course.' He grinned. 'NAAFI manager.'

Drummond found he had become completely relaxed, remote from any sort of tension. 'What else?'

The Norwegian came back with Wingate. He was holding a mug of cocoa.

'All arranged, Captain. We meet a fishing boat a mile or so out. We must leave the exact position to her skipper. An old friend. He will guide us past the point. The rest will be, er . . .'

Wingate remarked, 'Busy?'

'Yes. *Very* busy.'

Drummond asked him quietly, 'Do you have papers to explain *your* presence on board, if we get into trouble?'

He shrugged. 'I will not be taken. Have no fear of that.' He sounded weary. 'One more risk is no matter. Not if it means a victory.'

Sheridan crossed the bridge. 'Any orders, sir?'

'No. We remain at action stations. But see if you can rustle up some hot drinks for the lads. Go round the ship yourself. Have a word with as many of them as you can. Especially the green ones. You remember what it was like for you. The first time. The grand slam.'

'I will.' Sheridan turned up his collar. 'Funny about Captain (D) though.'

'Funny?'

'Keeping well back, I'd have thought, sir.' He pointed above the screen. 'Mist is getting worse. Met reports said there could be a pea-souper closer inshore. Still, I suppose he knows what he's doing.'

Drummond said as he made to leave, 'And take care, Number One.' What she had said. 'No heroics, just a good, clean job.'

Sheridan showed his teeth. 'I don't know about *clean*, sir. But thanks. And the same to you.' He was gone.

Drummond settled himself in the chair. A quick time check, although he had already seen the watch in his mind.

'Here we go, Pilot. Revs for twenty knots.'

He heard him speaking into the voice-pipe to the wheelhouse, knew the other ships astern were waiting to follow. Like a bloody cavalry charge. Just over four hours to go. Provided the poor old girl didn't shake apart as she sliced over the swell. But the sea was smoother now. That could mean that the fog was drawing nearer.

Drummond felt the deck shudder and then begin to vibrate more steadily under the chair. Faster, faster, the old screws slashing the sea into a sharp-edged line which was cut short astern by the swirling mist.

He pictured the destroyers on *Warlock*'s quarters. *Waxwing*, commanded by the flotilla's most junior skipper, Lieutenant James Lovat, R.N.. Son of a rich brewer. Young, but deadly in a pitched battle. On the other quarter, Lieutenant-Commander Bill Selkirk in his *Ventnor*, a tough reservist, a professional sailor in peacetime. The only one to voice doubt at Drummond's action which had left *Warden* to perish with most of her company. They had worked very little together, but Selkirk had a reputation for getting things done. The hard way.

Still the revolutions mounted, and he could imagine Galbraith in his rattling, screeching world below the waterline. Watching his gauges, shouting or singing unheard in the din.

And Rankin above the bridge with his fire control team, and Vaughan sitting with his gleaming instruments and his effeminate S.B.A. Noakes in the T.S., Keyes at the plot table, young Tyson with the secondary armament aft. And Sheridan. He would be keeping the ship afloat if things went very wrong. Or sitting in this chair if a shell put paid to the *Warlock*'s captain.

But all in all it was a good team, he thought. Perhaps better than average. He smiled to himself. Each individual captain would be saying just that. He had to, if he hoped to stay sane.

The nearer they drew to land, the more the Norwegian officer seemed to come alive. He stood beside Drummond's chair, gripping the rail below the screen with both hands, his head moving occasionally from bow to bow, as if he could smell the approaching channel.

'Depth?'

'Thirty-seven fathoms, sir.' Hillier bobbed down to await the next question or command.

Drummond did not look at his watch. He could *feel* the dawn probing up across the port bow. Apart from the feeling, it was such an unreal situation that the Norwegian's confidence was reassuring, to say the least. They were dashing through thick, milky fog at twenty knots, with nothing to guide them but Lyngstad's unwavering skill and local knowledge.

'Bring her round a point to port, please.'

In the strange light he looked like the statue of an old Norseman. Tall and gaunt, with a ragged beard thrusting above his fisherman's jersey.

'Course one-four-zero, sir.'

The Norwegian said calmly, 'My friend's boat will be appearing any minute now, I think.'

Drummond did not say anything. He felt it might break the spell and leave them all helpless. He hoped to God that the other ships astern were still on station. For with shallowing water to starboard, and the end of the minefield to port, any deviation could be final.

Lyngstad added, 'Be clearing soon, too. But the work will be—'

He swung round as a lookout snapped, 'Ship, sir! Fine on port bow!'

'*Half speed!*' Lyngstad waved his arms wildly as the grubby little trawler loomed out of the mist. 'I *knew* he would be here!'

The trawler was already gathering way, her hull pirouetting round as she swerved to take over the lead. If her skipper had been shocked to see the destroyer dashing straight for him, he gave no hint as he handled the little boat with apparent panache.

Archer was standing on the port gratings. 'The enemy's R.D.F. station is over there, high up on Vannoy Island. Our friends ashore must have done their work all right. We'd have had all hell down on us otherwise, fog or no bloody fog!'

'Ten fathoms, sir.'

'Good.' Lyngstad looked at Drummond. 'Tell your helmsman to keep as close to the fishing boat as he can.'

Wingate stooped over the voice-pipe as a messenger called, 'X gun report they can see *Ventnor* following astern, sir.' He grinned with sudden relief.

Wingate looked up. 'Did you think we were all alone? Tch, tch!'

Drummond felt the movement of cold, misty air against his face. Lyngstad was probably right about the fog clearing. He made a sudden decision.

'Hoist battle ensigns, Yeoman!'

Lyngstad drew his gaze from the small patch of clear water ahead of the bows and said simply, 'I have a flag, Captain, I was hoping . . .' He did not finish it, but pulled the rolled flag from under his reefer.

Drummond said, 'Yeoman. Run up this one beside ours.'

He watched the white ensigns breaking out on the masts, the other, smaller flag, red with its blue cross, rising firmly to the upper yard. He saw the Norwegian's face and guessed what this small gesture meant to him.

Lyngstad said, 'Now I know we will succeed today! Thank you.'

The Norwegian flag licked out abeam, and it was like a signal.

Very slowly at first, and then with gathering haste, like a first curtain, the mist started to edge clear, laying bare the tall green side of an island, a strip of glittering channel and a solitary, anchored patrol boat.

Lyngstad said harshly, 'She is yours now, Captain!'

Drummond gripped the rail. *'Open fire!'*

12

In Deadly Earnest

It seemed to take an eternity before the two forward guns responded to the tinny fire gong. They recoiled on their springs almost together, the double explosion echoing and smashing back from the nearest land as if they, and not the anchored patrol boat, were under attack.

Drummond held his glasses jammed against his eyes, feeling the deck buck, his ears taking in Rankin's voice across his intercom, the startled cry from a lookout as the explosions shook the bridge.

'Range oh-one-oh! *Shoot!*'

Again the guns spat out their tongues of flame, and Drummond saw a tall waterspout rise directly alongside the little vessel, another burst skyward far beyond.

'Down one hundred! *Shoot!*'

The next pair of shells smashed into the vessel together. She must have been built entirely of wood. Timber and jagged fragments were hurled into the air, and the oily water of the fjord pockmarked with scattered debris. There was fire, too, long plumes of it licking from abaft her small, boxlike bridge, where a few frantic figures were emerging like frightened insects.

Drummond shouted, 'Secondary armament! Fire when ready!'

Immediately, as if anticipating the order, the bridge Oerlikons rattled into life. Drummond saw their lazy lines of scarlet tracer lifting away ahead of *Warlock*'s bows, before criss-crossing and intermingling like hammers of hell across the stricken patrol boat. The twenty-millimetre shells completed what the heavier ones had begun. Sparks and flames enveloped her from stem to stern, and while here and there a forlorn swimmer was trying to splash away from the listing hull, others were being forced into the inferno between decks under a fusilade of tracer and metal.

'Port ten!' Drummond moved his glasses slightly. 'Midships. Steady as you go!'

He heard Rankin yell, 'Cease firing! Shift target Green four-five! Range double-oh-eight!'

From somewhere astern he heard the jarring crash of gunfire as the other destroyers followed through the narrow entrance to the fjord. Shells were exploding everywhere, the results mostly hidden in the retreating mist.

He saw Rankin's new target even as the first gunlayer shouted, 'Layer on!'

It was a high-sided freighter of some five thousand tons. From what he could see in the drifting mist and gunsmoke, he guessed she was the depot ship. There were small derricks lining her main deck, and alongside he could just make out the outline of a moored pontoon.

Lyngstad shouted, 'The submarine tender! Many of the crews under training live in her!' He was wildly oblivious to the crashing detonations, to the harsh rattle of automatic weapons which made thought a painful effort.

'Shoot!'

The four-inch shells made bright red eyes in the ship's side, and then, as they exploded deep within the hull, deck fittings and whole sections of steel were hurled high into the air.

Someone was firing back from her high bridge with a machine gun. Drummond's mind recorded its impartial rattle, the almost gentle sound of a Spandau. Then he felt the impact of bullets below the bridge, the banshee whine of ricochets, before another shell slammed into the depot ship and ignited either a paint store or a locker full of signal flares.

Warlock lurched drunkenly and then picked up speed again, and as he glanced over the screen Drummond watched the bow section of the smashed patrol boat bouncing away in a welter of spray and tiny splintered fragments. A man who had been clinging to a broken hatch-cover was plucked away and down into *Warlock's* churning screws, his mouth wide in a silent scream as he vanished into the white froth.

He snapped to Tucker, 'Make a signal to *Waxwing*. *Attack with torpedoes!*'

'Sir!' Hillier was staggering across the swaying gratings. 'Midget submarines on the port bow!' His face was like chalk. 'Must be a hundred of them!'

Drummond swung round, his eyes and mind recording everything in the same second. Tucker's lamp shuttering his signal to Lovat's ship which was careering across *Ventnor*'s stern. The strange, sharp-edged slipways of raw concrete which had been built for the sole purpose of launching and training the German crews. Up, partly hidden by camouflaged nets and low trees, he saw the long huts, workshops and stores which had made an idea into a reality which would soon have been used against the Allies. He recalled in the same instant the dead crewman in the Falmouth mortuary. His slitted eyes. The girl who had leaned against his slab without even a flicker of interest.

He yelled, 'Depth-charge attack! Minimum setting!'

Wingate shouted into the handset and then added, 'Shallow there, sir! No more than twenty fathoms!'

Someone else had finally been roused from his bed ashore. Bullets made thin, harmless-looking weaves of tracer as they probed above the mist and smoke, the tiny balls of fire so deceptively slow until they reached their apex and then lashed down on the advancing ships with the fury of bandsaws.

Further inland he heard duller thuds, grenades or mines, he did not know. Only that the Norwegian underground were doing their part, pinning down German outposts as they were awakened by the frightening roar and thunder of exploding shells.

Drummond seized Wingate's arm. 'Tell the yeoman to warn the other ships to keep clear!'

He ducked as a glass panel was shattered from the screen. He felt tiny pointers stinging his cheek, the taste of blood on his lips.

The two after guns were bearing now on the depot ship and other installations nearby. The slender barrels rocked back on their mountings, and once Rankin yelled wildly, 'Look at that one go up! A hit, the bloody bastards!'

Even in all this Drummond's mind noted that he had not known Rankin to lose his show of calm so completely.

'Depth-charges ready, sir!'

He craned over the screen, seeing an Oerlikon gunner directly below him, strapped by his harness, while his gloved hand beat an urgent tattoo on the breech as his assistant hoisted a full magazine into place. Right aft he saw the crouching shapes of the depth-charge parties, bent double like athletes as they tried to stay away from bright sparks which were being struck from the metal decks by an invisible machine gun.

'Fire!'

The port charge was hurled from its thrower in a puff of smoke to fall within a few feet of the outer trot of moored submarines. A squad of soldiers suddenly came around the nearest building, rifles at the high port, their helmets bobbing up and down as they skidded to a halt at the sight of a destroyer surging past the slipways with every weapon firing.

The depth-charge exploded violently, shaking *Warlock* from stern to bow like a terrier mauling a rat. Men fell cursing and yelling as she swayed dizzily away from the blast, and almost before they had recovered, a pattern of charges rolled from her stern and blasted the water a hundred feet higher than the mainmast truck.

Tucker was yelling, 'Signal from *Ventnor*, sir! *More gunfire astern!*'

'Captain (D) coming in to support us.' Wingate dashed some fragments of grit and flaked paint from his face. 'About bloody time!'

Drummond kept his eyes on the creeping, dodging figures which were darting through the smoke towards the remaining submarines. The crews which had been berthed ashore would be trying to save their craft. As any trained sailor would. They must be stopped.

'Slow ahead both engines!' He coughed in a down-draught of greasy smoke from the funnel. 'Tell Guns to shift all he's got to that target!'

A deafening roar came at them across the water and bounded against the hull like a living thing. Through the trapped smoke and haze within the fjord he saw a spreading sheen of red and gold, spilling out until it had covered every inch of water in a fierce, throbbing glow.

'Torpedo attack completed, sir.'

Lovat would have enjoyed that. Each of his three torpedoes must have made a direct hit on the depot ship. At that range it would need an idiot to miss.

Even through the roar of gunfire, the echo of Lovat's own

salvo, they heard the groan of fracturing plates and frames, the eager thunder of inrushing water.

Wingate crouched over the compass, with Lyngstad shouting directions into his ear.

Occasionally the hull jerked to a blow from some well hidden cannon ashore, and high above the bridge the air seemed to be constantly alive with tracer and shrieking steel.

Astern, Selkirk had manœuvred across their wake again, and was pouring a devastating fire into the jumble of midget submarines. It was impossible to tell the difference between those which had been capsized by the depth-charge attack and those which, if handled properly, might still escape. Shells were bursting everywhere. On land, in the water and dead in the middle of the low black hulls.

Figures ran amidst the bursts of smoke and fire like demented beings, others were plucked away by the machine guns' scythe of tracer which swept back and forth with relentless efficiency. The guns cut down running men and wounded alike, picked up smoking corpses and tossed them about like bundles of bloody rags before moving on again. Several huts were ablaze, and from one came the crackle of exploding small-arms ammunition until a direct hit blew the building into pieces.

All the bridge party ducked and looked up as a twin whistle, sharp and abbreviated, ripped overhead, followed immediately by a violent bang. The hull gave a long shiver, and the water alongside danced in tiny white feathers of spray.

'Shore battery!' Lyngstad had to shout before anyone looked at him. 'They must have been able to repulse our people!'

Again the shriek of shells, and an even louder detonation. The first fall of shot was clearly visible. Two great oval necklaces of salt spray where two shells had burst side by side. Like huge, melancholy eyes.

Drummond shouted, 'Call up Captain (D). Tell him I require support *now*!'

Again the shells ripped above the vibrating mastheads and the streaming flags. Almost flat trajectory. The guns must be firing from a site on the island directly abeam.

Rankin was snapping, 'Shift target! Red eight-oh! Range oh-one-five! Commence . . . commence . . . commence!'

The four guns were swinging round, their hooded crews work-

ing their wheels so fast that hands and metal where blurred
into one.

'Shoot!'

Rankin again. 'No! It must be behind those trees!'

More crashes, and a louder bang which rebounded into the
lower hull like a club on an oil drum.

Hillier called, '*Waxwing* has been bracketed, sir!' He gasped.
'She's slewing round!'

Drummond ran across the bridge, his boots crunching on
broken glass as he peered through the long trailers of smoke.
Waxwing had received more than a straddle. He could see the
deadly pattern of splinter holes at the break of her forecastle,
the larger smoking puncture right below B gun. The gun was
pointing at the sky, its crew strewn around it like old clothes.
He saw thin lines of scarlet running down from the dead gun
crew, and a single figure dragging itself towards the ladder, its
legs ablaze like torches.

Several of the men on her bridge must have been killed or
wounded, too. At the vital moment as she had made to turn after
Ventnor. She had charged out of control to run full aground on
a hard shoulder, and was even now heeling over, showing her
decks, the unmanned torpedo tubes, empty and pointing abeam
where they had hit the enemy depot ship.

'Shoot!'

'A hit, sir!' The lookout was yelling wildly as a whole line of
dark trees burst into flame and another explosion ran down the
hillside like molten fire.

'Too late for *Waxwing*!' Archer, the man from intelligence,
was trying to light a cigarette, but the ship and all else was shaking so badly he looked like the victim of shellshock.

Drummond saw the small Norwegian fishing boat was already
churning towards the grounded destroyer, small figures waiting
with heaving lines to haul the survivors clear. Poor Lovat. He
loved that clapped-out old ship.

Hillier was shouting into a voice-pipe, one hand over his ear.
He said dazedly, 'W/T reports that *Lomond* is remaining outside
the fjord, sir! There has been a signal from Admiralty. *Moltke*
is out of Trondheim. Probably left yesterday and heading north.'

Wingate said, 'Jesus! That's all we need!'

A bright glare joined with a single explosion, and when Drummond looked again at *Waxwing* he saw that the fishing boat had been cut in half by a heavy shell, probably from another battery. She was sinking and ablaze, the fires reaching out and spreading along the stranded destroyer.

Tucker said, 'From *Ventnor*, sir. *Am taking off survivors.*'

The deck shook as Rankin's guns fired again and yet again. The hillside was covered in smoke and blazing trees, but to seek out and destroy a well-sited shore battery was almost impossible.

He said, 'Half ahead. Take her to the end of the fjord.'

His mind was cringing, rebelling against the panorama of shell-bursts and crackling trees, of bobbing flotsam which parted across *Warlock*'s stem. All he could understand was that Beaumont had decided to stay out of the fight with the bulk of the flotilla. Because *Moltke* might be even now steaming round the next headland. And what if she did? Did he think the flotilla could survive against her for more than minutes?

Lyngstad was shouting, 'Just another mile, Captain! You'll see the fuel dump at the foot of the hillside!'

Drummond snatched up a handset. 'Guns, this is the captain. In a moment you will sight the main target. Keep shooting at it, no matter what.'

'Understood.'

Drummond raised his glasses and studied *Ventnor* as she altered course diagonally above the hidden bar which had caught Lovat's ship. There was smoke everywhere, but he could see figures floundering against Selkirk's scrambling nets, others swimming independently amongst corpses in lifejackets and the telltale spurts of machine-gun bullets.

A great glowing eye glittered in *Ventnor*'s side and expanded to a longer array of splinter gashes. But every one of her guns was angled towards the land, and she was maintaining rapid fire, despite her inner hurt. More shells exploded near her, hurling up tall waterspouts which seemed to take an age to fall. Each time she was still there, the work going on as before. But there were more splinter holes. Fewer men helping to haul aboard *Waxwing*'s survivors.

'Target in sight! Red oh-five. Range oh-two-five.'

'Shoot!'

Drummond clung to the screen as flaked paint and rust flew

up from the detonations. He could not see the target at all, even with his glasses.

'*Ventnor's* under way again, sir!' A signalman was pointing vaguely into the fog of gunsmoke. 'She's following us!'

Drummond nodded, his throat raw with shouting and coughing smoke. A stronger eddy of wind cleared a narrow road which ran almost parallel with *Warlock's* course, and he saw two trucks and a car blazing fiercely, some uniformed corpses close by, and the bright glitter of automatic fire higher up the hillside.

Lyngstad seemed satisfied. 'Our people are hitting them hard, too!'

Wingate pushed against him. 'Time to alter course, sir.'

'Yes.' Lyngstad had to drag his eyes from the ambushed patrol. 'You steer east now, towards Arnoy Island, there you will alter course once more to the north-west channel, and open water.'

A tank had appeared on the end of the road and was training its turret towards the hidden Resistance men, when its commander must have sighted the destroyers in the fjord below him. Before he could come to a decision *Ventnor's* forward guns opened up on him, hurling the turret one way and the rest of the tank down and down into the deep water below.

Archer said breathlessly, 'Probably the only duel between tank and ship!'

Drummond felt the Norwegian's hand gripping his arm like steel. He needed no words, for as Rankin's second salvo ploughed into the prescribed piece of land the whole bank of green and brown seemed to fall apart in a torrent of blazing fuel.

Drummond kept his eyes on the spreading wall of fire, but said harshly, 'Ask *Ventnor* if she can maintain full speed.'

He was thinking of the next part. The dash through the wider fjord and out into open water again.

'From *Ventnor*, sir. *Just say the word.*' The lights were blinking again like cats' eyes through the funnelling smoke. '*Have recovered eighty survivors. Lovat killed.*'

'Acknowledge.'

He looked at Wingate, seeing the deep lines of strain around his eyes and mouth.

'Now. Take her round.'

'Port fifteen. *Steady*. Steer zero-nine-zero.'

Warlock swayed upright again and headed towards the next

198

blur of land. Hundreds of eyes must have been watching, but apart from a few hurrying soldiers on the nearest spur of headland, there was not a living soul in sight.

'Steady on zero-nine-zero, sir.'

Drummond nodded. The stored fuel was still flooding into the calmer water at the head of the fjord. Fuel for *Tirpitz* and *Scharnhorst*, for Hitler's tanks and lorries. The very stuff of the whole war machine.

Hillier yelled, 'Those soldiers, sir! I think there's a mobile gun—'

Drummond snatched up the handset. 'Guns! Shift target! Mobile gun at Red four-five!'

Then the world seemed to come apart, like a picture being ripped into meaningless fragments. No noise, and little feeling beyond a great, blanketing pressure.

Wingate was the first to recover, and tried to drag himself to the voice-pipe. He was speaking aloud, but could hear nothing at all.

'Bridge— Wheelhouse!' The smoke was getting thicker. Blotting out everything. He could not even breathe. 'Send help. *Direct hit!*'

Then he rolled over and fell against Archer. He had just time to record that Archer still retained the unlit cigarette in his mouth, even though most of his body below the waist was like pulp. Only then did he fall unconscious.

Keyes clung to the plot table with all his strength as the bridge rang and trembled to the crash of gunfire. Although he had heard guns before, he had never dreamed it could go on like this. No sort of obvious control or objective, just an unending stream of intermingled sounds and voices. From above and below, from pipes and microphones. It was like the worst part of a nightmare, except that here there was no escape, no reprieve.

The navigator's yeoman blinked at him through a film of falling paint flakes from the deckhead, his face set in a wild grin.

'Not like they tell you it's goin' to be, is it, sir?' He looked slightly mad. Desperate.

Keyes shook his head as the plot table gave a violent shiver and the glass top cracked into several pieces. He groped for the voice-pipe.

'I'll tell the bridge it's out of action.'

He saw Rigge's hand on his wrist and heard him say hoarsely, 'Leave it, sir! They've got enough trouble up top by the sound of it!'

The heavy canvas curtain which separated the rest of the wheelhouse from the plot table bucked and heaved as if alive and in torment. Keyes could hear the familiar creak of the spokes going this way and that, the occasional jingle of telegraphs as speed was increased or reduced to order. The wheelhouse party said little, and only cursed and gasped as splinters cracked against the sides, or an extra loud explosion burst nearby and seemed to suck every bit of air from their confined, deafening world.

Keyes tried to think of Georgina, imagined her close against him, her eyes welcoming and a little in awe as he took her in his arms. But it was hard to keep her in his mind, harder to hold on to his wits.

The coxswain was shouting, 'By God, I've 'ad a bloody jugful of this lot!'

Then came the bang. It seemed to come from right beside the canvas curtain, blasting away reason, overwhelming in its intensity. The whole bridge rocked over as if tearing adrift, and when Keyes opened his eyes he could see nothing, could barely draw breath in the volume of choking smoke.

He had gone blind! Terror, despair, the need to find help, all swept through him as he rolled over, clawing with his hands until he realised that the blindness was caused by the big curtain. The blast, or whatever it was, had wrapped it round him and Rigge, bundling them in the wheelhouse corner like packages in a shop.

As he fought it away and staggered to his feet, he could barely stop himself from screaming.

The light through the steel shutters revealed a mercifully small picture across the fallen bodies, but it was enough to show the great spreading pattern of blood, the way one of the men was glaring at him, pleading in silence, the eyes dying even as he stared at them.

'Get up, Rigge!'

He turned, terrified, hearing a disembodied voice calling, 'Send help! *Direct hit!*'

Then he realised that Rigge was not moving, that his skull

had been smashed against the steel side and crushed like an egg-shell. One eye was still open, amazed, hostile. The rest was gone in the force of the blast.

Keyes clung to the shattered plot, retching helplessly, trying to stop from bursting into tears.

He wanted to call her name, but when he found his voice he said brokenly, 'Oh, Mother! Mother, what shall I do?'

A tattered apparition slipped through the shaft of smoky light and grabbed his arm. It was Mangin, although how he had survived it was impossible to know.

'Get up top! The bridge is a bloody potmess!' The coxswain seemed to realise that Keyes was on the verge of complete breakdown and added roughly, 'Come on, son, jump about. You can manage. I'll try an' sort this lot out.'

A man groaned in the darkness. It was Jevers, pinned beneath a broken locker, but apparently unhurt. He sounded dazed as he croaked, 'Christ, 'Swain, are we done for?'

'Take the wheel!'

Mangin stepped deftly above a gaping corpse and peered at the compass. It was intact and ticking quietly amidst the death and despair.

''Old 'er at due east, lad.' Mangin was already groping for a telephone beside the door. 'I'm goin' to call Jimmy th' One.'

Keyes knocked off the clips and staggered over the coaming and into a seemingly blinding sunlight. An Oerlikon gunner was hanging in his harness, gyrating jerkily as the ship plunged over the water, his face set in its last mask of agony, his shoulders smouldering from the impact of splinters.

Keyes pulled himself up the ladder, dreading what he might see. Shells exploded nearby, and once he was almost knocked from the ladder by a wall of falling water. It tasted more of cordite than salt.

He raised himself into the open bridge and peered round through half-slitted eyes, terrified, sick and helpless. He saw a figure moving away from the compass platform and dragging itself towards the voice-pipes. It was the captain.

Keyes ran to him, his eyes brimming with tears, blind even to the grotesque thing with the unlit cigarette in its mouth, or Hillier face-down on the deck across a bloodied signalman, of Tucker sitting with his back against the flag-locker, his hands interlaced across his stomach and the crimson mess which seemed to defy his fingers in its efforts to reach the deck.

Keyes sobbed, 'Oh, sir! You're *all right*!' He peered at his face, searching it as if still unable to accept he was no longer alone. 'I came to help . . .'

Drummond gripped the voice-pipes, cutting his fingers on the torn brass where a splinter had banged through it like a bullet.

He said, 'I'm fine, Mid.'

He slipped one arm round the boy's shoulder. To test his own legs, to stop Keyes from giving in to his terror. There was pain, but not enough to mean anything fatal.

Drummond gasped, 'Wheelhouse?'

Keyes nodded. 'Jevers is on the wheel, sir, the coxswain is taking charge.'

'Good.'

He tried to think, to react to the dull brown puffs of smoke above the island, the roar of fans as his ship continued her headlong charge.

Another voice croaked, 'Christ, my bloody arm!' Wingate sat up and touched his elbow with a look of stunned surprise. 'I've broken the bloody thing.' The sight of Archer, the others sprawled nearby, seemed to change him into a piece of machinery. Gritting his teeth against the pain, he rasped, 'Damage control party at the double!' He glared at Keyes, 'Go down yourself and tell Number One we may be in trouble!' He forced a grin. 'Or I'll let on to Georgina you wear frilly pyjamas in bed!'

'But I don't . . .' Keyes seemed to realise what Wingate was trying to do and nodded violently. 'I'll go.'

He ducked as more bangs echoed around the hull and steel clashed into the bridge like hail.

One splinter hit Tucker, but he did not change his expression. Wingate said thickly, 'Poor old Yeo has bought it, sir.'

'Yes.' Drummond trained his glasses over the screen, drawing strength from a sense of movement. 'Call up the chief. Stand by for full revs if we're not badly holed.'

Voices were yelling below the bridge, and he heard axes and hammers as the damage control party blundered into the forecastle.

Keyes had certainly had a grim blooding, he thought.

He said, 'Check each section.'

A signalman emerged from somewhere, dabbing blood from his forehead. He gaped at Tucker's body and said, 'I'll take over, sir.'

Nobody answered, so he dragged a pile of bunting from the upturned locker and covered the yeoman as best he could.

'We can turn now, if you wish, Captain.'

Drummond stared. It was Lyngstad, just as before, with not even a scratch. The Norwegian glanced at Archer without expression.

'If you follow this side of the fjord you may steer for open sea. I suggest greater speed. The bombers will be alerted by now, even if my people were able to cut the telephone wires to the bases.'

Drummond nodded, his head throbbing with pain. 'The gunfire has eased off a bit.'

Lyngstad sighed. 'There is another battery on Arnoy Island. But if you use smoke you should be safe. The battery is for visitors, not those about to leave.' He said it without a smile. Instead he looked at the splinter holes, the crude splashes of blood against the bridge, and added softly, 'Our people will not only have seen your sacrifice. They will have shared it.'

Rankin's voice cut through the other sounds. 'Cease firing. Check . . . check . . . check.'

The cease-fire gong rattled around the various mountings, and the crews paused to stare at each other, the litter of used shell cases, the wounded who crouched, whimpering quietly while they waited for help to come.

Wingate held out the handset. 'It's the chief, sir.'

Drummond turned his back on the others, shutting out their pain, their dumb despair.

'Captain speaking.'

'You're all right then, sir.' Galbraith seemed satisfied. 'I've got my pumps going, but the intake seems fair enough. I've had a report from damage control that the shell exploded just inside the fo'c'sle and then spent itself downwards into the stokers' messdeck. Bit too close to the fuel tanks for my liking. I gather there's a fire blazing there, but the lads are having a crack at it now.'

'Thanks, Chief.' If only the pain would go from his head. It was blinding him. 'I'm glad you're okay, too.'

'Aye. A few bruises, and the chief E.R.A.'s got a nose-bleed, but it's none too bad.'

'Yes, Chief.' He replaced the handset.

No point in telling Galbraith there was a long way to go yet, and maybe much worse to endure. He knew without a lecture. He was like that.

Sheridan pushed his way amongst the damage control party, his sea boots skidding on foam from fire-extinguishers, dripping spray, and a concoction of jam and butter which must have been blasted through one side of the main galley. It now lay with all the litter of pots and pans, broken crockery and, incongruously, a dazzling bright apron which the cook must have hung to dry.

Smoke pumped past him, but was thinner than when he had first arrived in response to the coxswain's call. He glanced quickly at Keyes, who had kept so close to him since he had brought the news that the captain was safe and in control, that he was like his own shadow.

The sight of Keyes' white face, his nearness to incoherence and collapse, had made him think the worst. That Drummond was either dead or too badly wounded to retain command. For a few seconds he had been almost too numbed to think in sequence. All his old ideas of command, of some special gift which he had within him, had been lost in the bellow of gunfire, amidst the cries and curses from vague shapes who had rushed past him in the smoke towards the tall column of vapour which had followed that savage shellburst under the bridge.

'Follow me!'

He pushed a man out of his path and peered down the oval hatch which led to the lower deck, the stokers' mess which had been turned into a shambles of blackened tables, smouldering clothing and hammocks. He hurried down the ladder, aware that the rail was still hot from the explosion, that there was far more light than there ought to be.

He paused, gripping the foot of the ladder, and stared at the gash in the side, the telltale splinter holes from some earlier damage. The white, frothy bow wave was streaming back from the stem and seemed only a foot or so below the gash in the hull. It made the familiar privacy of a messdeck fade, brought home to him the frailness of their daily protection.

'God, what a bloody mess!' He heard Keyes beside him. 'But the fire's out for a while.'

He knelt down and sniffed, catching the tang of oil fuel right beneath him. More punctures there, too. All around him there were other, more personal things scattered and burned, soaked in filth and foam. The large pin-up of a full-breasted girl in a sailor's cap and nothing else. That belonged to Leading Stoker 'Tosh' Harding. The picture had often called for a joke or a smutty remark when an officer did rounds in this cramped messdeck. There was a bundle of letters written in a shaky, untrained hand. A needle and thread still attached to a gold badge which someone had been sewing on a best uniform when the alarm bells had sounded. These sights, and others, made him suddenly bitter and angry, more even than those he had witnessed on the upper deck. It was an invasion of the men's lives. God knows, they had precious little else.

He looked up the ladder. 'Tell the bridge the fire's out. I'll get the buffer's party to do something about this gash right away.'

Sheridan glanced at the midshipman. It was strange, he thought. That moment of unreasoning anger had helped to steady him. Yet it did not matter now. One more good battering and they would have to bale out.

But to Keyes he said, 'This will be a dockyard job.'

One of the stokers in the damage control team stood staring emptily at his messdeck. But all he said was, 'Good thing ole Badger went on a run ashore after all.' He picked up a bundle of sodden letters and put them into a locker. 'They won't be read no more.'

Sheridan hauled himself up the ladder and strode along the opposite side of the forecastle. The forward messdeck seemed untouched, and he found two seamen having their wounds dressed by the S.B.A., and another who lay covered by an oilskin, one clenched fist sticking out as if to express his last moments of hate for those who had destroyed him.

He paused by the break in the forecastle, gulping in salt air, staring fixedly at the nearest strip of land, brown and green in the daylight, as it received the backwash of *Warlock*'s screws. He leaned over the rail below the whaler's davits and saw *Vent-*

nor close astern, her battle ensigns white against the smoky sky, the big hole in her side very obvious even at this distance. There was a towering wall of black smoke around the nearest spit of land. Right up to the hill-tops and far beyond that. Thick, greasy, solid. It looked as if it would stay that way forever.

Their visit would be long remembered, he thought dully. All that burning fuel. It would have reached *Waxwing*'s stranded hulk by now. A suitable pyre for those who had been left behind.

A voice exclaimed, 'Not *me*, sir!'

He turned and saw two men carrying a seaman on a stretcher whose arm was heavily bandaged. The doctor was striding beside the stretcher, his face expressionless.

The man tried to hold up his shattered arm. 'You *mustn't*, sir! Oh, dear God, why don't they listen?' He fell unconscious, his head lolling across his cap which they had used as a pillow.

Vaughan saw Sheridan and said flatly, 'It's got to come off. Now.'

Sheridan looked at the man on the stretcher. A plain, homely face. One you would never notice at Divisions or when inspecting the libertymen. He found he was gripping his own arm. What would he do if it happened to him?

He said to Keyes, 'Better go up to the bridge. Seems to be a lull.' He saw Keyes' face as he stared after the little forlorn group which followed Vaughan's white coat towards the screen door. He said, 'Don't think about it, Mid. I expect it was like this at Jutland. Trafalgar, too, probably.'

Sheridan found Drummond sitting in his chair, one leg thrust out stiffly and resting on a steel bracket.

'Finished your inspection, Number One?' He sounded calm. Too calm.

'Yes, sir. Six dead, fifteen wounded.' He thought of the man's eyes as he had cried, 'Oh, *dear God*, *why don't they listen?*' Someone should. He looked round the stained bridge. 'How many here?'

'Four. Two wounded.'

Wingate held up his arm which was wrapped in a crude sling. 'They don't call *this* a wound, apparently!' He grinned, the effort making his face even more strained.

Hillier was sitting on the steel step below the compass platform, his head in his hands.

Drummond added quietly, 'Shock. He'll be all right when he's needed.'

'I've got some matches, sir.' The signalman stepped over the yeoman's body and struck one carefully.

Drummond took it and held it to his new, shining pipe. It was amazing how steadily he could hold the little flame. Despite *Warlock's* rise and plunge over the inshore current, the vibration from her engines, he could still do it. And yet he felt as if every fibre in his body was cringing and shaking, beyond control.

He saw the match flame reflected in each of Sheridan's eyes. Like someone looking out from another mask.

He blew out a stream of smoke. It was strange. Cruelly unnerving. But he could not recall having enjoyed a pipe more.

Lyngstad called, 'Another ten minutes, Captain.' He gestured towards the starboard beam at the smudgy shape of an island. 'The battery there will try to hit you as you clear the swept channel.'

'Yes.' He tried to think. To stop enjoying the smoke. The firmness which the pipe seemed to give his whole body. 'Tell the chief. We'll need a thick screen. Good thing the wind's in our favour, what there is of it.'

The signalman said, '*Ventnor's* on station, sir.' He was trying not to look down at Tucker's feet. They had done so much together. So many watches, so many signals.

Rankin's voice droned from an intercom. 'All guns, load . . . load . . . load.' A pause as around the ship the weary crews stirred into life again. 'Short-range weapon crews prepare to repel aircraft.'

Good thinking. It would keep them occupied.

A bosun's mate lowered a telephone. 'Petty Officer Owles is callin' from aft, sir. Says he can fix some tea. Enough for the 'ole ship's company, if he can 'ave a couple of extra men.'

'See to it, Mid.' He watched the boy hurry away, looking neither right nor left. He was managing well, considering.

To port the other strip of land was curving away, losing its firm outline in the haze of persistent smoke and some stubborn patches of mist. Beyond it the sea looked like a great pewter wilderness. He tried not to shiver.

'*Lomond* in sight, sir!'

A lookout who had dashed to the bridge to replace one of the wounded, added vehemently, 'Took 'er long enough!'

Wingate snapped, 'That'll do! What are you, a bloody expert?'

Drummond raised his glasses and watched the lean flotilla leader as she steamed from behind the landspit. How clean she looked in the dull light. There were the others following astern. *Whiplash*, *Victor*, and slightly further back the heavily laden *Whirlpool*. Their people would be watching, he thought bitterly. Studying the splinter holes, expecting *Waxwing* to appear at the end of the fjord.

He said, 'Make to *Lomond. We are passing within range of battery to starboard. Suggest increased speed, and make smoke.*'

He heard the lamp clattering, and turned to see a man throw a bundle over the ship's side and into the wash.

Sheridan said dully, 'A man's arm. It had to come off.'

Drummond turned to watch the other destroyers. A light was blinking back across the water.

'To *Warlock*, sir. *Operation well executed. No sign of major enemy unit. Discontinue the action.*'

Wingate said quietly, 'Well, for Christ's sake.'

Drummond looked at him impassively. 'What are you? A bloody expert?'

The navigator leaned against the side, his arm smearing against some drying blood.

'Sorry, sir.'

There was a hollow boom, followed quickly by a bright flash on the starboard bow. Drummond watched the falling curtain of spray. Just to show us they mean business. But they had fired too soon. It gave Rankin time to adjust his defences. Galbraith's would be more reliable in this case.

'Tell the chief. Make smoke.'

'Char, sir.'

Owles was staring at him, holding out a great mug of tea. He stooped down and eased off Drummond's sea boot. It was sodden with blood.

'Can't 'ave this, sir.' He shook his head, oblivious to the repeated boom from the shore battery, the choking smoke from both funnels. 'Won't do at all, sir.'

'From *Lomond*, sir. *Increase to maximum speed.*'

Drummond massaged his forehead as another heavy shell exploded nearer to the starboard bow. High trajectory. Must be fired from the far side of the island. There was still hope. Not much, but . . .

He pounded the teak rail with his fist, not seeing Owles' anxiety as he bandaged the deep cut on his leg, nor Sheridan's look of despair. *Come on, old girl, come on!* He heard Wingate's voice, level and precise as he spoke to the engine room, the responding increase of jerks and rattles as the ship worked steadily up to her full revolutions.

He trained his glasses abeam, wincing as the pain in his leg became a reality. There was *Lomond*, making a fine sight as she plunged through the spray and spindrift from her own bow wave. He thought of *Waxwing*, of Archer, the unknown intelligence man, the little Norwegian fishing boat which had tried to help. The Resistance men who had done their part with complete courage and self-sacrifice. Long before those fires abated, or the wrecked midget submarines were salvaged, there would be many people clinging together in their homes. Waiting in dread for the knock on the door. The black uniforms. The agony.

And all the while *Beaumont had stayed out of it.*

If he lived through the next few days, Drummond was determined of one thing. To discover the truth about Beaumont. Once and for all.

'Both engines full ahead, sir. Course three-three-zero.'

Hillier got to his feet and lurched slowly to the shattered screen. He said, 'That was the best cup of tea I've ever had in my life.'

The intercom intoned sharply, 'Aircraft. Red one-one-oh. Angle of sight two-oh.'

The guns were already swinging round, sniffing at the air.

Drummond bit on his pipe, following the guns with his binoculars. There they were. Like little silver darts above the humps of land.

'Barrage . . . *commence!*'

The after guns fired first, joining with *Ventnor* as she opened fire at extreme range, the little brown puffs of smoke dispersing gently across the planes' line of flight.

Rankin said, 'Six aircraft. 88's by the look of 'em.' He had left his switch down. 'Well, here we go, my little ones! A doll for the pretty lady who hits the target!'

Drummond looked down as Owles dragged his torn boot into place.

'Thanks for the tea. Now go and get out of sight.'

The rest was lost and forgotten as the other weapons rattled and cracked into life.

Here they come.

Drummond watched the leading aircraft, imagined the pilot between those twin gleaming arcs of his propellers. Like his companions, he would have been sleeping. Safe from the convoys, from the Russian front, from everything.

Now he was up there, flying in deadly earnest.

He thrust the pipe into his pocket and said, 'So let's see what *you're* made of!'

13

That Bloody Hell

WHEN they were level with the nearest line of hills, the aircraft swung in two separate arcs, three in each wing of the attack. Drummond watched them warily, noting the way that the leader of the nearest group was waggling his wings, gaining height, with the watery sunlight behind him.

The barrage increased as *Lomond* and the rest joined. *Crump . . . crump . . . crump.* The sky was dirty with brown puffs of smoke. Rankin had been right. They were Junkers 88's. Twin-engined, and the largest of the German dive-bombers. He was picturing them in his mind as if studying the recognition diagram in the chart room. Two hundred and eighty-five miles an hour, and highly manœuvrable.

He held his breath as the leader he had been watching put his plane into a steep dive. Even above the roar of fans and the protests from the vibrating bridge structure he heard the rising whine of those engines. Only when the gunfire blotted out all other sound did the aircraft become less real, less hostile.

He imagined the pilot, his whole being screwed in tight concentration on the destroyer which was leaping up into his sights.

The *Ventnor* needed no additional warning, and was putting up everything she had, even light machine guns, which were making delicate threads of tracer across the German's wafer outline.

He saw the glint of metal as the bombs tumbled from the plane's belly, shared the agonising wait until the waterspouts exploded in a ragged line, the end of which was almost alongside the heeling destroyer. He heard the last bang, the telltale clatter of steel as the splinters smashed through *Ventnor*'s hull plating.

The bomber was already clawing out of her dive, pulling and circling away for her next attack. This time she would use her other bomb load beneath each wing. As it flashed across *War-*

lock's stern the dive-bomber opened fire with her machine guns. From its bulbous canopy to the extra gun which poked from its curved belly, the tracer rattled viciously, making dancing patterns across the water before clashing over the quarterdeck and beyond.

Wingate yelled, 'Here come our three!'

The deck jerked violently as the other bombers screeched into the attack. Every gun was firing with barely a break, the empty shell cases clanging unheeded around the crews' straddled legs, the automatic weapons cracking more sharply, scraping the inside of the mind as first one and then a second shadow swept right above the ship.

'Hard a-starboard!'

Drummond saw water rising to meet the onrushing ship, felt the body-blow of a bomb bursting close to the hull. More splinters, and somewhere a man screaming like an injured animal.

'A hit! Got the sod!'

The second bomber lifted on its tail, smoke funnelling out of its fuselage where it joined one of the wings. A flash, something black whirling into space, and then the plane fell apart, the pieces splashing in a diagonal trail and almost as far as *Lomond*.

'Cease firing!'

Drummond ignored the harsh shouts and concentrated on the pelorus sight above the gyro.

'Starboard fifteen.'

He heard the bombers' engines growling in the distance. Gathering their strength. Licking wounds.

'Midships. Steady.'

He saw the gyro ticking into line again.

'From *Ventnor*, sir. *Still able to maintain full speed*.' A pause as the light blinked again through the smoke. '*Your bird, I think*.'

Drummond smiled grimly as he turned to watch the progress of the smoke-screen. What with the great fog left by the blazing fuel tanks in the other fjord, and their own combined screen rolling away abeam, it was as if the destroyers were charging between two unfolding banks of black filth.

He heard the shore battery firing from somewhere on the starboard quarter. He peered at his watch. Half an hour. It had seemed like seconds since they had increased speed to regain the open sea.

'Two men wounded in the last attack, sir.' Hillier looked haggard. 'One badly.'

Drummond nodded, raising his glasses to seek out the bombers. What the hell would they do next? He thought of Hillier's dull voice. The hurt. If he could remember correctly, it meant they had lost about ten killed, and nineteen wounded.

He snapped, 'Aircraft! Port bow!'

This time the bombers were going to try a head-on attack on the other column of ships. More chance of being hit by shellfire from the heavily armed destroyers, but a better opportunity to straddle one, if not more, of them.

Lomond was already zigzagging violently, her after part hidden in a great white bank of spray and wash. Her guns made bright pin-pricks of light against the billowing smoke, and astern the rest of the ships were cutting the sky apart with closely knit tracer and shellbursts.

The leading aircraft side-stepped, recovered slightly, and then flopped helplessly on to the sea in a welter of smoke and spray.

The second fared little better, pressing on with its attack, until a shell exploded directly in its path, blasting the nose to fragments and hurling the blazing carcass down after the first one.

Drummond thought he saw a man fall kicking from the wrecked bomber before he, too, was flung into the water with the other fragments.

'*Whiplash* has caught one, sir!'

Drummond shifted his glasses, drawing in his stomach muscles as he watched the ship astern of Beaumont's veering out of line, smoke belching from her main deck even as the spray stopped falling from that last bomb. Cromwell, her captain, was doing his best to avoid a collision with *Victor*, which had been following close in his wake.

The signalman shouted, '*Lomond*'s calling up *Victor* to take 'er in tow!'

The bomb must have put *Whiplash*'s engine room out of action. It did not matter how temporary it was. So close to the land, it would be fatal if they could not get a tow aboard her.

'To *Warlock*, sir. From *Lomond*.' The signalman cursed as a spent bullet clanged against the bridge and whimpered plaintively over the other side. '*Assist* Whirlpool *immediately. Remainder form column on me.*'

Ventnor was already altering course to join with *Lomond* and the other ships.

Whirlpool was maintaining a good speed, despite her lethal cargo of mines.

Drummond wiped his forehead with his sleeve.

'Acknowledge. Pilot, take her round to join *Whirlpool.*'

God, he felt raw from noise and shouting. Even from thinking.

'Signalman. Make to *Whirlpool. I am coming to join your party.*'

Poor old Mark Kydd. It might cheer him up.

'Aircraft, sir! Green one-one-zero!'

'Two of the bastards.' Wingate cradled his good arm round the voice-pipes.

Very low this time, the bombers swept purposefully towards the scattered formation of ships.

'Barrage *commence . . . commence!*'

Warlock's guns were joining in, trying to maintain a tent-shaped area of exploding metal.

'Bombs coming down!'

There was a great sigh from somebody as two bombs burst alongside the crippled *Whiplash*. Her companion had been about to draw alongside to fire heaving lines across, but was now churning away, trying to give cover, to defend herself at the same time. Great shooting columns of water were all around and amongst the ships, and the sky was almost blotted out by shellbursts.

The second bomber droned steadily above its own reflection, the machine gunners spraying the ships as they pressed on.

Drummond saw cannon shells from *Victor*'s Oerlikons ripping through the Junkers' belly like claws, saw her falter and then plunge headlong. A cheer from B gun changed into a groan as the bomber crashed into the unmoving destroyer in a great fan-shaped curtain of fire.

'From *Lomond*, sir. *Recover survivors if possible. Repeat if possible.*'

Wingate said thickly, 'Christ, what a foul-up!'

Drummond looked at him. 'Tell Number One to prepare scrambling nets. Warn the doctor. This will have to be done rather smartly.'

Relieved of her earlier task, the *Victor* was already turning away to take station on the flotilla leader with *Ventnor*. They were all firing, so could probably see the remaining aircraft beyond the edge of the smoke-screen.

'Slow ahead both engines.'

Drummond watched the listing destroyer as she settled down more deliberately, half of her completely engulfed in flame. In the shattered bomber he saw an airman trying to get out. Like a trapped fly. He vanished in one great ball of flame.

'Stop engines.'

He heard voices yelling in the sudden quiet, the clatter of ropes and other gear as the deck party lowered the nets along side.

The stench and heat were overpowering, and the other destroyer was still fifty yards away.

A few survivors were swimming towards the side, others floated motionless, too dazed to help themselves.

Lyngstad said, 'We are clear of the minefield now.'

As if it matters. Aloud he replied, 'Thank you.'

He looked for *Lomond* and her consorts, and saw that they were already moving away in a small, tight line, the distance between them and his own ship growing more apparent with every second.

He listened to the coughing, retching figures who were being hauled aboard on either side. The yells of encouragement from gun crews, who moments earlier had been too stunned by noise and danger to take their eyes from their weapons.

'Come on, mate! Grab 'old of this then!'

Lyngstad said slowly, 'She may take hours to sink completely.'

Drummond tried to freshen his mind. He knew what the Norwegian had implied, but it took time to put thought into action.

'Yes. Commander Cromwell may not have destroyed his secret orders.' He swung round. 'Tell the torpedo gunner's mate to prepare one fish. Right now!'

They were all too shocked to move in sequence. He saw Sheridan on top of the port ladder by the gate. Like Frank had been when the shells had cut him down.

'Well?'

Sheridan stared at him, surprised by the edge in his tone.

He said, 'Can't reach any more of them. There's burning fuel on the other side of *Whiplash*. It could reach round here in minutes.'

Drummond ignored him.

'Slow ahead together.'

He waited, seeing the blazing wreck swinging slightly across his bows, tasting the stench, the misery. A ship like his own. Dying.

'Stop engines.' He turned and eyed Sheridan's smoke-blackened face. 'Are you still here?'

'But this is madness, sir!' The words seemed to pour out of him. 'The enemy will have a whole strike force of destroyers here at any moment. Bombers, too! All this is a waste of bloody time!' His arm waved above the screen, as if to encompass the burning ship and everything else. 'What's the use of making a senseless, selfish gesture?'

Drummond replied, 'They don't think it's senseless.' Then he turned sharply, his voice like ice. 'So get down there and help those poor bastards aboard! It'll probably be your turn in a moment, and then you'll know what it's like to see your friends leaving you to fry!'

He knew Sheridan had left the bridge, but was almost blind with anger and despair. He felt Lyngstad touching his arm, his voice calm and steady.

'Easy, Captain. *Give yourself time.*'

He looked at him. 'Time?' He smiled, the effort painful. 'I don't think that the choice is mine.'

'Torpedo ready, sir.'

'Very well.'

Hillier called, 'They've picked up *Whiplash*'s commanding officer, sir.' He was hanging over the screen, his hair steaming from the great heat across the strip of littered water.

'Send help for him.'

Drummond gripped the rail until the pain steadied him. *He will want to come up here. He knows.*

The other captain was a reservist like Selkirk. A merchant sailor who had found a place in war.

He was half carried up the internal ladder by the S.B.A. and a seaman. He was soaked in oil-scum and sea water, and there was dark red blood over his legs, mingling with the fuel.

Drummond helped to ease him into the bridge chair.

'Hello, Charles.' He looked at the S.B.A. 'See what you can do.'

Cromwell groaned and tried to sit upright, the pain returning to freeze him motionless.

He gasped, 'Sorry about this, Keith. But we did it. We hit the buggers, eh?'

The S.B.A. insisted, 'I'll *have* to get him below, sir.'

Cromwell shook his head. 'Too late. Done for.' He coughed and more blood ran over his chin. 'Put her down, Keith. For God's sake, *don't let her lie there like that!*'

Drummond looked at Wingate. The lieutenant said thickly, 'Picked up everyone we could get near, sir.'

'Yes. Slow astern together.' He waited, sensing the pain all around him. 'Port fifteen.'

Cromwell was saying wearily, 'My number one bought it. Lot of others, too.'

'Stop together.' Drummond wiped his eyes again, watching the other ship falling away as *Warlock* thrashed clear. 'Fire torpedo.'

He felt the slight shudder as the torpedo leapt from its tube and started to cut through the oily water like a snake.

'Hard a-starboard. Full ahead together.'

Cromwell said desperately, 'Lift me up!' He was scrabbling at the rail, his hands leaving stains of oil and blood.

The explosion rocked the hull as *Warlock* gathered way, her wash churning aside some wreckage and a few bobbing corpses.

Cromwell opened his mouth as if to shout, a last word perhaps. But his head fell forward and he said nothing.

The S.B.A. beckoned to his stretcher party. 'Dead.'

'Course to steer is three-three-five.' Wingate watched as the dead man was taken from the bridge.

Drummond felt for his pipe. Ahead, through the thinning smoke, he could just see *Whirlpool*, getting closer as his own ship reduced the lead she had just made. When he glanced astern the other one had sunk.

He felt very cold and sick. *Two down. Five to go.*

Sheridan had returned to the bridge. 'We picked up fifty, sir.' He looked round as if expecting to see Cromwell. 'I've put most of them in the wardroom. There's no more space.'

'Now go down to the messdecks and see how the repairs are coming along.'

Over the rear of the bridge screen he saw Sub-Lieutenant Tyson crouching beside the pom-pom platform. He was wearing a steel helmet, and seemed about to be sick.

He wondered vaguely how Keyes was managing, and Galbraith. All of them.

Wingate said, 'Must have really caught them on the hop. We're building up a bit of distance.' He did not sound very convinced.

The signalman called, 'From *Lomond*, sir. *Keep closed up on me.*'

'Acknowledge.'

Wingate raised his eyebrows. 'But we're going all out now, sir. I've never known the old girl move like this.'

'I know.' And Beaumont knows it, too. He's just got to say something. To show his control. 'But we'll keep with *Whirlpool* as originally ordered.' He trained his glasses on the other destroyer's racks of mines. 'He will have to dump those anyway.'

There was a drawn-out whistle and then a violent explosion, the sea bursting upwards within half a cable of the port side.

'What the *hell*?'

Drummond crunched over broken glass to peer abeam. But the smoke was still too thick to see anything. One shell, medium size. Fired blind perhaps.

Perhaps Sheridan was nearer the truth than he knew. Enemy surface ships from Altenfjord or Narvik, or an incoming patrol. It might even be Beaumont's *Moltke*. Up here amongst them to settle the vendetta once and for all.

He knew he was dangerously near to laughing. Or weeping.

'Tell Guns. No shooting until I say the word. Make a general signal to the flotilla.' He was straining his eyes, willing himself to see through the smoke. '*Am being fired on from south-west.*'

He heard it coming again. *Whooooosh—Bang!*

The waterspout was no nearer.

Lyngstad said quickly, 'I think it must be a patrol from outside the minefield. Older destroyers for the most part.'

'Like us.' Drummond winced as a third shell detonated astern of *Whirlpool*, deluging her quarterdeck in spray.

'From *Lomond*, sir. *Close on me*. Whirlpool *will discharge mines forthwith.'*

Hillier asked, 'What does it mean?'

Wingate was leaning painfully on his chart table. 'Captain Beaumont intends to leave a small field of mines to delay pursuit.' His eyes were hard as he looked up. 'Right, sir?'

'Yes.'

Drummond saw the frantic activity on *Whirlpool*'s decks, the falling away of her wash as she reduced to a safer speed for laying the mines.

'Ship at Red one-five-oh! Range oh-six-two!'

Drummond said sharply, *'Open fire!'*

He saw the V-shaped cleft in the drifting wall of smoke which had been made either by a freak down-draught or some new offshore wind. Through it, almost end-on, was the other ship. Chunky, low-lying, and firing again, even as he watched.

'Shoot!'

The jumbled voices across the intercom were drowned by the two aftermost guns firing together.

Drummond shouted, 'Make to *Whirlpool. Get rid of those mines now!'*

A shell rumbled over the bridge like an express train and burst far away in the smoke left by the fading screen.

'Port ten!' Drummond gritted his teeth. 'Midships.' He had to give the two forward guns a chance to bear on the target.

Whoooosh—Bang!

Splinters clinked on the deck, and one struck the motor boat with the sound of an axe.

Wingate called, 'The first mine has been dropped, sir!'

Whirlpool had altered course, exposing her full broadside as she steamed at right angles to Beaumont's little column. Splash. Another mine dipped and then vanished in *Whirlpool*'s wake

'From *Lomond*, sir. *Repeat. Close on me.'*

They were all looking at him.

He said, 'Disregard that signal.'

A shell exploded between the two destroyers, and seconds later Drummond saw several dead fish float to the surface.

'Shoot!'

Somebody yelled, 'A hit!'

A bright orange eye showed itself in the centre of the other vessel's low outline and then disappeared.

The mines were dropping from the little rails more rapidly now. The seamen had obviously been trained very well.

Just a few left and then . . .

Wingate said, 'It might cause a delay, I suppose.' He looked at Hillier and added wearily, 'I know. I just said that.'

Then came the explosion. It must have been heard for many miles. The great red glow which fanned out and surrounded the *Whirlpool* had such intensity and span that it looked like a hill of glowing lava.

When it had finally subsided there was nothing of the other ship to be seen.

Drummond felt the bridge closing in on him, crushing the life out of his body, his mind.

He said slowly, 'Make a signal to *Lomond*.' He stared at the churning patch of water until his eyes streamed. The shell must have burst amongst the last few mines. She had disintegrated. As if she had never been.

The signalman was staring at him. 'Sir?'

'Say, *mines laid as ordered*. Warlock *is rejoining you now*.'

Wingate said shakily, 'That's it then.'

'Yes.' Drummond slipped on to his chair, not seeing the other captain's blood. Not really seeing anything. 'It certainly looks like it, Pilot.'

Within an hour of *Whirlpool*'s violent end there were two more air attacks.

At full speed, zigzagging as they had not done for many years, with total disregard for safety-gauges and hull strain, the four surviving destroyers had fought back. Time had become meaningless, distance measured only by the span of a gunsight, the closeness of a bomb burst.

Victor and *Ventnor* shared a bomber between them. *Lomond* sent another racing for the Norwegian coast with a long trailer of smoke behind it.

And then, quite suddenly, it was over. Finished.

Drummond clung to the side of his chair, the tinny echo of the cease-fire gong still in his ears as he stared over the screen towards the other ships. Battered maybe, and each with her share of wounded, but there were still four of them.

He thought of *Whirlpool*, of Kydd's face at the meeting when he had been told about the mines.

He walked slowly to the rear of the bridge, surprised that he could move without the chair's support. Of the land there was no sign, and only a dull smudge along the blurred horizon showed the extent of the fight, and the cost to both sides.

The bodies had all gone from the bridge, and he realised dully that they must have been taken below during the ceaseless din of gunfire and barking anti-aircraft weapons. Tucker's cap lay in a corner, his old brass telescope nearby. It was unbroken.

'From *Lomond*, sir. *Reduce to cruising speed.*'

'Acknowledge.'

He glanced at the navigator who was sitting on his chart table, his arm-sling very clean against his leather jacket.

'Did you hear that, Pilot?'

Wingate nodded. 'Yes, sir.' He moved to the voice-pipe. 'Half ahead together.'

Feet moved on a ladder and Vaughan appeared in their midst. He was hatless, and his white coat was spotted with blood. Like a butcher's. He removed his rimless glasses and blinked at Drummond.

'Another has died, sir.' He shrugged. 'Did all I could.' He looked at the sea, realising that there was no enemy. No land either. 'What happened?'

Drummond eased his shoulders. He felt filthy and dead-beat. His mind simply would not react beyond simple matters of duty.

He said, 'It worked, Doc. Caught them completely by surprise. I'm sure there must have been other reasons, but surprise was one.' He thought of those who had been left behind, and of the gallant Norwegians. Of Archer, a man who had risked so much to make the raid a reality. 'And courage.'

Wingate said, 'There's a long way yet, sir. We may be running head-on into a whole Jerry squadron!'

Hillier grimaced. 'D'you know something? I think my ribs are cracked.' He looked so stunned that even Vaughan smiled.

'Take your coat off. Let me have a look.'

Drummond turned away, brushing unseeingly against a look-out who was resting his elbows on the stained metal to keep his binoculars level. Below the bridge he heard the scrape and clang of metal as the guns' crews cleared up the mess of empty cases and checked over their weapons for the next attack. They could not take much more. If another ship were to be sunk, the remainder would be unable to support each other. Perhaps that was what the enemy was trying to do. He stopped his racing thoughts with something like physical effort. The enemy was not a master-brain. It was people. Like himself and Wingate, Beaumont and Admiral Brooks. They could not always be perfect. Ready for everything.

Sheridan climbed up to his side on the gratings. He did not look at him as he reported, 'The splinter holes are plugged as best we could manage, sir. The buffer's party are going round the rest of the lower hull now.'

'Thanks, Number One.' He watched his profile. 'What about you?'

Sheridan replied flatly, 'I'm all right, sir. Glad we're getting away from the land. Away from all that'—he shuddered, despite his heavy coat—'that bloody hell.'

He turned suddenly, his eyes bright and feverish.

'Well, sir, *was* it worth it?'

'Strategically, of course it was. The Navy lost more ships at Narvik and achieved far less. More destroyers were sunk at Crete with nothing to show but a cruel evacuation job because of somebody's blunder.' He nodded slowly. 'This will rate as a success.' He hardened his voice. 'Even if we never see land again.' He gestured to the other three ships. 'Any of us.'

Sheridan licked his lips. 'If we do get back, sir.' He looked away. 'I'd like to apply for a transfer.'

'You would?' Drummond tried to feel something. To react or to care.

'I don't happen to think this sort of operation warrants such . . .'

'*Energy?*' Drummond gripped the rail as the deck canted unevenly. 'Is that what you object to?' He smiled. 'Perhaps a war without pain would be more in your line. I know it would be in mine.'

'That's unfair, sir. I've done my share.'

Drummond saw Wingate drawing away, leaving them isolated on the gratings.

He said quietly, 'There are no shares, can't you see that? We want to *win* this bloody war, not come in at the end as a nice, clean second! A lot of good men, and women, are depending on it. A whole lot have died already trying to make it come true.' Weariness, anger, the edge of shock made his voice suddenly bitter. 'D'you know, Number One, your reasoning astounds me. When the *Warden* went off like a bat out of hell after that alleged U-boat, you thought we should have supported her, despite all the things which were, and still are, expected of us. But when I stopped to pick up survivors today, you thought it was a *selfish gesture.*'

Sheridan swallowed hard. 'I didn't mean it to sound like that.'

Drummond groped for his pipe. 'I am very pleased to know that!' He added harshly, 'I wish you could have been up here to see Charles Cromwell's face when his ship was destroyed. I knew what he was thinking. And I thought you had it in you too when you joined this ship.' He tamped the tobacco into the bowl, much of it falling unheeded to the gratings. 'Transfer? If we get out of this lot, you can have it, and with my blessing!'

Sheridan stepped down, his face as shocked as if he had just been hit in the mouth.

The intercom rasped, 'Aircraft! Bearing Green four-five! Angle of sight two-oh!'

Sheridan was still at the foot of the gratings, his face working as he said, 'Here is your answer, sir.'

The intercom said curtly, 'Disregard. These are friendly, repeat *friendly* aircraft.'

Drummond did not know what to do with his pipe, as first one and then another of the men around the upper deck, behind gun-shields and at ammunition hoists, below the belching funnel, or right aft by the depth-charges, began to cheer.

'I think you may be right, Number One. It is an *answer*, for now.'

Wingate strode across the littered deck and gripped his hand. 'We *made* it!' He was half grinning, half choking. 'Never mind *for now*. Never mind that some jokers in high places think we're expendable. We did the job, and we got this far.' He squinted up as the first of the promised air-cover roared low above the mastheads, rocking its stubby wings in salute. 'And that, sir, shows what can be done, given a bit of faith!'

Lyngstad said quietly, 'Light your pipe, Captain.' He put his arms round Wingate and Hillier. 'We salute you, too.'

Sheridan looked at each of them. 'I suppose I spoke out of turn. I'm sorry.'

Wingate eyed him calmly. 'Forget it.'

Vaughan said, 'Your ribs are a mite buckled, Sub.' He seemed oblivious to the small drama, the ecstasy of survival.

Hillier said, 'Well, for God's sake.'

Drummond sat in his chair and leaned back to watch the aircraft as they circled overhead. There would be a carrier somewhere over the horizon, other ships to see them safely into harbour. Rendezvous with the oilers, a check on damage. Talk with Galbraith about the fuel level. Most important, speak with the wounded from his own and the other ship. So much to do. He pictured his cabin right aft. The bunk. A long, overwhelming drink. Oblivion.

He slid from the chair, the sound of his boots on the gratings making the others forget their own emotions and reactions.

He said, 'I'll speak with all heads of departments. Tell the yeoman . . .' He hesitated and looked at the discarded cap and telescope by the bloodstained flag-locker. 'Tell Ordinary Signalman Murray to find some cups and fetch the bridge party something hot.'

The spell was broken, and the others began to move outwards from him again, like spokes on a wheel.

He said, almost to himself, 'Well done, old lady.' He touched the teak rail. 'I never doubted you.'

He thought suddenly of Beaumont and added bitterly, 'Unlike some.'

Ten days later, after a wearying and circuitous route to avoid further attempts by the enemy to seek out and destroy their depleted flotilla, the ships anchored in Seydisfjord.

Drummond had spent a large part of that time in his chair on the open bridge, leaving it only occasionally to snatch short naps in his sea cabin. During the passage he had become almost an automaton, carrying out his duties, dealing with requests and managing his ship while his mind ached for rest and any sort of temporary release.

He had had to endure the tense and demanding moment of a

mass sea burial. It was never an easy thing to do, especially when so many of the pathetic bundles had been men he had known. Some a long while. Others only as faces or mannerisms. It was hard not to look for Tucker on the bridge, plucking at his beard, or putting right some junior signalman. Others who had been *Alf*, and *Ginger*, *Billy* or *Ned*, had taken their turn below a grey sky, gone deep down into the same darkness which Keyes had often contemplated during his times on watch.

He had received several lengthy signals from the Admiralty, and had wondered what Beaumont would think about them. His old enemy, the *Moltke*, had not come further north after all, but had re-entered the Baltic. She had, it appeared, been more severely damaged by bombing than anyone in intelligence had realised. Her brief cruise up to the Norwegian port had merely been a trial run, to readjust her and her company in readiness for the future. More to the point, and this was the part which must have affected Beaumont, the *Moltke*'s unexpected movements had been partly responsible for the raid's success. Every available destroyer not required by Group North had been sent down to ensure that the British would not interfere with the big ship's safety.

Another signal from Admiral Brooks had been congratulatory but brief. Like everyone else in the know, he was saying very little. The people in Britain had been told only that a daring raid had been executed against shore installations in occupied Norway. One newspaper said, '*In the tradition of Nelson*'. Another, '*In the spirit of Drake*'. Either way, it made encouraging reading for a population worn down by war.

To a special few, however, the routine statement on the B.B.C. meant something else entirely.

'*The Secretary of the Admiralty regrets to announce the loss of His Majesty's Ships* Waxwing, Whiplash *and* Whirlpool, *which were sunk during a gallant action against the enemy. Next of kin have been informed.*'

Once at anchor in Seydisfjord, the work of tidying-up got under way. The wounded were ferried ashore, temporary replacements were borrowed from the naval base at Reykjavik for the next passage, which was to be Rosyth in Scotland, when all immediate repairs had been completed.

The replacements had come aboard looking with awe at the

splinter holes and fire-blackened plating. The *Warlock*'s company had put aside some of their own feelings, if only to show the newcomers that there was nothing to it. Drummond had seen it before. The swagger, the reckless way that men who had fought for their lives could put on a show. If only for a short while. Later the pain would return. Old faces would emerge in memory. Losses would be seen more clearly than at the moment of death.

Drummond sat in his day cabin listening to Owles running his bath, knowing that if he paused in his pile of letters and signals he would not be able to go on. He had to write to every family whose son, brother or father had died. He looked around the quiet cabin. *In this ship*. It did not seem possible.

Through a scuttle he saw the repair ship almost alongside, and through the sheeting, incessant rain which had greeted their arrival, and had not stopped since, he saw a seaman carrying a basket carefully towards the gangway. He smiled, despite his inner feelings. Badger was returning to his ship. Unofficially, as usual.

There was a tap at the door, and Wingate entered the cabin with a batch of decoded signals.

'Orders for sailing, sir. Rosyth it is. Definite. It'll mean a long refit, I shouldn't wonder.'

Drummond nodded. 'You should have gone to the hospital, Pilot.'

'Not me, sir. This sling assures me of a hero's welcome. No, I've got this far, and it only takes one hand to draw lines on a chart.' He grinned.

He placed the papers on the desk. 'Top one says that Captain (D) is flying direct to U.K.' He hesitated. 'With the journalists and cameraman.' He held out a small note. 'This was sent aboard, sir.'

It just said, '*I was thinking of you. Will see you when you get there. Sarah.*'

'Thank you, Pilot.' He re-read the little note. 'Very much.'

Wingate sighed. 'It'll mean that you will be in command of the flotilla, sir.'

He leaned forward and seized the desk with his good hand. For a moment Drummond thought he had been taken ill, but when he saw Wingate's face he knew the real reason.

Wingate said tightly, 'What's left of it.' His eyes were blurred with emotion. 'God bless 'em, eh, sir?'

Owles was looking in the other door, and asked softly, 'Some brandy, sir?'

'Yes.' Drummond reached over and gripped Wingate's wrist. 'Yes. God bless the lot of them.'

14

A Spot of 'Leaf'

'ALL secure fore and aft, sir!'

Drummond leaned over the screen and studied the mooring wires as the dockyard workers snugged them over the big iron bollards. Ahead and astern the other destroyers were also making fast to the various berths, and waiting in little groups and peering up at the ships were the other dockyard men, specialists in repairs, experts who would decide if a ship required immediate isolation in a dried-out basin, or could manage with only superficial patching-up. In Rosyth dockyard they were very used to this type of work.

Drummond rubbed his eyes with the back of his wrist. The run from Iceland had been uneventful and strangely sad. It would have been better if they had endured bad weather, or warned of stalking U-boats. Anything was better than having time to brood on what they had suffered together.

They had had plenty of company. Aircraft, both carrier-borne and land-based, had rarely left them unattended. Several times they had made contact with a force of three cruisers. It was all part of the service to get them home.

Whoever had made these arrangements, and Drummond guessed Admiral Brooks had had a large hand in it, had been right in his assumption that such help was needed. Drummond knew that their strength and morale had never been at lower ebb. It was often so when returning from an operation of any size. Especially one which nobody had really expected to survive. Only when they had steamed in line ahead into the Firth of Forth and passed slowly beneath the great span of bridge on their way to Rosyth dockyard had they realised that things were different yet again.

Several tugs and harbour craft had puffed alongside, their crews waving and cheering. A small launch with a crew of Wrens had come so close that Drummond had had to sound his siren to warn them of the danger of *Warlock*'s whirling screws and their great undertow. But the Wrens had been cheering like the rest. Waving their caps and laughing. One had been crying and smiling all at once. It had been both moving and confusing.

'Ring off main engines.'

Drummond stepped down from the gratings and removed his cap. He was still unused to the bright gold oak leaves around its peak. It was like playing a part, he thought. Totally at odds with its newness against all the stained steel and jagged splinter holes.

Wingate said, 'It's beginning to rain, sir.'

'So I see.' Drummond smiled at him. 'And I don't care, do you?'

Below, on the iron deck, a brow was being made fast to the shore. A postman waited with his sack of mail, peering up at the bridge and tattered ensign. All along the jetty and pier men ambled up and down, calling out to the busy seamen, or merely pausing every so often to study the damage. The true scars of war.

Nosing amidst the confusion of railway lines, puddles and rusty bits of forgotten ships Drummond saw a shining staff car. It would all be starting again now. Explanations, questions, advice, worst of all, sympathy.

Feet pounded up a ladder, and Rankin burst on to the quiet bridge.

He held out a newspaper and said breathlessly, 'Got this from a chap on the jetty, sir. Thought you'd want to see it right away.'

Drummond unfolded it and held it by the chart table. He could feel the soft rain on his head and neck, but was aware only of the paper's great headlines. The print was large, as was the picture of a smiling Beaumont in the centre of the page.

'*The Hero of the* Conqueror *evens the score! After a relentless battle with everything which the enemy could hurl against him, Captain Dudley Beaumont, sole officer survivor of the battleship* Conqueror, *showed what the Royal Navy could do. In one of the most dramatic and heartening actions, much of which is still secret, Beaumont threw his small force of destroyers against a heavily defended German base on the coast of Norway. Regardless of danger, indifferent to the awesome odds against survival, he was able to complete this daring raid deep into enemy territory with absolute success. Under his skilful control and leader-*

ship, the destroyers taking part in the raid were able to wipe out many shore installations, shipping and several enemy aircraft for good measure. Our ships sustained some damage and casualties in the operation. But as Captain Beaumont told our correspondent at an Admiralty briefing, "Theirs was a great sacrifice. Mine the honour of being privileged to lead such men." '

Wingate said quietly, 'Well, I'll go to the top of our stairs!'

Rankin exploded, 'It's not right, sir!' He stared round at the untidy bridge. 'Not bloody true either!'

Drummond folded the newspaper. There was more. A whole lot more, with special pictures on the inner pages. Mostly of Beaumont, and one with what looked like a burning ship in the background. It was incredible. Unnerving.

'Must be like this when you come down from heaven to see what they've written on your gravestone.' Wingate watched the staff car as it ground to a halt by the brow. 'Will you deny any of it, sir?' He seemed dazed. 'I mean, you should be the one . . .'

Drummond said, 'Some of it is window dressing, of course.'

But the words seemed to stick in his throat. He kept seeing the flames and smoke, hearing the amazed voices around him when it had been learned that Beaumont was staying outside the fjord.

'Chief Operations Officer and Captain of the Dockyard are coming aboard, sir.'

'Very well. I'll come down and meet them. Tell Owles to get some drinks ready.'

At the brow he found Sheridan waiting with a hastily mustered side party. As they raised their hands in salute to the distinguished looking visitors Drummond looked at Sheridan's expression. Just for an instant he thought he saw something like triumph. *What did I tell you?*

The senior captain strode forward and gripped his hand.

'Welcome, Commander Drummond! To you and your ships! The whole country is proud of you!'

The operations officer added quietly, 'Captain Beaumont has spoken well of your part. Your efforts played no small part in the final success, I gather.' It sounded like a question.

'Thank you, sir.' Drummond gestured towards the lobby door. 'If you will come below. Out of the rain.' He beckoned to Sheridan. 'Send a quick R.P.C. to the other commanding officers.'

He glanced at the two captains. 'If you have no objection?'

'I should think not indeed. Brave chaps, the whole lot of them. From what Captain Beaumont has already said, I think they followed his ideas very well.'

Galbraith had been on his way aft from the engine room hatch. He was even dirtier than usual. He heard the captain's last words and exclaimed, 'Some might even have been *ahead* of his ideas, sir!'

The operations officer studied him coldly. 'What was that?'

'Carry on, Chief.' Drummond shook his head. '*Later.*'

To the others he said quietly, 'My engineer officer has had very little rest.'

Some of the offended look disappeared from the captain's face. 'Oh yes. I quite understand.'

Oh no you don't. He said, 'Now, if you will follow me, gentlemen.'

In the wardroom the air was thick with noise, excitement and smoke. Apart from *Warlock*'s officers, there were a few dockyard officials, a visiting lieutenant or two from H.Q., and one hazel-eyed Wren second officer from the signals department on the admiral's staff. Against the scuttles the rain was sheeting down, blotting out the other ships nearby, the dockyard, everything.

Wingate tossed back a neat gin and let it burn his mouth before swallowing it completely.

He said to Rankin, 'Drink up, Guns. Helps you to forget.'

He listened to the base electrical officer who was pumping Tyson for information.

Tyson said stiffly, 'It was touch and go for a bit, I can tell you. The Jerries were pretty mad after they found out what we were doing. Threw everything at us but the kitchen sink.' He gave a dramatic shudder. 'I've seen some sights, I can tell you.'

The electrical officer, who had only been to sea once in his life, nodded gravely. 'I can imagine.'

Rankin said, '*Jesus!*'

Wingate turned slightly to call for a steward and saw Keyes just inside the door. They had been almost too busy to speak beyond matters of routine during the long haul from Seydisfjord, but Wingate knew the reason for Keyes' disappointment. There had been no letter waiting for him when the ship had returned to Iceland. Nothing from Georgina. Naturally.

He watched the midshipman narrowly. Keyes had changed without anyone noticing. But then they had been rather busy. He felt the same prick behind his eyes as he had when he had almost broken down in the skipper's cabin. It must have been a million times worse for Keyes.

Keyes looked older. Leaner.

He called him over. 'Here, Allan. Come and join the drunks!'

Keyes pushed past the chattering visitors. 'I couldn't decide. I thought I might stay in the cabin.'

'*Rubbish!*' Rankin was halfway to oblivion. 'Don't you read the bloody papers? We're all heroes!'

Wingate said, 'Leave it, Guns.' To Keyes he added, 'What's the trouble?'

'I had hoped to see Georgina.' He kept his voice down. 'She didn't seem to remember.'

Wingate made a decision. One he might regret later. 'What a damned idiot I am!' He fumbled with his wallet and dragged it through his sling. 'She gave me her card to hand you, and I completely forgot!' He pushed it into the boy's hand. 'Here, look for yourself. She even put her phone number for you, how about that?'

Keyes turned the card over and said quietly, 'Georgina. *Georgina Dare.*'

Wingate swallowed. 'Yes. A nice name.'

He wished the bloody steward would come quickly. What with Keyes' gratitude and Rankin's owlish stare, he knew he needed another drink very badly.

Keyes looked up. 'Do you have a girl, Pilot?'

Wingate sighed. 'I'm not much use like *this*, am I. With a cracked arm?'

Rankin smiled toothily. 'S'right, Pilot. As a gentleman, you would always take the weight on your elbows, of course!'

Wingate grinned. 'Get stuffed.'

In another corner Sheridan was talking to the doctor, his back towards the others.

Vaughan was saying, 'I must say that I never thought I'd see this country again.'

Sheridan swirled his half-empty glass round and round. 'It's incredible. They're all relics. All of them.'

'Who?' It was a mild question, but behind the glasses Vaughan's eyes were very sharp.

'Well, look for yourself, Doc.' He waved the glass towards the noisy throng. 'The pilot, the chief, certainly the old man.' He looked at the crest. 'The ship most of all.'

'But not you, Number One. You've managed to stay free of, er, becoming a relic?'

'I've been a part of this sort of war, too. But I think you should try and keep your own personality. Stay clear of sentiment if you can.'

'Sentiment, or do you mean just *caring*?'

'Don't you start, for God's sake!'

Vaughan gave a small smile. 'I'm only a quack. I leave the heroics to my betters. And talking of which . . .' He placed his glass on a table. 'I have been watching that Wren. I think it's about time I moved in, so to speak.' He eased through the nearest bodies and confronted her.

Sheridan sighed. The doctor had not touched his drink at all. He stared round the crowded wardroom. God, it would be impossible to get rid of this lot. It would be the first dog watch before they had lunch at this rate.

He wanted to be on his own. To decide what to do. He had been to Drummond's quarters the moment the two senior officers had left the ship. An hour ago. Both of them had been pretty merry. Drummond had seemed much as usual, as far as he could tell.

Drummond had told him about plans for leave, docking and duties while the ship was having repairs carried out. Matter-of-fact, almost remote in his manner.

Sheridan had blurted out suddenly, 'The newspaper report, sir. You see what Captain Beaumont has done, don't you? He's taken all the credit for himself!'

Drummond had stood up, patting his pockets as if looking for something.

'If you try to bring discredit on a senior officer, Number One, the chances are you'll bring it more on those you care about. *Waxwing*'s people, all the rest who were killed. Press even harder, and nobody will believe anything. They might even start to think the whole raid was a fake. Would you like that?'

Sheridan could remember very clearly the expression on Drummond's face at that moment. Like a man burning up inside. Being driven to the limit. Not knowing what to do.

He had said, 'Well, I think it's wrong, sir.'

Drummond had not seemed to hear. 'The raid was a success. Seen in a dispassionate, cool-headed way, it was a *complete* success. More than anyone could have hoped. And the casualties? Considering that the numbers involved, directly and otherwise, were many, our losses were minimal.'

'You don't believe that, sir?'

Drummond had picked up his pipe and tapped the stem on the desk.

'There was a carrier put at our disposal with, presumably, some escorts. How many's that? Two thousand people? There were the oilers, the submarine, airmen, and probably hundreds of others who were working to make our task a success. Against those numbers, our losses must be seen as small.' He had looked round the cabin, his face strangely sad. 'I think you once implied that this ship was expendable, too?' He had slumped down, the pipe unlit. 'But it hardly concerns you. Now that you are applying for transfer.'

It had been like a slap in the face. A dismissal.

He had said, 'I need time to decide, sir. All I ask—'

Drummond had swept papers from his desk and upended some glasses as he had shouted, 'All *I* ask is for you to *leave me alone!*'

Someone touched his arm. It was Galbraith, almost unrecognisable in his best uniform. He smiled.

'I'm off, Number One. Home to the wife, if she'll have me!' He glanced at the others. 'When I saw the leave list, I thought I'd not stop to waste a second. There'll be enough work to do when I return. Putting right all the things the dockyard tiffies have done.' He held out his hand. 'So long. I guess you'll be in another ship when my leave's up.' He walked away, nodding to Wingate and Rankin.

Sheridan clenched his fists. They had written him off already. They had never even taken to him in the first place.

He saw Noakes, the gunner (T), squat and sweating freely, swilling drinks as if his life depended on it. He was surrounded by willing listeners. Sheridan felt lost. Bitter. Even Noakes was enjoying himself.

Rankin drawled thickly, 'Still here, Number One?'

'What the *hell* d'you mean by that?'

Several visitors fell silent and stared at him.

Wingate said sharply, 'Guns is not in our orbit. Just ignore him.' He looked round to make sure the interest had gone elsewhere and added, 'Anyway, I'd have thought you'd be sharing a bottle with the skipper. It's customary, and after what you've just shared with him, it's even necessary!'

'He doesn't need me.' He thought of Drummond's angry eyes. 'Or anybody.'

Wingate shrugged. 'If you say so.'

Sheridan murmured quietly, 'I know that some of my ideas have been unpopular since I took over as number one. I didn't fit in. Even you were a bit peeved by a reservist being appointed over your head, right?'

Wingate put down his glass and took Sheridan's elbow. Outside the wardroom door he said evenly, 'I can't move my arm, as you know. It saves me from being court-martialled for punching your face through the back of your stupid neck!' He swayed slightly but regarded him calmly. 'You still don't understand, do you? You came aboard *Warlock* believing that you had been done out of promotion because of the enquiry into *Conqueror's* loss. Victimisation, scapegoat, and what you just said about reservists. It never occurred to you at all that your last captain was letting you down as gently as he knew how, did it?'

Sheridan said coldly, 'In what way?'

'Don't say I didn't warn you.' Wingate drew a deep breath. 'The fact is, Number One, you're not bloody well good enough for command!' He hurried on before Sheridan could speak. 'When that shell hit the ship, and I got thrown across the bridge like a lump of pusser's duff, my last recognisable thought was, *Please don't let the skipper have bought it!* I just knew you'd never get us out of that mess, nor any other!' He stood back, his eyes blazing. 'Your last C.O. knew you weren't able to hold down command. Sooner or later you'd have believed someone *had it in for you* again, God help you.'

Sheridan replied angrily, 'That was quite a speech.'

'I did warn you. Now I'll go and get drunk, if you'll excuse me.' He paused by the door. 'Your predecessor in this ship was pretty useless. Nice bloke, but not up to the job. The skipper carried him, because they were good friends. And there were other reasons. When you came aboard, I thought, Here comes a stranger, one who might be able to help share the load.' He looked at Sheridan with contempt. 'God, it's like telling the pack to carry the mule!'

The green curtain swirled across the door, deadening the voices, and leaving Sheridan alone.

Drummond closed the door of the operations room behind him and stood uncertainly in a long passageway. Wrens hurried back and forth with signals and mysterious packages. Officers of every shape, size and rank bustled past him. Even here in Rosyth, Drummond had that same feeling he had known in the Whitehall bunker. That the H.Q. war, wherever it was, would continue with the same vigour without any ships at all.

He straightened his new cap and saw two Wrens watching him, whispering behind their papers.

He smiled, and one of them said, 'We saw your ships coming under the Forth Bridge, sir. It was all lovely!'

The other said, 'But they were so knocked about. So small-looking.'

He nodded. 'They felt a bit small at times, too.'

Another voice said, 'Hero-worship, how terrible!'

He turned and saw her standing in an open door. She was smiling at him, but her face was like a beautiful mask. He crossed the passage and held her arm.

'It's good to see you. I never know where I'm going to see you next.'

She pulled him into the empty office and slammed the door. For a long moment she studied him, her smile gone, her eyes brittle with tears.

'Oh, Keith!' She threw herself against him, burying her face on his chest. 'What have they done to you?'

He held her tightly, unable to think, to speak. He only knew that they were together. It was real. Not some sustaining dream to make a man do the impossible. She needed him almost as much as he did her.

She said softly, 'When I saw you just now. Your face. I couldn't believe that you could hide such feelings from those around you. All day. Every time you appear before your men. You must appear perfect. A man without fear or feelings.'

He held her more tightly.

'Don't. It's all right really. I'm all right now.'

She eased herself away and looked up at him.

'Oh, yes.' She tried to smile. 'I can see that.'

He released her hands and said, '*Warlock*'s going into dock tomorrow. I'll have to be nearby. In case anything goes wrong with her.'

She moved her head from side to side.

Her mouth was moist as she said, 'I could hate that ship, if I didn't know I could never compete with her in your heart.'

He continued, 'I want you near me. If you'd like it, that is ...'

'*Like* it?'

She stepped towards him and put her hands against his face. They were very warm.

There were voices in the passageway. There was no more time.

He said urgently, 'Edinburgh. There used to be a good hotel ...'

The voices were getting closer. She lifted herself on her toes and kissed him on the mouth.

'Do it, Keith. I can get away from work.' She pushed her face on to his shoulder, hiding it from him. 'Don't think badly of me. But I want you all to myself.' She gripped his neck with both arms. 'Just us.'

The door opened and a bespectacled clerk asked awkwardly, 'Is it all right to come in?'

She turned to the window, dabbing her face with a small handkerchief.

'Yes. Of course. I was just asking the commander a few questions.'

She could not keep it up, and when she faced him he saw that she was smiling at him. Really smiling this time.

God, I love you. He said, 'I'll call you then.'

She tried to be serious. 'You do that, *sir*.'

Drummond nodded to the astonished clerk and left the room. She hurried after him and caught his arm.

'You've got lipstick on your face.' She was laughing and crying at the same time. 'No naval officer worth his salt can walk about like that!' She rubbed his face with her handkerchief. 'And don't you go off with any of those Wrens either! A ship is bad enough, but I'll scratch their eyes out if they start anything.'

He held on to her wrist. 'Sarah. Oh, *Sarah*.'

She nodded, a tear started down her cheek. 'I know, Keith. I *know*. But it will be all right.' She touched the back of his hand. 'I'll make it so.'

When Drummond reached the main doorway he looked back. She had gone, but he could still see her.

She stood just inside the wide doorway and looked slowly around the room, as if unwilling to break the spell.

As the hotel porter shut the door she exclaimed, 'It's *huge*! How did you manage it?'

'Rank has some privileges.'

He put her small case by the bed and crossed to the windows. It was getting dark, but the rain had stopped, leaving only streamers of black cloud across the first small stars. Below, in Princes Street, the traffic sounds seemed a long way off, the cars groping like little moles, trying to get home before blackout.

He turned and looked at her. Against the big door, the room's air of a past, extravagant age, she seemed frail, like a child. She had changed into a dress which he had not seen before, and was watching him soundlessly, her arms limp at her sides.

She said suddenly, 'Oh, Keith, I'm almost afraid to believe it's true.'

He smiled. 'I think the hotel nearly changed its mind about giving us the room. It's *very* respectable.' He walked to her and held her against him. 'But I liked the look of it. *Commander and Mrs. Drummond*.'

Together they walked to the bed. It was high off the floor. Massive. She tightened her grip on his hand.

'I feel like Emma Hamilton!'

There was a discreet tap on the door and a servant peered in at them.

'Will you fix the blackout curtains, sir, or will I?' He looked at the girl. 'Does, er, Mrs. Drummond have everything she needs?'

Drummond gave him ten shillings. 'Yes to both questions, thank you.'

He waited until they were alone. 'I expect they've seen our ration cards already.'

She pulled herself up, her arms around his neck. 'I don't care. Not about anything.'

He sat her on the bed and opened his case.

She laughed. 'Champagne!'

'I told you. *Rank*.' He grinned, sharing her excitement. Feeling his mind melt with each of her movements, her voice. 'Actually, Owles got it from somewhere. I didn't ask.'

Owles had packed it carefully in a piece of oilskin, blurred with moisture and ice-cold. He had said, 'Do you good, sir. This and a spot of leaf.'

'He sounds nice.'

She followed him into the bathroom where he rummaged for two glasses.

He answered, 'Like a mother to me. Most of the time.'

The cork made a cheerful sound, and for a long time they stood by the window between the curtains, watching the shadows, unwilling to speak.

Then she said, 'I don't want you to think that I . . .'

He replied gravely, 'I *think* you are beautiful. I *think* I will try to make you love me.' He held his glass against hers. 'As I do you.'

She would not look at him. 'Cheers.' It was all she could manage.

She added, 'I could get to like champagne.' She looked at her case. 'I want to go to bed.'

He said, 'I have to telephone the dockyard.' He grimaced. 'I'll be ten minutes.' There was a telephone beside the bed. 'Be as quick as I can.'

He walked down the stairs and around the busy lobby, seeing nothing. He was barely aware of the many uniforms, the atmosphere of escape and gaiety. A holding on to a past which would never be the same again.

When he returned to the room the bedside light was on. She was in the centre of the bed. Her eyes were on his face as he sat on the blankets, her lips moist in the small yellow glow.

He said quietly, 'You look lovely. I wish I could give you more. Everything.'

She kept her eyes on his as he pulled down the sheet, tensed as his hands moved around her pale, uplifted breasts and across the smooth skin of her belly. He saw that her fingers were bunched into tight fists at her sides, saw the fierce pumping of her heart beneath one curved breast, beating to match his own.

He threw his clothes blindly on the floor and made to turn off the light, but she said huskily, 'No. Let me see you, too. Please.'

They came together slowly at first. All sound was blotted out by their hearts and blood, all vision obscured but each other.

Still and still he tried to prolong it, seeing the urgency in her eyes, the way her body was trembling as he knelt above her, feeling the soft smoothness of her in the space she had offered between her knees.

She gasped, 'Now! Keith, *now!*'

He touched her, raised her to him, and then felt her lifting, arching her spine to draw herself even further around him.

It was pain and darkness, ecstasy and passion, which left them breathless and spent. Like a single being. A piece of living sculpture.

Later, as he switched off the light and moved from the bed, he knew she was awake, watching him as he opened the curtains and let the hazy moonlight explore their private world.

He saw her, her pale limbs almost silver in the strange light. He returned to the bed, stroking her, feeling her coming alive again, sensing her longing, his own immediate response.

She sat beside him, pushing him back on the bed, her voice muffled in lost words as she bent across him. It was like another perfect torment. Her hands, her mouth, her whole being were everywhere, until once more they were spent.

When she leaned above him she saw that he was at last asleep, his legs relaxed, his breathing regular and untroubled. Gently she smoothed his hair from his face and then took one of his hands, watching to make certain she had not awakened him.

She held the hand against her breast and said simply, 'Sleep, my darling. I am here.'

With a minimum of haste the majority of *Warlock*'s ship's company hurried ashore to make every minute of their liberty count.

Some, like Galbraith, went home to their wives. Galbraith was a Scot, but like many of the flotilla's officers, lived in the South, near Canterbury. His wife was a sturdy, uncomplaining woman, and she had given him two girls. They were all his pride and joy, and the only thing which spoilt every leave was knowing that he would soon have to go back to a ship.

Others, like Rankin, were less happily married. He had taken his wife too soon, before he had 'bettered himself', as his mother had observed more than once. As he sat in a badly ventilated train speeding south to his home on the outskirts of London he pictured her face. Once very pretty, as all barmaids were supposed to be, she had become slovenly, even sluttish. He was equally certain that she shared several beds when he was away. He would have it out with her. He sighed, edging away from a snoring army officer. No, he wouldn't. He never could. But when the war was over he would not go back to her. He yawned, tasting the vast amount of gin which had kept him aboard long after the last libertymen. Perhaps, this time, she would be different. Kind to him.

In an hotel room not far from the one where *Warlock*'s captain lay in a heavy, dreamless sleep, Vaughan was cursing himself for drinking too much. He drank very little as a rule, but the Wren officer had made it sound like part of a bargain. 'I've met men like you,' she had said. 'Get you sloshed, and then take advantage.' But she had got sloshed all the same, and so, unfortunately, had he. He slung his jacket on a rickety chair and looked down at her sprawled on the bed. She was still in uniform, and her hair was in abandon as she tried to see what he was doing.

She said, 'I'd better be going.'

He sat beside her and unbuttoned her jacket. She seemed to sober up, and gripped his wrists, staring at him with something like horror.

'But you're a *doctor*!'

He fumbled with her shirt, feeling her breast hot under the material, the blood thundering in his brain. She struggled, and the cloth tore open.

She gasped, 'My shirt! What'll my girls think!'

He pulled the torn shirt up and over her shoulders with a kind of madness.

She said as he half fell across her. 'Anyway, I can't. Not at this time of the month.'

Vaughan jerked up violently and glared at her.

'You *silly bitch!*'

He slipped and fell against the table, knocking an ancient wash-hand-basin into clattering fragments.

Someone banged angrily on the dividing wall. 'What have you got in there, mate? A ruddy tiger?'

Vaughan and the girl stared at each other, stunned and confused.

Then with a rueful grin she threw the rest of her clothes on to the floor and said, 'Come here, *Doctor*! We'll make the best of it!'

He saw himself in a mirror, flushed and wild-eyed. He grinned down at her. 'Coming, Tiger.'

Another train which was already nearing London well ahead of Rankin's contained at least two more of *Warlock*'s company.

One was Able Seaman Jevers, going home, despite all his plans and caution. To be absolutely certain. To know he was safe for all time.

Another was Midshipman Allan Keyes, wide awake as he enjoyed the luxury of an almost empty first-class compartment. He did not want to fall asleep in case any of the next few hours and days might be marred by his dreams. Nightmares.

He concentrated on his destination, and the girl who had not forgotten him after all. Georgina Dare.

Opposite him, his eyes half asleep and red-rimmed, was a merchant navy chief officer. He watched Keyes' fresh face, the way he kept looking at a photograph. He sighed. Poor little sod. His sort never stood a chance. Not for long.

15

Time for Thought

VICE-ADMIRAL NICK BROOKS held a cigarette in one of his wizened hands and studied Drummond coolly. In the big map room deep below the Admiralty the air was dry, like the admiral. Almost lifeless.

Drummond tried to glean something from the charts on the walls, but there was nothing to give him a clue.

It had been a strange, unreal four weeks since *Warlock* had gone into dry dock at Rosyth.

Other commanding officers had often known such an existence, but he had just not considered it. He had seen fellow captains sharing their lives between ships in for repairs and their other demands of homes or families, but it had been outside his true understanding. Until Sarah.

Beyond the dockyard and the hotel, life for the rest of the world had continued. The promised and expected invasion of Italy had got under way, and after the grim and deadly conflict at Salerno the Allies were now beginning to make real headway. But to the *Warlock*, and others like her, that was a war apart. In the busy dockyard, affairs were only concerned with putting right damage done by enemy and weather in the Atlantic, the North Sea and on all the urgently required convoys.

He knew that in earlier days he would have felt restless, fretting at the delays which were keeping him and his ship on the sidelines. This time it was totally different. His need for the girl, her responding love which she had given completely, had made a new life for him, something real and precious.

She was out there now, waiting for him, in a London little different from his last visit when he had met her at Beaumont's press conference.

Brooks said, 'No captain can expect to get much rest when his command is in dock for repair and overhaul. I would have been to see you myself in Scotland, but affairs here and in the Mediterranean have kept Special Operations rather occupied.' He blew out a stream of smoke and patted ash from his crumpled grey suit. 'But in view of your work, the splendid dash of the attack into Norway, I would like you to hear some news from me now.' He gave a wintry smile. 'Yesterday our midget submarines were able to penetrate all the net defences and minefields, and laid their charges beneath the German battleship *Tirpitz* in Altenfjord as planned. Actual damage is still unverified, as we had losses, and Norwegian reports say that some of our midget submarine crews were taken prisoner. However, there is no doubt at all that *Tirpitz* is out of the war for a considerable while. Long enough for us to concentrate on her remaining large consorts. Long enough to plan her final destruction by more conventional means.' He showed his long upper teeth. 'But for your attack, and the destruction of the fuel dump, *Tirpitz* would certainly be ready to put to sea when we could least contain her. As for the German midgets, "Negroes" and the like, there again, the damage and losses you inflicted will have put the enemy well behind in training and supply. It was a fine piece of work. Imaginative in planning, determined in execution.'

Drummond tried to relax. It was like a carefully rehearsed lecture. A sales talk.

He had not set eyes on Beaumont since the raid, but had heard of him quite a lot. In the newspapers he had been shown making a speech at a warship week, when people paid their hard-earned savings towards building another ship for the Navy. At factories on war work, his cheerful, confident face had been seen from Tyneside to Cardiff. The man of action taking time to encourage the many thousands who worked behind the scenes and without much praise.

Once, he had been in an Edinburgh cinema when the inevitable had happened. Beaumont had been shown on one of the newsreels, pointing at some vague strips of film, showing how it was done. One minute excited, the next grave and sad for those who had died in battle.

Sarah had squeezed his hand in the darkness and had whispered, 'Let's get out of here. He makes me feel sick.'

He said, 'I had wondered about the *Tirpitz*, sir. I'm glad it went off well. I'm afraid I'd never make a submariner. I like to see where I'm going.'

'Quite so.' Brooks lit another cigarette. 'I keep out of the limelight. Have to. But I don't miss much. Can't afford to in this business.' He eyed him calmly. 'I've heard a few things about you and Captain Beaumont. Things I'm not too happy about.'

'It's not come from me, sir.' Drummond felt immediately on guard. 'I have not even *seen* Captain Beaumont since the attack.'

'I know. But there's more to it than that. In war, there are many different threads you must weave to complete a victory. Bombing and convoys, tanks and infantry, and all the lines of supply it takes to keep them coming. But no less important, Drummond, is *confidence*. A belief, an absolute faith in final victory. It's no good telling a man who has to struggle to work every day on train or bus, regardless of air-raids and the fact his house has just been bombed flat, that all is well. He must be made to believe it. To hold on when everything looks at its blackest.'

'I thought that was more for the propaganda people than us, sir.'

Brooks shook his head. 'The *enemy* has propaganda, Drummond. The Allies have *sources of information*. Quite different.' He winked. 'But you are correct in seeing the importance of close contact between the few who fight and the greater mass which has to suffer if the country is to survive.'

'I'm not sure I understand.'

'No. You are a seagoing officer. Not a politician. You see, Drummond, when the *Conqueror* went down, it was not merely another ship going to the bottom. You know that. She was a symbol, like the old *Hood*, the *Royal Oak*. The country had come to rely on them, even though most people had never laid eyes on any of them. *Conqueror's* destruction came at a bad time. Heavy losses in our convoys, severe shortages at home, almost nightly bombing in our cities, some of which will never recover. In the field, too, our troops were faring badly for the most part. *Conqueror* might well have been the stone to tip the scales. Instead, she offered us a living symbol. Someone who could endure the very worst and still fight back. A man of war.

Somebody we could all recognise, in whom we could see something of ourselves.'

'Captain Beaumont?'

'Just so.'

There was a long silence and then the admiral said, 'When we decided to create a little flotilla under the auspices of Special Operations, I, for one, had no idea of its capability, its chances of success. That, I must admit, is why I selected older, less valuable vessels for the task. Also, from my experience, the older, harder-worked ships inevitably produce the best and most determined companies and captains. They *have* to be to survive. You don't get much drive by swinging round a buoy in Scapa Flow.'

'I think we all realised that, sir.'

'I am sure. I am equally positive that you would not wish to upset the apple-cart at a time when this damned war has taken a turn in our favour.'

'If you mean the raid, sir . . .'

'Well, you said it.' Brooks searched for a fresh pack of cigarettes. 'I have heard that some of your people are feeling bitter about the manner in which the raid was carried out. Not about the manner in which you and your ships were asked to perform a miracle.'

Drummond eyed him steadily. 'I can't speak for anybody else, sir. But I did think that the attack should have been executed as originally planned. If the enemy had been bringing up heavy units, including the *Moltke*, and some fleet destroyers, we'd have been done for anyway. Surprise was all we had.'

'You are being too modest.' Brooks frowned. 'You are suggesting that as Captain (D), Beaumont should have sent the whole flotilla into the fjord, regardless of any threat which might have been coming from elsewhere.'

He paused, watching Drummond's grave features. 'That is what you would have done in his place?'

'Yes.'

In his mind it was suddenly very clear. The destroyer slewing round and going aground, the heavy fall of shells from the hidden shore battery. *Ventnor*'s side steaming from a massive explosion, the Norwegians dashing along the hillside above burning German vehicles.

He added simply, 'My three ships could have been knocked out without getting to the major targets at all.'

Brooks tapped his knee as he perched on the corner of a table. His face was grave and thoughtful.

He said slowly, 'It's water under the bridge as far as that's concerned.' His face relaxed slightly. 'I have to tell you that the Distinguished Service Order is being awarded to you for your part. Others will be recognised, too.'

'Thank you.'

'You don't seem too impressed?' Brooks eyed him curiously. 'Are you afraid of becoming a hero?'

'Of becoming something I'm not, sir.' He thought of the *Whirlpool* vanishing in one blinding explosion. 'I was as scared as the rest of them.'

'That I can believe. I was not always a crabby old admiral, you know. Another war, and I was much like you. Only the methods change.'

'Is that what you wanted me for, sir?'

'Of course not. I wanted to hear it from you, naturally. But also I needed to know how you feel about another operation.'

Drummond tensed. 'We'll not be going back to general service, then, sir?'

'Is that an answer?' He showed his teeth. 'In a way, I suppose it is. But you see, I cannot merely order you to perform another of our little miracles. It will be a hard one, it could easily be a complete failure.'

'In your opinion, sir.' He was torn between his emotions like a piece of flotsam. He kept seeing her face, knowing what she meant to him. She was his future now. Everything. 'Is it a plan which has a real value?'

Brooks smiled wryly. 'It's not for propaganda, if that's what you're implying!'

'Something like that, sir.'

He tried not to think of Beaumont. *The symbol.* He recalled her words when they had first met. *The image-makers.* Maybe Beaumont was still the same man inside. The one he had known all those years ago. The one which Sarah's brother had described in his letters to her. Perhaps he had been unable to resist creating a myth, and in so doing had become just that himself. He chilled, remembering the few moments when he had seen through Beaumont's guard. Uncertainty or guilt, or had it really been fear at what he was building, and what might in turn destroy him with it?

'Would Captain Beaumont be in overall command of this new one, sir?'

'Fair question.' Ash fell unheeded on his suit as he snapped, 'And, I think, a fair assumption. Afterwards,' he gave a weary shrug, 'he will no doubt be asked to accept flag rank, where his talents for rallying enthusiasm will be of great value.' He coughed. 'Well?'

'How long have I got, sir?'

Brooks smiled. 'A few weeks.' The smile vanished. 'Top secret. So watch your words with *everyone*.' He added sharply, 'You're not married, are you?'

'No, sir.' *He knows about Sarah.* It was obvious. Just as it was that Beaumont had been talking about him with Brooks. 'But I will be as soon as I manage to arrange certain matters.'

'Splendid.' He looked away. 'I'll not keep you any longer for now.'

As Drummond walked towards the thick iron doors he heard the admiral ask, 'Do you ever think about *your* future?'

He smiled and half turned. 'Now, I do, sir.'

'It's nice to be back in Edinburgh.'

They laid side by side looking into the darkness above the bed.

She added, 'Going back to London made the war seem more real. Closer.'

Drummond slipped his arm round her shoulders and placed the palm of his hand against her spine. Outside the hotel windows and drawn curtains it was pouring steadily, and the air held the bite of an early winter. He thought of Brooks in his sealed bunker, the activity aboard *Warlock* when he and the girl had returned to Rosyth that morning.

Warlock's latest scars had all but disappeared under fresh welding and paint. He had seen some ratings being shown round the ship by Petty Officer Abbott, the way they had fallen silent as he had walked past. New hands to replace the killed and badly wounded. Men who had watched him, their captain, the holder of their destinies perhaps.

She turned on her side, and he could feel her watching him in the darkness. Against his body her limbs felt like cool silk.

She said, 'You've got a big operation coming off soon?'

He squeezed her shoulders. 'I thought you were the one who knew everything that was going on?'

She did not respond to his joke. 'I forgot to tell you. When my leave is up I will be doing some other work for Miles Salter. He told me while you were at the Admiralty. Checking back over records for a factual film about convoys.'

Drummond thought about it. 'So you're still with Salter's department. But you're not being given the run of information about our flotilla.'

'That's it.' She raised herself on one elbow. '*Why?* Is it important?'

He tried to think of an easy way. Then he said flatly, 'You mentioned that survivor from the *Conqueror*. The seaman called Carson. Do you know where he is at the moment?'

He heard her intake of breath. 'Yes. At a small hospital at Manchester. There are quite a few like him. Shellshock, loss of memory, that sort of thing.' She added softly, 'You think my story was a true one? About Tim being on the raft with Beaumont?'

'There are several things about Beaumont which are worrying me.'

She wriggled closer as the wind-driven rain slashed against the windows, running her hand across his chest, holding him.

'Tell me, Keith. I love you so much. I can't bear to see you worried. Things are bad enough as it is.'

'That last operation. It was rougher than anyone knows.' He felt her body-warmth moving across him, as if she was trying to cover him, protect him from memories. 'At one point I thought he would kill the whole lot of us.'

It was out in the open, but he felt no relief.

She said urgently, 'I had a feeling about it. Once or twice you've tossed and turned in the night. Like a man in fever.'

'Sorry.' He pressed her spine, feeling her body tremble, the pressure of her breast against his chest.

'Don't talk about it any more. Try not even to think about it.' In a smaller voice she asked, 'How long do we have?'

'Two or three days and *Warlock* will be ready to take on fuel and stores again.' He hesitated. 'And then I'm not certain.'

She hugged him and ran her fingers lightly across his thigh. 'I hate the thought of leaving this hotel.'

He smiled. 'The manager thinks we've taken root!'

She was looking at him now, her hair brushing his mouth. 'I *want* you, my darling.'

'And I you.'

Midshipman Allan Keyes stood on the road opposite the theatre and examined it carefully. It was not quite what he had expected, and was not in the West End of London either. In the middle of a seedy-looking street, flanked on one side by a bombed-out fish-and-chip shop and on the other by a boarded-up shoe factory, it bore all the signs of a Victorian relic.

But he crossed the road and thrust his way through the black-out curtain and past a sign which announced 'House Full', where he was confronted by a heavy-jowled man with a cash box.

'And where the hell d'you imagine you're going, my lad?'

Keyes said stiffly, 'I am expected.' He held out the little card. 'See for yourself.'

The man took it and looked from it to Keyes with apparent surprise. Then he grinned. 'Well, I'll be damned!' He recovered and said, 'It's the interval in a few minutes. I'll show you round the back to her dressing room.' He looked at the midshipman again and shook his head. 'Well, well!'

Keyes didn't care what the man thought or why. He had had a terrible leave. Shunted back and forth between his parents' friends and relatives, made to recount the story of the action again and again, until he was heartily sick of it. The parts he wanted them to know, he found were too private. Too personal when it came to the moment of telling. His mother usually burst into a fit of sobbing and said. 'My poor boy.' His father followed up with, 'Must have been a proud moment.' Or something of the sort.

And every single day of his leave he had telephoned the theatre to speak with Georgina. To begin with, the persons he was able to talk to had seemed doubtful. Then as he had persisted, somebody had looked up some bills and had agreed that Miss Georgina

Dare would indeed be coming to this theatre with *Forces Frolics* in due course, although God alone knew how *he* had discovered the fact! It restored his faith, made him glow to realise that he knew more than the theatre.

It had not helped his nerves. He had lost his appetite. Got drunk twice, and had made his mother remark severely, 'I don't know what they teach you in the Navy, but I don't like it, Allan!'

His father had, as usual, taken the neutral course. 'Don't harass the lad, Mother! He has to spread his wings a bit.' But he, too, had seemed a bit worried.

And now he was here, at the theatre. He was reminded of the old films he had seen in his boyhood. The 'bloods' and stagedoor-johnnies waiting to escort their girls of the chorus to the Café Royal, or somewhere like it. But he was visiting one of the *stars*. Through the sealed doors he heard the thump of an orchestra, the responding chorus of male voices in 'Let's all go down the Strand'. It could have been Grand Opera to him at that special moment.

The man returned and gestured to some narrow concrete stairs. 'Up the top. First door.'

As Keyes hurried up the stairs the stage-doorkeeper said, 'Bit of a change for Georgie, ain't it?'

The man with the cash box rubbed his chin. 'Must be more to him than shows at a glance, eh?'

Keyes hesitated outside the flaking door. There were telephone numbers and messages scrawled over the wall. An air of decay, smells of grease and powder, of dust and sweat hung in the narrow passageway like part of the building itself.

He rapped on the door and heard her call, 'Just walk right in, sailor!'

She was sitting at a dressing table, the large mirror of which was surrounded by different coloured light bulbs, as well as wads of postcards and old telegrams, the flotsam of previous occupants. She had her back to him, and was wearing a short, very flimsy coat with a collar of pink feathers. The coat was open almost to her waist, and as he stared at her reflection in the mirror, spellbound, she looked up at him for the first time.

She swung round on her stool. '*You!*' She pulled her coat together. It only helped to reveal her breasts as well as uncover a larger portion of bare thigh. She swallowed hard. 'Where—I mean . . .'

He held out the card. *She was so overcome by his arrival that he wished he had telephoned her first.*

'I'm so sorry.' He hesitated, feeling the flush rising to his face. 'Georgina.'

She took a very deep breath. 'Of course. Iceland.' She patted a chair, giving herself time. 'Sit down. You sound all in, er . . .'

'Allan.' He looked round the dressing room. 'You look marvellous.'

'I seem to recall that I gave the card to one of your lieutenants.'

'Yes. He'd forgotten to pass it to me. Otherwise . . .'

She nodded slowly. 'Otherwise. Yes, I get it.'

He decided to try again. 'I thought we might go out somewhere. To a restaurant. Have dinner.'

She studied him gravely. He had changed in some way. He looked strained. Desperate. She thought of the pilot officer called Mike, and gently eased him from her mind.

'Well, Allan. Where's it to be?'

'I thought perhaps you'd know of a decent place.'

She looked in the mirror, seeing the way his hands were gripped together, and was suddenly moved by what she saw.

Georgina Dare, aged twenty-six, whose name on a birth certificate described her as Grace Wilkins of Shoreditch, London, who was married to a soldier in the First Army, and knew more about ways to excite men than most, was actually touched by the sad-faced, eager boy in a midshipman's uniform than she would have believed possible.

Gently she asked, 'How much cash have you got?'

'Three pounds, and a bit.'

She took a deep breath. She could not allow him to escort her to one of the local places. Someone would spoil things. And up West, after the theatre had closed, the price would be three pounds just for a glass of watered wine.

She said firmly, 'There's a place down the road. They sell drinks. Tell them I sent you. They'll let you have some Scotch.'

He stared at her, completely lost. It was getting out of control.

She stood up and touched his hair with her hand. She was very close to him and he could see her neck and shoulders, very white, through the flimsy coat.

She added softly, 'After the show we can go back to my flat. It's not far.' She hesitated. 'Unless you really *want* to go to a restaurant?'

He replied, 'No. Whatever *you* want. Really.'

'That's settled then.'

She touched her hair with a comb. Anyway, it would make certain that they did not bump into Mike.

By the time they reached her flat Keyes' mind was in a complete whirl. They had stopped on the way at a small backstreet pub where they had had quite a few drinks and exchanged greetings with some other jovial characters. 'Showbiz people,' she had explained casually. A couple of old-timers from the Hackney Empire, a chirpy comic from the Mile End Road. It was another existence to Keyes.

She unlocked the door of her flat. Picked two letters from the floor, remarking, 'Damned bills, I expect!' and switched on the lights.

It was a tiny flatlet, with a kitchen and bathroom opening like large cupboards from either end.

She nodded towards the sideboard. 'Some glasses in there.' She saw his uncertainty and crossed the room to face him. 'What's the matter? Is anything wrong?'

He put his arms round her, like someone handling a piece of priceless porcelain, and answered shakily, 'I've wanted to see you for so long. And now . . .'

She pushed him firmly into a battered sofa. 'Drinks first. Then some music.' She was groping amongst a pile of records. 'Geraldo. He'll do.'

Keyes' head revolved as he watched her moving busily round the room. Drinks appeared, and Geraldo's orchestra provided a muted accompaniment.

She said, 'Hang your nice coat on that chair.' She leaned over the back of the sofa and ruffled his hair. 'Here's to you then, sailor. Now, I must get out of this dress. It belongs to the show anyway.'

She vanished into the bathroom, humming in time with the gramophone.

Keyes loosened his tie and poured another drink. He had only had whisky once in his life. At his aunt's funeral. It was hot and fiery, but not as bad as he remembered.

She came back in a white négligé and stood by the door, eyeing him calmly, a small smile on her red lips.

She asked, 'Approve?'

He nodded and said hoarsely, 'You look lovely.'

She nestled beside him, sensing his sudden confusion and despair. In another moment he would make an excuse and leave. His moment and dream shattered. And her evening wasted.

She touched his face and then pulled his head round towards her and kissed him hard on the mouth. He was as stiff as a board, but she was not one to give in easily. She said into his ear, 'Hold me, Allan.'

He reached out blindly, his eyes buried in her hair. The négligé was wide open, her breasts and supple body right here under his hand.

She gave a small sigh, her hands tugging at his shirt and exploring his chest. She could feel his agitation giving in to something far stronger. She thrust him away and stood up, letting the négligé fall to the floor.

'I'm waiting, Allan.'

She watched him as he struggled with his clothing, and reached out to help him.

'My poor darling.' She did not know why she had spoken. 'Let me do it.'

She laid down beside him and kissed him again. This time he was ready. She sighed with catlike satisfaction. And very able.

Two miles from the room where Midshipman Keyes was being led deliciously into manhood, Able Seaman Jevers stood in a crowded bar staring at his beer.

Back to the ship tomorrow.

He downed the beer and gestured to the barman. And everything was quiet. As it should be. Nobody had said much about his wife, and he guessed they were too embarrassed. Funny that. The whole bloody city falling in bits under the bombing, yet these daft buggers still bothered about unfaithful wives and unhappy marriages.

He'd go back to the ship and try for his leading rate. He was due for promotion, which would make him eligible for chief quartermaster. He had it all worked out. As Leading Seaman Harry Rumsey, *Warlock*'s chief Q.M., had somehow survived the shellburst, his job would not be vacant. He'd apply for a draft chit to another ship. There would be no questions asked that way. It would be the natural thing for a matelot who was trying to better himself. He grinned and swallowed another glass of watery beer.

In the other bar, the Snug as it was called, Sergeant Matthew Wagner kept out of sight behind a bottle-glass partition. The thin-haired railway porter at his side nodded firmly.

'That's 'im, all right, mate.'

The American gestured to the barman. 'Scotch for my friend here. Make it a triple.'

The barman showed his teeth. 'Where you bin, chum? *Scotch?* I'll give Bert a large gin, s'all I can manage.'

The elderly porter smiled at the American's grim face.

'There was this article in the *Hackney Gazette*. Had a bit about Jevers. Local bloke an' all that. Got a mention in despatches for stayin' at the wheel in the middle of the battle, or summat.'

He laid the newspaper cutting on the wet bar. It was an old picture of Jevers, but there was no mistake.

The porter named Bert said, 'It's 'im all right. The same chap as I saw that night when 'is wife went missin'. Right 'ere, on the manor.'

'Thanks, Bert.' Wagner felt the surge of rage again. 'I'll not forget.'

Bert said, 'Well, I said I'd phone you, didn't I? I promised!'

'Sure you did, old-timer. And I'm grateful.' He peered round the partition but saw the space at the bar was empty.

Bert said, 'S'all right. 'E'll 'ave gone to his old 'ouse, I 'spect.'

The sergeant nodded and pushed his way towards the door, his mind racing. Now he would be able to get it out of Jevers. The porter would give evidence if necessary that he had been at his home on the night he'd claimed to be elsewhere. What a bit of luck the picture in the paper had been.

He hesitated, his eyes blind in the blacked-out street. Then he heard Jevers' uneven steps in a narrow alley, saw the pale rectangle of his blue collar.

He called harshly, 'Hold it, fella! Right there!'

An off-duty policeman and an air-raid warden found the American's body half an hour later. He was still alive, but a knife-thrust had almost certainly punctured a lung, and he was barely breathing. As the warden ran to call an ambulance the policeman stayed with Wagner, shielding his face from the rain which had just begun to fall over the East End of London.

Once the American opened his eyes and managed to gasp one word. It sounded like a girl's name. *Janice.*

The policeman sighed. Another fight no doubt. Local boy and Yank. Brawling over a girl.

He would telephone the American provost marshal. He was better at this sort of thing.

Down the alley in the little pub the porter called Bert heard the ambulance roaring past, its gong going for all it was worth. He sipped his large gin and thought about Wagner. Nice chap. One of the best.

Lieutenant David Sheridan sat in a deep chair with his feet on the wardroom fender watching the glow in the stove. It was almost welcome to feel the ship moving again, lurching occasionally against the piles of the jetty where she had been since leaving the dock. Tomorrow the bulk of the hands would return from their long leave. He had already been aboard for four days, sorting out new faces, fitting them into watch-bills and duty rotas.

Beyond the steel hull he heard the wind moaning across the blacked-out basin, the tap of heavy rain on deck.

Soon *Warlock* would be putting to sea once more. Another mission like the last? Or back to convoy? He found he did not care. Either way. He had not applied to leave her after all. He was still the first lieutenant.

He had had a strange leave. He had taken long walks in the countryside. Keeping away from uniforms, searching for solitude in small pubs and within himself. It had been like therapy, he thought. Self-inflicted.

He had met the captain only twice. Neither of them had mentioned a change of appointments. Drummond had seemed younger. Relaxed. That would be the girl, he thought. Despite everything, he grinned. *Lucky beggar.*

Sheridan looked round as the coxswain peered through the door. He was wearing an oilskin and carrying a torch.

'Ready for rounds, sir.' Mangin glanced at the empty wardroom.

'Right, 'Swain. Anything doing?'

'Nah.' Mangin rubbed his wet hands. 'Duty part of the watch 'ave cleared up the messdecks. Most of 'em are too shagged out to stay on their feet.'

'Have a tot while you're here, 'Swain.'

The coxswain took off his cap and stepped quickly to the fire. 'Tha'd be just fine.'

Sheridan handed him a large gin. 'Well, I'm still here.'

The coxswain took a swig and smacked his lips. 'Knew you would be, sir. First day you come aboard. Knew you was a *Warlock*, like the rest of us poor buggers!' He grinned. ' 'Ere's to the next time!'

The coxswain became formal. 'Some of the lads is off shore already, sir. A.B. Jevers is one. 'E's slapped in a request to see the old man about gettin' 'is 'ook and transfer to another destroyer.'

Sheridan nodded. He had forgotten about Jevers.

Mangin added, 'The *Lomond*'s got a vacancy for chief Q.M., sir. 'Ers 'as gone to the depot to sit for cox'n.' He showed his uneven teeth. 'Smart chap!'

They both turned as Sub-lieutenant Hillier stepped over the coaming, his cap and raincoat dripping wet. Hillier was holding himself very erect, and was obviously still recovering from his cracked ribs.

'All right, Sub?'

Hillier smiled. 'Yes, thanks. I'm not sure how *you* are going to be in a few minutes, Number One.'

'Are you a bit stoned?'

Hillier tossed his cap on to a chair and held his hands by the fire.

'I just saw Captain Beaumont on the jetty. He seems to be making for this ship.'

Mangin snatched his cap.

'Wot? At *this* time o' the night?'

Sheridan scrambled to his feet.

'Are you sure? I thought he was supposed to be in London.'

Hillier sat on the fender, pleased with the storm he had caused.

'Well, he's here now. More to the point, Number One, I'd say he was rather sloshed, too!'

Sheridan dashed out and up the ladder, to be met by the duty Q.M. and gangway sentry. He saw the figure at the end of the brow. Hillier was not mistaken.

Beaumont walked very slowly and carefully across the brow, and as he moved into the tiny glow of the quartermaster's police light Sheridan saw that he was without a raincoat. His immaculate cap and uniform shone in the feeble light like blue metal. He was sodden.

Sheridan said, 'In here, sir. Out of the rain.'

Beaumont did not move. He said, 'The captain, where is he?'

'Ashore, sir. He's not due back until . . .'

Beaumont swayed and seized the guardrail for support.

'Fetch him, telephone him. Do what the bloody hell you like. But I want him here *now*!'

Sheridan stood aside as Beaumont swayed towards the lobby door.

'Yes, sir. I'll attend to it right away.'

Beaumont had vanished, and he heard him scrambling down the steep ladder, breathing hard and cursing with each step.

Mangin murmured, 'Somebody's for it, sir.'

'Hmm.' Sheridan groped through the gangway log. 'What was that number?'

A returning libertyman was staggering towards the brow. Looming forward and swaying back again into the persistent rain. Mangin knew from the man's tipsy voice that it was Petty Officer Owles.

'It's goin' to be one o' them nights.'

Mangin yanked the P.O. steward on to the deck.

To the sentry he rasped, 'Take the P.O. to 'is mess and pour as much coffee into 'is guts 'as they can 'old.' He gripped the beaming Owles by the lapels. 'You'd better sober up, matey. The skipper is goin' to need you, 'eaven 'elp 'im.'

Owles replied stiffly, 'Can't a chap enjoy a song when he feels like it?'

He started to bawl again but allowed the sentry to lead him towards his mess.

Sheridan was on the shore telephone. 'I want to speak with Commander Drummond, please.' He pictured them together and felt vaguely ashamed. 'Captain, sir? I think you'd better get down here as quick as you can.'

16

Old Friends

DRUMMOND sat in his day cabin watching Beaumont's bulky shadow as it soared back and forth across the white paint like an angry spectre.

It had been hard to get a taxi from Edinburgh at this time of night, and all the way to the dockyard he had wondered what was so important to bring him back. Sheridan had said little on the telephone, other than to assure him that there was nothing wrong with the ship.

He had found Beaumont fuming by the wardroom stove, his jacket drying on a chairback while he sipped repeatedly from a silver flask. To see him in such disarray, something which had never happened before, suggested a really serious situation.

Now, as he watched the other man and listened to his barely controlled anger, he found he was able to match it calmly, instead of feeling the resentment he might have expected.

Beaumont was saying, 'By God, I thought I knew about men, and in you I believed I had found a loyal, trustworthy officer.'

Drummond said sharply, 'Look, sir, I've listened to you for ten minutes. I still don't know what was so urgent to get me out of bed.'

Beaumont glared at him. 'Bed? Yes, I expected you to be with *her*!' But as Drummond made to rise to his feet he hurried on, 'No matter! I don't give a damn what you get up to. All I know is that people have been plotting against me behind my back, creating a vendetta, when I have, through my own efforts and trust, given them nothing but success and pride.'

Drummond eyed him coldly. 'I was interviewed some days ago by Vice-Admiral Brooks. He asked for my opinion. I gave it. I still believe that the plan of attack was right, but wrongly executed.'

Beaumont paused in his movements and stared down at him, his face flushed and triumphant.

'It bloody well worked, didn't it?'

'Good men died unnecessarily, sir.'

'In *your* opinion!'

'Yes.'

Beaumont seemed momentarily confused by the bald reply. He exclaimed, 'And another thing. You went to see that rating in a Manchester hospital. *She* put you up to it, didn't she?' He shook both fists in the air. 'After all I've done!'

Drummond thought of their visit to the small hospital. The thing which had made it worse had been the quiet. Absolute. Until it had seemed to press on the eardrums like thunder.

And the man, Carson. Lying in a steel cot, hands exactly placed on the neat bed-cover. Like two lifeless claws.

A doctor had already admitted that the hospital had been able to do little for him. Or for many of the others. Drummond had felt the girl gripping his arm, as if fearful of being separated from him as they had followed the doctor past silent wards.

Gaunt-looking men in dressing-gowns. Leaning on sticks and crutches, or merely standing by the windows watching the rain without any sort of recognition. It was strange how their suffering had moulded them. They all looked the same age. The same build.

Carson had showed a tiny flicker of recognition when his eyes had finally settled on Sarah.

Drummond had said quietly, 'I want to ask you something.'

The contact had gone instantly, like the snapping off of a light.

But she had whispered, 'You can speak.' She had reached out to take Drummond's hand. 'Trust him, please.'

Carson's eyes had ventured round very slightly. Then in a strange, tuneless voice he had muttered, 'It was true. We was on the raft. I was almost done in, but I could 'ear 'em shoutin' at each other. Like madmen they was.'

'Who?'

'Beaumont.' The man had closed his eyes tightly. 'The bloody bastard!' A clawlike hand had groped over to touch the girl. ' 'Im an' your brother. I was a messenger on *Conqueror's* bridge. I 'eard the admiral askin' Beaumont's advice about some signal

261

or other. Beaumont kept sayin' over an' over, it was right to send the destroyers away.'

The doctor had interrupted worriedly, 'I think that's enough. It's weakened him quite a lot. You'll have to go, I'm afraid.'

That same doctor had probably telephoned higher authority. Beaumont. Brooks. Anyone.

Drummond said quietly, 'You're not the only one with responsibility, sir.' If he had hit Beaumont he could not have affected him more. 'I have my own ship to consider. The lives of all the men who are working with me at any given time. You must realise that? There's more to fighting a war than medals.'

'Of course I do. D'you take me for a complete fool?'

It was almost dawn. In a few more moments the cook would be roused, anyone might hear Beaumont shouting. Drummond stood up quickly. It was too late to turn back. Too much depended on it. On him.

He said evenly, 'When you took the flotilla on exercises, and we had the luck to capture a German midget submarine, one which up to then had been virtually unknown to the Allies, I believe you saw your way clear. I did not really understand what could happen to a man caught up in a system of ideas not of his own making. But I do now. Part of it anyway.'

He expected Beaumont to shut him up. To put him under arrest. The silence was like that at the hospital.

He continued, 'You wanted to use your reputation to gain advancement. It's not uncommon. But you did not see that every man has his limitation, beyond which he's a menace. A threat to everyone who relies on him.'

Beaumont sounded hoarse, as if his collar was too tight. 'You dare to suggest that I would risk lives for my own benefit?'

'I think, sir, that you saw the midget submarine as a useful lever for your next appointment. Far more senior officers than you have been tempted, sir.'

'Go on.' Beaumont sat down in a chair, never taking his gaze from Drummond's face for a second. 'I can't *wait* to hear your verdict!'

Drummond said quietly, 'Try to think about it, sir. Before it's too late. You've allowed yourself to be used. Used beyond your scope. When you consider the odds against success on that last raid, I think we are all being driven beyond it.'

'*Really*.' Beaumont dragged on his coat, breathing heavily. 'I'm glad I came now. I needed to cut through red tape. To treat you fairly. As a man, not a subordinate.' He smiled to himself. 'I didn't expect you to be pleased at the visit, but I did anticipate you would do me the favour of understanding. Of *understanding* that our work must arise above personal and petty ideals.' He paused and glanced at himself in the mirror. 'However, I know the strain you have been under. Some react differently from others in such matters. Far too much depends on the efficiency of this unit to waste time and labour on you. You do your part and obey orders, and I'll ask nothing more. Use your present *fame* to damage me, or to gain rewards for yourself, and you will regret it. As will others.'

He faced Drummond, apparently composed, and with nothing to show for his heavy drinking. 'Sarah Kemp's brother was a fool and a coward. I tried to save his life, as I did others. After *Conqueror* went down, when I met Sarah Kemp and saw her despair, how could I tell her that her brother was a screaming, yellow-bellied coward?' He sighed. 'Even at the risk of damaging my own reputation by lying about what happened, I could not bring myself to hurt that woman further.'

Drummond watched the returning power in the man. Like sunrise on hard metal. Beaumont had found a weakness and would use it ruthlessly if pushed further.

He said, 'Thank you for confiding in me, sir.' He did not hide his disgust and contempt.

Beaumont picked up his cap. 'Don't try to dislodge me.' He looked round sharply as Owles appeared in the doorway. 'Sorry. Can't stop for coffee.' He smiled at the steward's confusion. 'But I daresay your captain needs one. *Now*.'

The days which followed Beaumont's unexpected visit to the ship were surprisingly empty of incident. Drummond expected a summons to naval H.Q. at Rosyth, even to the Admiralty. To be told he was being transferred to other duties. To be reprimanded by Brooks. Almost anything. But nothing of the kind happened.

The worst part had been parting with Sarah at the railway station. Drummond had seen so many like it in the past. Two faces separated by a few inches. One on the platform, one in the train window. So many words which never came until it was too late and the contact broken. The station had been packed with uniformed figures. Some saying goodbye, like himself, others being joyfully welcomed home on leave.

She had been ordered to report back to the ministry in London, and the thought of her enduring the nightly raids worried him more than his own immediate future.

He had watched her waving until the train had pulled around a curve, and had returned to the affairs of his ship. With Beaumont back in London, he was in control of the flotilla's remaining ships.

Captain Kimber, the admiral's right-hand man, was a regular visitor to the dockyard. He was usually accompanied by several staff officers and base engineers, and he rarely discussed the operation which Brooks had hinted at in London.

In fact, a complete security screen seemed to hang over the four survivors of the Scrapyard Flotilla. *Lomond*, the leader, was an outstanding example. She had remained in her basin, heavily guarded, and with only dockyard personnel allowed on board.

Lieutenant-Commander Dorian de Pass had exclaimed more than once, 'Damned cheek, I say. Don't they trust me or something?'

And then one day, while Drummond was writing a letter to Sarah in his cabin, Selkirk of the *Ventnor* came aboard to see him. He came straight to the point.

'Look, sir, I know you're only temporarily in charge of us while Captain (D)'s away, but I'm worried. I'd like to ask you something.'

'Go ahead.'

Like the rest of them, Selkirk had been more withdrawn since the raid. At the best of times he was a difficult man to know.

Selkirk said, 'Captain Kimber's *experts* have been aboard my ship again. She had a real battering from those Jerry guns, but I thought the repair work was finished. It looks very sound to me.'

'Well then?'

Selkirk shifted in his chair. 'I got hold of a chap I know in the yard. Ordnance artificer. Been a friend for years.' He shrugged. 'I *know* all about security. That I'm not supposed to speak with anyone.' He looked hard at Drummond. 'How would you feel, if it was your ship?'

Drummond asked quietly, 'What did your friend tell you?'

'That they're putting my *Ventnor* back in dock. Like the *Lomond*, she's got to have something else done to her. When I touched on the matter with one of Kimber's staff he told me, politely, to mind my own business!'

Drummond lowered his eyes, seeing the top line of a letter she had sent him yesterday. *I have written to ask him for a divorce.* It was like a dream coming true.

He shook himself and said, 'I'll see what I can find out. Probably some new weapons being fitted.'

Selkirk shook his head. 'No. They'd put us down the other end of the yard.' He stood up. 'You will try and find out, won't you?' He was pleading. It could not be easy for him. 'I want to finish this bloody war in *Ventnor*. She can be a bitch, but I've got to know her. It's different for you. You're a career officer. But me, well, it's one war and one ship. Then I go back to freighters and clapped-out old tramp steamers.' He grinned. 'Maybe I'll make master of one of them!' He went out without waiting for Drummond to reply.

Drummond picked up a telephone. A voice answered, 'Officer of the day, sir?' It was Hillier.

'I'm going ashore to H.Q. in a while, Sub. Send the doctor down here.'

Vaughan arrived as he was running a comb through his unruly hair.

'Sir?' The pale eyes watched him emptily. 'I'm afraid I can add nothing to what you heard about Jevers. He seems to be telling the truth.'

'It's not about Jevers.' Drummond turned to face him. 'I believe you're fairly friendly with a Wren officer?' He held up one hand. 'No, I'm not nosing into your private affairs, Doc.'

Vaughan smiled gently. 'It's perfectly all right, sir. I am quite proud of the affair actually.'

Drummond grinned. 'I'm glad to hear it. But I want you to go and see her right away. She's a signals officer, right? So you will have to go up the ramp between two basins. I need to know something about *Lomond*. You will have to pass some guards, but if you're going to the signal tower by that route they'll have to let you through.'

Vaughan was interested. 'What am I supposed to be looking for?'

'Anything. Everything. I'm not certain.'

He scribbled some notes on a pad. 'Here, take this. Tell Signals I want that pamphlet.'

Vaughan beamed. 'My cover, sir. I feel like a spy!'

It seemed to take an age before the doctor returned.

He said, 'They didn't even stop me, sir. Saw my scarlet stripe, I expect. Doctors are not supposed to know anything about ships.' He became serious. '*Lomond*'s forecastle is completely open to the sky. Welders and all kinds of people swarming about like flies. Seems to be some sort of steel framework being put into the front of the hull.'

'Strengthening it, do you think?'

'Yes.' He nodded. 'Exactly.'

'Thank you. Get Owles to fix you a drink. I'm off to H.Q.'

He walked out and up to the iron deck. It was very cold, with a stiff wind ripping at the overnight rain puddles and making the ships' flags stand out like painted metal.

After the usual delays, showing passes, waiting for messengers to return from delivering trays of tea to all the various offices, Drummond was eventually escorted to a small office below the operations room. It was steamy with heat from a radiator, but the walls were running with condensation. As if the room were submerged.

Captain Kimber greeted him cheerfully. 'God, you must be a damned mind-reader. Was just going to pop over and see you.'

Drummond said, 'About our orders, sir?'

'Yes. Up to a point.' Kimber lit his pipe methodically. 'Vice-Admiral Brooks was here this morning. Flew up.'

'I didn't know that.'

'Not surprised. He moves very quietly.' It seemed to amuse him. 'He put me in the picture about the latest events. By the way, what did you want to see me about?'

'*Lomond*, sir. And I've heard a rumour about Selkirk's ship, too.'

Kimber frowned. 'Can't keep anything secret up here. Well, I can tell you part of it. We need two destroyers. *Lomond*'s keel was damaged by that last bombing. Had several near-misses, as you know better than I. She's had a long life.' His eyes were distant as he continued, 'Served in her myself as a young subbie.' He became businesslike again. '*Ventnor* was knocked about, too. She is the next obvious choice.'

'For what, sir?'

He could feel his muscles tightening. He had imagined that it would be different the next time. It never was.

'Sit down, Keith.' Kimber perched on the edge of a desk and studied him thoughtfully. 'I know you can keep a secret. I know, too, that you've already agreed to go on this next operation. The admiral wanted you from the start. I don't know if that makes it better or worse!' He added, 'We're planning a raid into occupied France. We've got full backing from the P.M. downwards. It's important. It could also be damned dicey for those who are taking part. *Lomond* and *Ventnor* will be manned by *volunteers only*. For them it will be a one-way trip.'

'Bill Selkirk came to see me, sir. He had heard rumours, too.'

'Yes. He would.' He sighed. 'He loves that old tub of his. But . . .'

Drummond asked, 'What about *Warlock*, sir? And *Victor*?'

'You will be going, too, of course. But in a more conventional role. There will be troops and commando taking part. Air cover. The lot.'

'Can you give me any idea when, sir?'

'Around Christmas, I should think. Long dark nights. Foul weather. Be easier for you in the long run.'

It was about two months away.

As if reading his thoughts Kimber added, 'I'll want you and *Victor* to go round to the west coast. To Greenock. You can exercise from there, up through the Minches. The Army have several special training camps on the islands. Your orders will fill you in. It's kid stuff to you, but it should help your new men, the, er, replacements, to settle into the team.'

Drummond nodded. 'It'll keep everyone's mind off it, too.'

'I'll see Selkirk myself. It will come better from me. I'm not involved. It will give him someone to blame, if that's what he wants.' He hesitated. 'Of course, I'd rather he remained in command.'

Drummond eyed him gravely. 'Don't worry. He will.'

'As for *Lomond*.' Kimber looked away. 'Captain (D) will be in command of her, I imagine. As it's his show, so to speak.'

He glanced at his watch and Drummond knew it was time to leave.

A Wren officer, not Vaughan's, caught up with him.

'Commander Drummond?'

He looked at her. She was pretty, but strained.

'Yes.'

'We've just had a signal phoned to us from Chatham. It was for you. We were going to send it to the ship, but I knew, we all knew you were in the building . . .' Her voice trailed away and she blushed.

Drummond asked, 'What was it about?'

She said, 'I'm awfully sorry, sir. It's about a friend of yours. Lieutenant Frank Cowley died last night in the hospital at Canterbury. His widow wanted you to know.'

Drummond looked away, his mind shocked. Poor Frank. All these months. Lying there, or trying to learn to walk on artificial legs. Probably reading about the flotilla, the *Warlock*, and all the rest of them, or hearing about them on the wireless.

Aloud he said, 'I should have gone to see him.'

The Wren replied quietly, 'Perhaps I shouldn't have told you. Like this.'

He touched her arm. Wishing she were Sarah, so that he could tell her about Frank.

He said, 'No. You did right. You made it seem more human. Thank you.'

Drummond walked towards the entrance doors, knowing the Wren was still staring after him.

That night he was sitting in his cabin drinking and thinking of all the things which had happened since he had been given the old *Warlock*. The ship moved restlessly at her moorings, pushed by a mounting wind. She was very quiet, as most of her company were ashore on local leave. Tomorrow forenoon, off to sea again. But tonight he would be alone. And think.

Feet banged on the ladder and Selkirk thrust aside the door curtain and said gruffly, 'Can I share a drink with you?' He seemed dazed. 'I've seen Kimber. He told me.'

Drummond said, 'Sit down, man.' He poured some brandy into a glass. 'Here.'

Selkirk stared over the glass, his eyes misty. 'They're going to make her into a bomb. A *floating bomb*.' He tossed back the drink and added savagely, 'In God's name, how can they do that to a ship!'

'I'm sorry. You know that.' He watched the man's anguish. Despair. He asked, 'Will you be staying?'

Selkirk stood up violently. 'You bet. You never know. There might be a chance of saving her.' The spark died just as quickly and he said brokenly, 'Poor old girl. What a bloody thing to happen!' And he slammed out of the cabin.

Drummond sat down heavily. A ship condemned. Elsewhere a man had died.

Sheridan appeared in the doorway, his shoulders glistening with rain.

Drummond pointed to a chair. 'Sit down, Number One.'

The other man sat, watching curiously as Drummond poured him a large drink.

He said, 'It's blowing up a bit, sir. Be a rough passage tomorrow for any weak stomach.'

Drummond did not seem to hear. He said softly, 'Your predecessor has just died.'

He had telephoned the hospital himself after leaving Naval H.Q. The doctor on the other end of the line had been evasive until he had told him that Frank had been his friend.

The doctor had said awkwardly, 'I am afraid that Lieutenant Cowley killed himself. There was nothing we could do.'

Sheridan replied, 'I'm sorry, sir. I did not know him, of course, but I have heard that you were both very close.'

Drummond said, 'We are going on another operation shortly.' He did not look at him. 'I just want you to know that I'd like you to be with me. I've treated you harshly, often unjustly. Perhaps it was because of Frank. Anyway, I'm sorry.'

Sheridan stared at him. He knew well enough that most of the trouble between himself and Drummond had been of his own making. He recalled Wingate's words. *Not fit for a command*. And now the death of a man he had not known had changed everything. Cowley's presence had remained in the ship, like an invisible barrier. Now it was gone. He was accepted. He saw the strain returning to Drummond's eyes and cursed himself. More than that, he was needed, just as Galbraith had implied all those long weeks ago.

He said, 'I don't think I'd be any good as a commanding officer anyway!'

Drummond looked at him and then poured another drink.

'If you can say that, there's hope for you yet.'

Vice-Admiral Brooks entered his map room by a small side door and nodded amiably to his chief of staff. The room was packed with officers, hardly one of whom was of lesser rank than captain, or its equivalent in the Army and R.A.F. Brooks held up a wizened hand.

'Smoke if you wish, gentlemen. And at the same time pray that the air-conditioning does not fail. It would be a grievous loss to our cause if all the top Service brains died from tobacco smoke.'

It brought a wave of chuckles. Brooks was always a popular speaker, and the fact he was well aware of it helped considerably.

He said, 'First, I would like to thank all of those present who have worked so hard with my department over the past weeks to make this plan a possibility.' The wizened hand gestured to a large table, discreetly covered by a cloth. 'The possibility is about to become reality.'

He paused long enough to allow an aide to light his cigarette, and for the assembled staff officers to settle themselves in their uncomfortable folding chairs. Inside the bunker it was damply warm, and it could have been any time of the day. In fact, it was evening, and up above in London there was an air-raid commencing over the south bank of the Thames, and several streets blazing to mark the fall of incendiaries. November was always a bad month for air-raids. Cloud cover, the natural misery of cold and short rations. It was no joke spending the night in an air-raid shelter with a blanket and a Thermos of weak tea, Brooks thought.

Beyond the air-raid he could visualise the other theatres of war. Italy, where the first stirring advances had slowed into a stalemate of snow and slush. And a German army, which even in retreat was still hitting back, and hard. On the Russian front it was the same tale. Vehicles and men in a white panorama of chilling, agonising endurance. The Allied victories in North Africa and Sicily, the Pacific and the great naval feats against the *Tirpitz* and the Norwegian fjords had become part of the past. Something in favour, but still the past. Next year. In the next few months the Allies would move against northern Europe. Every officer in the room knew it, almost to the date, and the millions beyond the steel doors were equally certain that there was no other way to a complete and final victory.

Brooks coughed. 'And now, gentlemen. Operation Smash-Hit is poised in the wings.'

He could feel the excitement like a drug. He did not like the code-name, but a member of the War Cabinet had expressed the opinion that it would appeal to the younger people. They, after all, had to do the fighting. It was a fair point, Brooks conceded.

In a way it was rather sad. All these familiar faces. Men who had dropped into occupied Europe to arrange supplies and to organise the Resistance from anyone who could pull a trigger or light a fuse. There were many no longer here, who had paid the price of daring. There were others who had commanded raids on enemy coasts, trained men from peaceful walks of life who became professional fighting men who did not need an order to kill. They acted by instinct now, playing the enemy's game, and making up for so many retreats and an inability to grasp that war is not for amateurs.

Once the final invasion of Europe was begun, his special force of inter-service experts would be scattered to individual sections. It was sad indeed. Like the breaking up of an old and tested college.

He saw Beaumont sitting with his arms folded, eyes straight ahead. Behind him, the only one in civilian dress, Miles Salter, puffy-eyed, as if he had slept badly for weeks.

He said, 'Uncover the table, Thompson.'

The officer removed the covering with a splendid swirl, rather like a matador, Brooks thought.

He forgot him and everything else as the table and its miniature coastline and port installations were laid bare in the overhead lights. The model was said to be perfect. It should be, too. R.A.F. reconnaissance planes had provided pictures, and a wealth of information had been amassed from such varying sources as peacetime travel agents and amateur yachtsmen.

'There, gentlemen. St. Nazaire. A German base of some importance, as last year's attack will bear out.' He took a pointer and held it above the sprawling concrete installations. 'The Normandie Dock, so called because it was built to hold the great French liner of that name, and still the best for repairing the largest enemy warships. Despite last year's attack, and the damage done by our valiant sailors and soldiers, much work has been done to put the dock area back into commission. Further, the German engineers have constructed another docking area, much along the lines of their highly successful U-boat pens, for the sole benefit of their new midget submarine arm.'

The air buzzed with excited comment, but when Brooks glanced at Beaumont he saw he was staring ahead of him as before, his forehead shining damply in the glare. Beaumont did not need to examine the model. He had looked at it every day since it had been made.

Brooks continued dryly, 'The time is now ripe for Smash-Hit to be put into operation. Only by an immediate frontal attack from the sea with a massive charge of explosive and the subsequent havoc of released water can this objective be destroyed, or at least crippled until after an Allied invasion. Bombing from the air has proved ineffective. The concrete emplacements are too strong, the losses of men and aircraft too savage to continue in any sort of strength. But if we fail to put this complex out of action, the enemy will be able to continue using it for her remaining capital ships like *Scharnhorst* and *Moltke*, and for all the other surface war vessels which could be employed against our invasion forces. What chance would frail landing craft and heavily laden transports stand against even one sortie by such ships? Just one setback would be enough for the enemy to recover from the initial surprise. After which . . .' He gave a narrow shrug. 'Frankly, we cannot endure another failure. It is as simple as that.'

Like an actor taking up his cue, Captain Kimber stepped up to the table.

'As you know, we have been assembling men and studying the objective carefully. Unlike last year's raid, we will have two destroyers instead of one, each of which will be loaded with explosives. To all intents, floating bombs.' He shut the picture of Selkirk's face from his mind. 'Two other destroyers, *Warlock* and *Victor*, will accompany them. To cover their attack and render any sort of aid they might need. Both of the latter have been in training with the commando units.' He saw an army brigadier nod to confirm it. 'And are now on their way to Falmouth.' He glanced at the clock. 'In fact, they should have arrived there an hour ago.' He looked at Brooks, wondering if the admiral was thinking how it had all begun in that Falmouth mortuary. He said, 'Coastal Forces are supplying M.T.B.s to combat fast enemy surface craft. M.L.s will be used to ferry the commando ashore to attack shore installations in depth.'

He glanced at an air vice-marshal with grey hair. 'The Royal Air Force will, needless to say, be supplying a full range of background bangs and grunts to keep Jerry fully occupied!' It brought some laughs, as Brooks had said it would. He became serious. 'Because of the enemy's vigilance, and the fact that once our surprise has been overcome he will see the attack as a near copy of the last raid, both *Lomond* and *Ventnor* will be fitted with *short fuses*. I do not have to explain to everyone here the importance of timing and co-operation.' Nobody was smiling now. 'Without them, this could turn into a bloody sacrifice to no good purpose. With them, and a lot of courage besides, it might well prove to be the first chink in the enemy's West Wall.'

As he paused, both to draw breath and to recall if he had left anything out, there was a burst of clapping. Magnified by the bunker's massive walls, it sounded like a stampeding mob of barefooted madmen.

He held up his hand. 'Captain Dudley Beaumont,' he paused, seeing their faces, watching their new confidence, 'will be in overall command. If any man can pull it off, he will.'

He hated the way they clapped and cheered. It was almost obscene when you stopped to consider what it would cost in lives whether it was a success or failure. Perhaps he had been working too long on Brooks's many projects. Or maybe he was too old for this sort of thing. He watched Beaumont's shining face as he stood and then bowed very slightly to the excited gathering. Perhaps it was just Beaumont.

Miles Salter caught the captain's eye and excused himself through the little side door. He had a lot to do, a report to prepare for immediate release if Beaumont succeeded with Smash-

Hit. He grimaced and rubbed his eye. It would not stop blinking since that terrible raid on the fjord. Even though *Lomond* had stayed outside, the air attacks had been terrifying. Salter had been crouching with his cameraman, gasping and retching as each stick of bombs had whistled and exploded on every hand. And when the *Whirlpool* had gone up with all those mines aboard, the cameraman had run below to hide. One result was that they had had few useful films, other than those taken in Iceland and off Bear Island. All the actual raid had been hidden by the land, and he still could not believe that *Warlock* and *Ventnor* had been able to do it on their own and still fight their way back to the others.

He paused by the press room and saw the usual weary gathering of war correspondents. As he turned the other way he heard a girl's voice and knew it was Sarah Kemp.

'Just a moment, Miles! I must speak with you!'

He turned heavily and waited for her to catch up. God, she was beautiful, and after the talk of death and destruction she looked particularly fresh and desirable.

'I've been trying to get hold of you for days!'

He grinned. 'Here I am, darling! Ready and willing!'

She did not smile. 'I'm serious, Miles. You've been avoiding me.'

'Yes.' He sighed. 'You've got your new assignment. I thought you'd be busy enough.'

She looked at him anxiously. 'A stupid job. Anyone could do it. I've been cut off from the Special Operations, I've even had my pass taken away. But I'm still on your staff, Miles, so what the hell is going on?'

Salter watched her worriedly. She was really concerned. Near to tears, which was not like her.

He said abruptly, 'Canteen. Cup of char.' He took her arm. 'We can talk there.'

He watched her stirring the awful canteen tea, the way her perfect breasts were moving under her dress. Just imagine it. With her. Pushing aside her protests, and then . . .

Salter asked wearily, 'What's the trouble?'

'I'm not a child. I know there's a big one coming off. I want to be involved with it. Because of . . .' She dropped her eyes. 'I don't have to spell it out to you, Miles.'

'True.' He studied her for several seconds. How wrong he had been about her. He said, 'You don't get it at all, do you?' He played with his spoon. 'Captain Beaumont doesn't trust you. Because of your brother. Because of Keith Drummond, too, in many ways. I wanted to get rid of you months ago. To transfer you to a nice department where you could work with sane, every-day people. I thought you'd be safe that way. Out of his reach.' He knew she was staring at him incredulously but could not stop. 'I'm as much to blame as anyone. When you're a real-life journalist, and you get dropped into an organisation like this, you can't help yourself. You make a story, and then the story makes you.' He added bitterly, 'Beaumont would not hear of your being transferred. He wants you where he can manipulate you. Like he does me, and damn near everyone else.'

'You sound as if you hate him?'

'Hate?' He looked at her and gave a crooked grin. 'He scares me to death. Like Frankenstein's monster. We've made it, and can't do a goddamned thing to control it.'

She gripped his hand across the stained table. 'Thanks, Miles. But I must see him. I love him. It's real this time.'

He nodded, watching her hand on his. 'I can see that, my love.' He made up his mind. 'A minesweeper came into port yes-terday. It had shot down a Dornier with one ancient machine gun. Either that or the German pilot had heart failure.' He saw her desperate eyes, and for a moment longer enjoyed her need of him. 'The boat is down in Falmouth. I can get you a special pass and travel documents for that. All you need.' He took her hand and examined it closely. 'Falmouth could be just what you want.' He squeezed it. 'And Christ help us if you let the cat out of the bag!'

She stood up and said huskily, 'Thank you, Miles, I'll never forget this.'

He watched her go and called, 'I'll still want that story about the minesweeper's bloody Dornier!' He gave a great sigh. Well, why not? It would probably be the last time they ever met.

17

Smash-Hit

DRUMMOND thrust open the wardroom curtain and stepped inside. He had just come from the chart room by way of the upper deck, and had noticed how treacherous everything was underfoot. Sleety rain had left a layer of slush on decks and fittings which could hurl the unwary into something hard or jagged. It was strange he could consider such minor injuries, he thought. With Operation Smash-Hit now firmly fixed in his mind.

The two destroyers had tied up in Falmouth that evening, and almost before the engines had fallen silent Drummond had received the next draft of his orders. He was glad of one thing. That Kimber was prepared to leave the briefing to him and nobody else.

Now, as he saw their expectant faces glowing in the comfortable wardroom lights, he was not so sure. Some of them would soon be dead. Perhaps all of them.

He had already told Sheridan. It was the beginning of a new trust, a bond between them. Carefully begun, handled like something fragile but infinitely precious.

Sheridan said formally, 'All present, sir.'

Drummond gestured around him. 'Please sit down. I'm the visitor here.'

He thought of the *Victor* alongside, of her R.N.V.R. captain, Roger North. He would be telling his people now. In his own way, as Drummond was about to do. Not treating them like machines, as a remote staff officer might have done.

He began, 'The last weeks of training have brought us all very close together. The old hands teaching the new. The new bringing fresh ideas to replace some of ours. Working in and out of Greenock, seeing the marines and commando doing their exercises, has told you that we're getting ready for something big.

Even Midshipman Keyes must have found time between writing letters to realise *that*!'

They all laughed, and even Keyes overcame his embarrassment at being the centre of attention.

'So I'm going to put you in the picture. It's soon now. In fact, we must be ready for the signal to move at any time from now onwards.'

He paused, watching them as they glanced at each other, smiled, or tried not to show too much concern.

'A special flotilla of ships is going to attack the German installations in St. Nazaire on the Bay of Biscay.'

Something like a great sigh went round the wardroom.

He continued, 'Two of our friends, *Lomond* and *Ventnor*, have been stripped out and filled with high explosives. They will proceed under their own steam, but with reduced complements of picked volunteers, all of whom have been chosen.' He looked down. 'Lieutenant-Commander Selkirk has remained with his ship.'

There was utter silence around him, and he could feel the ship noises intruding like whispers, as if *Warlock* was trying to say her piece.

'A force of torpedo boats, another of motor launches, will be employed as escort and for landing a shore demolition party. Fleet destroyers will be around to keep inquisitive Germans out of the way—' Someone, probably Wingate, gave an ironic cheer. 'And air cover is being laid on. The target will be the new dock installations. The method, to ram *Lomond* and *Ventnor* into them and fire the charges. Support craft will land and evacuate as many of the shore-party as possible. We will then withdraw.'

For a long while nobody flinched, each man immersed in his own thoughts, examining his own part of it.

Sheridan said slowly, 'I think we're all glad you told us like this, sir. Keeps it in the family.'

Galbraith added wryly, 'Aye, like the 'flu.'

'What is our role in things, sir?' Rankin watched him glassily.

'To assist the two ramming ships.' He let his words sink in. 'In any way we can. Two other destroyers will be accompanying us for some of the way, towing M.L.s, as we will, so as to conserve their fuel.'

It seemed that Brooks and his staff had thought of everything.

He looked at each officer in turn. Except of these living men, who would have to do it all.

Rankin, closing his mind to everything but what his guns would have to achieve. Wingate, tense, alert. Resigned, perhaps? Tyson and Hillier, side by side, yet a world of difference between them. The clean-cut New Zealander was probably composing one of his enormous letters. *Dear Dad. Today we were told about the big raid.* He and Keyes were always writing. Tyson was sitting with his chin on his chest, eyes fixed on the faded carpet. He could be shaking. He had not recovered from the last one. He was obviously terrified. Mr. Noakes, grim and unsmiling, a man without warmth or further ambition, no matter what he proclaimed. But he would not crack. His sort never did. Maybe war was endurable only for the unimaginative. The doctor was outwardly untouched by what had been said. His pale eyes were far-away, and only his scrubbed fingers moved in a small, restless tattoo. Young Keyes had grown up a lot. But not so much that he could hide his feelings. Anxiety was there. Pride, too, at being part of it. He looked at Galbraith and they exchanged quick smiles. As the engineer had said more than once, *you up there, me down here. We'll get the old girl through. Hell or high water.*

He turned as Sheridan asked, 'Will there be any leave for the ship's company?'

'I'm afraid not, Number One. I'll tell them about this business tomorrow. Then they can write their letters, and the port admiral will put them under lock and key until it's over.'

There was a discreet cough, followed by a tap on the door, and Petty Officer Ives, the new yeoman of signals, showed himself around the curtain.

Ives was a lean, stern-faced man, with the quick movements of a terrier. He had transferred from a light cruiser at his own request, and Wingate's description of his being 'very pusser' and like greased lightning with his work, had already proved correct. But it was hard not to look for Tucker's bluff outline, his shaggy beard and ready laugh on the bridge.

Ives snapped, 'Signal, sir. Thought you'd want it immediately.'

He did not relax or even glance at the watching officers. His hair was trimmed so short and so high above the ears that when he was wearing his cap he could have been completely bald.

Drummond could feel them all looking at him.

There was to be a top-level conference at the temporary H.Q. building in an hour's time. The last one when they would see each other as faces, before the balloon went up. The final line was the only one he revealed to the others.

He said quietly, 'The flotilla will proceed to sea tomorrow at 1800.'

Keyes' voice broke the stillness. 'But, sir, we will be away for Christmas!'

Surprisingly, most of them grinned at his horrified face.

Drummond said, 'Never mind. We'll make up for it later on.'

Sheridan asked, 'Will you stay and have a drink with us, sir?'

'No. I have to go ashore.' He smiled. 'But thanks. Have one for me.' He left the wardroom.

Vaughan crossed to Sheridan's side and held out a glass. 'Here, you should be congratulated.'

'What the hell for?' Sheridan was still thinking of Drummond's eyes. Like a man under sentence.

Vaughan smiled. 'I was talking to my Wren. About this and that.'

'I can imagine!'

'*Seriously*, old chap. She told me that the skipper has recommended you for command.' He stood back, enjoying Sheridan's astonishment. 'So here's looking at you, eh?'

Sheridan drew a deep breath. 'Well I'm damned.'

'Most probably.'

Drummond had reached the brow, and pulled up his great-coat collar as more sleet probed across the darkened deck towards the jetty. Rankin, who was O.O.D., had somehow managed to beat him to the gangway, and stood with the quartermaster to see him over the side.

Another officer was waiting with him. North of the *Victor*, who had just crossed the deck from his own ship which was on the outboard side.

He said, 'I'll walk with you, sir?'

He was a serious-looking man, very slim and contained. In peacetime he had been a solicitor as well as gaining recognition as a first-class yachtsman. He had even found time to join the volunteer reserve, and to get married to a stunning-looking girl called Elinor.

Drummond nodded. 'Glad of your company, Roger.'

They walked through the clinging sleet, hands in pockets, heads down.

North said suddenly, 'Pity about Christmas. Still, I've not had one at home since the war.' He laughed, the vapour spurting from his mouth like steam. 'God, this is going to be quite a show!'

Drummond replied, 'It is. How did your officers take the news?'

The other man chuckled. 'Reluctantly. My number one is convinced he's going to get the Victoria Cross!' He added quietly, 'Just so long as it's not a marble one.'

In due course they arrived at that same dreary-looking building. It was still like a mortuary. Armed sentries, sandbags and bustling personnel did not seem able to change it.

They were ushered into a crowded room. Drummond flicked down his collar and shook his cap on the floor. They were all here. Not the planners or strategists. The ones who were going to fight.

Then from across the room he saw Beaumont. He was staring at him, his pink features set in concentration.

He nodded curtly, 'Ah, Keith. Take a pew. We're all here now, I think.'

His eyes did not leave Drummond for an instant. A question, a warning? It could have been both.

Beaumont said loudly, 'Sorry about the weather, chaps. Even I couldn't fix anything up there!'

Drummond sat back in his chair. The main act was beginning at last.

The following evening, anyone who was foolish enough to brave the worsening weather, or still employed in the dock area would have seen the ill-assorted flotilla getting under way.

With *Warlock*, followed by *Victor*, in the lead, the motley collection of motor launches, two small Hunt class destroyers and a heavy salvage tug slipped from their moorings and pushed into a diagonal downpour of grey sleet.

Drummond buttoned his oilskin more tightly around his throat. Beneath its collar he had already wrapped a clean towel.

It was wringing wet before they cleared the harbour precinct and turned south-west towards the Lizard.

Sheridan lurched across the heaving bridge and reported that he had checked the blackout and been round all parts of the ship himself.

He said, 'We will be meeting the others tomorrow then?'

'Yes. The M.T.B.s are coming round from Bristol where they've been exercising for their part in things.'

Sheridan watched him narrowly, seeing Drummond's face shining in the sleet and falling spray.

'I'm sorry for the blokes in the M.L.s, sir. They'll be bobbing about like corks before much longer.'

Drummond lifted himself on his chair to watch the bows wallowing deeply in a trough, almost as far as the bullring. Around B gun the oilskinned seamen were crouching like pieces of black statuary. He had already thought about the small craft. Crammed with commando and marines, they might find it easier once they were in deeper water where the troughs were further apart. He hoped so, for all their sakes. Men keyed up to fighting-pitch were one thing. But to arrive at their objective bruised and demoralised by heavy seas would lessen their chances even more.

The weather was foul everywhere. The met reports had gloomily prophesied that the heavy snow which was now falling in the North Sea and English Channel would reach the Bay by tomorrow.

He tried to push his apprehension aside. They had been wrong plenty of times in the past.

'We will exercise action stations in fifteen minutes, Number One. Make a signal to *Victor* to that effect.'

After which it will be in deadly earnest, he thought.

Ives snapped, 'At once, sir!' It sounded as if he were clicking his heels.

Down on the messdecks the off-duty watch sat or crouched in their seagoing gear, knowing the alarm bells would soon be sounding.

Leading Seaman Rumsey, the chief quartermaster, went methodically through his own arrangements. Tin of fags, well wrapped in a bit of oilskin. Matches. Bar of nutty. He grinned lazily. And a lifebelt.

From the opposite mess, Leading Telegraphist 'Dolly' Gray called, 'You'll be going up to the wheelhouse, won't you, Harry?'

Rumsey glared. 'Where did you expect? To the bloody ward-room?'

The telegraphist grinned. 'Keep your hair on, mate! It was just that there was a message about your Q.M., Jevers. Has he been up to something?'

Rumsey pricked up his ears. 'Why?'

'Oh, maybe nothing to it, but the harbour police were making enquires about him. On behalf of the London coppers and the American provost marshal.' He shrugged and tightened his belt. 'We didn't tell them much, of course. Signals department was restricted until this lot's over.'

Rumsey stood up, gauging the distance to the vertical steel ladder to the deck above.

'I'll tell him anyway.'

The tannoy squawked. 'Hands to exercise action!'

Rumsey was the first up the ladder and through the small oval hatch before anyone had moved. He had never missed yet.

A few minutes later Sheridan reported, 'Ship at action stations, sir.'

Drummond had been listening to the staccato voices coming into the bridge from guns and magazines, from each section of his ship. Beyond them he had heard the regular ping of the Asdic, the surge and plunge of *Warlock*'s stem across the bustling white-caps. Sleet and leaping wavecrests, while astern he could just make out the dull blobs of the other vessels. Beaumont was back there in one of the accompanying Hunt destroyers, ready to transfer to a motor gunboat which was to be used as a com-mand vessel once they had joined *Lomond* and *Ventnor*. Far abeam he saw a winking green eye. Wreck buoy to mark some unfortunate encounter in the past.

'Thank you, Number One.'

They had gone to their stations quickly, considering it was only the usual exercise. They were behaving well. As they had when he had spoken to them about their part in Smash-Hit. Every captain thought his own company was different from all others. To everyone else *Warlock*'s people were probably very ordinary. In a street, or in their home towns, they would not even stand out. He ran his hand along the ice-cold rail below the screen. Nevertheless, this company seemed very different.

He said, 'Fall them out. Port watch to defence stations.'

In the sealed compartment below Drummond's chair, Leading Seaman Rumsey stepped up on to the grating and relieved the coxswain at the wheel.

He peered at the gyro repeater and said, 'Course two-two-five, 'Swain.'

Mangin grunted. 'I'm off then.'

As the men pushed away from the various action stations in response to the tannoy, groping irritably with each plunge of the deck, Rumsey said to Jevers, 'There was a call about you from the boys in blue. From London.' He watched the ticking gyro but heard Jevers' quick intake of breath. 'Something to do with the Yanks.'

Jevers scoffed, 'Gorn, you're makin' it up!'

'No. On the level, mate. Leading Tel. Dolly Gray took the message. Ask 'im, if you like.'

Jevers replied, 'I'm not bothered. Why the 'ell should I be any-way?'

Rumsey groped with one hand for his chocolate bar. He heard Jevers staggering down the internal ladder, his oilskin scraping against the wet metal.

He called up the voice-pipe, 'Wheel relieved, sir. Leadin' Sea-man Rumsey.'

Wingate's voice, almost lost in the slashing sleet. 'Very good.'

At the foot of the ladder Jevers paused and clung to a hand-rail. He felt hot and ice-cold in turns, and it was all he could do to think properly. Rumsey's casual mention of the police ex-plained everything. That bloody Yank must have been alive. He could feel him now, as he clung to the swaying ship. The tall sergeant's anger falling away to a choking cry of agony and dis-belief as he had driven his knife into him, twisting it with all his strength until the man's weight had pulled it clear as he fell.

He stared round the dim companion-way like a trapped ani-mal. Even now the wires would be humming. Perhaps the skipper already knew.

A bosun's mate lurched into him, and Jevers snarled, ' 'Oo the 'ell are you lookin' at?'

The seaman stared at him. 'Sorry, chum, I was just takin' the milk for old Badger. Didn't seem right to leave him behind this time.' He watched as Jevers blundered away into the darkness. 'Bomb-'appy sod!' he muttered.

Back in Falmouth the town and harbour settled down for a long night of sleet and probably snow. But they were used to it, and had been since ships had first gone around the headland. To meet the Armada, to fight under Nelson at the Nile, to fish, or to carry cargo to the other side of the globe.

Some of the berths were empty now, strangely derelict under the layers of slush.

In the dock office, where in happier times Customs officials and harbour pilots shared vast quantities of tea, the duty operations officer yawned over tomorrow's arrangements for an in-coming fleet repair ship.

The telephone broke into his thoughts, and on the other end of the line he heard the O.O.D. say, 'Sorry to bother you, sir. But there's a young lady from the M.o.I. here. She's got the right passes and everything, but . . .'

The operations officer said, 'Put her on.'

She had a very nice voice, he thought. She said, 'I was asking about the *Warlock*, sir. I wanted to see Commander Drummond. I thought . . .'

The operations officer recalled his own feelings as he had watched the strange collection of ships heading away from the land, the lump he had felt in his throat. And that was after four years of it.

He said, 'Wait there. I'll come up and see you.'

At the other end of the line she handed the telephone to a young lieutenant.

He asked, 'All right, was it?'

She looked at him and replied, 'I was too late.' She walked to the window and lifted one corner of the blackout to stare at the streaming glass. 'But I'll wait.' She was oblivious to the man's curious eyes. 'I'll be here when he comes back.'

Drummond awoke, ice-cold and shivering in his chair with some-one gripping his shoulder. It was Wingate, his eyes red-rimmed in the dull light, his face squinting against the unrelenting rain and sleet.

'Some nice hot tea, sir.' He gripped the voice-pipes as *Warlock* swayed heavily to one side, and watched Drummond take the first sip. Then he said cheerfully, 'Merry Christmas, sir!'

Drummond felt the scalding tea exploring his stomach and waited for his mind to level off. How could he or anyone else sleep in this? he wondered. But he had managed it. On an open bridge, and with his oilskin coat clattering to the steady downpour.

It had been pitch-dark when he had dozed off in the chair. He looked at his watch. Six in the morning. Funny how you could forget Christmas.

'Where are we, Pilot?'

Wingate gestured vaguely over the screen. 'One hundred and fifty miles south-west of Land's End, sir. Not bad, considering.'

Drummond lurched to his feet, stamping his seat boots to restore the circulation. All greys. Dull or pale. Interspersed at irregular intervals with breaking wavecrests, although mercifully the sea had eased out into long, ungainly rollers. If only the sleet would go, too.

He put the mug down and asked, 'How are the others?'

'All with us, sir. The two Hunts have had difficulty with their tows. Ours are okay so far.'

He waited until Drummond had peered aft to where two shining M.L.s veered this way and that on their tow lines. It was still very dark and overcast, and he was ravenously hungry.

He said, 'We should rendezvous with the others at 1100.'

'Yes.'

Drummond wondered what Selkirk was thinking as he conned his ship through the foul weather towards her final gesture. What had they told him? That Selkirk's ship has been loaded with some thirty depth-charges, which in turn had been sealed in concrete and supported by a mesh of steel frames just abaft her forward gun support. *Lomond*, being slightly larger, carried an even greater amount of explosives. Primed with special army fuses, their combined effect would be devastating.

Sheridan appeared on the bridge, his cap dripping, his face raw with blown salt.

He managed to grin. 'Happy Christmas, everyone!'

As time wore on the other ships and small craft took on shape and personality, and although no signals were exchanged, *Victor* had hoisted some kind of green garland to her foremast as a defiance to their circumstances.

Drummond thought of his sea cabin, the chance of rest. Even a shave. But it was not the time. Not yet. He munched a soggy corned-beef sandwich and drank more tea than he could remember doing before.

The watches changed, weapons were checked and tested as the little force headed slowly but purposefully south-west into the Atlantic. On either beam, out of sight and beyond contact, two separate groups of powerful fleet destroyers would be carrying out sweeps in case a solitary U-boat was trying to keep tabs on the strange flotilla.

Drummond looked at the sky. It would take another day to work into position. And then . . . He sighed and dabbed his sore face with a towel. The chiefs of staff were certainly doing them proudly, he thought. A force of bombers would make a strike to the south of St. Nazaire, another would cause a diversion further north towards the U-boat pens at Lorient. Heavy, but not unusual. Enough to keep the Germans busy, Christmas or not.

He thought about the letter he had written for Sarah. The hardest thing he had had to do in his life. If he were killed she would have to read it. It was more like a last will and testament, he thought.

It did not get much brighter, even during the forenoon. The patterns of grey merely got paler.

'Signal from *Victor*, sir! Ships in sight to the nor'-east!'

Down the lines of vessels the guns swung on their mountings, although like Drummond everyone was expecting the rendezvous.

A light winked briefly through the sleet and Ives said, 'From *Ventnor*, sir. *Nice to be back*.'

Drummond thought about Christmas, but decided against anything flippant. It would not help Selkirk at a moment like this.

'Tell him. *Good to have you in the family again*.'

But as the two other destroyers loomed through the grey murk everything else seemed to fade. For a moment Drummond thought it was a trick of the light, or that he had been too long on the bridge. But as the destroyers drew nearer he was aware of a sense of discomfort, something akin to the embarrassment you felt when you were confronted with a disfigured or badly burned man.

Sheridan was the first to break the stillness.

'What have they done to them, for God's sake?'

Ventnor was in the lead, but her outline was entirely changed. Extra metal plates had been welded to her bridge, and her un-equal funnels raked right back from the foremast. The forward gun was missing, and had been replaced by a small pair of twenty millimetres. Astern of her, the *Lomond* showed the same sort of crude surgery.

Drummond said quietly, 'The attack will be in semi-darkness. They will have all the outward appearances of German escort destroyers.'

The explanation did not really help.

He added heavily, 'Make the signal, Yeoman. *Take station as ordered.*'

He lifted his glasses to watch the two ships manœuvring to follow *Victor's* lead. In the misty lenses he saw Selkirk's face above *Ventnor's* screen, some others just behind him.

A Sunderland flying-boat, glinting like a wet whale, circled slowly overhead, dipped its wings and started back towards England. The pilot had watched over his charges and delivered the goods, while two screens of fleet destroyers had done the rest.

Hillier remarked, 'If the Jerries get the jump on us before we make our attack, it will all be wasted.' He sounded strangely moved. 'I'll never forget this. *Never.*'

Wingate gave a crooked grin. 'I'm sure we're all glad to hear that, Sub. Now go and fetch the next chart for me, eh?'

'Signal from Captain (D), sir.' Ives had his glass trained astern 'Reduce flotilla speed to ten knots. Execute Plan Baker.'

Drummond felt for his pipe, although it would be impossible to light it.

'Acknowledge. Tell the chief.' He looked at Sheridan. 'At seven o'clock tomorrow morning we will be in position to begin the final run-in.'

Wingate said, 'I've got the charts set up, sir.'

Drummond tried to consider his feelings. Not what he had expected? Perhaps even to the last he had imagined Beaumont would delay the attack. The weather and visibility were poor.

But if it got no worse it might act as an ally. Then, as evening closed in they would go about and steer south, and then east, deep into the Bay towards the Loire estuary. *Just like that.*

Sometime during the night the motor torpedo boats would come growling out of the darkness as additional support, and tomorrow they would move in for the kill. He gripped the pipe hard between his teeth until his jaw ached.

Owles appeared on the bridge, his features pinched in the bitter air.

'I'm makin' some nice stew, sir. Just the thing to keep out the cold.'

Drummond looked at him and smiled. 'Thank you. I'll have it in the sea cabin.'

Owles seemed surprised but pleased. 'That's the ticket, sir.' He grimaced. 'With all them squaddies down aft, you've got to watch every blessed spoon!'

He was referring to a platoon of grim-faced commando who had been put into the wardroom and passageway. Tough, heavily armed, their heads covered in khaki stocking-caps, they looked for all the world like bandits. Throughout the small force of vessels there were about three hundred soldiers and marines. Specialists.

Drummond said to Sheridan, 'I'm going down. For my Christmas lunch.'

They all ducked automatically as a great wash of spindrift sluiced into the bridge, and Wingate said, 'I wonder what I got in my stocking this year?'

Later in the tiny sea cabin Drummond stared at Owles' stew with something like nausea. His stomach contracted violently to the motion, but he knew he had to eat before something happened. He also knew it was not the motion which was making him the way he was. It was fear.

Drummond left the upper bridge just once more the following morning to check his calculations in the isolation of the chart room. As promised, the M.T.B.s had made contact, and the whole collection of vessels were now moving on schedule. He looked at the stained chart spread between his hands. Forty-seven degrees north six degrees west, and the coast of France some two hundred miles ahead of the corkscrewing bows. It was incredible that they had got this far without any sign of discovery.

The regular signals from the Admiralty suggested that the weather was too bad for German air patrols. They did not mention that the R.A.F.'s Bomber Command might also be grounded.

As Wingate had remarked, 'They won't want to spread alarm and despondency!'

He returned to his chair on the bridge and considered their situation. They had formed into their new formation. *Lomond* and *Ventnor* in the lead, steaming abreast, about half a mile apart. His own ship and *Victor* followed closely in their wakes, while the launches and M.T.B.s made two large arrowheads even further astern. The two Hunt class destroyers and the heavy tug had steamed purposefully to the south. Would-be rescuers, undertaker's men, their roles could change very quickly.

He turned to watch the command vessel, a motor gunboat, streaking up the starboard side, making a superb wash as she dashed past. He saw Beaumont's oak-leaved cap on her small bridge beside her commanding officer. He looked vaguely theatrical, he thought.

The sleet had changed to flurries of snow, much as the met men had promised. It seemed almost warm after the wet, soaking downpour.

He heard footsteps behind him and saw the senior commando officer, a trim lieutenant-colonel, watching the M.G.B. carrying Beaumont to the head of the procession.

'Good morning, Colonel. I hope you slept well.'

The soldier smiled bleakly. 'I spent most of the time trying to identify the creaks and bumps. Give me a field anytime.' He grinned and looked about ten years younger. 'Different from North Africa!'

Drummond turned to look for Beaumont's command vessel. He should be transferring to the *Lomond* before dusk. The M.G.B. would be needed by the marines' senior officer to watch over and control the demolition party.

The colonel asked, 'How do *you* rate our chances?'

'Evens.' He tried to smile. 'It's all a matter of timing.'

'Isn't everything, old boy?' The colonel yawned. 'I'm going to have some breakfast. In that sphere the Navy does have the edge on us.'

Down in the wheelhouse Midshipman Keyes heard the colonel

laugh, the clatter of his boots on the ladder, and then turned his attention back to the plot table. Like the navigator's yeoman, it was new, and it was only too easy to recall Rigge lying with his head smashed against the side, the bodies sprawled in the smoke.

The new man said brightly, 'There, sir, that's fixed it.'

Keyes nodded. He was thinking of that last leave. Georgina's perfect body above and below him, consuming him until he had been like a man possessed. He had written to her several times while the ship had been at Greenock, but had only had a post-card in reply. But then she was a star. She would be working all hours. He wondered if she was thinking of him at this moment. What his mother would say when he took her home on the next leave. He would soon be eligible for promotion, too. The picture built up in his mind. The veteran sub-lieutenant, and, all eyes turned to watch him pass with this dazzling girl on his arm.

Tyson staggered through the door and rasped, 'Get down aft. Number One wants you to help Mr. Noakes with the heavy towing gear. It's got to be ready for emergencies.' He glared. 'Well, don't just stand there, chop bloody chop!'

A signalman was busily cutting open a large canvas sack, tumbling bright bunting all over the wheelhouse deck.

Tyson asked sharply, 'What's all that?'

The signalman did not bother to look up, but spread out the uppermost flag. A big naval ensign, scarlet, with black cross and swastika.

He said, 'All ships will hoist German colours in fifteen minutes, sir.'

He said it so importantly that Rumsey, who was on the wheel, muttered, 'An' God bless us, every one!'

Tyson stared, his eyes bulging from his head. Each thrash of the screws, every dragging minute was clawing at his entrails like hooks. The sight of the enemy flags, here inside their defences, was like finding the Germans right amongst them. He felt the bile in his throat, an icy chill on his skin.

Rumsey darted him a glance and snapped, 'I'd get up to the forebridge, Bunts, afore the new yeoman starts a-barkin' for you!'

He did not like the look of Tyson. Toffee-nosed little bastard.

Rumsey had seen plenty of supposedly hard-cases crack open after their first taste of battle.

Drummond watched the flags breaking at masts and gaffs throughout the flotilla. They made the only patches of colour in the formation against the sea and the swirling flurries of snow.

All that day they had headed towards the French coast, but apart from sighting the conning tower of a British submarine they had the sea to themselves. The submarine had been positioned as a final marker. Once contact had been confirmed, she had flooded her tanks and dived deep, her part completed.

They were right on time, and despite poor surface visibility were keeping in their tight formation like Roman troops on a field of battle.

Towards dusk Sheridan stood beside Drummond on the gratings, moving his sea boots restlessly and dabbing his wet face with a piece of rag.

Drummond said, 'They'll be setting the time fuses aboard the *Ventnor* and *Lomond*.'

Even as he said it he was conscious of the finality. One of the officers on each ship would be down there now, squatting amidst their tons of high explosive, putting the whole thing into operation. Acid upon copper, like the ticking of a clock.

He added abruptly, 'Hands to action stations. Section by section. Check them yourself. Then come back here.' He hesitated and said simply, 'If anything happens to me, Number One, I want you to do your damnedest for the others.' He avoided Sheridan's eyes. 'Right?'

'You can rely on me, sir.' He added firmly, 'This time.'

It was almost midnight when the lookouts reported flashing lights dead ahead. But in fact they were the bursts of anti-aircraft fire reflected and distorted by snow and low cloud, many miles away. The R.A.F. had managed to do part of their work anyway. It was strange. Eerie. With the engines pounding away and the fans giving their confident purr you could hear nothing outside the ship. The snow was like a great damp curtain, so that the rippling red pin-pricks of the flak were without menace or substance.

Sheridan peered at his watch. It was nearly time.

He said quietly, 'We're in, sir. I don't know if we'll get out again, but the Germans have been caught napping up to now.'

Drummond looked at his own watch. It was just after one in the morning. What the hell was Beaumont doing? He should have left the M.G.B. and boarded *Lomond* for the final run-in. Drummond found he was sweating badly, fearing he was right, dreading the possible consequences. If Beaumont stayed in the command vessel, de Pass would have to take *Lomond* in on his own. Just thinking about it made him feel sick. De Pass could never do it. Not in a thousand years. Selkirk would be all right, but even he needed instructions.

He heard the colonel say, 'I've got my lads ready to disembark.' He was carrying a Sten gun and chewing on a sandwich. 'By God, it's thick up ahead.'

Drummond looked at Wingate. 'Have the battle ensigns hoisted. Get those Jerry flags down!'

A light blinked feebly from somewhere on the port bow. A challenge.

Drummond heard the squeak of halliards as the flags soared to the yards. By the time it was light enough to see them, the ship might be on the bottom.

Another light gleamed against the snow as *Lomond* flashed a quick reply. De Pass had put out his recognition signals as ordered. He was keeping his head so far. They were all largely guesswork, but would give the flotilla time to get that little bit closer.

A searchlight licked out from starboard, swept like a scythe over *Lomond* and *Ventnor* and then, surprisingly, vanished.

Drummond snapped, 'Carry on, Number One.' He heard him run for the ladder, and added, 'They'll be on to us any second now.'

A blue light winked brightly from water level, and Drummond knew that the command vessel was in sight of the main objective, the great concrete wall and iron caisson which formed the centre-piece of the dock area.

On either beam the M.L.s were moving forward like dark wings, their machine guns and cannon swinging to cover the darkening mass of land which was at last showing itself through the snow.

Drummond said tightly, 'The M.G.B. will lead us through the outer defences. *Ventnor* will take the caisson, *Lomond* will sheer off for the submarine pens.'

Tracer crackled over the masthead and whistled away through the snow.

In the shuttered wheelhouse Mangin gripped his spokes and muttered, ' 'Old on, me lads!'

Behind his heavy curtain Keyes turned his head slightly to look at the navigator's yeoman. His name was Farthing, and he seemed a nice chap.

Farthing was fiddling with the plot, and said between his teeth, 'Christ, I'm bloody scared, sir.' He forced a grin, which only made him look worse. 'I'm not like you, sir, this is the first real scrap for me.'

Keyes heard the impartial mutter of machine gun fire, and then an insistent thumping sound which puzzled him.

Farthing said hoarsely, 'Heavy mortars, sir. There used to be an army range near my home.'

Mangin and the others looked up at the deckhead as the first shells exploded close by. The detonations were muffled, but beat against the hull like hammers wrapped in sacking. *Boom. Boom. Boom.*

Rumsey, Jevers and the others stared at each other, eyes gleaming in the compass lights.

A loud bang rocked the ship violently, and somebody cried out with alarm.

Then Mangin heard Drummond's voice, *'Full ahead together!'*

A piece of metal struck the bridge and rattled down on the deck below.

Mangin listened only to the engine room bells, and then shouted up the voice-pipe, 'Both engines full ahead, sir!'

Reaching out on either bow the land was at last coming alive, like a great beast awakening to an impudent intruder. Red and green tracer lifted and slashed down through the snow, and from further inland came the heavier bark of artillery. Shells shrieked overhead, and one exploded aboard an anchored tender, setting it ablaze from stem to stern and lighting up the scene like a picture of an inferno.

Some of the M.L.s had already landed their shore parties on the mole and along one of the great concrete slipways and were heading towards *Warlock* and *Victor* at full speed to collect the rest of the troops. One M.L. was listing badly, her low hull partly concealed in a mass of red sparks and smoke. The air was alive with gunfire, the *Warlock*'s four-inch weapons adding to the din as they poured a regular barrage into the defences beyond the submarine pens.

Drummond watched the nearest M.L. swinging round to run parallel.

'Half ahead together!'

He heard Sheridan yelling through a megaphone, and prayed that none of the soldiers would slip and fall between the pitching hulls at the one, brief contact.

Very lights and flares drifted overhead, and Drummond saw fresh lines of tracer probing down from the tops of warehouses and the pens themselves.

Rankin's voice was harsh on the intercom. 'Pom-poms and Oerlikons shift target. Machine gun at—' His words were lost in the immediate crack and thump of cannonfire as his crews poured a devastating fire towards either bow.

'*Ventnor*'s cracking on speed, sir!' Hillier was yelling like a madman. 'Twenty knots at least!'

The old destroyer with the strange outline was pushing well ahead of the others, her churning wash and bow wave giving testimony of her increasing efforts to reach the target.

Slightly to starboard *Lomond* was being bracketed with shell-bursts, and she was replying as best she could, although her gun crews must have been blinded by smoke from the shore and burning harbour craft alike.

Wingate exclaimed in a choking voice, 'God, will you listen to *that*!'

An M.L. was thrashing clear of the side, her deck crammed with troops, some of whom were already firing Brens and other light automatic guns towards the shore. Above the insistent, ear-scraping clatter came the jubilant skirl of bagpipes.

Wingate said, 'How can he play the damn things in all this?'

More metal clattered over the bridge and a lookout cried sharply, 'Oh, Jesus!' Then he fell down on his face.

Ives snapped, 'Dead.' He dragged the body to the rear of the bridge, adding to one of his signalmen, 'Well, don't stare, lad! Take his bloody place!'

Drummond heard it all. The first of his company to die.

He levelled his night-glasses on the great mole and tried to find the command vessel. The blue light had gone, and the whole stretch of water seemed to be alive with darting M.L.s, drifting wrecks, a few men swimming towards the land.

'Direct hit on *Ventnor*, sir!'

An M.L. was already speeding after the destroyer which had slewed off course in a great curtain of falling spray and sparks.

Drummond let out a sigh as *Ventnor* swung drunkenly back on course. Nothing could prevent her from hitting the caisson now, unless her packed charges exploded prematurely. He watched the M.L., wondering briefly if she would be able to lift off *Ventnor*'s small steaming party.

A great flare exploded directly overhead, blinding him, and holding the ship between the glaring clouds and bright water like a vessel made of ice.

'Hard a-starboard!' He heard Wingate shouting in the voice-pipe. 'Midships!' He winced as a shell exploded in the water alongside, raking the hull with splinters.

Aft, by X gun, Sub-lieutenant Tyson was clinging to a stanchion and straining his eyes through the smoke when the shell burst. Water and snow burst over him, choking him with salt and the stench of H.E. The communications rating was crouching beside him, pressing his headphones against his ears as he repeated what Rankin was telling him from the director.

'Shift target, sir! Shore battery at Red one-one-oh!'

A splinter slammed him in the chest and he sprawled over his seat, choking and gurgling, while Tyson stared at him with frantic horror.

The gunlayer swung his brass wheel and yelled, 'Red one-one-oh!'

Another man slammed a shell into the breech and jumped clear as the gun roared back on its mounting, the bright shell-case clanging away unheeded amongst all the others.

The gunlayer paused in his efforts to look at Tyson. 'That's all we bloody well need now!' he shouted to his friend the trainer. 'Dick's gone for a burton and the sub is spewin' 'is guts out!' He tensed, his eye pressed to the sight. 'Layer *on*!' He held his breath. '*Shoot!*'

Sheridan ran with his damage control party to check the towing gear. To make sure the last shell had not blasted it away. He mopped his face. Like the rest of his body, it was burning like fire, and yet there was thin ice forming on guardrails and along the depth-charge racks. He squinted at his luminous watch.

'God, we've only been under fire for twenty minutes!' He shouted aloud, unable to believe that the battle had not been raging for hours.

He was thrown against the shield of Y gun, feeling his skin pushing over his jaw like a mask as a tremendous explosion tore the night apart.

A seaman called, '*Ventnor*'s blown up, sir!' But his voice was lost in the unending roar of the combined charges.

Men crouched like animals as the air became filled with flying fragments, and some were knocked senseless by metal and lumps of concrete which rained down through the glowing red ball of fire which had been the *Ventnor*.

Sheridan shaded his eyes against the glare, feeling the deck swaying this way and that as Drummond conned his ship wildly through the tell-tale waterspouts and criss-crossing tracer.

His brain was still able to record everything. The M.T.B.s snarling past the ship, guns hammering, as they charged into the attack, the leaders already firing their torpedoes towards the pens where the midget submarines were said to be moored.

He could see the *Victor* quite close by, her side glowing red and orange in the reflected explosions, her guns high angled as she fired again and again towards the warehouses and the riverside jetties of dockland where the Germans' resistance was visibly strengthening.

He felt the *Warlock* shuddering as if in a great tide-race, and stared with amazement at the complete stern-half of a German supply ship which was being carried past on a torrent of seething water. The dock area must have been blasted wide open.

A man was shaking his arm. 'Sir!' He was waving a handset. 'Captain wants you!'

He pressed it to his ear, covering his other ear with his glove.

Drummond sounded miles away. 'We're pulling out, Number One. General signal to break off the action immediately.'

Another great bang, and a section of the quartermaster's lobby buckled inwards like wet cardboard.

Sheridan shouted, 'What about *Lomond*?'

'Engine trouble.' He sounded almost matter of fact. 'We'll grapple her and take her in tow if we can.'

Sheridan shifted his smarting eyes to the clutter of towing

gear on and around the quarterdeck. It was just as if Drummond had known all along.

Drummond added tersely, 'Quick as you can. *Ventnor*'s done her part. The M.L.s are taking off the landing parties.'

Sheridan asked, 'Did they pick up any—'

'No. *Ventnor* received a direct hit as she rammed. Both she and her M.L. bought it.' The line went dead.

Sheridan saw the chief boatswain's mate crawling towards him.

'Right, Buffer. Jump about. Towing job!'

Petty Officer Vickery gripped a bandage between his teeth and tightened it round his wrist.

He said, 'I'll get the lads, sir.'

Sheridan stuck a cigarette between his lips and lit it, his fingers shaking badly. It didn't matter now, he thought. What with bursting torpedoes hurling shattered piers, hunks of metal which had been midget submarines and towering banks of flame right up to the clouds, one more light would not make much difference.

Men blundered past him, groping for wires and tackles, and he hurried to join them. He saw a man crouching by two inert bodies. It was Tyson, rocking from side to side, sobbing and whimpering like a child.

Someone gripped his sleeve, but when he looked down he saw it was not a human touch. A splinter had ripped through his clothing, laying bare his arm from shoulder to elbow without even bruising the skin.

Bullets hammered sparks from the side and deck plating, and he saw his men falling back.

He felt strangely calm, even elated, and found that he could walk right aft without stooping. He was going mad. It had to be that.

He turned his back towards the clattering machine guns and yelled, 'Move yourselves! Nobody lives forever!'

18

Reunion

SEVERAL great fires had begun to explore the immediate waterfront and jetties, so that the falling snow gleamed in bright orange hues, as if each flake was hot to the touch.

Drifting smoke, the confusion of spitting tracer helped Drummond considerably as he brought his ship alongside the crippled *Lomond*.

Wingate shouted, 'If her charges go up, we've all had it!'

Drummond ignored him. The charges would have exploded by now if things had gone as planned. *Lomond* should have been wedged into the nearest overhanging concrete cliff, her small passage crew speeding to safety in one of the M.L.s.

'Stop starboard!'

Shadows danced through the glittering snow, and he saw some of his men clambering across to *Lomond*'s deck with heaving lines as *Warlock* nudged firmly into her bulging fenders.

'Stop port!' He craned over the screen to peer aft. 'Tell number one to *get a move on*!'

He felt something fan past his shoulders and smack into the forward funnel. He found he could ignore most of it, concentrate on the immediate situation.

Cable and wire hawsers were clinking across decks, and several men fell sprawling on the slush and ice.

He thought he saw Vaughan climbing on to the ship alongside, and gritted his teeth as a motor torpedo boat surged abeam and fired her fish towards the dock area.

The explosions roared back, and more debris, pieces of wood and metal rained down on every side.

Ives said imperturbably, 'Signal from senior officer M.T.B.s, sir. *All torpedoes fired. Am proceeding to assist in general evacuation.*'

'Tell him. *Many thanks.*'

He forgot Ives and his small winking light as Hillier yelled, 'All secured aft, sir!'

'Very well. Slow astern port.'

He watched the ships angling apart, the apparent tangle of wires and shackles dropping into place as *Lomond*'s bows slewed round to follow in *Warlock*'s wake.

'Slow ahead together. Port fifteen.'

Sheridan dashed on to the bridge, his face streaked with sweat in the reflected fires.

'De Pass's gunnery officer broke the fuses, sir. Just in time. She's holed below the bridge, but the pumps will be able to cope if they can get the engine room cleared.'

He seemed to realise that the bulk of the fires were swinging away across the starboard beam as *Warlock* continued to turn towards the open sea.

'Good.'

Drummond raised his glasses, searching for the command vessel. Maybe it had been sunk with some of the M.L.s, and Beaumont killed.

'Midships. Steady. Steer two-five-zero.'

Sheridan watched him. He was remembering his brief visit to the ship which was now following obediently astern.

De Pass, teeth bared in agony while Vaughan did what he could, seemed to have lost most of one leg and was cut about the face in a dozen places.

He had said between groans, 'Beaumont should have been aboard. He knew what to do. I signalled for assistance when we got disabled, he acknowledged, and that was all he bloody well did do!'

The pain and the morphia had mercifully released him from his despair.

Drummond said, 'De Pass did well. Better than I gave him credit for.'

Ives called sharply, 'W/T office have urgent signal from Admiralty, sir.'

'Must be for Beaumont.'

He listened to the steady thump of gunfire through the snow and smoke, and wondered how the little boats were getting on with the evacuation. The wounded would have to be left behind to spend the rest of their war behind barbed wire. It was to be hoped they knew that their suffering was not for nothing.

Ives said, 'No, sir. Restricted. To you.'

Sheridan remembered the wounded who had been brought off the *Lomond*.

'I'll see to it, sir. Doc's busy.'

Drummond nodded. An urgent signal in the middle of hell. He had the sudden desire to laugh out loud. Probably an announcement about clothing issue for Wrens.

He saw *Victor* steaming abeam, her guns firing up and over the nearest M.T.B.s which were heading out from the land. They would have to get a move on. Their fuel must be running out fast.

When he looked at his watch he saw it was barely half past two.

Ives called, 'Command vessel closing to port, sir.'

'Tell the buffer to get a side party to haul Captain (D) aboard.'

If he wants to come, he thought bitterly.

He gripped the vibrating screen and threw back his head to let the clinging snow cover his face. It helped to steady him. To realise that the gunfire was less rapid now, the pale waterspouts further away. They had gone in with little hope of completing the mission, still less of getting away. The snow had saved them. That, and a whole lot more.

He heard the snarl of engines alongside, the scrape of wood against steel as the M.G.B. surged along the hull before lurching away again, her skipper waving his hand towards *Warlock*'s seamen.

Beaumont clambered on to the bridge, his face glowing in the strange reflections.

He shouted, 'Why didn't that fool de Pass get closer to the pens?'

'It was too late. He cut the fuses just in time. My doctor says he's dying.'

Beaumont moved restlessly round the bridge, his feet catching on broken glass and some severed halliards.

Drummond watched him calmly.

Beaumont swung on him. 'I think most of the troops are away. Had some losses, of course.' He glared as Sheridan appeared by the chart table. 'What d'*you* want?'

Drummond listened to his voice. He could barely recognise it. Flat, toneless. 'Urgent signal from Admiralty.' He looked at Sheridan's dull shadow. 'Read it under the chart screen.'

Even Sheridan sounded different. 'To commanding officer Warlock. *Discontinue the action immediately and withdraw as planned. Due to weather conditions, no air cover is at present available, but surface support is on way.*'

Beaumont rasped, 'In God's name! Now tell us something we didn't know!'

Sheridan continued, '*Yesterday off North Cape the battle-cruiser* Scharnhorst *was sunk by units of the Home Fleet under command of Admiral Fraser. During recent bad weather in English Channel remaining battlecruiser Moltke passed unobserved westward towards Brest. She was damaged by Bomber Command but still able to maintain ten knots. She is now believed to be somewhere in your vicinity with two destroyers in company.*'

Beaumont murmured thickly, 'In God's name! After all this time!'

Sheridan reappeared from beneath the chart screen and said sharply, 'There's more yet, sir.' He was looking at Drummond.

Drummond said, 'Let's have it then.'

He was thinking back over the months and years. Now, with *Scharnhorst* sunk, *Tirpitz* trapped and impotent in her Norwegian lair, there was only the *Moltke*. She was coming south to the dock which now lay astern, shattered and out of action. The German battlecruiser was rendered as helpless as her consorts. She had nowhere else to go.

Sheridan's voice touched his mind like a hot wire.

'*Commander Keith Drummond will take all steps to evacuate landing parties without delay. He will assume overall control of Smash-Hit until otherwise instructed.*' Sheridan stared at him. 'End of signal.'

Beaumont spoke first, his voice brittle with doubt and anger. 'What in hell's name do they think they're doing? Why, that would mean—'

Drummond said flatly, 'That you are relieved, sir. As of now.'

He sought out Ives. 'Make to *Victor. Follow my instructions.*'

He watched Beaumont, half expecting him to attack him. He

felt neither elation nor surprise. Everything seemed planned and inevitable. They all had parts, and he wondered what Beaumont's lines would be next.

Beaumont shouted, 'You can't do it, Drummond! How dare they treat me like this! After all I've done!'

'*Victor*'s signalling, sir. *M.T.B.s withdrawing now. Six M.L.s in company. Remainder sunk or captured.*'

Drummond nodded. To Beaumont he said, 'We will tow *Lomond* clear and if possible make contact with the salvage tug. She's not too badly damaged.'

Beaumont seemed unable to grasp what was happening.

'The *Moltke* is coming! I'm not running away, even if you are!'

Wingate and Sheridan watched silently as Drummond swung round and replied bitterly, 'Nobody's running, sir. After the way you left de Pass to do your job, I'm surprised you've got the gall to suggest it! That's *your* ship we're towing back there! While you were dashing about in the M.G.B. and looking grand, men were dying. Like they did in the fjord because you stayed outside.' He took a quick breath. 'Like they did in the *Conqueror* when you advised your admiral to scatter the convoy and escort.'

He knew the others were staring at him but could not stop.

'You thought that a German cruiser was coming between the screen and the convoy, didn't you? That *Conqueror* would smash her to scrap before her captain knew what had happened? You didn't bargain for a bloody battlecruiser!'

Beaumont's mouth was hanging open. He stammered, 'It's a lie! You've been conniving with that woman, with that lying rating Carson. The ungrateful—'

Drummond snapped, 'Yes, we know. *After all you've done.*'

A great explosion rolled out of the darkness and made the snow swirl up and around the dripping lookouts like steam. Another of the commando's charges must have burst to add to the general havoc.

When he looked at Beaumont again he saw that he was standing very stiff and straight on the gratings.

Drummond said quietly, 'The pity is that so many had to die because of your folly in the first place, and so many afterwards to cover your deception.'

Two motor torpedo boats scudded between the destroyers, decks black with exhausted troops and marines.

Wingate cleared his throat as they all caught the brief intrusion from the solitary piper.

'I'm glad *he* made it okay,' he said.

Drummond said, 'Pass the word to keep a close watch for small surface craft until we get clear. E-boats, anything. Although I doubt they'll be hereabouts. More likely they'll be following the *Moltke* to see her safely to her dock.'

Hillier said, 'Well, we spoiled things for that one!'

Sheridan said, '*Lomond*'s wheelhouse is a shambles, sir. Most of the hands were wiped out by shell-splinters.'

'Ask for volunteers. Just enough to manage her until we know what's happening.'

His mind strayed elsewhere. Weather and distance. No air-cover as yet, but surface vessels on way. But what and how many?

Beaumont said dully, 'I'm going aft.' He flipped the peak of his cap very casually. 'It's not over yet. Not by a long chalk.'

'Carry on, Number One.' Drummond could feel the exhaustion sapping him down. 'Now it's done, I can almost feel sorry for him.'

Sheridan shrugged. 'I just can't believe it, sir. It's like a bloody nightmare.'

'Signal from Admiralty, sir.'

'Read it.'

He saw Sheridan hovering at the top of a ladder, one foot swinging in space.

'*Moltke and escort reported as being to north-west of your estimated position. Weather clearing in same vicinity. Air cover will be despatched as soon as possible.*'

'Phew.' Wingate rubbed his chin. 'Let's hope the high-fly boys get to us before she does!' He looked round the bridge. 'Two old ladies against that big bastard! Not for me, thanks!'

Drummond was thinking busily. He must keep to the original plan as much as possible. Otherwise the supporting ships and aircraft would lose valuable time looking for them. And those overcrowded craft from Light Coastal Forces, many of them crammed with wounded troops, despite the order to leave them behind to the enemy's mercy, could be wiped out in a single broadside.

If only they had some M.T.B.s with their tubes still full. At least they might then tackle the two German destroyers. They would be fast and powerful. But that was normal enough. They had been fighting those sort of odds for years.

But the *Moltke*. Nothing could shift her. Damaged or not, she was a formidable fighting machine.

Sheridan had been right. It was like a nightmare. Each piece seemed to be linked to something else, a tiny incident, a fragment of memory.

Like the man Carson. Their visit had not been in vain after all. Perhaps the fact he had taken the trouble to accompany Sarah to his bedside had helped the man to rally. Enough to make a fresh statement, enough to have someone like Brooks believe it.

Drummond had worked some of it out for himself, and guessed the rest. Beaumont had not denied it this time. Not in his usual style. It would be interesting to see which way the Admiralty jumped when they were back in the cool sanity of Brooks' bunker.

He thought of Selkirk dying in his ship. Of the colonel with a sandwich in his fist as he had gone ashore with his raiders.

Suppose he himself had been killed? To whom would control of the operation have been handed then? he wondered.

He looked up, off guard. The snow was passing away towards the starboard quarter, leaving the bridge and rigging shining in the gloom like icing on a giant cake.

He peered at his watch. It was four-fifteen in the morning. When daylight came to them again, it was impossible to know what might be waiting.

Drummond wiped the rail with his glove, feeling the snow crisping into ice.

Who touches me dies. A good many had discovered that, he thought grimly.

Wingate called, 'Bosun's mate wants permission to bring some cocoa to the bridge, sir.'

'Never more welcome.'

He walked aft to watch the *Lomond*'s narrow hull veering back and forth across the stern.

Lomond's engineer might even be able to raise steam soon. It would help considerably.

He sat in his chair swallowing the thick, glutinous cocoa, his body aching, his face raw from the cold.

Beaumont would probably be transferred to some obscure shore duty where his actions would pass unnoticed. It would not do to drop him altogether. Unless the question of Sarah's brother was reopened.

Drummond rubbed his sore eyes with the back of his glove. It all seemed remote and unreal.

The first hint of daylight came with a gradual streak of grey far astern where land had been. As it strengthened, and the weary men at guns and lookout stations rubbed their eyes and tried to keep warm, *Victor*'s lithe silhouette took on shape again, her battle ensigns still flying, very white against the full-bellied clouds.

Drummond left his chair to make a full sweep from horizon to horizon. The Bay was lined with endless, unbroken rollers which cruised down from the north-west, lifted each ship in turn, held her uncomfortably for a few moments before allowing her to sway upright again.

He walked to the rear of the bridge, seeing *Lomond*'s bows pale and sharp in the growing light, the lines of splinter holes which marked her forecastle from waterline to bridge.

The Bay was theirs. Somewhere, far beyond the destroyers, the M.L.s and M.T.B.s were pushing ahead on their own. If they failed to make contact with the Hunts and the big tug, they would be as helpless as *Lomond*.

He took a searching look down the length of *Warlock*'s iron deck. At the men, still anonymous in their heavy clothing, as they crouched behind their gun shields or waited patiently on the quarterdeck watching over the towing wires. Tired out. Their resistance would be very low now. Cold, and remembering the night's work. The sights and the sounds. It was a pity they could not be given more than stale sandwiches and mugs of tea. They deserved a banquet.

He walked back to his chair, his legs taking the uneven rolls without conscious thought or effort. He nodded to Wingate, who lounged against the voice-pipes, and to Hillier, who was wiping the gyro compass with his sleeve. Around him the others took shape for another day. Ives, like a thin ramrod, his cap worn at the perfect angle. His signalmen and the lookouts, a bosun's mate and a spare seaman who was cleaning away the bits of broken glass and the dark stain where a man had died.

Drummond leaned forward to look through the screen. The men on B gun were banging their hands together, while one poured tea or cocoa into their filthy mugs. Below on the fore-castle he could just see the muzzle of A gun moving very slightly as its crew tested the mechanism. And far, far away he saw the dull blur of the Atlantic horizon. It never seemed to get any closer. Like a fool's landfall.

Midshipman Keyes stood beside Sheridan on the quarterdeck with Petty Officer Vickery and some shivering stokers. He watched the tow dipping and tautening while the *Lomond* continued to follow in their wake. The strain of the night action, followed now by a sort of dull acceptance of survival, left him limp and excited. He thought of Georgina. How she would look at him. How she would feel as they embraced and clung together.

Vickery said wearily, '*Lomond*'s calling us up, sir.' He squinted at the small stabbing handlamp. Then he exclaimed, 'She's got steam up, sir!'

Almost immediately the quarterdeck telephone buzzed, and a seaman called, 'First lieutenant, sir! The cap'n says to prepare to slip tow. Volunteer passage crew to be sent over by Carley float as soon as you're ready.'

'Thank you.' Sheridan gripped the midshipman's shoulder. 'Get those blokes aft on the double. With the sea and wind as they are, a float will drift across with very little sweat needed.' He found to his astonishment that he could joke about it. 'I think we're going to be all right.'

Able Seaman Jevers hurried aft with the other volunteers. He looked neither right nor left, but concentrated instead on what he was going to do. When he had heard that a helmsman was required for the *Lomond* he had started to make plans. This additional move might help him when the time came. His mind was blurred, his thoughts overlapping like loose pages. He kept telling himself that nothing had altered. The Yank was dead. Nobody on this bloody earth could touch him. And yet . . . it was just possible. He felt the sweat running over his neck again.

Sheridan shouted, 'As soon as you are across to the *Lomond*, secure the raft. It might come in handy if you have to bale out.'

A seaman said dourly, 'We could paddle all the way to Blighty, lads!'

Lieutenant Rankin had turned himself on his steel chair to watch as the Carley float was warped alongside, bobbing up and down in the wash like a toy boat. High in his director position above and abaft the bridge he could see just about everything. The *Victor* steaming calmly abeam, the men below on the iron deck, like busy moles as they ran with lines to guide the float further aft. It was nearly over. Help was on the way. They would get a well-deserved rest after it was finished, he thought.

It would mean seeing his wife again. He sighed, so that one of the spotting ratings below his chair turned to glance up at him curiously. She was definitely being unfaithful to him. Not the casual affairs like before. Someone more permanent had come into her life. It had to be true. She had barely tried to conceal the fact. Had even laughed at his confusion.

His mother had exclaimed angrily, 'Why don't you knock the little slut's head off?'

He leaned further over to watch Beaumont's familiar figure striding aft to the quarterdeck. He had picked up most of the gossip about him within seconds of the confrontation on the bridge. It must be a hell of a lot worse than he had imagined for Drummond to risk his career by clashing with a man like Beaumont. He sighed again. Perhaps that was what was wrong with his own life. He did not take risks. He was a 'hoper'. He hoped that his wife would somehow change. That he would so impress her she might start all over again. It must have been all right once, surely?

He heard raindrops pattering against the wet steel like pellets. Christ, it was cold.

Rankin felt the chair biting into his spine as a great explosion rocked the ship drunkenly to one side, and felt the hull quiver from keel to bridge as a vast column of water shot above the starboard side before cascading down across the forecastle like a tidal wave.

Below on the bridge Drummond pulled himself across the gratings, his boots slipping in inches of seething water. He heard men shouting, the buzz of telephones, and above all the tell-tale *swoosh* of another great shell falling, it seemed from the sky itself.

He shouted, 'Get me the first lieutenant on the telephone.'

He groped for his glasses, sweeping them over the screen where *Victor* was steaming as before. Only her four guns, swinging with sudden agitation towards the leaden horizon, showed that everything had changed.

A man gave him the handset, and he had to count seconds before he could trust himself to speak.

'Number One. This is the captain. Tell Captain Beaumont to transfer with the volunteer steaming party forthwith. *Lomond* has enough power now to fend for herself. Tell Beaumont to scuttle the ship and stand off in a Carley float. I'll not risk men's lives on the top of that floating bomb.'

He tensed, gritting his teeth, as yet another massive projectile burst abeam. The opposite side, and well away this time. The invisible enemy was shooting blind.

He heard murmurings on the line and then Beaumont's voice. Very calm. Completely at ease.

'I shall, of course, take command of *Lomond*. There is only a sub-lieutenant aboard her at present.'

Drummond cut him short. 'We might be able to slip past. If not, you will fire scuttling charges and abandon ship.'

He felt the pain pricking at the back of his eyes. Beaumont would survive this way. It was ironic. As a prisoner of war he would receive more kudos than at the hands of Admiral Brooks. It was strange that the Beaumonts of this world always prospered.

Beaumont said suddenly, 'By the way. I did not know about *Lomond*'s original hull state.' He sounded as if he was stifling a laugh. 'I wanted *Warlock* to be used in the ramming job.' The line went still.

Drummond swung round, his face uplifted as another shell ripped above the masthead like an express train. *He wanted me dead.* It had meant that much to him.

He felt the ship surge forward and down and a man yelled, 'Tow 'as bin slipped, sir!'

Then Rankin's voice on the intercom. 'Enemy in sight. Capital ship bearing Green one-one-oh. Range one-two-oh.'

Drummond glanced up at Rankin's steel perch. Six miles. When the light strengthened still further the German gunnery officer would pick them off at leisure.

The voice of the senior radar operator was already confirming Rankin's assessment. Except that despite the bad conditions he had located two smaller blips on his screen. The destroyers. Not that numbers meant anything now.

He said, 'Make to Admiralty. *Enemy in sight to the north of our present position.*'

He walked aft again and saw *Lomond* steaming away very slowly, her hull rocking drunkenly on a steep roller. She would be an onlooker after all.

Ives watched him sternly. 'That all, sir?'

Drummond shook his head and looked up at the two streaming ensigns above the bridge. How white they were. The only clean things today.

He said, '*I am engaging.*'

He turned to look at Wingate. 'Increase to maximum revs. Alter course to two-six-five.' He found that his mind was suddenly clear, although it could see nothing, feel nothing beyond this single moment. 'Signal *Victor* to take station astern.'

Drummond strode to the table and threw the screen to one side. 'By altering course we might head the enemy off long enough for the M.L.s to get clear. Those Jerry destroyers could catch 'em in no time, or drive them into the Atlantic until they run out of fuel.'

Two tall waterspouts shot into the air directly ahead of *Victor*'s bows as she turned steeply to obey his signal.

She made a fine sight, he thought. Like we do from her decks. Dazzle-paint shining with flying spray as she worked up to full revs, her out-of-date lines momentarily lost in speed and purpose.

Beaumont intruded into his mind. *He wanted me dead.* Now, if he stayed out of range, he might be able to watch it happen.

He lifted his glasses, and for just a brief instant he saw the bright stab of gunfire through the horizon murk. Seconds passed, and then came great double explosions. He felt the ship buck beneath him, and tried not to think of the *Moltke*'s armament. Nine eleven-inch guns, ten five-point-nines. A heavier armament than the whole of the Scrapyard Flotilla put together. And now there were only two of them left to show defiance.

Rankin again. 'Bearing Green nine-oh. Range one double oh.'

It was no use. The range was falling away rapidly, and *Warlock*'s gunners could not even mark the giant.

He shifted his attention to *Victor*. She was directly astern now, her bows making a giant moustache of creaming foam.

More shells hurled tall columns of water beyond the two destroyers. He saw the spray reaching out in vast white circles to mark the power of each one.

The Germans would be eager to destroy them, no matter how frail they were by comparison. *Moltke*'s captain had spent most of his war dodging the R.A.F. or sneaking out of his base to chase and destroy a rare convoy. He had almost certainly been informed by Group West that his hope of a safe dock had been denied him, just as he would know that these two relics of the Kaiser's war were the culprits. What he would not expect was a direct challenge.

He found he was sweating badly.

'Make to *Victor*. *Prepare to alter course ninety degrees to starboard*.' He saw the flags darting aloft and added shortly, 'Hoist Flag Four.'

Wingate looked round as Ives snapped to his signalmen, 'Flag Four. *Engage with torpedoes*.'

'*Victor*'s acknowledged, sir.'

Drummond trained his glasses astern and saw Roger North standing upright on his open bridge. Would his wife, the beautiful Elinor, blame him, too, for what was about to happen?

He snapped, 'Execute!'

He heard the flags coming down the halliards and Wingate say, 'Hard a-starboard!'

The ship tilted violently, pushed still further as more shells exploded near the bows. Drummond felt the splinters hammering along the hull and knew he had judged it to the split second. *Warlock* should have been steaming where those last shells had fallen.

'Midships!'

Wingate was having to shout above the din of engines and fans as the ship swung in a tight arc and then steadied on a course towards the enemy. But not two long targets any more. They were on equal terms. Bow to bow.

'Steady as you go!'

Wingate was peering along his gyro, coughing as spray deluged over the screen.

Drummond said, 'We will engage to starboard.'

Wingate stared at him, his eyes without emotion. 'Yes, sir.' He was probably thinking, six torpedoes between two ships. If they reached that far.

The sky came apart as towering columns of spray roared above the forecastle. It was like a body-blow, the shells exploding almost as the stem sliced through the falling curtain of spray.

In Galbraith's engine room it would feel like a mine going off.

'Range oh-nine-oh.'

'*Open fire!*'

The two forward guns reacted immediately, hurling their puny shells through the rain and spray to burst in line with the enemy. Throughout the racing, trembling hull the men would know they were trying to hit back.

Rankin was shouting into his intercom. 'Short! Deflection seven left!' More distorted voices over the pipes and telephones and then, '*Shoot!*'

Abeam, her ensigns still stiff in the wind, *Victor* was also using her forward guns.

Drummond could see the oilskinned figures grouping around her triple-mounted torpedo tubes, the purposeful way they were even now turning athwartships.

More violent explosions announced the last fall of shot, and Drummond felt despair in his heart as he watched the neat pattern of waterspouts.

The battlecruiser must have been using her two forward turrets alternately. Two by two. Feeling the range. Judging the moment.

Then it came, and he had to hold the rail with all his strength to prevent his being flung on his back. Choking spray and whistling fragments whirled above the bridge, and he heard the violent clatter of breaking glass as the radar lantern was blasted away. A man fell past the starboard Oerlikon, and was lost kicking and screaming in the water alongside. He could smell the stench of explosives, taste it in his lungs as if he were drowning in it.

But he could only stare at the *Victor* as she ploughed slower and slower into a great creaming backwash from the last shell-bursts. She had lost twenty feet of her bows, and the sea was surging into the gaping, jagged hole like a high-pressure hose. If North could not stop his engines the sea would smash through the bulkheads like a battering ram and she would continue her brave charge right to the bottom.

More shells exploded on either side of her, bracketing her in a vice of iron. Holes appeared along her side, and her upper deck and superstructure seemed to wilt and shake as if in a great wind.

'Port ten.' Drummond could not take his eyes from her. 'Midships.' To Wingate he added, 'We will stand off a bit to show ourselves to the enemy. It may give *Victor* time to recover.'

There was a chorus of shouts as two shells exploded directly on the labouring destroyer. The effect was instantaneous and complete. Funnels and masts, boat davits and deck plating were hurled about like sticks in a gale, and then as some internal explosion sparked off her torpedoes, the *Victor* seemed to fold up, the stern half sinking immediately in a welter of spray and steam, the forward half, complete with bridge and one un-manned gun, remaining afloat for a few more desperate minutes before it, too, rolled over and vanished.

'Tell the chief to make smoke!' He had to repeat the order as Wingate and the others stared dazedly at the vast circle of spreading oil.

More shells were falling now, creeping nearer and nearer while Drummond swung his ship towards the enemy on a narrow zigzag.

They must have hit the battlecruiser more than once, although with so much smoke and falling spray, rain and noise it was hard to tell.

He watched the *Moltke* with cold fascination. Tall from the sea, bridge upon bridge, she was rushing towards him headlong, firing as she came.

The two escorting destroyers were steaming away to the west-ward, probably to seek out the escaping M.L.s, or to cut off *Warlock*'s only chance of escape.

He shouted, 'Stand by to fire torpedoes!'

He watched the oncoming ship and wondered how *Warlock* would look to her captain.

'All ready, sir!'

'Port fifteen!' He felt the ship heeling hard round. '*Midships!*'

It was a bad angle of attack, but the German made a big target. It was all they had anyway. Apart from surrender.

'Steady!' He crouched against the gyro, pressing his eye to the ice-cold sight. 'As you bear! *Now!*'

He kept his eyes fixed on the other ship, saying nothing until Hillier yelled, 'All torpedoes running, sir!'

'Starboard twenty!'

Round again, and more great shells blasting the sea into towering walls of spray and foam.

'Original course, Pilot. We'll keep at her—'

He coughed as a great bang seemed to come directly against the hull. Water cascaded over the decks, and he saw two men hurled from their gun and smashed lifeless against the wet steel.

He blinked the spray and sweat from his eyes and watched as the big battlecruiser lengthened in his glasses. *She had seen the torpedoes and was turning away.* He saw the ripple of flashes along her side and knew that her captain was bringing his secondary armament into action. Then he had *not* seen the torpedoes!

Almost as he considered the fact, two things happened. A thin column of water raised itself in line with the enemy's bridge, and as his brain recorded that one of his torpedoes had found a mark, *Warlock* gave a great convulsive leap and began to slow down.

On every side men were yelling and responding to orders. When he looked aft, Drummond saw that there was a great gap where the mainmast had been. X gun and its crew had been wiped away, and there was a crater across the hull big enough to hold a tank.

Some men were already running aft, cringing as shells screamed overhead and burst angrily alongside.

Wingate yelled, 'Flooding in boiler room, sir! Fire in tiller flat, and sixteen casualties aft!'

Hillier shouted hoarsely, 'The chief says he can give you half-speed until—' He ducked as more explosions rocked the ship.

'Tell him, thanks.'

Drummond clung to the rail, watching the great battlecruiser circling round, her turrets swinging for the last salvoes. One torpedo might have slowed her still further. But it was not enough to save the *Warlock*.

'The enemy's signalling, sir!' Even in all the bedlam and danger Ives managed to sound surprised.

Sure enough, the enemy's big signal lamp was winking busily from one of her high bridges, and when Drummond turned he saw the reason.

Steaming rapidly through *Warlock*'s screen of greasy smoke was the *Lomond*. Half submerged in funnel smoke and that from all the gunfire, it was hardly surprising that *Moltke*'s captain had mistaken her for one of his own.

More crashes made the hull sway dangerously, and Drummond saw several of his men drop even as they dragged fire hoses to the growing plumes of smoke above the quarterdeck.

He watched the *Lomond* increasing her speed as she turned slightly and headed towards the enemy. What was Beaumont thinking of? he wondered. If his intention was now obvious, his reasons were not. Watching the lone, battered *Warlock* trying to fight the impossible giant, or seeing in his own last gesture a chance to redeem himself?

As he watched he saw something come adrift, leaping and swaying in the *Lomond*'s wake. It was the float, with some dozen figures clinging to it as it was almost capsized in *Lomond*'s wash.

Wingate shouted, 'That only leaves three on board, sir!'

Drummond had already guessed who they were. Apart from Beaumont, there would be Jevers on the wheel and *Warlock*'s chief gunner's mate, Abbott, the man who had lost everything when his home had been bombed.

He felt a lump in his throat as he watched *Lomond*'s challenge. She was doing nearly thirty knots, and despite her changed outline held a kind of beauty.

Two men who had everything to lose. One who had lost everything.

The Germans had at last realised what was happening. Their five-point-nines were being divided between *Warlock* and *Lomond*, so that by swinging his ship from side to side Drummond was able to continue to close the range.

A shell slammed into the deck beside the wheelhouse, and he felt the pain lance up to his spine as if to break his neck.

He shouted to Hillier, 'Get down there!'

Seconds later he heard a new voice from the wheel and then Hillier returned to the bridge, his uniform splashed with blood.

He reported dully, 'Direct hit, sir. All killed. Keyes, Mangin, all of them.'

Wingate rubbed his eyes and said harshly, 'Not Allan, too!'

'*Lomond*'s hit, sir!'

The German captain had left it too late. By sending his two escorts away to search for the M.L.s, by seeing in *Lomond* only what he had expected to see, he had given his ship too little time to avoid collision.

Lomond, blazing from a dozen points, her funnels buckled and broken, her hull a mass of splinter holes, charged the battle-cruiser's flank within yards of where *Warlock*'s torpedo had exploded.

There was a sudden stillness, broken only by the distant rattle of automatic weapons as the Germans raked the listing, battered destroyer which was held like a ram against her hull.

Perhaps then, and only then, did the enemy understand why a solitary ship had acted as she had. When they realised that no men ran from their action stations to surrender or jump overboard, then they could measure time in seconds alone.

Abbott had always known a great deal about fuses.

As he lay, bleeding from a dozen small splinters, he could see the great wall of depth-charges in their concrete emplacement quite close to his feet. He could see his wife and little daughter, too, even more clearly.

In the shattered wheelhouse Jevers was trying to drag himself up the tilting deck towards the buckled door. He was sobbing quietly, willing the explosion to come and relieve the agony.

Beaumont lay on his smashed bridge, his cap spattered with his blood, his hair moving across his dead face as the rain hissed across his wide, compelling stare.

In his mind's eye Drummond could see the three of them, so that when the explosion came it was almost a relief.

The brilliant flash was seen many miles away by the force of fleet destroyers which were speeding into the Bay in search of Drummond's little group of ships.

It was seen and heard by the captains of the two German destroyers, who turned and headed towards the land, knowing that help was on the way for the remaining elderly ship with the unmatched funnels.

Moltke had gone. Wiped away as if she had never been created.

Hours later, as Ives read the flashing signal lamps from the line of destroyers, Drummond found time to wonder about all of it.

Ives said, 'From *Caistor*, sir. *All evacuated personnel have been recovered. Your courage did the trick.*'

Drummond saw Sheridan leaning against the signal lockers, his cap in one hand, his head held back to suck in the air and drizzle. Wingate was by the compass, his face lined with strain. Hillier, too, was holding on to the screen, the fight gone out of him.

Throughout the ship the company sat back and drew breath. They watched the oncoming destroyers, and later the arrow-head of escorting bombers. They were *that* important, but at the moment it did not seem to count. Some were thinking of friends killed or wounded. Others watched the dull sky and thanked God they could still see it.

In the wheelhouse, its side torn open to the sea and sky, a seaman held the spokes and listened to Wingate's helm orders.

At the rear of the wheelhouse, the coxswain, Tommy Mangin, and the chief quartermaster, Rumsey, lay together, arms and legs entwined, where they had fallen. A man had been blasted to fragments, another barely marked. One of the latter was Midshipman Keyes. He was found by the plot table, with the navigator's yeoman on top of him. Keyes had had his eyes tightly closed. As if, Vaughan explained, he had heard the shell coming. In his hand was a picture of a showgirl. Like those you saw in the foyers of lesser-known theatres.

When the doctor told Wingate about it later, he had said harshly, 'She was Allan's girl.'

Above the bridge Rankin bandaged one of his spotters and thought of his wife. After this he would really change things.

Mr. Noakes had died in the battle, cut down by a white-hot splinter even as he had shouted angrily at a cowering seaman. It seemed only fitting he should die angrily and bitterly. As he had lived.

Tyson's body was never found, and had probably gone when the shell had struck the ship by X gun.

Owles took a pot of hot coffee to the bridge for his captain, but when he had been unable to pour it because of his hands shaking so badly, he had broken down and cried.

For Drummond it had been almost the worst part. The final revelation of battle.

He said, 'Course for Falmouth, Pilot. Then we'll make a signal to Admiralty. *Smash-Hit completed.*' He touched Owles' arm, trying to help him. '*Moltke destroyed.*' He hesitated, recalling the *Lomond's* wild attack. '*By Captain Dudley Beaumont.*'

Ives wrote it all down and then took Owles by the sleeve. 'Come down with me. I could use a tot.'

Many hours later, as the escorting destroyers reduced speed and allowed *Warlock* to complete her entrance into Falmouth alone, Drummond read through a whole sheaf of signals which had accompanied his ship as faithfully as any escort.

Congratulations. Questions. Orders.

He glanced sideways at Sheridan and said, 'I'm being given another command, David.'

Sheridan watched him, seeing the emotions crossing his strained features.

'Congratulations.'

Drummond continued quietly, 'Something new. Not even completed yet.'

He watched the land sliding out to greet them, the crowds lining the shore to watch the little destroyer creeping past the buoys. How silent they were when they saw the scars, the cruel marks of their sacrifice.

She would be there waiting for him. He just knew it. *She had to be.*

He said, '*Warlock's* new skipper is already appointed.' He ran his hand along the teak rail, pausing to touch a jagged splinter-mark as if he was feeling a wound. 'The ship will be going into dock for repair and conversion to long-range escort. Like your last ship, David.'

'I see, sir.' Sheridan hesitated, knowing there was more, feeling Drummond's sense of loss. 'But to me she'll always be a destroyer, sir. In the best sense of the word.'

Drummond could not look at him. 'She's *yours*, David. Your promotion and appointment have come through.' He reached out impetuously and added, 'Take care of her.'

Wingate had been watching them from the compass platform. He said quietly, 'Ten minutes, sir.'

Sheridan stepped away. 'I'll go forrard, sir.'

Drummond nodded. He saw a seaman carrying Badger's

familiar basket along the iron deck. So many had died, but the cat had survived.

Later, as the mooring wires went ashore and the waiting on-lookers surged as near as they could get to the listing ship, Drummond stood alone on the deserted bridge.

He took one last long look around, feeling the ship dragging at him and then just as quickly letting go.

As he walked down the ladder a signalman held out a stained battle ensign. 'The only one left, sir.'

'I'd like Keyes' girl to have it. Give it to the navigating officer.'

It might help her to understand. To know what she had done to make a boy's last days on earth happy.

He paused at the brow, seeing Sheridan and Wingate, Rankin and Galbraith in his filthy boiler-suit.

Sheridan said quietly, 'I relieve you, sir.'

Drummond shook his hand. 'Then I will leave the ship.'

He knew that there were many people waiting to see him, and he thought he saw Sarah being helped through the crowd by Kimber and Miles Salter. But for a moment he looked up at the battered ship and then gave a slow salute.

As Sheridan had said. She was a destroyer. Now and always. They could never take that away from either of them.

Also by Douglas Reeman

PATH OF THE STORM

It was 1943. On the Black Sea, the Russians were fighting a desperate battle to regain control. But the Russians' one real weakness was on the water: whatever they did, the Germans did it better, and the daring hit-and-run tactics of the E-boats plagued them. At last the British agreed to send them a small flotilla of motor torpedo boats under the command of John Devane.

Devane had been in the Navy since the outbreak of war. More than a veteran, he was a survivor — and the two rarely went together in the savage war of MTBs. Given command at short notice, Devane soon learned that, even against the vast and raging background of the Eastern Front, war could still be a personal duel between individuals.

BATTLECRUISER

Conceived on paper as an invincible defence against enemy commerce raiders, the battlecruiser was hailed as a triumph. Romantically described as the fleet's greyhounds, these great ships, remarkable for their size and speed, were designed to outrun and outshoot any of their heavier opponents.

But the Battle of Jutland exposed their fatal flaw, the weakness of their armour, which could be pierced by a single enemy shell. At the outbreak of World War II, only four of their class remain.

In 1943, when Captain Guy Sherbrooke joins HMS *Reliant*, he knows he may be her last captain. The battlecruisers *Hood* and *Repulse*, household names, have been destroyed. But *Reliant* is both legend and survivor, a lucky ship, and as Britain prepares to invade occupied Europe, one of the last battlecruisers must enter the conflagration. And Sherbrooke, who commands her destiny, cannot alter the bitter truth: that for one of her ill-fated class, there can be no half measures. Only death or glory await HMS *Reliant*.